"IF I WERE PLANTI_____**TO GO**
off when the car started," Oliver said quietly _____ ___ moved to
open the door, "I'd absolutely figure the new mother would want
her baby's car seat."

Kyle's hand froze. "That makes sense to me. You think Kitty's
the target? Or the baby?" He growled this last question. I liked
overprotectiveness toward my child from our new bodyguard.

"As I already told your superior, I don't know who the target is.
However, Missus Martini is on the guest list for the President's
Ball, ergo, she's a potential target."

We quickly moved our little group across the street and back
down the block. "How long for the bomb squad?" Oliver asked.

"Not too much longer," Kyle, who'd made the call, said. He and
Len were busy looking all around. We weren't exactly being subtle,
but no one really seemed to be around to notice.

I dug my phone out of my purse. Jeff answered immediately.
"What's going on? Reynolds has been making urgent calls for the
past few minutes and his stress is off the charts."

"Len found a too-convenient parking place and we're all waiting
for some folks to come and let us know if our limo's been rigged or
not."

"Reynolds says his people will be there in another minute. How
far from the limo are you all?"

"We can still see it."

"Get farther away."

"Jeff, really—"

I was going to tell him he was overreacting. Only the limo exploded before I could finish my sentence. . . .

"If you like your futuristic adventure with heapings of over-the-top
fun and absurdity, Koch has the series for you. . . . A rip-roaring
and outlandish romp!"   —*RT Book Reviews*

DAW Books Presents GINI KOCH's
Alien Novels:

TOUCHED BY AN ALIEN

ALIEN TANGO

ALIEN IN THE FAMILY

ALIEN PROLIFERATION

ALIEN DIPLOMACY

ALIEN VS. ALIEN
(coming in December 2012)

ALIEN
DIPLOMACY

GINI KOCH

DAW BOOKS, INC.
DONALD A. WOLLHEIM, FOUNDER
375 Hudson Street, New York, NY 10014

ELIZABETH R. WOLLHEIM
SHEILA E. GILBERT
PUBLISHERS
http://www.dawbooks.com

First Printing, April 2012
1 2 3 4 5 6 7 8 9

To Dixie, for begging me to "write funny" for years, in every diplomatic way possible, until I finally broke down and listened— I wouldn't be here without you.

ACKNOWLEDGMENTS

I realize why authors stop thanking their agent and editor after a few books—not because the agent and editor, in my case, Cherry Weiner and Sheila Gilbert, are any less amazing and awesome now than they were for the prior books. No, it's because you start running out of adjectives and end up repeating yourself when you say, "You two are the best in the world!"

That goes as well for my crit partner and main beta reader, Lisa Dovichi and Mary Fiore. It's hard to keep coming up with synonyms for "fabulous" and "best ever."

But I persevere.

I don't think it can get old, though, saying thank you with all my love to Team Gini, all those on Hook Me Up!, and all the Alien Collective Members in Very Good Standing around the world— y'all make all the work, the deadlines, the late nights, the pre-release stress, and the general insanity that is my writing life worthwhile. I have the best fans in the world, and you all constantly rock my world.

Many thanks again and always to the legion of book review bloggers who continue to support books in general and my books in particular. *Smoothies* to all my Twitter peeps and Facebook folks, just 'cause. And, as always, thanks to all I've thanked before, anyone I've missed somehow (DAW's copy editor assures me this seems impossible, given the length of my acknowledgments for every book), and anyone on or added on to my own Alpha Team between the time I wrote this and the time the book comes out— love and appreciate you all.

Special shout outs to: Marnie Walski, for making me almost stop breathing when you asked if you could start an official fan site for me (The Alien Collective Virtual HQ) and then making such an awesome one; all the mods and members at said fan site (did I mention the name? The Alien Collective Virtual HQ, in case you missed it.); Paul Sparks and Kenton Schassberger for putting a lot of time and creative energy into scientifically proving that my science ain't all that soft after all; the Queen Creek Writer's Group for being an awesome writer's group and having me out to run the yap live so often; my sis-in-law, Akiko, for letting me use her company, Akiko Clothing, as Kitty's Washington, D.C. designer (even though Akiko Clothing is located in Los Angeles—hey, it's fiction, right?), and my little bro, Danny, for being understanding about why Blackhearts Brigade didn't make this particular cut; Mysterious Galaxy Bookstore, for being awesome and supporting me and my books constantly; and everyone who came to see us before, during, and after Comic-Con, effectively creating little areas of fun and calm around that awesome but always overwhelming event.

Finally, thanks to my husband, Steve, for always supporting me, even when I probably sound insane or incoherent, and patiently listening to me ramble on about characters and plot points; and to my daughter, Veronica, for being my utility player in all of this and always being there when I need your help to handle whatever the crisis—beta reading, contest naming, promotional ideas, plot nightmares—with efficiency and understanding, as well as snarky wit (I have no idea where you get that from). You're both the best and I love you even more than I love writing or the pets. Put together. Honest.

THEY CALL BOXING THE SWEET SCIENCE. I have no idea why. It's not like two guys beating each other up can be called sweet in any culture, and it's hard to buy the science part when there's not that much scientific theory involved in "hit harder, longer, until the other guy goes down."

Now diplomacy, there's your sweet science. You have to be sweet even when you don't want to be. Or your husband has the little "representing an entire race" chat with you. And figuring out the many layers, links, connections, and conspiracies attached to just one diplomat is hard enough. Try doing that with every diplomat on Earth. Then expand past Earth. Then wonder why your husband can keep it all straight when you can't and await the "if you'd only read the briefing file" chat.

Diplomacy has opened up a whole new world of chatting for Jeff and me. So far, I haven't enjoyed any of them, but hope springs eternal.

Being one of the head diplomats for Centaurion Division's Diplomatic Corps is quite the honor. Kind of wish I'd had a little more time to transition from marketing manager to superbeing exterminator to newlywed to new mother to retired superbeing exterminator to full-time diplomat. More than two years start to finish would have been nice. But, hey, I'm good with change and a challenge, right?

Of course, nothing could really have prepared me for the superpowers that were my parting gifts for labor and delivery of our daughter. Like the Alpha Centaurions from Alpha Four, I now have hyperspeed, faster healing and regeneration, improved vision, and superstrength. Other abilities show up when I least expect them. I don't have two hearts like a real A-C or any special talents, such as dream and memory reading or empathic skills. But being a super's pretty much all it's cracked up to be.

Sadly, when it comes to diplomacy, superpowers don't really help. At all. But that's where my winning ways and charming influence over others come in.

Hey, when it comes to diplomacy, I *do* practice the sweet science. Yeah, okay, the kind with boxing gloves. What can I say? Washington's a tough town.

CHAPTER 1

"MISSUS MARTINI, CAN YOU PLEASE EXPLAIN the proper way to greet a visiting dignitary from China when you are also in the company of dignitaries from Japan, Russia, Thailand, and Bangladesh?"

"This is a trick question, right?"

My Washington Wife course instructor glared. "Hardly." Mrs. Darcy Lockwood, a proud Daughter of the American Revolution, wife of the influential senator from Maine, and all around know-it-all, wasn't fond of me. I'd only been in her class a few weeks, but the feeling was incredibly mutual.

"I suppose a cheerful howdy-do isn't it, right?" There were titters throughout the class. Sadly, I knew they were absolutely not laughing with me.

Another glare. I wasn't sure which one of us hated the other more, me or the instructor, but there was less than no love lost between us. To date, this summed up my entire experience with Washington, D.C.: I didn't like it, and it didn't like me.

"Missus Martini, your husband's career is affected by you—what you say, how you present yourself, how you act. As the wife of an ambassador, I'd think you would have more interest in representing yourself and your principality well."

"I'm also an ambassador." I chose not to argue about the principality thing. I was representing the Alpha Centaurion, or A-C, population, and it was never clear to me what our exact status really was. It wasn't as if we could tell the general population that most of those who called themselves A-Cs were aliens from Alpha Four in the Alpha Centauri solar system, with a goodly group of human agents and a few intermarried humans thrown into the mix.

I'd been told we were like the American Indians, with reservations a little more spread out all over the United States and the world in general. I'd heard we were like Puerto Rico, only our islands were all landlocked. I'd also gotten the younger A-Cs listed as political refugees, and every A-C born on Earth was considered a legal U.S. citizen with all the rights thereof. I had no clear idea how this worked or who knew, or thought they knew, what, so I tended to just nod and forge ahead. This worked everywhere but in certain situations, the Washington Wife class being Exhibit A.

"Missus Martini, as we've discussed, you are not the ambassador. You are part of the diplomatic mission, true, but you are not the ambassador, nor are you his Chargé d'Affaires. You are an ambassadress, the wife of the ambassador."

"No, as I keep on explaining to you, I am one of our ambassadors. My husband, the other head ambassador, says so."

She snorted. It was delicate and ladylike, but it was a snort, nonetheless. "Please. As *I* keep explaining to *you*, there can only be one Chief of Mission. Charming as it is of him to make you feel as if you're his equal, the Chief would be your husband, not you. Now, let's try to get back to decorum, shall we?"

I opened my mouth to share that, as I kept explaining, we did things differently at our Embassy, but Eugene nudged me and I snapped it shut. Eugene was the only person in this horrid class who didn't hate me or laugh at me, because he was as lame as I was with this stuff.

"Besides," Lockwood went on, "if you were the actual ambassador, this greeting would carry even more impact. Therefore, who can tell me what the proper procedure is?"

One of the gay guys politely raised his hand and shared the proper greeting procedure. He did it perfectly. Everyone in class did everything perfectly other than me and Eugene. We were both washing out, and neither one of us could afford to.

What made this worse was that Amy hadn't even had to take the class. Oh, sure, she'd come from money and I'd come from covert ops masquerading as dull middle class, but it still wasn't fair. I'd saved the world in the double digits, easy, and yet, here I was, the Class Dunce.

Amy had breezed in, spent about an hour with Lockwood, and bam, there she was, already approved and back in the Alpha Centaurion Embassy, all snug and secure and not being picked on.

She'd tried to help me, but I wasn't really excited about studying this stuff when I was released from the prison that was this class, and all it had done was make us snap at each other, so she'd given up, and I'd resigned myself to spending time in Hell every week for the rest of the foreseeable future.

Class droned on, and I reminisced about the days when I was happy and carefree, killing parasitic superbeings for a living. Or when I was averting intergalactic war. Running away from scary creatures, both human and extremely not, that were trying to kill me. Saving the day. Those days were only three months ago, really, but they seemed like a lifetime away, especially when I was in the Washington Wife class.

It didn't help that my husband and my two best male friends had both insisted that I take the stupid class in the first place. With Jeff, Chuckie, and Reader aligned against me, I had nowhere to turn. That my husband was the head of the A-C Diplomatic Corps, Chuckie was the head of the C.I.A.'s ET Division, and Reader was now Head of the Field for Centaurion Division made the directive to attend sort of unavoidable.

Oh, sure, they'd insisted after I'd inadvertently insulted the Prime Minster of England, but how could I have known he wasn't willing to admit that the Rolling Stones weren't half the band Aerosmith was and never would be?

Lockwood droned on, and I surreptitiously checked my watch. Fifteen more minutes and I could escape. If only A-Cs weren't deathly allergic to alcohol, I'd get drunk both before and after this class, but, sadly, I was restricted to nothing harder than Coca-Cola or iced tea. I never wanted to risk Jeff not being able to kiss me. Him kissing me was still on my Top Three Things To Do At Least A Dozen Times Every Day list. Kissing tended to lead to my other top two things to do. My mind wandered happily to our sex life and stayed there.

"The President's Ball is in two days," Lockwood reminded us, yanking my mind away from Pleasure Island. She had a happy smile for all, until her eyes hit the back corner where Eugene and I sat. We got a pitying glare. I was kind of impressed. I didn't know how you learned that look, but Lockwood had it down.

I'd spent much more time learning how to imitate my mother's intimidating smile. I was getting really good at it. Pity that, so far, it hadn't worked on the diplomats, lobbyists, or politicians I'd run across these last few months.

My mother being the head of the Presidential Terrorism Control

Unit had come as a shock two years ago. Sure, she'd been lying to me my whole life, but it was pretty cool to find out that my mom was basically the Annie Oakley of antiterrorism. In my new career as a diplomat, however, my mother being the head of the P.T.C.U. wasn't a threat; it was a liability, because many of the people I had to deal with knew her, and, therefore, were more than happy to tell her how I screwed up.

"Please remember that while you haven't finished the course yet, I expect all of you to do us and your spouses proud, and charm one and all."

Class was dismissed, and the others all wandered out in groups, happily chatting about what they were going to wear, who they planned to cut dead, who was the "get" politico to hang with. Eugene and I looked at each other.

Eugene was the husband of the junior senator from New York, who was on the rise. The woman was an animal, meaning she was just what Washington ordered. Eugene, however, was a sweet, mild-mannered man who looked like an actuary because he was. He was of average size, average looks, and average intelligence. And he, like me, had fallen in love with, in that sense, the wrong person at the right time and ended up here.

"We're doomed," he said finally.

"Dude, you speak the truth."

We got up and headed for the door. "You two," Lockwood said before we could escape, "come here." We did. It was like being back in high school, but we did. She shook her head. "I truly don't understand what's wrong with you two. If I didn't know better, I'd think you were both trying to sabotage your spouses' careers."

Eugene and I both started to protest, and she put up her hand. "I'm not actually accusing you." Her expression softened, and she looked almost kind. "I just want to ask one small favor of both of you."

We looked at each other. This was a new one. Maybe I'd been reading her wrong. Maybe she just wanted to help, and our failing hurt her. Maybe teaching was her calling, and we were her greatest challenges and, therefore, would be her greatest triumphs. Maybe she wanted to be the Annie Sullivan to our Helen Kellers.

Eugene and I both leaned closer. "Sure," I said. "What can we do for you?"

Lockwood cleared her throat. "Saturday night, at the President's Ball?"

"Yes?" Eugene asked.

Lockwood gave us both a tight smile. "The reputation of the Washington Wife class is extremely precious. My graduates go on to help their spouses to achieve great things." We both nodded—we'd heard this Day One. Lockwood sighed. "Look, it hurts me to say it, but somewhere along the line at that gala event, one or both of you is going to blow it in a horrible way."

I blinked. "Excuse me?"

She shrugged. "I'd appreciate it if you wouldn't mention to anyone that you're in this class. I'm certainly going to deny it, if anyone asks."

CHAPTER 2

EUGENE AND I SLUNK OUT OF CLASS. The class was held at Georgetown University, so we got to wander through the beautiful campus. It was the end of March, but it was still cold here. I hated cold.

"Well, that sucked," I said as we put our coats on and trudged outside.

"Like every week." Eugene heaved a sigh. "You think we're going to blow it at the ball?" He sounded both depressed and hopeful. Washington really brought out the dichotomies.

"No," I said as firmly as I could. "Lockwood just doesn't like us 'cause we walk to the beat of our own drums."

"Yeah. Unfortunately, my drummer is making it embarrassing for Lydia."

"My husband's okay with it." This wasn't a total lie. I hoped.

We walked along in silence, enveloped in our mutual misery. "Maybe we can both get an intestinal ailment and be forced to stay home." Eugene actually sounded like this was a plan to be hoped for.

"It never works like that. If we get sick, we'll toss the cookies right onto one of those people you never want to throw up on."

"Are there people you do want to throw up on?"

"I'm all for barfing on Lockwood."

We were still chuckling when we rounded a corner to see a number of our classmates sitting or lounging in an appropriately cool way at a couple of tables. "Hey," one of them called, "come on over!"

I didn't really want to, and I was sure Eugene didn't, either, but it was a certainty that if we cut them dead, Lockwood would be discussing it at the next class and using us as the examples of the types of people who gave those in the political lifestyle a bad name.

I shoved a smile onto my face as we reached them. "Hey, what's up?"

"Oh, we just wanted to talk to you guys for a minute," Abner Schnekedy, who'd called us over, said. He pulled out a chair for me with a flourish, meaning I had to sit or create an incident. While creating the incident sounded like a better plan, I decided to play nicely just in case and sat down, dumping my purse at my feet.

Despite having a name that should have ensured he was the butt of every single joke in the world, Abner was insanely popular in class. Possibly because he was married to Lillian Culver, who had wisely kept her maiden name for business and who was one of the top lobbyists for some major defense contractors. He was also an artist, at least according to his business cards that he'd shoved at all of us on the first day.

"What about?" Eugene asked warily as Abner pulled out a chair for him too. I couldn't blame him for being wary. Abner had now separated us, so we were on either side of him.

"What did Darcy want to talk to you two about?" Marcia Kramer asked. She was a big-breasted blonde bimbo type married to a Congressman from Illinois. She was his third wife, so even though he was on something like his eighth term, she was brand new to Washington. Somehow she felt this made her better than his former wives, as opposed to merely the next trophy in line. I relished the thought of the day her husband would get tired of her and move on to number four. It couldn't come soon enough.

"Oh, just giving us some tips for Saturday night," I lied cheerfully.

The rest of them looked at each other. Jack Ryan, who actually insisted on us acting as if he were really the main character from the Tom Clancy books, even though the only resemblance he had was in name, cleared his throat. "Come on, Ambassador. Give us the real word. Maybe we can help you."

Ryan calling me Ambassador was a real tip-off that this wasn't so much a gathering of adults discussing the next political event, but rather a lovely return to high school, with Eugene standing in for Chuckie. No one in class other than Eugene considered me an actual ambassador, so one of them using the title indicated they wanted to play. Fine with me, I'd been here many times before.

"Oh, she just wanted to reassure us," Eugene said hopelessly.

"Now, now," Ryan said with a conspiratorial wink, "you know you can't fool Jack Ryan." In addition to the rest of his delusions, his wife worked within the C.I.A., though not in the Extra-Terrestrial Division, for which I thanked God every day. So Ryan fancied himself Mister Superspy, even though he actually ran a car dealership in Silver Spring.

He looked like a guy who ran a car dealership in Silver Spring, too. He was less than six feet, had a good start on a middle-aged gut even though he was in his mid-thirties, and tended to dress just a little too flashy for the occasion.

"It wasn't a big deal," I said casually, hoping Eugene would keep his mouth shut and not volunteer.

"What was Darcy reassuring you about?" Vance Beaumont asked Eugene. He was the one who'd answered the greeting question I couldn't have gotten right if I'd actually wanted to. His husband, Guy Gadoire, was a lobbyist for the tobacco industry, making Vance one of the Big Men on Campus for the Washington Wife class. Vance didn't work. I had no idea what Vance actually did with his time when class wasn't in session, but gainful employment wasn't on his schedule.

"What we're going to be wearing," I answered before Eugene could say anything.

"Oh?" Nathalie Gagnon-Brewer asked, suddenly interested. She was the only non-American in the Washington Wife class, and I still wasn't sure why she was there, other than for something to do. She'd been a model in Paris and married a wealthy California vintner, Edmund Brewer, who'd just come on as a junior Representative. She and Eugene should have had a lot in common, but the few times she ever glanced at him, it was as if she were looking at a cockroach. "What are you wearing?"

"I have no idea. Lockwood just wanted us to be sure to dress nicely." I figured this one was a safe bet.

"Oh." Nathalie lost interest and went back to examining her iPhone.

"You should go for something really low cut," Vance suggested. "Really show off your assets."

I shot him what I really hoped was a withering look. "Thanks for the tip. I'll be sure to take it into consideration."

Leslie Manning and Bryce Taylor came over, carrying trays of drinks from the student union. She and her partner were supposedly closeted, so she represented as the best friend of the Chief Aide for the Secretary of State, Marion Villanova. Their story was that Leslie lived with her to help out because Marion was too busy to find Mister Right and start a family. Everyone played along, even me and Eugene, because, well, some things you didn't use against a person.

Bryce was "single" and supposedly only the personal assistant to Secretary of Transportation Langston Whitmore. As with Leslie, everyone knew, but again, we all faked it. Leslie and Bryce had become besties, in part because they could pretend to be dating.

As a "couple" they proved the adage that people tended to date those who looked like they did. Though Bryce was taller, they both had stocky builds and a similar taste for modified mullet haircuts and pink polo shirts. They were both attractive, though, in their ways, with a vaguely non-American look indicating they were both probably first-generation citizens.

Leslie's eyes widened when she saw me and Eugene. "Oh, I'm so sorry. We didn't know you were joining us." She actually sounded sincere, and I believed it. Of all of them, Leslie was the least offensive. I would have liked to hang out with her, if not for her friends.

Bryce, on the other hand, was a tool. "So, what prompted you two to grace us with your presence?" he asked as he handed drinks around. He finished and put his arm around Leslie's waist. She snuggled next to him with a smile. I had to give it to them—they did come off as a real couple whenever they wanted to.

"Abner asked us over," Eugene said.

Bryce and Abner exchanged a look. I recognized it. It was the "goody, fresh meat" look. I stood up. "It's been real, but I graduated from high school a long time ago. Eugene, let's go, I need to get home."

"Ambassador business to handle?" Vance asked. "Or are you going to race out to find a Wet Seal to get your dress?"

It took every ounce of my self-control, but I didn't flip him the bird. "No, actually. I'm going to go home and hang out with people who, in point of fact, have manners."

Jack shook his head. "Be careful. Wouldn't want you to cause an international incident on your way home."

Eugene looked as though he didn't know if he should stay or go. Why he wanted to be tortured I had no idea, but I decided not to let him make a potentially bad decision. "Eugene, you're my ride. I need to get home to my daughter."

"Right!" Eugene stood up as I grabbed my purse, which had gotten shoved under the middle of the table somehow. "See you guys Saturday night."

"Oh, we can't wait," Marcia said.

Vance nodded. "We're so looking forward to seeing what you two wear."

"And what you two do," Abner said, managing to control a snicker. "We can't wait for that."

Bryce did snicker, Leslie looked as though she wanted to be anywhere else, and Nathalie didn't look up from her phone. I got the impression she was playing Angry Birds and really couldn't tear herself away for anything less than a nuclear threat.

"I'll bet you can't."

Abner gave me a slow smile. "My money's on you doing a strip-tease after you've had one drink. You are named for a stripper, right? Your mother, perhaps?"

I wanted to punch his face in, but that actually would cause an international incident. Besides, I'd grown up watching people taunt Chuckie this way. He'd never let them goad him into something stupid, and I did learn by example.

I leaned closer to Abner, however, and got right into his face. He clearly hadn't expected it, at least if I took his eyes widening and shifting all over as proof. "Abner? You and *your* ridiculous name better pray that my mother and I don't decide to strip your ass down for parts. Though I have to bet you'd only be useful if we needed some manure really quickly."

With that, I spun on my heel and left, Eugene, thankfully, coming with me.

"See you Saturday night," Bryce called. "If you survive that long."

"My Glock, my Glock," I muttered as we strode off. "My kingdom for my Glock." Like so many things, I wasn't allowed to carry it to the Washington Wife class, presumably because everyone knew I'd use it.

"What?" Eugene asked.

"Nothing. Just having another really nostalgic moment."

Eugene sighed. "I miss my old job and where we used to live. No one ever acted like this."

"Dude, you're speaking to my soul. I miss my old job like you wouldn't believe."

I wondered if there was any way to lure a few parasitic jellyfish over, toss them onto those people, and then kill them, all in the name of saving humanity.

Probably not. I never lucked into good things like that.

CHAPTER 3

"WELL, THAT WAS HELL ON EARTH," I said finally when we were far enough away that I knew there was no chance they could hear us.

"Sorry," Eugene said. "I knew we should have pretended we didn't see them."

"Like we had a choice? But not to worry. I plan to spill something that stains permanently on all their clothes at the ball, so it'll all even out."

Eugene stared at me. "Seriously?"

"Dead seriously."

He grinned. "Punch?"

"I'm thinking of some kind of oil, like WD-40, possibly mixed with dirt, breast milk, foundation, and chocolate. Very, very hard to get out."

"I might enjoy the ball after all," Eugene said almost cheerfully.

I looked around as we walked on. The riot of spring was in full force, but while the colors were pretty, they weren't desert colors, and I was a desert girl.

I noted someone lounging against a tree that was bragging to the other trees about how it was a proud Maple of the American Revolution and explaining how its leafy branches made the rest of them look inferior. I'd have missed him if I hadn't been doing a morose study in comparative botany.

He was a big guy, built along Jeff's lines. As he smiled and gave me a nod, I realized he was someone from our class, Malcolm Buchanan, one of the few who didn't really "group" with anyone. He was sporting the tall, blue-eyed, brown-haired, big and brooding hottie look. I had to admit that if I were single, I'd have been interested in seeing if he was interested in hanging with me.

However, I wasn't single, and, if he was in the Washington Wife class, he wasn't either. So I went for the semi-friendly wave. He grinned as Eugene turned to see who I was waving to. "You friendly with him?" Eugene asked, sounding displeased.

"Not really. Not enemies, either, though."

"Oh. I don't like him."

"Why not? Has he been a jerk like the people we just left?"

"No. He just . . . he makes me nervous. He's always watching us."

I turned around. Buchanan was indeed watching us. He didn't seem fazed by the fact that I was looking back at him. In fact, he winked. I felt my cheeks get hot.

I turned around, and we kept moving while I worked to stop blushing like an idiot. These days I wasn't used to anyone but my husband making me blush.

We walked on and reached the parking lot Eugene used in a couple of minutes. He drove himself. I would have, but the A-Cs were against it for a variety of reasons, the biggest being that A-C reflexes were so fast that they couldn't actually drive, fly, or use other human machinery safely.

I wasn't an A-C, despite the lovely parting gifts that having our daughter, Jamie, had given me. We'd done the mother and child feedback thing, and since her daddy was a mutated alien thanks to some of our many enemies, Jamie had shared some mutated alien genes with me. I could still drive and fly. But as the Co-Chief of Mission, no one wanted me to.

I was used to it. When I'd been the head of Airborne for Centaurion Division, Tim Crawford had been my driver. Tim had my old job now, and, from what he told me, he was having a great time. It wouldn't be hard to have more fun than I was having, I had to admit.

Of course, we hadn't found a human driver I clicked with yet. And since I was already miserable, Jeff was going out of his way to try to find someone, anyone, to make me a little happier about our major job changes and their required location. So far, not a lot of luck, but then again, there was only one Tim, and he was busy saving the day and kicking evil butt.

Normally Eugene dropped me off at the A-C Embassy. I got to avoid upsetting the latest human operative who'd been given Driving Miss Kitty duty, and it gave us more time together without anyone else telling us we sucked. But today there was a gray limo at the curb, parked, with the motor idling.

A big, tall, droolingly handsome man with rather broad features and dark brown eyes under a great head of dark, wavy hair was leaning against the side of the car. He was in a black Armani suit, crisp white shirt, and black tie, with a black overcoat on. He gave me a wide smile.

I ran and jumped into his arms. Jeff pulled me to him and kissed me. As always, his kiss was amazing, and it washed away any thoughts about my inadequacy, the horrible high school reenactment we'd just gone through, or other men. As also always, my thoughts instead happily turned to getting our clothes off as soon as possible.

He ended the kiss slowly, eyes smoldering. "How're you doing, baby?"

I sighed. "Much better now. What brings you here?"

He shook his head. "The two of you are giving off suicide-level depression," he said in a low voice Eugene was unlikely to hear. In addition to his other talents and with the assist from some drugs he'd been unwittingly given by those aforementioned enemies, Jeff was the strongest empath in, most likely, the universe. He always monitored me, and, again due to the mutation said drugs had caused, he could read much of my mind. He'd started monitoring Eugene, too, because Eugene was with me when no one else Jeff trusted was.

Jeff kept one arm around me and put his other hand out to Eugene, who was politely waiting nearby. "How's it going?"

Eugene shook Jeff's hand. "It's going as well as it ever does."

"That bad, huh?" Jeff shook his head again. "You two can't be doing that poorly."

"We suck. We're trying hard not to care, but it's true. And Lockwood wants to disavow all knowledge of us at the President's Ball. Do we have to go?"

"Yes," Jeff said firmly. "Both of you." He gave Eugene a commiserating smile. "It could be worse."

"How?" Eugene asked. "I certainly don't want to humiliate Lydia, but it seems as though that's all I do. I'm not an outgoing person. She used to like that."

"I'm sure she still does. I mean, Jeff still likes me the way I am. Right?" I tried not to sound worried about his reply.

Jeff laughed. "Yes, baby, I love you for exactly how you are." He sighed. "Try not to worry about Saturday night, either one of you."

We exchanged some more meaningless chitchat, then Eugene went to his car. "So, why are you really here?" I asked as soon as Eugene waved and drove off.

"Just wanted to see you. Like I said, suicide-level depression." Of course, A-Cs couldn't lie, at least, not most of them. Jeff was awful at it, though he tried hard. Like now. I had yet to share that looking at your shoes was a dead giveaway—I mean, why help them with it?

"I'm willing to bet we give that off every class. So there has to be a reason other than that, or you'd pick me up every week. Or, better, refuse to let me go. So, what's going on?"

Jeff sighed. "I'll explain in the car. Or, rather, he will."

"He who?" I asked as Jeff opened the door and helped me inside.

"Me, who."

I knew the voice better than I knew Jeff's, but only because I'd known it a lot longer. "Hey, Chuckie, what brings you by to watch my latest shame?"

He shook his head as Jeff got in next to me and shut the door. "Nice to see you're dealing well with it."

I snorted. Unlike Lockwood's, it was neither dainty nor ladylike. "Dude, you'd hate it, too, trust me. Especially the people in class with us. You'd loathe them."

"So you've whined to me for weeks. I know most of their respective spouses, so I'm sure you're right. However, I'm hoping I have at least a partial solution."

"I can take this class from someone else?"

Chuckie laughed. "No, sorry, you're stuck. But I think it's your overall attitude that's the problem."

"I'm doing just fine in the Diplomacy for Beginners class."

"Because it's taught by someone you like," Chuckie said patiently.

"True." My mother's best friend, my Aunt Emily, had been a senator's daughter. She still lived in the area and occasionally taught the diplomacy class. In honor of my ascension into the ranks of all things political, she'd enthusiastically taken it upon herself to train the entire new A-C Diplomatic Corps on the ins and outs of our new jobs. She wasn't aware that half of the Corps were aliens, nor that the former Diplomatic Corps had been eaten. Some things I tried not to share with my mother's oldest friend.

Speaking of that which had eaten the Corps, a bundle of cuteness peeked out from Chuckie's coat pocket. It saw me, purred, and leaped into my lap. "Hey, Fluffy. How's a Poofy thing?" Fluffy purred loudly while I petted it and relaxed a little. The Poofs had been among the cool things we'd gotten during Operation Invasion, or, as others insisted on calling it, my wedding. Jeff was part of the Royal Family of Alpha Four, and, as such, the Poofs were a part of that whole deal.

The Poofs looked a lot like tiny, fluffy kittens with no ears or tails, but with shiny black button eyes. They were fluffy balls on tiny legs and paws, and I loved them. I had one, but the Poofs, like my Glock, were off limits at the Washington Wife class, so Poofikins had to stay home. Which was a pity, because I found the Poofs very soothing. And since they could go Jeff-sized and quite toothy when danger threatened, they were wonderful personal protection bundles of cuteness.

Despite being Alpha Four animals, in the Poofs' world, if you named it, it was yours. Ergo, a lot of Poofs belonged to humans, Chuckie being one of the first, but certainly not the last, to get one.

I noted something while I petted Fluffy and enjoyed its purrs. The limo wasn't moving, and Jeff wasn't arguing with Chuckie, glaring at him, or giving off any kind of "go away you bother me" vibes. This was rare when they were together, especially if they were together with me. Jeff still wasn't quite over the fact that Chuckie had proposed, and I'd considered it, while Jeff and I were sort of broken up. Operation Drug Addict had some good memories attached to it, but not nearly enough to make me reminisce often.

"Why aren't we moving?" I looked forward, at the driver. There were two men up there, but they were facing front. No one I recognized from the back, but I knew for sure that whoever was driving hadn't been the one who'd brought me to class.

The driver looked fairly tall, big, and built along Jeff's lines. The guy who had shotgun was bigger. They were both in suits.

Chuckie grinned. "I don't know. Why don't you tell your driver where you want to go?"

I didn't get it, but I knew that look. When you've been best friends with a guy since ninth grade, you know his looks. And this one was saying "I know you're gonna like it" quite clearly.

I leaned forward. "Excuse me, but can you take us back to the Embassy?"

The driver turned around and flashed me a grin. "Of course. Trojan football always here to help."

CHAPTER 4

I COULDN'T HELP IT, I squealed. "Len!" The bigger guy turned around and grinned, too. "Kyle! What are you guys doing here?" Len and Kyle had been on the USC football team and, thankfully, in Vegas when Jeff and I were doing the pre-show entertainment of saving the world before we got married. They'd helped us, me in particular, in a big way.

Len laughed. "We're out of college and working for the C.I.A."

"Just like we told you we'd do," Kyle added. "I've been completely clean, too. No drinking, no carousing, no threatening women, just studying and prepping."

"True enough," Chuckie said. "He's not only been clean, he spent the last year running USC's Take Back the Night program, volunteering for their escort service and teaching girls what to look for to avoid a date rape situation and also what to do to get out of it safely."

"Excuse me—escort service? Kyle became a pimp or a gigolo, and you're all okay with that?"

Jeff coughed, Chuckie started laughing his head off, and Len leaned his head on the steering wheel he was laughing so hard, while Kyle turned bright red.

"No," Chuckie gasped out. "It's the program where someone can get Security or similar to walk them back to their dorm, apartment, sorority house, and so on. It's a protective service. We had it at ASU."

"Oh. Maybe we did. I never needed it—I used CPS."

Chuckie started laughing again, though Len got himself under control. Kyle was still blushing.

"What are you talking about?" Jeff asked.

"My campus escort was always handled by Chuckie Protective Services."

"I don't want to hear about it," Jeff said, with a half-groan and half-growl.

"Also," Len said quickly, "Kyle was one of the main representatives for our sports program's preventive counseling service that works with athletes to keep them from becoming the kind of bastards who think they can do anything to any woman at any time."

"Really? Wow."

"Really," Len said. "You don't want to know what he did to anyone on any of our teams who even looked at a girl slightly funny." Len sounded proud of Kyle. Considering he'd been more than fed up with him when we'd met, this, more than the listing of Kyle's protective resume, impressed me.

"You'd appreciate it, however," Chuckie added.

Kyle's blush was still on full. "I just wanted you to be sure you could trust me," he mumbled.

"Nicely done." I figured saying that I'd already trusted him would sort of diminish all his achievements, so I kept it to myself. I congratulated myself on the fact that I could be diplomatic, at least sometimes and with certain people.

"So, meet your driver and bodyguard," Chuckie said. "If you want them, of course."

"Totally! But, um, why them, why two, and why C.I.A. operatives and not Centaurion agents?"

Jeff sighed. "I know why you haven't liked the other drivers we've tried—you didn't recruit them or go through a danger situation with them. They're just random men to you. Human agents help us blend in more easily, and you're away from me far too often these days—in addition to someone who can drive, I want someone with you I know will break necks if you're threatened. I also want someone smart enough to recognize danger before it blows up in your faces."

"Makes sense."

"Thanks," Jeff said dryly. "Because we need to use humans here in D.C. as much as possible, Reynolds, James, and I discussed it, and two makes more sense because while they can't do all we can, they can double the protection if needed. These two know who we are, what we do, and why we're here. You've hated every Centaurion agent we've given you, and Reynolds insisted these were the two who would make you happy."

"Aw, you got that out without growling. I'm so proud. And, yeah, Chuckie, you're right, great choices! So which C.I.A. division are they part of?"

"They work for me. Directly, I might add. I wanted someone I felt I could trust near you. Under the circumstances, Reader and your husband agreed."

"Awesome. Home, please."

Len winked at me, then he and Kyle turned around, and we drove off. While I basked in the glow of finally having people who were more likely to actually want to discuss sports and music while driving, I ran this event over in my mind. Something didn't add up. What circumstances was Chuckie referring to, and why was Jeff suddenly so concerned for my safety, when he'd told me only this morning to go to class and stop whining like a baby?

I looked up at Jeff. "What's coming that has you two so worried that you're working together like actual adults?"

Bingo. His eyes started shifting. "Nothing."

"Nothing my ass." I looked at Chuckie. He had a poker face on, but I still knew him too well. "Spill it."

Chuckie sighed. "I told you she'd figure something was off."

"She doesn't need to worry," Jeff growled.

"Worried now. I did mention that I liked you acting like adults, though, right?"

"Right." Chuckie looked at Jeff, who heaved a sigh and nodded. Chuckie looked back to me. "My sources have determined there's going to be an assassination attempt, quite soon, most likely at the President's Ball."

CHAPTER 5

WE DROVE ON WHILE I let that one sit on the air for a bit. Many questions were banging around in my head. I went with the obvious first. "The President?"

"Possibly, but he doesn't sound like the actual target. Your mother has her team on full alert, of course, and they'll be working with the Secret Service."

"So my mom will be at the party Saturday night, too?"

"And your father," Jeff said. "We have a team assigned to him, since he'll be more in the background."

"A-C team or human team?"

"Combination," Chuckie replied. "C.I.A. and Centaurion."

"Which C.I.A.? Your team that wants to keep us alive, or the other C.I.A. that wants to turn us into the War Division?"

"Both." Chuckie didn't sound happy about it. "I can't keep Agency personnel out, not with this threat level. Especially since we have no clear idea who the target is. Or targets."

"Who do you think?" Chuckie's nickname in high school had been Conspiracy Chuck and, insulting though it was, it was also accurate. He was the smartest guy in any and every room, and pretty much if he had a solid theory, he was right. Of course, if he didn't know, we were flying blind.

He shook his head. "I have no idea."

"We're so screwed."

Jeff sighed. "I see you're really getting a lot out of that Washington Wife class."

"Can I drop it?"

"No." Chuckie and Jeff said this in unison. I hated the unison thing. I never won against it.

I pondered other options. "Does it have anything to do with the various conspiracies we discovered during Operation Confusion?"

Chuckie shrugged. "It might. But we're still tracking people down." He grimaced. "As you know, I had most of my team working on following those leads. However, I've had to pull them in because of this threat. How much this will delay us, I have no guess, but I'm not happy about it. Then again, averting an assassination is probably in everyone's best interests."

We'd discovered that the former Diplomatic Corps had been working with several divisions of the C.I.A. on a variety of nasty plans, all of them aimed at turning Centaurion Division into the War Division in some way, shape, or form. Chuckie was having to work slowly and carefully, because his investigation was pitting him against the people who wanted to destroy us and kill him. He also hadn't been able to confirm who higher up in the C.I.A. and the various world governments was in on which plan or plans, and who wasn't a lying sack of excrement. So far, this had meant a lot of strategic maneuvering I'd been too busy being indoctrinated into the D.C. lifestyle to be a part of.

"Can't argue with the 'let's not let anyone get murdered' logic."

"If only we knew who the anyone was," Jeff said. Chuckie grunted. I got the impression they'd been stressing about this the entire time I'd been gone.

We pulled into the garage for the American Centaurion Embassy. It was underground, but that didn't mean it wasn't spacious. Like everything else the A-Cs did, the Embassy was big and had a lot going on underground.

The Embassy was a full city block, long and wide, and it went up seven floors and down one. Well, it went down more than one, since we'd discovered a hidden elevator and a really hidden secret lab during what I referred to as Operation Confusion. Chuckie and I had destroyed the lab with the help of Richard White, in his last days as the Pontifex of the A-Cs, or, as I thought of it, their Pope With Benefits.

White had retired to the active lifestyle and, on the rare occasions when we got to do something other than smile at politicians, was now my partner in the butt-kicking. Which, sadly, meant he was getting a good chance to catch up on his reading.

The parking garage was under the basement level, meaning it was two stories down. That it only took up three-quarters of the block should have been a clue to someone that there was something going on at the far side, but apparently these things only occurred to me. Then again, my specialty was thinking like psychos and megalomaniacs. A skill that should have made fitting into Washington a breeze, when I thought about it.

Of course, the A-Cs didn't care about cars like humans did, and the former, now eaten, Diplomatic Corps had been deeply involved in that secret lab and all the horror therein, so that had undoubtedly had a lot to do with everyone else's dimness.

We got out of the car and a new bundle of cuteness appeared out of nowhere. "Poofikins!" And then another. "Harlie!" Poofikins was mine and Harlie was the head Poof and belonged to Jeff, though the Poofs all seemed to prefer females to males. They both seemed to know I needed the extra Poofiness when I got back from class.

The Poofs had their little purrfest, then Fluffy went back into Chuckie's pocket, job, presumably, done. Poofikins and Harlie stayed on my shoulders. Poof adornments were not an issue.

Of course, there was one bundle of cuteness severely lacking. Even if I hadn't been thinking about her, my breasts were sharing that it was time to feed my baby. As per usual, I didn't actually have breasts at the moment, I had torpedoes. "Jeff? Can we let Chuckie and the boys get upstairs by themselves?"

"Sure, I know the way," Chuckie said with a grin. "Go take care of Jamie."

Jeff grunted, grabbed my hand, and we took off at hyperspeed. I could do the hyperspeed now all on my own, but I was having some issues with control, so it was wiser to have an A-C holding onto me, preferably Jeff.

For whatever reason, there was no elevator to the parking area—stairs only. I'd run track in high school and college under the most dedicated, and sadistic, coaches in history, so stair charges had been a part of my life for a long time. Having hyperspeed was better, but I'd spent the last three months discovering that the effort was the same even with the cool A-C powers.

However, going up the nine flights to get up to the top floor was only about a quarter of what I used to run routinely, so we zipped upstairs. We'd discovered it was bad and embarrassing to take the elevator when I was ready to feed Jamie. The milk stains were gone, and the smell hadn't really lingered, but the ribbing from everyone was still going strong. That Jeff and I were basically incapable of being in an elevator alone together and not making out was, in my opinion, a good thing.

I could hear Jamie crying as we reached the top floor of the Embassy. Half of this floor was our living quarters. The other half belonged to Christopher White and Amy Gaultier. Amy had been one of my best girlfriends in high school and had gotten pulled into the fun and frolic of my new life only three months ago. They'd made the Action Love Connection during Operation Confusion and were officially engaged.

We entered our rooms or, rather, our palatial suite of rooms tons bigger than the house I'd grown up in. Though the Embassy was one of the A-C showcases, where they most easily pretended they were "just folks," I still wasn't fully comfortable in it. However, having a huge nursery connected to the master bedroom was a big plus that came with living in a place large enough to house a small country.

I was glad of the space when I realized we didn't just have Christopher and Amy with Jamie, but a whole lot of others as well. "What's going on?" I asked Christopher. "You two couldn't handle one three-month-old baby for a couple of hours and had to call in all of Alpha and Airborne to assist?"

Christopher was Jeff's cousin, though he was smaller and shorter, with straight, lighter brown hair, green eyes, and more wiry than buff and brawny, albeit with the family rock-hard abs.

He also had glaring down to an art form and was hitting us with Patented Glare #2. This one was rarely used and indicated severe stress. "You're late," he snapped. "Jamie's been crying for fifteen minutes straight. Nothing we did worked. I was about to call your mother."

"I still pump enough milk to qualify as a dairy cow. You're suddenly incapable of giving her a bottle?" I asked as I reached for my squalling offspring.

"She wouldn't take it," Amy said. "I think she knew you were late."

Jamie quieted the moment she was in my arms. "Awww, Mommy's little Jamie-Kat likes her routine, doesn't she?" I cooed. I took another look around while I kissed her head. I'd seen right the first time—all of Alpha and Airborne teams were lounging around my living room, as were White and his replacement, our new Pontifex, Paul Gower, who doubled as another of Jeff's cousins and Reader's mate. "Seriously, a crying baby isn't exactly 'call the cavalry' worthy. What's going on?"

Jeff sighed. "Assassination threats, however, are something we all pay attention to, baby."

"Oh." The realization that they'd been having the big powwow while I was being tortured during and after the Washington Wife class sauntered up and waved at me. "I'll, um, just take care of the baby then, while you all figure out how to save the world." I rushed into our bedroom as fast as I could. Crying in front of everyone didn't seem like my best plan.

As I stepped into the room, I heard purring, and Jamie heaved a big sigh. There were a number of luxurious cat trees that I called Poof Condos in our bedroom, filled to capacity with Poofs.

Due to our marriage, we'd gotten a starter set of six Poofs. They were androgynous and could mate with each other, supposedly only when a Royal Wedding was imminent. Right after Jamie was born, and also right after a set of power-mad lunatics had tried to kill us all, we'd had a major Poof explosion. No one knew why, beyond Christopher and Amy hooking up, but we had a *lot* of Poofs. No one minded. Poofs for all was my viewpoint, and more Poofs for me was my other viewpoint.

We had all the spare, unnamed Poofs living with us—I called it the Privilege of Royalty whenever Jeff couldn't hear me, and my right as the co-head diplomat when he could. Jamie had her own Poof. She wasn't exactly speaking at three months of age, so I had no idea how she might have named it to claim it as hers, but this one Poof in particular liked to be near her, so we let it. It did the Poof "there one moment and here the next" thing and snuggled up against her tummy, purring. She wrapped her little hand in its fur and gurgled happily.

Jeff came in behind me, and the purring increased. "Why wasn't Jamie's Poof with her?" I asked as I headed into the nursery. It seemed a safer question than "what were you all talking about before I got here and ruined the summit meeting."

"No idea. Baby, you're upset for nothing."

Right. Empath. Two years in, you'd think I'd remember that he always knew what I was feeling. "I know. I'm not the head of Airborne anymore."

Jeff took Jamie while I settled myself into the lounger in her room and got ready to feed her. He shook his head as he checked her diaper. "No, you're not. I'm not the head of the Field anymore, either, and Christopher's no longer the head of Imageering." He shot me a look I knew was suggesting I think instead of sulk.

I gave it a shot. It was me, and I thought best aloud. Fortunately, Jeff was used to it. "Everyone's here." He nodded, leadingly. "Waiting for you and Chuckie to get back." Jeff's eyelids lowered to slits.

This wasn't his sexy, jungle-cat look; this was his "you're really trying to be stupid" look. I pondered a little more. "And waiting for me to get back?" I asked hopefully.

He finished up with Jamie's diaper and helped get her eating. She'd been a chowhound from birth, and that hadn't waned; she was happily snorking down breast milk in a matter of moments. "Yes. We have no idea who the target is, but you and I will be at the President's Ball. Therefore, you and I are integral to whatever plans are put into place."

"So what was decided without me?"

Jeff heaved a sigh. "Not much. James wanted to wait for you to get back."

On cue he popped his head in. Reader was still the best looking human I'd ever seen in the flesh, and if he wasn't gay and married to Gower, my life might be very different. Seeing as he was, however, the cover-boy smile being flashed at me merely reminded me that someone thought my input was necessary.

"Girlfriend, while you feed the baby, want you thinking about a couple of key points I'm sure Jeff and Reynolds didn't tell you."

I tried not to visibly perk up but failed if the grins I got from both Reader and Jeff were any indication. "Sure, James. Lay 'em on me."

He nodded. "First, Reynolds' 'source' happens to be our favorite investigative reporter of all time."

"Really? Chuckie takes information from Mister Joel Oliver?"

Reader shrugged. "Per Reynolds, the guy's almost never wrong. The second point, however, is that we have no idea if it's a lone assassin, a group, or anything else you can come up with. I'd like you to come up with everything you can, though, because we have less than two days to avert God literally knows what."

CHAPTER 6

READER POPPED BACK OUT, and we switched Jamie to the other torpedo. "What *do* we actually know?"

Jeff sighed. "Sadly, baby, that's it."

"So you saved it all for me?" Things suddenly seemed more like they used to be.

He grinned. "Yeah. See? I said you were getting yourself upset for nothing."

"Humph. So, what are the chances that this is aimed at Centaurion Division as opposed to the President or another high-ranking human official?"

"No guess. Reynolds and I have already communicated with Alpha Four, just to be safe."

That we were able to casually talk to people in the Alpha Centaurion solar system had much to do with ACE, the superconsciousness I'd managed to filter into Gower during Operation Drug Addict. The rest had to do with the fact they were a lot farther along the advancement scale in that solar system and occasionally shared with us.

"What did Alexander and/or Victoria have to say?" I'd put Alexander on the throne of Alpha Four, and Victoria was, therefore, the Queen Mother. They were Jeff's cousins, though they were closer in the bloodline to Christopher. I liked them a lot, especially since they hadn't resented me or Tito for killing their other family members. Hey, some royal successions are bloodier than others. "Could this be our fave escaped megalomaniacs coming back to try to snatch our baby again?"

"As far as Alexander knows, all's quiet. All of the A-C system monitors for them regularly, and we do as well; happily, there's been no sign of either Ronaldo Al Dejahl or LaRue Demorte Gaultier, let alone my loser of a brother-in-law." Amy's stepmother had been the brains behind Operation Confusion and had hijacked an interstellar ship with the illegitimate son of the devil himself or, as we knew him, the Ronald Yates/Mephistopheles superbeing, in tow. As far as we knew, they'd also taken A-C Traitor at Large Clarence Valentino with them. Good riddance to all.

"Okay. So, more importantly, what did Councilor Leonidas have to say?"

"Per what he told Reynolds, if there's a threat, it's not coming from any agent outside Earth."

"Does Chuckie believe him?"

"Yes, as far as he's told me." I let go of the breath I hadn't realized I was holding, and Jeff grimaced. "It's so nice to know you still think he walks on water." Jeff's sarcasm knob went to eleven, though I put this response only around five. Personal growth, it was a good thing.

"Oldest friend. Brilliant. Massively successful in three separate careers. Risks his life to protect us. I'm not seeing the downside to valuing his opinion. You were doing so well with the jealousy. Let's go back to that."

Jeff sighed. "I don't think it's jealousy if it's based on fact, but I'll give you that this situation is more important."

I decided to merely enjoy the personal growth as opposed to comment on it. Jeff was massively jealous and possessive, but since he made up for that in any number of amazing ways, at least half of them sexual, I lived with it. Besides, it was still flattering that he was worried that someone other than himself was going to sweep me off my feet.

"So it's someone new. Or someone old. Or someone borrowed, and we probably can't rule out someone blue."

"Nice to see you're focusing on Christopher and Amy's wedding as opposed to our current situation." Jeff's sarcasm knob was heading toward eleven after all.

"Just adding some undoubtedly much needed levity to lessen the strain of a tense situation." Jamie was done, and Jeff took her from me, put her gently on his shoulder, and patted her back. "You're such a good daddy."

He smiled, and for the first time since we'd gotten back, he looked relaxed. "Glad you think so." Jamie burped rather hugely, then cooed. "And glad to see our Jamie-Kat thinks so, too."

We finished up, and I put Jamie into a cute Minnie Mouse sleeper, one of the many gifts from her A-C induction ceremony. Then we joined the others in what Jeff called the Great Room and what I called the Humongous Living Room.

I did a fast head count. I hadn't been wrong before—everyone in any position of power within Centaurion Division was here. It was a good thing the rooms in our penthouse were huge, because otherwise we'd have had to use video conferencing to talk to each other.

Alpha Team currently consisted of Reader, Tim, Serene—who was now the Head of Imageering—Gower, and, technically, me. I hadn't gotten a lot of time with the team over the past three months, but I held onto my Head of Recruitment title with both hands and at least one foot. White, as my now-partner and the former Pontifex, was still considered a part of Alpha, too, albeit a very nonpublicized part.

The rest of Airborne, also known as my five flyboys, were here as well, as was Tito Hernandez, though he'd been sidelined into Embassy life, too, as our official Doctor in Residence. He seemed to mind it the least, possibly because he was doing what he loved every day.

Lorraine and Claudia were both my best A-C girlfriends and had also assumed the positions Reader and Tim had vacated when they'd been promoted, so they were now Captains. They were also both extremely pregnant—we expected their babies to arrive, at most, days apart. It was fitting. They were besties, they'd married Joe Billings and Randy Muir, respectively, who were two of said flyboys and also best friends. That they were going to have their babies at the same time seemed right.

In addition to Alpha and Airborne teams, we also had several others represented. Brian Dwyer, my old high school boyfriend and now Serene's husband, was in attendance. Chuckie, Len, and Kyle had joined the crowd. And Kevin Lewis, my mom's right-hand man and another human giving the A-Cs a run in the looks department, was with us as well.

"Wow, the heck with the President's Ball. If someone wants to take us down, all they'd have to do is blow up the Embassy right now, and Centaurion Division would lose everyone who controls its protection." I got a lot of dirty looks. "I guess you're all hungry. We need to call Subway or something for a Party Platter."

I was saved from snide comments by a knock; Tito went to get the door. In came Doreen and Irving Weisman. Doreen was the daughter of the former head diplomatic couple and Irving was her human husband. She was handling her parents' "disappearance" remarkably well, probably because she'd come to loathe her parents by the time Operation Confusion went down. I couldn't blame her—I'd loathed them from my first minutes of meeting them, her late mother, Barbara, in particular.

"Geez, where's Walter? I think we have everyone else conceivable in here."

Brian shook his head. "Actually not. Michael, Naomi, and Abigail are on their way." These were Gower's younger siblings. Michael, like Brian, was an astronaut. Naomi and Abigail, like Jamie, were not only hybrids with an A-C and a human parent, but they also had stronger, mutated talents, which was something female hybrids had over the male ones. It made a lot of sense to have the girls here, and when we needed extra muscle we could trust, if he was on the planet, Michael was our go-to guy.

We'd originally thought Serene was a hybrid, but during Operation Confusion we had discovered she was another one of Ronald Yates' illegitimate children. She'd handled this news pretty well, mostly because it meant that White was her older brother and Christopher, therefore, her nephew, meaning she actually had family that cared about her.

That Ronaldo Al Dejahl was also her older brother was something we all did our best not to talk about too much. The rest of us were too busy trying not to worry about how many other illegitimate offspring, either hybrid or mutant-level talented, Yates had left around. Sadly, we had to figure there were a lot; when he'd been alive, he'd made Hugh Hefner look like a fuddy-duddy.

"And your mom and dad are with the President," Jerry Tucker, my favorite flyboy, shared cheerfully, thankfully pulling my mind back from thinking about Yates and his heinous ways. "But we can get them on speakerphone if we need to."

"Walter's staying in the Security Center," Christopher added. As our Acting Head of Security, this made sense. The kid was also still awed to be working with us and determined to be the best security chief anyone could find in any part of the galaxy. I really liked Walter.

"But I'm on the com, Chiefs."

"Nice to hear your voice, Walt. So, gang, what do we have?"

An alarm went off. "Sorry," Walter said politely. "But you don't have time for the briefing, Co-Chief Martini."

CHAPTER 7

"EXCUSE ME?" I KNEW HE MEANT ME. No one ever referred to Jeff as co-anything. The benefits of being in charge for his entire adult life.

"I'm in charge of your calendar right now, Chief, remember?" I did. This was because I'd conveniently "forgotten" the Washington Wife class, so Jeff had added this onto Walter's list of fun things to do. "You and Jamie have a Mommy and Me class to attend."

Of all the classes I went to, Mommy and Me was the only fun one. "I love going, but aren't we in a crisis situation?"

Chuckie nodded. "We are. But we also don't want anyone aware that we know we're in a crisis situation."

"So everyone's here having a powwow, and yet I'm going to do baby calisthenics?" I felt another pout coming on.

"Yes," Jeff said firmly. "Having the jocks along will be enough of a change to alert someone that things are off, but I don't want you going anywhere alone."

"You could come with me. They encourage fathers to attend."

"We need him," Reader said. "We need you, too, but Reynolds is right. We have no idea who the target is, but if we all go into lockdown, we'll alert the assassin that we're aware of the plot."

"And then they'd pick a new target event, and we'd have no head's up for that and would have lost our window of opportunity. I get it." I heaved a sigh. "Well, someone let us know if you figure out what's going on while we're off being our version of normal."

I trotted back into the bedroom to find Jamie's diaper bag all packed and sitting on the bed, along with a baby snowsuit with fluffy faux-fur-lined hood for her and a long, black coat with a less fluffy faux-fur-lined hood for me. Per Jeff, this was done by the Operations Team. Per me, it was the A-C Elves. I'd certainly never seen any of the Elves in person, at least to my knowledge, and they worked like magic. Christopher liked to try to explain this more comprehensively, but his explanation made my head hurt so I ignored it.

I changed out of my "appropriate" clothes—the Armani fatigues as I called them, white Oxford shirt and black slim skirt to everyone else—since I didn't have to pretend to be anything but a mom for Mommy and Me. I put on a clean pair of jeans and one of my long-sleeved Aerosmith T-shirts, the ones with the snazzy rhinestones creating the band's logo. I always felt better with Steven, Joe, and the rest of my boys on my chest.

Under the circumstances, I got my Glock out of the drawer Jeff thought he had it hidden in, made sure it was loaded, and shoved it and a couple of extra clips into the bottom of my purse, focusing on flowers the entire time. Jeff didn't come in and rip the Glock out of my possession, so I figured the flowers had worked their empathic avoidance magic.

Reader joined me and bundled Jamie into her snowsuit while I got my coat on. It was March but winter was giving spring a good fight to the death. Spring seemed to be winning in terms of flora and fauna, but winter was keeping the cold around until the bitter end. I let the homesickness for Arizona and New Mexico wash over me and then shoved it aside. Danger was back on the case, and that meant me longing for the desert wasn't going to do us any good.

"I mean it, girlfriend," he said as he snuggled his goddaughter and got a happy coo in return. "I want you thinking. Reynolds, Kevin, and your mother have run down intel on every terrorist organization known, the ones only the C.I.A. and P.T.C.U. know about and our personal favorites included, and nothing's coming up. If the threat is real, and we all think it is, then we have to get some kind of handle on things before Saturday night."

"I'll do my best, James." I sighed. "At least you have the others to bounce ideas off of."

"Use your new personnel. Reynolds says they're trustworthy, and they certainly helped in Vegas. He also says they're smart, and we need all the smart we can get now."

I nodded. Reader wasn't empathic, but clearly my sulking was obvious, because he put his hand under my chin and moved my head so I was looking at him. "No one's trying to shove you or Jeff and Christopher out of this. We may have all taken new positions, but we're still the same team we were before." He flashed me the cover-boy grin. "And you know I work best with my best girl helping me."

I hugged him. "Thanks, James. That makes me feel tons better." It did. I slung the diaper bag over one shoulder, my purse onto the other, and took Jamie, feeling more cheerful about things. Her Poof was clearly coming along for the ride, and as I checked, so were Poofikins and Harlie. Poof hitchhikers were not an issue. "The Martini Girls are ready for action."

Reader laughed as he escorted me out. Jeff took Jamie, and Len had her stroller with him. Not only was it top of the line, but there were a lot of A-C bells and whistles on it, including an invisibility cloaking device and a laser shield. Anyone touching the stroller or touching someone in contact with the stroller was in its protection range. For some this would be ridiculous overkill. For us it meant Jeff didn't have an ulcer from worrying whenever Jamie and I were out of his sight.

We took the elevator down to the first floor, then trooped the rest of the way downstairs. Jeff ensured Jamie's car seat was secure, then pulled me into his arms and kissed me. I did my best not to grind against him but, as always, it took effort.

"Be good, baby," he said softly. "Remember that we don't know who the target is, and that means it could be you."

"Or you. Or any one of the others." I leaned my head against his chest. "I have to wear some fancy dress I don't have to the ball."

"Go shopping after class."

"Yeah, it's the only way I can be assured of getting something in a color other than black and white and from a designer other than Armani." A-Cs loved formality, black and white, and Armani, not necessarily in that order. I was all over the wearing of Armani, but sometimes a girl liked a change. "That means shoes, too, you know."

Jeff grinned. "Happily, you have two men assigned to be with you and ensure your safety. That includes shopping."

"You and James are the ones with great taste, though."

"So, if you like more than one thing, get them all, and we'll decide which one you're wearing to the party."

When offered a shopping spree as opposed to a war room summit meeting, I'm sure most girls would vote to head to the mall. But their skills probably didn't run toward figuring out what the psychopaths and megalomaniacs were up to. Besides, there were hair, jewelry, and makeup concerns I didn't want to share with Jeff. I did my best to focus on flowers.

Jeff hugged me. "You're going to be late. We're all a phone call away. Now, stop feeling sorry for yourself, go enjoy class, and go show that we at American Centaurion like to shop just like everyone else."

"So shopping is an undercover assignment?"

"Yes." He patted my bottom and tucked me into the limo.

Kyle closed the door then got in as shotgun. Len took the driver's seat. Not quite what I'd become accustomed to, but still a lot better than this morning.

"Ready, Ambassador?" Len asked.

"Dudes, seriously, it's me. And it's just us in here."

It might have been a limo, but I could still see Len's grin in the rearview mirror. "Got it, Kitty. You ready to rumble?"

Kyle turned the stereo on, and the melodious sounds of Aerosmith's "Back in the Saddle" wafted through the speakers.

Ah, that's what my driver and bodyguard were supposed to act like. Maybe this day wasn't going so badly after all.

CHAPTER 8

PARKING WASN'T REALLY PLENTIFUL in the D.C. area. The nice thing about having a driver was that I didn't have to worry about it. Len pulled up in front of the building where Mommy and Me was held while "Can't Take Me Home" from Pink blared on the stereo, turned on the emergency flashers, and Kyle helped me and Jamie inside.

Class was fun for both me and Jamie. While there were still plenty of moms and babies dressed for serious Washington success, there were plenty in jeans and tracksuits, too. I hadn't really made any friends in class yet, but no one was unpleasant, and it was generally one of my favorite hours of the week. That the instructor allowed us to have our iPods on, on low, of course, was an added bonus. I usually played my Steely Dan mix playlist, since mellow was the order of the class day.

I didn't fret about what was going on. This was time for me and Jamie, and I let my subconscious wander while "Pretzel Logic" played in my background, and I focused on lifting her up and swinging her around and she focused on giggling.

She was only three months old, but per her doctors, Jamie's brain functions were highly advanced. So she was doing some things early, but not too many. Fortunately I had Erika Gower on speed dial, as well as Melanie and Emily, Lorraine and Claudia's respective mothers. Not that my own mother wasn't perfectly equipped to handle any concerns, but some things about a hybrid baby even my mom wasn't prepared for, hyperspeed being only one of them.

So far, Jamie's hyperspeeding issues had been handled by Jeff and ACE. I didn't ask how because ACE didn't like to talk about it, and Jeff's attempted explanation had confused the hell out of me. I was satisfied with the results and let it go at that.

"Hi!" A mom about my age with a boy a couple months older than Jamie plopped down on the empty mat near us. "I'm Bernice. My friends call me Bernie. And this is Jordan." She was dressed in jeans and an Abercrombie & Fitch T-shirt. Jordan was sporting a Donald Duck motif. They were clearly our kind of people.

"I'm Katherine, and my friends call me Kitty. This is Jamie."

She grinned. "Cool. I think we're supposed to team up for the next stuff. You two want to buddy up?"

"Sure!" After my earlier experience, someone actually being friendly for a normal, nonvicious reason was a treat.

We passed our babies back and forth. I was glad my iPod was on low, because Bernie was a chatterer. She was small and dark-haired, with big brown eyes. Jordan looked a lot like her, though, per Bernie, not as much as Jamie looked like me.

Her husband was a professor at Georgetown, and she was an adjunct. He taught law; she was in the humanities department. "I'm a Jackie of All Trades. They float me where they need me. It keeps things interesting."

"Sounds like a great gig." It sounded a lot better than my gig, but I kept that to myself. "You must be happy to be here."

"Raul loves it here, I think it's okay, but I'm not convinced it's the right place to raise Jordan," she shared.

"Oh? What don't you like about it?" I hated pretty much everything, so I figured I'd let her lead this conversation.

"Pretty much everything," she said with a laugh. "I mean, it just doesn't feel like . . . us. You know?"

"Totally."

Exercises changed. Bernie gave me a sheepish look. "I forgot my iPod. Would you mind sharing earphones?"

I wasn't a germaphobe, and we could easily be close together. "Sure." I switched the headphones so I had one in my right ear and she had one in her left. "Any requests?"

"Oh, I like pretty much everything."

"A kindred spirit!" I figured we could move off of Steely Dan, so I turned off in the middle of "The Royal Scam" to switch to the random-select option. The melodious sounds of "Take On Me" by A-Ha came on.

"Oh, I love this song," Bernie said. "You like oldies and classic stuff, too?"

"I like everything."

"Wicked!"

We quietly rocked out with our babies for the rest of the time. Class ended far too quickly, but I felt a lot better about things. I'd made a friend who was, as near as I could tell, just like me, and that was worth all the crap I'd gone through earlier.

Bernie and I exchanged cell phone numbers. "You guys doing anything this weekend?" she asked as we packed up our stuff and I chased after one of Jamie's bottles that had rolled away from me.

"Yeah. I wish we weren't. We're going to the President's Ball."

"Oh, wow, you're so lucky. Wish we were going, but professors, even law professors, don't rate an invite."

I shrugged as I put the bottle away. "I'd prefer to stay home or go to a movie. I don't really expect to have a good time." I also expected some kind of assassination attempt, but that was definitely something I didn't think I should share with Bernie, and not just for security reasons. Why scare off the only girlfriend I'd made in this town in three months? I'd let her find out what my life was like after we'd had time to bond over more than Mommy and Me and my iPod.

"Well, maybe we can do something together next weekend. If your schedule allows for it."

"I'll do my best, believe me. Even if I have to insult a dignitary to do it." This was, sadly, not so much a Cool Chick thing to say as likely prescience on my part.

Bernie giggled. "Wicked."

"Only when someone pisses me off."

Bernie gaped at me for a minute, then she burst into laughter. "You're great. I can't wait for Raul to meet you. He's going to think you're to die for."

"Same back atcha. I think Jeff will get a kick out of you, too."

"Hanging with you," Bernie said emphatically, "is gonna be a blast."

CHAPTER 9

WE WANDERED OUT, EXCHANGING PLEASANTRIES with the other moms. No one appeared about to assassinate me or anyone else, so, while still possible, suspects seemed unlikely in my Mommy and Me class. And the instructor didn't tell me to disavow all knowledge of her or the class, so I counted this in the win column, too.

I had no idea where he'd managed to stash the limo, but Len was with Kyle in the waiting room, guarding the stroller, diaper bag, and Poofs.

Bernie sort of stared at the boys. We said our good-byes, and she hustled Jordan out. I hoped my having big bodyguards wasn't going to mess up our budding friendship, but there was only so much I could do about it.

"I'll go get the car," Len said as he stood up.

"Don't bother. I'm sure we can walk it." I had on my Converse, so I was prepped for walking. Besides, the various A-C assigned drivers had refused to allow it. Ergo, I wanted to walk to wherever the limo was.

Len and Kyle exchanged glances, and Kyle shrugged. "Mister Reynolds said she was the boss unless he had to override her for some reason."

I put Jamie in the stroller, happily surrounded by Poofs, and we headed out, the boys flanking me.

Something made me look across the street. There was a familiar figure there, leaning inside a doorway. Buchanan nodded to me, shoved off the wall, and walked off in the opposite direction from where we were going.

"Who's that?" Len asked.

"Someone from my Washington Wife class."

"Why's he here?" Kyle asked.

"No idea."

I pondered this weirdness for about half a block, when a familiar figure with black hair and beard stepped out of a doorway. He was dressed as I was used to, in casual, baggy, well-worn but clean clothes, big camera around his neck. I still couldn't tell if the clothes hid muscles or pudginess. He was under six feet and much smaller than Len and Kyle all the way around.

He beamed at me, blue eyes twinkling. "Here you are, my favorite alien lover."

"Mister Joel Oliver, always a pleasure. Meet Len and Kyle, my friends, who, like me, don't believe in aliens."

Oliver snorted. His snort was a lot more like mine than Mrs. Darcy Lockwood's. I wondered for a moment what her opinion was of Mr. Joel Oliver, then figured it had to be poor. He was the main investigative reporter for the *World Weekly News* after all, and I didn't have to ask to know what Lockwood thought of that kind of newspaper.

Len and Kyle nodded at him. "Nice to meet you, Mister Oliver," Len said, in a tone indicating he was lying.

Oliver smiled wider. "Mister Joel Oliver, please. As Missus Martini is well aware, a man in my position needs to ensure whatever shreds of respect he can garner. How are you, my dear?"

"I'm good. Why are we having this conversation?"

Kyle shoved past Oliver, gently, as Len took my arm and kept me and the stroller moving along.

Oliver wasn't fazed, of course. He trotted along with us. "I have more information," he said quietly.

"This is you barking. This is me being the wrong tree."

"I can't risk going to your oldest friend right now," Oliver said as he tried to get a couple of snaps of Jamie, which Kyle quite effectively blocked. Football players as paparazzi protection was rather brilliant. Not a surprise Chuckie had come up with it.

"And why is that?"

"I'm being followed." He said it calmly.

"Turn about being fair play and all that?" Hey, I had a sarcasm knob, too.

Oliver sighed. "I'm not your enemy. But I believe the people following me are."

We turned a corner and kept on walking. We weren't rushing; in fact, we were going quite slowly. I was used to having big guys around, but Len and Kyle were clearly adjusting to their new protection detail, and having Oliver along was causing some issues on the sidewalk. I considered if we should just run for it. It was a safe bet that Len and Kyle would have no problem beating Oliver over a short distance, and circumstances constantly ensured that my sprinting skills remained topnotch.

Jamie started to cry, loudly. We all stopped while I did a fast diaper check. Oliver poked his head around as I was doing this. "Oh, what a beautiful baby!" He sounded sincere, and the camera wasn't snapping.

Jamie looked right at him, gurgled, and smiled. He bent closer; she reached up and tugged on his beard. Oliver laughed and tickled her tummy, earning giggles. I cleared my throat and Oliver backed off. Jamie looked back at me. I decided to take the hint.

"Fine. Why don't you come along with us and share the latest?"

Len and Kyle gave me looks that said I was crazy. I was used to looks like that. Since meeting the boys from A-C, I got those looks on a very regular basis. "Jamie likes him." Which, because she had both empathic and imageering blocks implanted, courtesy of Jeff and Christopher, likely meant that ACE was giving me a hint.

Since ACE tended to leave us alone so it didn't interfere with our free will, I'd learned to pay close attention to whatever hints Jamie seemed to be giving me. I was all over getting an assist from the superconsciousness whenever possible. I liked being alive and keeping my nearest and dearest alive, too.

Len shook his head. "You're the boss."

We started off again, Len on one side of the stroller, Kyle on the other, Mr. Joel Oliver walking next to me while I pushed. If we went at a leisurely pace, this wasn't too bad. The limo appeared to be several blocks away, but even though it was cold, it was a pretty day, so I decided to enjoy our impromptu constitutional. "So, MJO, how did you find out about the assassination attempt?"

"MJO?"

"I like to save the breath when I can."

He gave me a look that said he didn't believe me. I glared at him. He sighed. "I have a network of informants. All of them agree that something big is going down, and the President's Ball came up as the likely location more often than not."

"That's it? Something big?" We had our entire network panicked over this? I began to wonder if Chuckie needed a vacation or something.

He sighed again. "Missus Martini, there's more to it than that. I have informants all over the world. When, worldwide, the same things start popping, you have to pay attention."

This I knew to be true. "So, why are we assuming assassination?"

"Every major political player will be there, foreign dignitaries, high ranking military . . ."

"Got it. It's essentially like shooting fish in a barrel, right?"

"So it seems. Thank you for listening to me," Oliver said quietly. "I appreciate you and Mister Reynolds occasionally treating me as more than an idiot annoyance."

I broke down and shot him a smile. However, I neither confirmed nor denied. No reason to let Oliver feel like he was a trusted member of our team, though he certainly seemed to want to be. "You said you had more news."

"I do. I haven't shared it yet because I still feel I'm being followed."

I faked a trip, stopped and checked my shoelace, taking the opportunity to do a quick scan around me. I saw no one and nothing suspicious; however, if they were good, I wouldn't be likely to spot them anyway. "So now whoever's following you knows you're with me," I said as we started up again. "How is this a good plan? If you have a plan, I mean."

"You have a beautiful little princess there, and I mean that quite literally. I'm negotiating for another *World Weekly News* exclusive. After all, we got all the pictures from your wedding. It makes sense that we'd want to gain the exclusive baby pictures. And of course I'm approaching you while your husband isn't around because he'd object, and you might not."

It was a good story, actually. I figured it was even one Chuckie would approve of, though Oliver was right—there was no way Jeff would okay pics of Jamie being published anywhere, let alone in the tabloid with the worst reputation around. "So, you spend time on that or are you just winging it?"

"Unlike you, I tend to think things out beforehand. However, a good investigative journalist has to be instantly adaptable."

I decided to let the comment about my ability to plan pass. After all, in some ways, he was right. "Who's following you?"

"I'm not sure." We finally reached the limo. Against all the odds, Len had found a street without any cars on it. "Please check the car before we get into it," Oliver said to Len.

"Why?" Len asked.

"You shouldn't have left it out of your control."

I coughed. "They're special cars."

"Yes, but even the most advanced car can be tampered with if it's left unattended."

Len looked like he felt he was flunking his first assignment. "Len, it's fine."

Kyle looked worried. "Not if there's something wrong. Mister Reynolds will be furious."

"Dudes, seriously, we leave the limos unattended all the time. But if you have some special way of checking for car bombs, let's be paranoid. Chuckie will be happy if we find a bomb, in that sense, and pleased with your precautionary instincts if we don't. Win-win all the way around."

The SUV we'd been in for a big battle during Operation Fugly had been tampered with. By an A-C. I'd learned early on that we couldn't really trust anyone and were probably not safe when we thought we were. While Len and Kyle made a couple of phone calls, I did what Reader wanted. I thought. The first thought that came to mind was that ACE had clearly allowed Jamie to share that she liked Oliver. Meaning, there was a reason ACE felt Oliver should be with us right now.

I looked up and down the street. "Why are we the only car on this street?"

"A good question," Oliver said. He sounded like he thought it was not only good, but that it had occurred to him, too, and he didn't like his conclusion. I was with him.

"We weren't when I parked it," Len said. "Two cars pulled out while I was cruising around, so I took advantage of the opportunity." He and Kyle exchanged a look. "I think we might want to move away from the limo."

I did a fast inventory. I had Jamie, my purse, the stroller, and her diaper bag. I didn't think we had anything of importance in the trunk, and the boys hadn't brought any paraphernalia with them that wasn't on their persons. "What about Jamie's car seat?"

"If I were planting a bomb that wasn't set to go off when the car started," Oliver said quickly, as Kyle moved to open the door, "I'd absolutely figure the new mother would want her baby's car seat."

Kyle's hand froze. "That makes sense to me. You think Kitty's the target? Or the baby?" He growled this last question. I liked overprotectiveness toward my child from our new bodyguard.

"As I already told your superior, I don't know who the target is. However, Missus Martini is on the guest list for the President's

Ball, ergo, she's a potential target." I realized we weren't even pretending that Chuckie was just a globetrotting millionaire playboy, nor were we pretending that Len and Kyle were merely along for the ride. Under the circumstances, I decided to table my worry about our lack of good security procedures and just accept that Oliver clearly knew all about us. No one believed him *other* than us, so really, it was back to the bigger issues for me, like getting away from a potentially rigged limousine.

We quickly moved our little group across the street and back down the block. "I'm not that new a mother anymore," I mentioned to Oliver as I took Jamie out of the stroller and held her tightly.

"Three months is still new," he said with a smile. "How long for the bomb squad?"

"Not too much longer," Kyle said shortly. He and Len were busy looking all around. We weren't exactly being subtle, but no one really seemed to be around to notice.

I dug my phone out of my purse. Jeff answered immediately. "What's going on? Reynolds has been making urgent calls for the past few minutes and his stress is off the charts."

"There's been a lot of that today. Your blocks okay?"

"I'm fine. I'm concerned about my wife and child."

"We're fine, as far as we know. We're with our personal paparazzo. Len found a too-convenient parking place and we're all waiting for some folks to come and let us know if our limo's been rigged or not."

"Reynolds says his people will be there in another minute. How far from the limo are you all?"

"We can still see it."

"Get farther away."

"Jeff, really—"

I was going to tell him he was overreacting. Only the limo exploded before I could finish my sentence.

CHAPTER 10

LEN AND KYLE LEAPED TO COVER ME AND JAMIE. Mr. Joel Oliver leaped and hit the Laser Shield button on the stroller. I felt it activate as I lost my balance, what with two big guys trying to protect the loose footballs that were me and Jamie.

Oliver grabbed me and held on, keeping me somewhat upright and his hand on the stroller. The boys were touching me, and because my vision was now A-C enhanced, I saw the shield go around all of us.

Just in time. Jeff had been right, we'd been too close to the limo, and a twisted piece of metal slammed against the shield and fell to the street.

"Everyone okay?" I asked as I checked Jamie. She gurgled at me, looked at Oliver, and smiled at him. "And yes, thank you, Mister Joel Oliver, for saving our lives."

He looked shaken. "I'm concerned I endangered them in the first place."

"You think that bomb was intended for you?" Kyle asked as he and Len tried to act like they weren't completely freaked out, with limited success.

"I think it's possible."

"It was our limo that had the convenient parking place on the suddenly cleared out street," I reminded him. Oliver didn't look convinced one way or the other. I heard someone shouting faintly. I looked around, realized I'd dropped my phone. Len handed it to me. "Jeff, we're okay."

"We're on our way." He sounded completely shaken. I couldn't blame him. "Baby, are you and Jamie really all right?"

"Completely unscathed, though scathing would probably have happened to the boys if not for Mister Joel Oliver."

"The jocks covered you?"

"Yes. They acted just like Secret Service." Len and Kyle perked up a little. "Chuckie's people aren't going to have a lot to look at."

"They're not there yet?"

"No. Probably a good thing. The bomb must have been on a timer, not an ignition switch."

Everyone looked at me. Oliver nodded his head. "I delayed you."

"Yeah, you did. And if you hadn't . . ." I counted in my head. "We'd have been home, or close to it."

Len was squinting at the remains of our ride. "I think the bomb was in the middle of the car."

"So it was in the car seat." Oliver and I looked at each other.

Jeff was growling, well past "rabid dog," already at "enraged bear," with "lion takes over the veldt" on the horizon. "They tried to kill my daughter?"

"We don't know who 'they' are, but I think they wanted to ensure we'd have the bomb with us." I checked my watch. "Did Chuckie order the really slow bomb service?"

"No. There's some accident on the Beltway, and there's street construction stopping them. It's stopping us, too. I could get to you on foot but Reynolds is saying no."

"He's right. For all we know, whoever did this is trying to flush you out." I looked around. People were starting to come out of the buildings, and I heard sirens in the distance. "Jeff, do we want to be questioned by the police? If they ever get here, that is." I was used to faster response times in Pueblo Caliente. And every other city we'd ever had a situation like this in, which were, by now, plentiful.

I heard him talking to someone. "Reynolds is against it. So is James. Can you hyperspeed out of there?"

"Jeff, I'm with Mister Joel Oliver." I also didn't want to test my hyperspeed control when I had Jamie, not to mention the others. I'd hit a couple of walls already, and while I had the snazzy fast A-C healing, it still hurt like hell. Now wasn't the time to slam other people into brick, let alone risk my daughter.

"I don't care anymore. I want you and Jamie back in the Embassy where it's safe."

"Wouldn't have been safe if we'd brought that bomb back with us."

"Good point. Look, get out of there. That's the overriding direction from me, Reynolds, and all of Alpha Team."

It was odd to hear that directive and not be one of the people making the decision. However, now wasn't the time for sulking. Now was the time for speedy casual walking—people on the streets were starting to notice us, particularly because there was car debris right where we were standing. "Dudes, we need to get our little flock out of this part of Dodge. MJO, you have a ride we can borrow?"

He shook his head. "I don't think we want to take the chance."

"Public transpo it is. Jeff, tell Chuckie his people should carefully find Mister Joel Oliver's car and check it out, too, just to be safe."

"Fine, where should we meet you?"

"Go back to the Embassy. Send a team or two to check out the remains and protect Chuckie's people. We're going to do what normal people do and take the bus." We headed off at a much faster stroll than we'd used to get here.

"Stay on the phone with me."

"I kind of have my hands full." I tried to send an emotional signal that I didn't want to have to share more with Oliver than I had to. I wasn't sure if I was doing it right—exploding cars tended to shake me up for some reason.

Jeff sighed. "Got it. I understand, you don't want to give away more than we already have to the so-called journalist."

"You mean the guy who's clearly right?"

"Yes, yes, Reynolds seems to think he's worth listening to."

"He's the reason we're alive."

"Fine, fine. I hate this," he muttered.

"I know. Me too." It wasn't the danger. It was the fact that we weren't able to do what we both wanted. In the good old days of three months ago, Jeff would already be here, our people would be cleaning up the scene, and we'd be off kicking butt and taking names. Now? Now we had to play pretend because there were a lot of people hiding in the shadows in D.C., literally and figuratively, and Jeff and I were no longer shadowy figures working in the background—we were the faces of American Centaurion.

"I love you, baby. Be careful."

"I love you, too, and we will be." We hung up, and I took a deep breath. "Do you boys know where a bus stop is?"

"Really? We're taking the bus?" Kyle sounded shocked.

"I have no better plan for how we're going to get back to the Embassy."

"Taxi?" Len suggested.

Oliver and I exchanged another look. "Do you want to do the honors or shall I?" he asked politely.

"I'll cover it. Dudes, you know all those conspiracy theories Chuckie undoubtedly drilled you on?" The boys nodded. "He's never wrong. So whatever he told you about exists, and therefore all the techniques to avoid capture he likely taught you need to be something you're taking very seriously. Also, someone's just tried to kill us. They either used a timer or they were watching us and decided we were clued in, hit the super-duper send button, and gave us a big, noisy message. In case the latter option is what's going on, the next assumption you make is that any taxi stopping for you is driven by one of the bad guys."

"Like in the movies?" Len asked skeptically.

"Just like. In all my time with American Centaurion, though, I've never, ever seen anyone take a bus. Ipso facto, we take a bus, we're reasonably safe."

The boys didn't look convinced, but they didn't argue, either. Len pulled up the bus routes on his cell phone and we walked on.

"We're a few blocks away from a bus stop," Len said uncertainly. "But I don't think it's a route that'll take us back to the Embassy."

He showed his phone to me. "Dude, I'm clueless here, still. The streets confuse the hell out of me." They did. Pueblo Caliente, Arizona, where I'd been born and raised, was set up on a nice grid system. It made the streets less "interesting," but it was hard to get lost there.

D.C., on the other hand, seemed to live for winding streets that turned into circular turns and ended up dead-ending when you'd swear they should take you somewhere. I could no more look at the bus routes Len was showing me and know which line we needed than I could design a rocket ship. I'd probably have better luck with the rocket.

Oliver took a look. "He's correct. Though we can do several transfers."

I considered this. Taking the bus and going somewhere made sense. Taking the bus and then transferring several times didn't seem like a way to stay under the radar. "Where would the bus we're close to take us?"

"One of the nicer shopping districts," Oliver replied. He looked at Len's phone again. "I believe the next bus will be arriving right about the time we'll reach the stop."

"Super." I pulled my phone out and dialed. "Hi, Jeff, where are you?"

"Still in the car, heading back to the Embassy. Where are you?"

"Heading to a bus stop. I'm taking the boys and going shopping."

"Why? You were all almost killed."

"Yes, but I don't have anything to wear to the ball. And unless a fairy godmother's going to show up and turn some fruits, veggies, and unsuspecting rodents into things to wear and ride, I need a dress."

"True. I just don't understand why you want to take care of that right now."

"We're not conveniently located, buswise. I figured we'd shop, and you could send another car to pick us up."

Jeff sighed. "Yes, fine." I heard someone talking in the background. "James wants to know if you've come up with anything."

"Someone doesn't like us."

"Other than that. He's stressing that time is of the essence."

"No. We haven't had time to get Mister Joel Oliver's intel."

"He's still with you?"

"Yep. We bonded over exploding vehicles."

"Fabulous. I'm going to have Gladys track you." He sighed again. "I mean, I'm going to ask Alpha Team to track you." I heard the voice in the background again.

"What's James saying?"

"That I'm allowed to sound like I'm still in charge." He sounded frustrated, worried, and depressed.

"You are. You always will be, no matter what title you have."

"I love you. Be careful, buy whatever you like, spend whatever you need. Go to good dress shops."

I sighed. "I know. I will. When will someone be coming to get us?"

"James says he has that taken care of already. Huh? Oh, he says to take your time."

"First it's hurry up, then it's take my time. A girl could get confused around here."

"I promise to clear up when to rush and when to hurry later tonight."

"I love how you think." We hung up and I gave the boys a bright smile. "Change of plans. We're going to kill two birds with a pile of gravel. MJO, lucky you, you get to help me find a dress for the President's Ball."

He grinned. "I consider it an honor."

"No photos."

"Of course not. At least, that you'll know about."

We still had a few blocks to walk, and I decided to make the most of the day. I pulled my iPod out and tuned to my Kick Butt Mix. I hadn't gotten to listen to this frequently over the past few months, but I figured us surviving our limo blowing up was a good reason to give it a whirl. As I clipped the iPod to my jeans, a taxi cruised by. The boys looked at it longingly.

We started off again, and another taxi went past us. Then another. As yet another taxi went by I looked harder. "It's the same taxi," I shared, while noting that Chuckie's conspiracy theories were again being proved true.

"The others behind it have circled the block as well," Oliver said.

The taxis got closer. "Want a ride?" the driver of the first taxi asked. He was wearing a cap and sunglasses, and he had a beard on that looked extremely fake to me.

"Nope."

"My rates are cheap," the man said as the other taxis pulled up behind this one. The drivers all looked like they were trying to hide what they really looked like and I was sure this guy was disguising his voice. Not good. "It's nice and safe in my cab," he added.

As the sounds of "Animal" by the Neon Trees came on, I made a command decision. Jamie was still in my arms, but I decided keeping her there was probably best. I put my purse around my neck, and ensured I had a good, safe grip on my baby, holding her body against my stomach and her head against my chest, in the age-old "fleeing from the evil overlords" pose so popular with pretty much every mother who'd ever had to run for it with child or children in tow. "Poofies, into Kitty's purse. Len, take the stroller. Everyone, follow me and stick together."

"What are we doing?" Kyle asked as the taxi drivers all started to get out of their cars.

"Running like hell for that bus stop."

CHAPTER 11

I **WANTED TO GO TO HYPERSPEED,** potential to slam into walls or no, but I didn't want to lose the boys or Oliver. It was hard to run holding Jamie this way, but that also kept me from hitting the internal hyperspeed button.

"Animal" was an exceptionally good song to run to, so that was a positive. The fact that the men in the taxis were back in their cars and chasing us, however, wasn't.

Oliver was a good runner. Clearly, being a paparazzo had certain fitness benefits attached to it. The boys had played football for their entire lives, so they were in great shape. And my track skills were constantly being kept up-to-date. We were good. Not able to outrun a car unless I took us all to hyperspeed, but as far as post-graduate track stars, we had a shot for at least the bronze for relay in the Extremely Amateur Olympics.

On the plus side, no one was shooting at us. Either they didn't have guns, weren't supposed to kill us, or didn't want to draw extra attention. I was just happy to have any small favor going for us.

The other thing in our favor was that the taxi drivers had no idea where we were going. Sadly, I had no idea, either. "MJO! You need to get us to our destination."

He ran in front of us and took a sharp left. We ran down an alley that was too small for a car. Oliver ran us down to another turning point, this time we went right. He slowed down. "Carefully," he said as we neared the street.

A taxi whizzed by. I was positive it was one of the ones after us. Oliver peered out. "Go!" He took off again, going back the way we'd come. The boys and I followed him.

We hit the intersection and the light was thankfully with us. We dashed through as the taxis came around again. They were now on the wrong side of the road, meaning they couldn't pull up to the curb, at least not without causing a major traffic incident.

Oliver was puffing, but we were still running at a good clip, him in the lead, then me and Jamie, with Kyle flanking us, and Len and the stroller bringing up the rear. As "Parade" by Garbage came on, the calm part of my mind mentioned that this had to look hilarious. The rest of my mind suggested we laugh about it later, when we were actually somewhere safe.

We turned again and seemed to lose the taxis. For about half a block. "Coming toward us," Kyle shouted, and this time the taxis were again on our side of the street.

All three taxis were heading for us, but they were several cars away when Oliver ran into traffic. The squealing of tires was impressive, but he wasn't hit. The rest of us followed him. I was shocked, and grateful, but just like in the movies, the cars slammed on their brakes to avoid hitting us. Amid a great deal of cursing from the various drivers and the distinct sound of slamming metal, we dashed on.

"Two of the taxis slammed into each other," Len shouted. "But one's still coming."

"Where the hell are the cops in this city?" We were fleeing in the streets with tires squealing all around us, yet there were no cops around, implied, or suggested.

"No idea," Kyle shouted back. "But I don't smell a whiff of bacon."

I managed a laugh but decided I'd tell Kyle how much I enjoyed that little saying once we were safe somewhere. Oliver turned right, and I could see the bus stop, and the bus, in the distance. We all sped up.

The remaining taxi reappeared, driving on the other side of the street, but keeping pace with us. That meant he was going slowly for the street, and there was again a lot of honking and cursing. I didn't know if all the attention we were drawing from the various drivers made us safer or not, but it certainly wasn't bringing out D.C.'s finest to investigate. I didn't want to be questioned by the police, but that sounded a lot better than whatever the taxis had in store for us.

I chose to hope that the only paparazzo around was running ahead of me. The thought of this little foot race making any kind of news was enough to make me want to go into witness protection.

Not that there were any law enforcement officers around to suggest it to.

We reached the bus stop as the bus pulled up. Oliver ushered me and Jamie on first. The bus driver stared at us. "You folks in a hurry?"

"Just didn't want to miss you," I gasped out as I rummaged around for some money.

Oliver shoved a twenty at the driver. "For all of us." He and I found seats in the back where there were no other passengers, while the boys got the stroller collapsed and it and themselves inside in record time.

I took Jamie out of the Fleeing Position. She cooed at me. "That's my good little babycat," I said as I kissed her nose. "You're my little ready-for-action girl, aren't you?"

I looked out the window as the bus doors closed and we started off. The taxi driver was still across the street. He tipped his cap to me and drove off.

The bus drove past the street where the other taxis had collided. They were still in the street, but the drivers were nowhere around.

Len cleared his throat. "Are you and Jamie okay?"

"Yeah. How about you guys?"

"Nice workout," Oliver said with a laugh.

The boys, however, looked sheepish, worried, and upset, and they didn't answer my question. I sighed. "Guys, really. You're still learning. It happens."

Len shook his head. "We're supposedly fully trained. If you'd let us, we would have gotten into one of those taxis."

"But I didn't let you." I patted his hand. "You did great."

"How so?" Kyle asked, clearly as upset as Len. "If it wasn't for Mister Joel Oliver here, we'd all be dead."

I patted his hand, too. "But we're not. We call this learning on the job."

"Our job is to protect you," Len reminded me.

"Yeah, it is. My job is also to protect myself, my baby, and anyone with me. I'm better at that job because I've been doing this longer." Happily, no one was with us who could contradict me. "MJO, were our, ah, friends the same ones you'd spotted earlier?"

"Sadly, no. At least, not that I could tell."

We all looked out the windows again. "I don't see anyone or anything suspicious." The men chimed in with the lack of suspicious. "So I guess we can sort of relax. For the moment anyway. So how long are we on the bus for?"

"Several miles," Oliver replied.

"I'm willing for that to take a while."

No sooner were the words out of my mouth than the bus pulled over. Doors opened, no one got on or off. We looked at each other. The bus started up again. And stopped at the next block. Same thing.

We lurched along, stopping at every block, listening to the other passengers mutter to themselves and each other about this ridiculous situation until my brain kicked. "Oh. Um. We can relax and let the bus driver drive the way he knows how to do. Best. And all that."

The men all gave me the "you so crazy" look. However, I hadn't been talking to them. Jamie sighed, and I could have sworn she gave me a "make up your mind" look. But the bus continued on, this time not stopping except for traffic lights and legitimate bus stops.

As we made our way, more passengers got on. We were no longer alone in the back. We all scrutinized said passengers, but none of them seemed either interested in us or a threat. Well, none of them were interested in us, but a couple of them made smiley googoo faces at Jamie. They appeared to be people who liked to smile at cute little babies, so we all smiled back.

"Do you want to call the ambassador?" Len asked quietly.

"No. Why stress him out any more than he undoubtedly is?" I didn't want to admit that I was actually trying to avoid a lecture or a fight. Jeff had wanted to come get us, which now seemed like it might have been the smart plan. But, oh, well. Improvisation was my middle name, right?

I focused on feeling calm and relaxed, so that if Jeff was monitoring he'd know we were all okay. My phone rang. "Do I want to know?" Jeff asked.

"Probably not. Not in a good place to fill you in, either."

"Everyone's safe?"

"Yes. Still heading to the shopping area."

He sighed. "Fine. Try to not burn down the shops."

"Oh, ye of little faith."

Jeff snorted. "Never forget, baby, I know you."

CHAPTER 12

WE JOSTLED ALONG. To be polite I put my iPod back into my purse. I didn't think discussing the limo's explosion, the potential assassination attempt, our chase through the streets of D.C., or who Mr. Joel Oliver thought was following him were wise topics, so we chatted about the weather.

Len, Kyle, and I weren't in favor of the cold. Oliver liked it because wearing coats gave him more places to stash film, media cards, cameras, and so forth. I refrained from making snide remarks, proving that at least Aunt Emily's Diplomacy for Beginners class was paying off.

Len asked why Oliver still used film, and we got a brief but informative lecture on why some shots still came out better using traditional photography methods and why some didn't. Oliver carried what seemed like every type of camera on him, so he was ready for any shot, at any time, whether it be artistic and up for a Pulitzer, digital and catching a celebrity without her underpants on, or anything in between.

In a short time we were at the shopping area, got off the bus, and started strolling around. "Okay, no one got on the bus with us, no one got off the bus with us, I see no taxis with poorly disguised drivers around, so if whoever else was following you is still on your tail, they'll need to park. So, who *is* on your tail?"

Oliver looked around. "I believe they're with the C.I.A."

Len shook his head. "Mister Reynolds doesn't tail you, and he doesn't have people tailing you."

"Ah, but you'd say that, even if he did," Oliver said pleasantly.

"However, I don't think they're on Mister Reynolds' side of the alien question."

"There are no aliens." Hey, I was going to do my best to get us back to some sort of security level.

Oliver chuckled. "Of course there are. You're married to one. But to make you feel better, let's just refer to them by the nice name everyone uses around here. I believe those who have targeted me are not friendly to American Centaurion. Nor are they friends of those who are friends of American Centaurion."

"That doesn't exactly narrow it down."

"Whoever's in charge will be at the President's Ball."

"To watch the fireworks, make sure nothing goes wrong, or to pull the trigger?"

"I have no idea. My informants were all clear about the ball being the place where the major situation is going to go down. And while I doubt whoever's in charge is the person or persons following me, I got a glimpse of shadowy figures and nothing more."

"Then why do you assume they're C.I.A.?" Len asked.

"It's a safe bet," Oliver said dryly. "Plus there was . . . something about them . . ."

"Lurking in nice suits?"

He shook his head. "No. C.I.A. field operatives are trained to blend in."

"They didn't blend if you saw them."

Oliver stared at me. "That's a very good point."

I considered this. "You think they wanted you to see them?"

"Why would they want that?" Kyle asked.

Len pursed his lips. "To flush him out, send him to whoever he thinks will protect him or want his information."

Oliver looked chagrined. "And I did exactly that."

We were in front of Cartier's, and I stared at the nearby dress shops. "Did you? Because I know who you wanted to run to, and he's not here or even close."

"So does that mean they thought he was?" Kyle asked. "Or did they think he'd run to you, Kitty?"

"Or did someone blow up our limo for an entirely unrelated reason?" It was a legitimate question. In my experience, there was never just one scheme going on around us at any time.

"Until we know otherwise, I'd assume that there was a connection," Oliver said. "Unless your limousines routinely explode."

"Not unless someone's trying to kill us. And who were the dudes in the taxis working for? Were they part of the blow-us-up gang, or were they merely trying to kidnap us for different, nefarious reasons?"

"No idea. I don't believe we have enough information."

"We should have grabbed one of them."

"I don't think either Mister Reynolds or the ambassador would have liked that," Len said.

"Oh, they'd have liked it if we'd gotten some decent, accurate intelligence out of the experience." Ah, well, another potential opportunity missed. I chose not to worry about it and instead made a command decision. "Let's hit this shop."

I forged in before the males could protest. It was small and loaded with expensive clothes. I had a little trouble getting in the door with the stroller. None of the salesgirls came to help, but, fortunately, Len was there to handle it.

For some reason, I expected to get someone asking me if I needed help finding anything. I wasn't exactly dressed up, but then again, I had three men with me, two of whom looked official, and we were in a town loaded with foreign dignitaries. But it was as if I weren't there as far as the salesgirls seemed concerned.

I looked at a few dresses, held them up and stared in a mirror, but I didn't feel enough love to try them on. The boys were on lookout, but Oliver was trying to help.

"That's pretty," he said for the tenth time as I held up the tenth dress I wasn't enamored enough to try on.

"It's okay. I guess." I liked shopping with Reader. I could trust his taste. I didn't think Oliver or the boys wanted me to look bad, but they weren't former top international male models, either. Football players and paparazzi had one thing in common, though—anything revealing I held up got the thumbs up sign. Great. I needed to look like an ambassador, or at least the wife of one per Mrs. Darcy Lockwood, not like I was auditioning to be the next Bond Girl.

I looked around. "Excuse me, could I get some assistance, please?"

One of the girls deigned to leave the clutch of salesgirls and come over. "What price range are you looking for?"

"I'm looking for something that looks good."

"Yes. How much are you planning to spend?"

I gave her a long look. She looked about twenty-one or so. "You ever seen *Pretty Woman*? The movie with Julia Roberts?"

She sniffed. "No, I don't watch old movies."

"Really? Wow. It's probably considered a classic of some kind now. You really should rent it or catch it the next time it's on TV."

"Why is that?" she asked, sounding uninterested in the reply.

"Because I'm going to drop a freaking fortune on clothes today. But not in this shop." I dropped the dress I was holding on the floor, grabbed the stroller, jerked my head at the males, and headed for the door.

Len opened it as one of the other girls came over. "Ma'am, I'm sorry, but our store is just likely too expensive for someone of your means."

"Excuse me?"

She gave me a patronizing smile. "There's nothing in here that's less than a thousand dollars."

"And your point is?"

"People who ride the bus usually can't afford to shop anywhere but Ross," the first girl snapped. She was holding the expensive dress I'd dropped and looked affronted by my treatment of it.

"Girls, I point you again to the educational film, *Pretty Woman*. Now, excuse me, we supposedly poverty stricken need to stop sullying your fine establishment."

As I said this, I heard the sound of a camera snapping. Sure enough, Oliver was taking pictures. He grinned at my expression. "Being with you is good for my career."

"How so?"

He shrugged. "I should get the lead with this story. Boutiques refusing to serve an ambassador? That's always good for the front page." He got some quick snaps of the salesgirls. "You mind waiting outside while I get their names?"

"Not a problem," I said cheerfully as I looked at their expressions, which were all kinds of horrified. "Wouldn't want them misspelled so their parents miss out on how well their daughters listened to their lessons on politeness and treating everyone pleasantly."

Len and Kyle escorted me out while the salesgirls started complaining that they'd been misunderstood, and my money was just fine. I took a deep breath. "Hanging with Mister Joel Oliver has its benefits."

"Yeah, but you still don't have a dress, we don't know what's going on, and we have to take the bus back to the Embassy," Kyle pointed out.

My phone rang. "Hey, James, what's up?"

"Hold your position, girlfriend."

"Why?"

As I asked this, a gray limo pulled around the corner and slid to a stop in front of us. "Because your ride is trying to find you."

CHAPTER 13

"IT'S HERE, I THINK ANYWAY." A man I vaguely recognized as one of the many human operatives I hadn't enjoyed got out of the driver's side and tossed the keys to Len.

"Good. Now, there's a surprise inside." Reader sounded pleased with himself.

"There was a surprise inside my last limo. I didn't care for it."

"You'll like this one. I hate the dress shop you were in, by the way. Great for going back to Vegas, completely inappropriate for the President's Ball."

"You don't hate it as much as I do. I didn't buy anything, don't worry."

"Good."

"I wish you were here. I need Gay Fashion Support. Desperately."

"I know. And, like Reynolds, I've got a fix that will help you not only with shopping but with the Washington Wife class, too."

"Oh, yeah? There's an Uzi in the backseat?"

Reader laughed. "Nope. Something much, much better."

"Yeah? What?"

"You'll find out. Love you, babe." Reader hung up.

The driver opened the door, and a slim, reasonably attractive man got out. I felt my mouth drop open. He smiled at me. "Kitty, darling, you look radiant. Motherhood agrees, I see."

"Pierre!"

"In the flesh, darling, in the flesh."

"What are you doing here?"

He grinned. "What I do best, darling. Saving the day."

I shoved Len at the stroller and ran and gave Pierre a big hug. "I can't express my joy."

He patted my back. "So Jimmy said, darling." He took my shoulders and held me at arm's length. "Still have our wonderful, feminine figure, I see." Pierre shot a derisive look at the dress shop. "But clearly Jimmy was right. You need a guardian before you get lost in the forest of heinous fashion choices."

I introduced Pierre to the boys as the limo's former driver, and his A-C shotgun, wandered off and then came right back, armed with another limo filled with A-Cs. Clearly Alpha Team had decided we weren't to be left alone, and Jeff had decided that Len was required to function as a shield when we weren't driving.

Oliver joined us, grinning from ear to ear. "That was fun."

"Pierre, Mister Joel Oliver, head paparazzo for the *World Weekly News*. MJO, this is Pierre, the best hairdresser, deejay, and all around fix-it man on the planet."

They shook paws. "Jimmy's told me all about you, Mister Joel," Pierre said. "I happen to love your articles. You also capture your subjects extremely well. You're a clear talent in a field filled with dilettantes."

Oliver opened his mouth, cocked his head at Pierre, and laughed. "Mister Joel is acceptable under the circumstances. And thank you. It's rare to find anyone who appreciates what I do."

Pierre grinned. "So pleased. And trust me, dearest, people do appreciate, particularly those of us in the beauty business. Clients do love to escape while they're under the dryer, don't they?" He rubbed his hands together. "Now, while you load up the car, I hear there's a precious little princess who needs to meet her Uncle Pierre."

I got Jamie out and let Pierre hold her. She cooed and giggled. "So, Pierre, not that I'm in any way unhappy to see you, but what are you doing here? We're a long way from Vegas. Are you vacationing or something?"

Pierre made a goo-goo face at Jamie, then looked over to me. "Darling. Please. Jimmy explained all about your new mission and how you and your compadres are not, shall we say, managing as well as we could hope."

"I'm kind of screwing up constantly, yeah."

Pierre snorted. "I doubt you're anything but practically perfect in every way, darling. Besides, from what Jimmy said, you weren't the one who planned the little soirée that went so very wrong."

"Oh. Right. Yeah." Mr. Joel Oliver looked like he knew about this, but the boys looked confused. "Amy threw a little party for our Embassy neighbors, just to sort of say hi."

"What's wrong with that?" Kyle asked.

Pierre coughed. "Your lovely Embassy is friendly with all, as I understand it. Your neighbors are not so openhearted."

"Apparently Latvia, Romania, and Egypt aren't really speaking to each other right now, and everyone's upset with Ireland for something. The folks from Luxembourg were really supportive, though."

"As I understand it, fisticuffs were exchanged," Pierre said flatly.

"There was a small brawl, yes. We were able to save the good china and crystal." Only because Jeff, Christopher, and Doreen had all used hyperspeed, but that wasn't important now. Besides, no one had noticed. They were too busy cheering for whichever side of the fight they felt they were on.

"First fight of the year," Oliver confirmed. "You started off in style."

"They're all really nice people, though. I don't get why they got upset."

"Too much alcohol, wrong foods being served, no understanding of the current relationship crises, unawareness of the variety of dalliances, forgot to invite several nearby and considered 'in your neighborhood' diplomats." Pierre rattled this off as if he were making a shopping list while the boys got the stroller into the car, confirmed the new car seat was securely fastened, and helped me lock and load Jamie into it. "I could go on."

"Please don't. Again, why are you here?"

Len got into the driver's seat, Pierre and I sat on either side of Jamie, with Oliver across from us, Kyle closed the door, got into the shotgun seat, and Len pulled away from the curb. The other limo followed us, the two human agents in the front seat, the A-Cs filling up the back to capacity. I hadn't been in a limo parade since Operation Fugly. I enjoyed the nostalgic moment.

Pierre looked at me as if it were obvious. "Darling, I'm your newest employee."

"Excuse me?"

"I'm the new Majordomo Concierge for the American Centaurion Embassy and its Diplomatic Corps."

My jaw dropped. "We have such a position?"

"You do now," Pierre said. He leaned forward and handed Oliver a piece of paper and indicated he should hand it to Kyle, which Oliver obediently did. "Len, darling, please head us to the address Kyle now holds in his big man-hands, if you'd be so kind."

Len nodded with a grin, Kyle grunted and I noted he was blushing again, and we headed off. "Where are we going?" I asked as Pierre tickled Jamie.

"Directly to a designer, darling." He shook his head. "Appalling, that a dignitary of your level was actually going to grace a chain establishment with your presence, let alone your money."

"I have a level?"

"You do, darling, you do." Pierre heaved a sigh—of contentment, I was pretty sure. "And now that I'm here, we're going to ensure you're aware of where and what it is, and then I'll handle all the little details while you and your Jeff get to relax and actually enjoy being attached to the exciting mission that is now yours to have and to hold."

Oliver leaned forward and shook Pierre's hand again. "Trust me when I tell you that you've arrived just in the nick of time."

CHAPTER 14

SHOPPING WITH PIERRE was an entirely different experience, one I was fairly sure the boys could happily never have again but that I enjoyed on a whole variety of levels, relief being the foremost among them.

I'd had no idea that D.C. had a thriving fashion industry, including some name and up-and-coming designers, but it shouldn't have shocked me. There was a lot of money floating around, and that kind of honey attracted its own level of really expensive and exclusive bees.

I sent some texts back and forth to Reader and Chuckie and was only somewhat surprised to learn that Pierre had been fully briefed on pretty much everything, including the fact that he was now working for a foreign principality—to take the term "foreign" to its most extreme form. Apparently Pierre would have been on board sooner, but Chuckie had run him through every security check he could think of and any other C.I.A. tests lying around, all of which took time.

Per Chuckie, Pierre passed with flying colors—and at a higher rate than most of Centaurion Division. I chose not to ask any questions, particularly where I'd landed on Chuckie's Super Secret Spy-o-Meter tests. If my luck was holding firm, I was at the bottom, with "why is she allowed security access to an ATM machine let alone more" on a Post-it next to my name.

Because Pierre was cleared at the highest security levels now, we could discuss the exploding limo, Mr. Joel Oliver's stealth stalkers, the NASCAR taxis, and the potential assassination attempt in front of and with him. When we were all in the limo. When we were out of it, more time was spent on my measurements, all of them, including feet, than anything else.

Fabrics, colors, and accessories came up, too. My input remained minimal. No one was interested in what I wanted, since all were clear that I had no idea. I knew better than to suggest something in an Aerosmith logo pattern, but nothing else I was coming up with seemed worthwhile, so I shut up, stood there, and listened to Pierre rattle off requirements like we were prepping to take to the Himalayas on some elephants and needed to look awesome doing it.

Somehow, Pierre expected the designers to come up with a fab ensemble for me, and ones for Amy and Doreen, whose measurements he already had, in about a day. Considering Doreen was ready to give birth at any moment, I was amazed the designers were doing anything other than laughing derisively, but they all seemed unworried, so I decided to focus on the scary picture of who was trying to kill whom and why.

Despite serious mental effort, by the last stop, I was still at pretty much zero. "My Psycho Meter is off," I said as we left the last designer and settled back into the limo for the ride home. "I'm coming up with nothing."

"I'm more concerned with what we're going to do with him," Kyle said over his shoulder, pointing to Oliver. "I don't know that Ambassador Martini wants him at the Embassy."

"I don't know that we want to leave him wandering alone." I didn't. I didn't want something bad to happen to Mr. Joel Oliver when he'd both come to warn me and then saved our lives.

"I'm right here," Oliver said dryly. "But I do agree with your concerns—both of them. I'm sure the ambassador isn't going to be excited by my appearance, but I'm also attached to staying alive."

A thought occurred, and I called Chuckie. "Any developments?"

"No, unless you count your husband's blood pressure rising."

"Nope. We're coming up with nothing here, too. But I wanted to ask what you wanted us to do with Mister Joel Oliver. Was his car okay?"

"His car was burned to a crisp when we found it."

I made eye contact with Oliver. "I hope you didn't leave anything important in your car."

He shook his head. "No. I assume it's not safe?"

"It's a crispy critter." I went back to Chuckie. "So, have you checked out his living quarters?"

"Yes. They've been rifled with extreme prejudice. So do what I know you want to, even though it'll mean I have to listen to another one of your husband's temper tantrums: Bring him to the Embassy. White will handle film and disk exposure, and Serene's team can fix whatever he doesn't catch."

"You got it. You know, Jeff doesn't exactly throw tantrums."

"In your opinion."

"It's been a crappy day for everyone, I see."

"Yeah, it has. You're all alive not due to anything your people or my people did, but rather because you, thankfully, listened to a tabloid reporter, who also happens to be my source, my *only* source, for putting a large number of operatives on the highest of alerts."

"Dude, our limo and his car are toast. I think he's got the goods, so to speak."

"Yeah. God alone knows what's coming next."

"Well, let me add more for the confusion grist mill and share what's already happened." I brought him up to speed on the taxis, including the fact that they hadn't seemed to want to kill us.

Chuckie groaned. "It's worse. Did anyone get a license plate on any of those?"

I checked and was able to confirm none of us had had the foresight to look. Chuckie managed not to say that he thought the four of us were idiots, for which I was grateful. He merely heaved a sigh. "Fine, I'll see what we can find out from other channels. Not that I expect to find anything."

"You're Mister Polly Positive."

"I'm not used to none of us having any idea of what's going on."

I thought about this as we sat in traffic. "Maybe it's because we actually have a head's up."

"Mind explaining that?"

"Sure. Usually, we're in complete reactive mode. Something bad happens, then we go into action. This time, we know the bad's coming, but that's all. We're all used to being reactive and this is a proactive thing right now."

"Wow, great to know you can still pull up the marketing talk when you have to."

"Blah, blah, blah. Think about it. I know I'm used to having more clues to work with. I think everyone else is, too. We had more even when Amy triggered Operation Confusion." Our last big mission had happened right around and after I'd given birth, when the creeps had been after my baby. "Think it's another attempt to get Jamie?"

"No, not the limo explosion, or if it is, it's the most roundabout plan ever conceived. She'd have been killed right along with you if you hadn't listened to Oliver."

"So it's not the 'control the A-Cs' team in charge, then."

"How do you mean?"

Amazing. I was running my mouth and the ideas were flowing. Some things never changed. "The ones who want to control Centaurion Division want at least one of us under their complete control. They don't want Jamie dead—they want her, and Jeff, and Christopher, and all the others doing what they want, not dead and buried."

"Makes sense. Only cuts out a third to a half of those who might be in charge."

"Well, they could still be involved. I can't think of a time when it was only one plan triggering against us."

He laughed. "Too true. And let's not forget that your taxi situation could have easily been a kidnap attempt in order to gain control of Jamie. So we're right back to everyone being a potential suspect."

"How nice. It's good to be popular."

He snorted. "How long before you're back at the Embassy?"

I looked around. We were stuck in a lot of traffic. "Not too long. At least, distancewise. No guess timewise. What's up with all the construction? I don't remember this all going on a week ago."

"Standard road work. It happens, you know."

"Yeah, I guess. It's a pain in the butt, though."

"Your husband's told me I can't think about or mention your butt."

"Yeah, but we both know that won't stop you." We both laughed, said our good-byes, and I hung up.

"I'm allowed to come with you?" Oliver asked.

"I think you need to come with us is more like it. Your car was torched and your place was tossed. You're in danger, clearly."

He nodded. "I wish I had more information to impart. I know Mister Reynolds is going to ask for more."

"Well, you have something you haven't really told us. I mean, not that I doubt for a moment that you'd like to get exclusive photos of my baby, but I have to think you were lurking outside my Mommy and Me class to do more than share that you were being followed."

"True enough. I feel there's something wrong with the intelligence I've gotten."

I groaned. "Chuckie will *not* want to hear that."

Oliver shook his head. "The threat is very real. It's the lack of a clear target that seems suspicious. I dug deeper with my most reliable sources, and they can't pin down anything more than the President's Ball."

"Maybe that just means the would-be assassins are really good."

"No one's actually that good. If your people weren't able to do what they do with photographs and the like, everyone would know what American Centaurion really was. Even the stealthiest and most clandestine organizations have leaks. Normally, this close to an operation of this magnitude going down, some names would be popping."

"But there are no weasels so identifying?"

Oliver gave me a blank look.

"Pop goes the weasel," Len supplied from the driver's seat.

"Oh!" Oliver chuckled. "I didn't catch that. Also, I doubt we'll end up considering the target or targets weasels."

"You never can tell, though it's usually the good ones who die young, true." I looked around again. "Are we even moving?"

"We could walk faster," Kyle said. "We definitely ran faster. They're moving us down to one lane."

I looked around. There were people in what looked like construction crew garb, but no officers of the law. "What is *with* the cops in this city? Isn't this kind of major road issue something the police take at least a passing interest in?"

"Police funding has been cut recently," Oliver said. "I did a full exposé on it a few weeks ago."

"I don't read your paper, sorry. Want to give me the CliffsNotes version?"

Oliver sighed. "Certainly. Due to the economic situation, funding has been slashed from a variety of programs, law enforcement being only one of them. Private security firms are attached to various Embassies and politicians, funded through something other than taxes."

"You mean kickbacks or campaign funds."

He shrugged. "Among other, legitimate means. There are several security firms who are trying to get contracts to protect our people in various unfriendly countries, versus having the U.S. military do it. D.C. is the test case."

"I thought it worked the other way around."

"Sometimes. Not this time. Titan Security has a lot of influence."

"They're the ones in charge?"

"Not in charge so much as assigned. Titan Security has the most contracts in place right now. There are others, of course, vying for the business; however, at this moment it's Titan's business to lose."

"Is that good or bad?"

Oliver shrugged. "I personally feel that giving any private company that much power is a bad thing. But Titan's leadership are very well entrenched within the political structure, and they have a strong lobbyist working for them. They're here to stay unless they screw up very badly and publicly."

"Lucky us. So, Titan has the bigwigs?"

Oliver nodded. "And some key properties, all the monuments, and so forth."

"Then who's protecting the regular people?"

"Supposedly there are enough police officers on the streets to do an adequate job." Oliver didn't sound like he agreed with this statement. After what had just happened to us with little to no police interest, I agreed with the sentiment. "However, that does mean there are fewer officers handling traffic duty right now."

"At least we're not on the bus. Speaking of which, let's at least have some tunes while we sit."

Kyle dutifully turned on the music, and "How You Like Me Now?" from The Heavy came on.

"I'd like it better if we were moving," Len muttered.

Due to the vagaries and joys of the current traffic jam, our other limo was next to us. Len motioned for them to go ahead as we all funneled into the one lane. We weren't the only limos in this jam—there were a lot of them, mostly black, but some white and even some other gray ones.

Things unsnarled, resnarled, and unsnarled again. I lost track of where our other limo was. There were several gray ones nearby. I counted. There were a lot of gray limos. In fact, we were now a little fleet of gray limos.

I looked closer. Centaurion Division's limos didn't look very different from any other limos out there, at least on the outside. Limo windows were tinted like every other limo, so it was close to impossible to see in. Drivers would be humans, and I certainly didn't know every human driver we had. But I also found it hard to believe that anyone, even Jeff, had decided we needed a fleet of limos to get home.

Len cursed. "We need to turn, but no one's letting us over."

Sure enough, we were in the middle of the group, like our own little mobile pod of gray whales. Only we didn't belong in the pod.

"Boys? I think evasive maneuvers are going to become a necessity." No sooner had I said this than I saw the windows of the limos next to us roll down. "Kyle! Hit the laser shield button!"

I hoped he'd been told where it was, because the guns pointed at us started firing.

CHAPTER 15

IT HAD BEEN A LONG TIME SINCE I'd actually been inside a laser shield, and now here I'd gotten to do it twice in one day. Not that I was complaining.

Actually, what I was doing was shielding Jamie. But, fortunately, Kyle had found the button in time, and we were treated to the interesting sight of watching bullets ricochet. The sound was different—a sort of deep pinging combined with a weird boing at the end. I decided I liked it a lot better than the sound bullets made when they hit people I cared about.

"Kitty, sit down!" Len sounded pissed, not that I could blame him. "I'm going to ram through. Keep the baby in her seat."

I sat and rebuckled. "I'm not so sure—" I wasn't sure it was a good idea to do this, but Len floored it and proved that concern to be a moot point. We slammed into the car ahead of us, but the impact didn't feel like too much. A-C technology had a lot of advantages, and every A-C vehicle had a lot of cool, high-tech after-market stuff in it. Which begged the question of how someone had managed to rig our former limo. However, I didn't have time to ponder that one at this precise time—I was focused on not getting whiplash.

"You sure they're all unfriendlies?" Pierre asked, with a lot more calm in his tone than I'd have expected.

"Don't care," Len snarled.

"I don't think American Centaurion would be firing on their own people," Oliver said. He sounded fairly calm, too.

Kyle was on his phone barking something to someone, and Len was snarling but driving really well, if I defined that to mean we

were going to totally win this demolition derby. Even Jamie seemed
to be handling this like a trooper. Leaving me to act like a normal
person. Always the way.

Of course, screaming wouldn't help anyone and would probably
scare Jamie. So I went for my other standby—running my mouth.
"So, Mister Joel Oliver, with all your contacts, you didn't spot
yourself as the assassination target du jour?"

"I'm with you," he pointed out as we rammed the car next to us.

My phone chose this moment to ring. I managed to grab my
purse as we jerked and slammed against the other car next to us.
The gunmen inside had recovered themselves and were now aiming
lower. "Len, they're trying to hit our tires," I shared as I flipped my
phone open.

"Great, that *is* your car on the news. Girlfriend, I can't let you
out of my sight."

"James, a little help would be appreciated."

"Serene's team is altering footage, and we just dispatched agents
to help."

"Could they help with the bullets flying?"

"What?" He sounded shocked and horrified.

"I thought you said we were on the news."

"Major traffic incident, that's all they're showing. No mention
of gunfire."

"Well, there's a lot of it. We're surrounded by gray limos, by the
way, so be sure the agents don't just randomly go help gray cars,
because the chances are good they'll be helping the bad guys or get
shot. No worries about police interference, though, so there's that
going for us. I guess." A few cops shooting back at the bad guys
wouldn't have gone unappreciated by me at this point.

Len broke us through and floored it. We weren't by our street. I
had no idea where we were by now, though I thought we were close
to Georgetown. Len either knew or didn't care. We careened down
street after street, weaving in and out of traffic as "Destination Unknown" by Missing Persons fittingly came on the sound system. I
cringed, waiting for us to run over some random tourist. "James,
where is that help that's supposedly coming?"

"They're with our other car." His voice sounded funny.

My stomach clenched. "They didn't activate their laser shield in
time?"

"No, they didn't."

We were too far away for me to have a hope of spotting them,
but I turned around anyway. There were several gray limos follow-

ing us. They all had guns. "We're doing okay, I think." I considered our options. "We'd have a better chance of getting away if we were on foot, I think. Using hyperspeed." A-Cs could drag anyone along with them if they were touching. I figured I could do it, too, since I had the powers if not the full control. Besides, slamming into a building had to be better than being shot, right?

"I can't authorize that."

"Um, why the hell not?"

"Serene says there's an unreal number of cameras trained on you right now. If you bolt, someone will catch it, and she's concerned Imageering will miss something."

"Great. Just great. Where are Jeff and Christopher?"

"At the Embassy."

"Where are you?"

"At the Pontifex's Residence." The Pontifex had digs in D.C., close by but not within or attached to the Embassy. Before we'd become the Head Diplomats, I'd never known it existed—Richard White had never used it. Since we'd changed jobs, Reader and Gower were there a lot. The implications of this were crystal clear—we were screwing up. A lot. However, right now what I cared about was getting some help.

"Okay, I'll call you back."

"What? Stay on the phone with me."

"Um, no. Gotta make a call." I hung up and dialed as Rihanna's "SOS" came on. "Jeff, where are you?"

"Tracking you."

"I thought you might be. James doesn't want us to run, and I don't want you or Christopher to get shot."

"Wow, I don't want my wife or child to get hurt. Guess what? I plan to win this argument. We'll be there in a couple of seconds."

I hung up. "Guys? Be prepared. Kyle? Unlock the doors, please. Now."

"What?" He sounded freaked. I didn't care.

"Unlock the damn doors!" He did. Jamie cooed and looked expectant. "I know, Jamie-Kat, Daddy and Uncle Christopher are here." Blocks or not, Jamie always knew when Jeff was nearby. About a second later, the doors on either side opened and shut. If I hadn't been prepared for it, I'd have missed it, enhanced vision or not.

No one else was prepared for it, of course. Pierre yelped, Oliver jumped, Kyle shouted, and Len spun the wheel to the right.

"We want them in," I shared as Len got the car under control. I realized he hadn't actually lost his cool. We'd gotten onto a dead-end street and had to get out of it. "Hi, guys. Missed you."

Jeff shook his head. "Only my girl. You okay, baby?"

"Yeah, we are. Per James, the other car wasn't as lucky."

"Luck had nothing to do with it," Christopher said. He was glaring, Patented Glare #3, but I had the feeling he was glaring at the situation in general, not at anyone specifically. He was a glaring impresario, after all, and had great range.

Jeff looked around. "Why is the reporter in the car with us?"

"Chuckie and I thought it was wise to protect him."

Jeff grunted, then nodded to Pierre. "Glad you're here. Sorry about the welcome."

Pierre waved his hand nonchalantly. "Darling, really. Bullets and a rather slow car chase? That's nothing. You're speaking to a man who spends his time in the midst of crises of epic proportions. Now, if the cars were manned with half-crazed and completely stressed-out mothers of the brides? I might feel a quiver or two of fear. Otherwise, this makes a lovely change."

Oliver shrugged. "I've covered wars. So far, he's right, this isn't too bad."

"I mention that it was really bad for the car of ours that didn't get its laser shield up in time, and we'll let it go at that. Good speed on that one, Kyle, by the way."

He turned around. There was a funny expression on his face. "Kitty, I didn't hit the shield button. It activated before I could reach it."

We all stared at each other. A suspicion niggled. Operation Confusion would have been a lot more confusing, and we'd have lost at least every guy on Alpha and Airborne, if not for the fact that Jamie had talents even Jeff hadn't been able to figure out yet. Hybrid girls were nothing if not exceptionally gifted. And, as had been pointed out to me frequently, while Jamie's blocks kept her from feeling everyone's emotions, her hearing was topnotch. After all, I knew why the bus had acted strangely earlier.

I looked right into her eyes. Jamie looked back and grabbed my nose. I laughed and kissed her head. "You're such a good baby."

CHAPTER 16

TO EVERYONE'S CREDIT, while they looked shocked, no one asked me if I was crazy. I didn't figure this kind of luck would hold, but I enjoyed the moment.

Then again, they might not have said it aloud, but their expressions showed a variety of "you so crazy" looks. I could understand why the others were surprised, but, really, Operation Confusion had only been three months ago. You'd think Jeff and Christopher both would have remembered that Jamie had had a tiny hand in helping to save the day.

Then again, they'd been tied up and tortured while most of that was going, so perhaps it wasn't foremost in their minds.

Or maybe it was because Len was skidding us around yet another corner. He avoided hitting the cars coming for us, I had no idea how, though driving onto the sidewalk had something to do with it.

"How are we getting out of this alive?" I asked.

Jeff grunted. "I plan to take care of that shortly." He turned around. "Kid, take the next three rights, then two lefts. You'll see a parking garage under renovation, head into it, barriers be damned."

"Yes, sir, Ambassador," Len said, teeth gritted.

"I'm glad Len has athletic reflexes." I was. He was doing things with the car I'd expect from Reader or Tim, or myself. But I hadn't seen this level of competence since we'd been relegated to the Diplomatic Corps.

"We had to take a course," Kyle shared. "Len got one of the highest scores ever, per Mister Reynolds."

"We'll cheer later," Christopher snapped as we skidded around yet another corner, narrowly missing a gaggle of students. "If, you know, we don't die or kill someone on the way."

I checked behind us. "We still have our pod of gray killer whales behind us. They don't give up easily, do they?" No police cars were anywhere in the near or far distance. So much for the idea that regular people would be adequately protected. Anyone around us right now was in danger.

"Killer whales?" Oliver asked.

"Don't ask," Christopher said. "You get used to the Kittyisms or you go insane."

"Thanks ever, Mister Happy."

"Limos are like the car version of whales," Len said, teeth still gritted, as he spun us toward Jeff's requested parking garage. "These are trying to kill us."

I sighed happily. "See? Someone understands me without a translator."

Jeff grunted. "I'm thrilled. Kid, head for a middle level, not the bottom, not the roof, spin our whale around, and have it ready to go either up or down."

"Yes, sir."

"His name is Len," I mentioned.

Jeff gave me a look that indicated he was close to having to have the jealousy chat with Len. I decided I liked who my driver was now, so shutting up was likely going to be the better part of valor. Besides, I had to cover Jamie's ears while I screamed as we careened through a barricade, drove up a small ramp, took to the air, and landed to the sounds of Saliva's "Click Click Boom." At least we had a good soundtrack going, though I got the impression I was the only one taking the time to enjoy it.

"Kitty, need the eardrums," Christopher said, wincing. "You're louder than the music, which is saying something."

"Don't care. I've needed to scream for what seems like hours now, and couldn't before."

"Why not?" Jeff asked as Len spun the car.

"It would have scared Jamie."

"You screaming your head off now didn't scare her?"

"No. You're with us now, so she knows Daddy will take care of it."

"Oh." Jeff looked extremely pleased. The car stopped, however, and his expression went hard. "I want us ready. Music off, I want you all paying attention." Kyle turned off the stereo just as Iron Maiden's "Dance of Death" was starting. I controlled my complaint as Jeff shot me the hairy eyeball look. I'd been paying attention but decided now wasn't the time to protest or demand musical accompaniment.

"Kid, Christopher and I are going to take whoever's coming, but just in case we get into more than we can handle, I want you heading the car down if you can get out safely, or to the roof if you can't."

"Len and I can handle ourselves in a fight," Kyle said.

"I want you doing your jobs, and that's driving and protecting Kitty and Jamie. Period." Jeff wasn't growling, but he was close.

The boys chose not to argue. I knew they were smart.

Mr. Joel Oliver cleared his throat. "Why don't you simply ask the baby to get us safely home?"

"Kitty was joking about what she said earlier," Christopher said, sounding strained. Or maybe it was because they were hoping I hadn't told Mr. Joel Oliver what he likely already knew.

Oliver, who was sitting between Jeff and Christopher, gave me a small smile. "I know, Mister White. You can stop pretending."

"No idea what you mean," Christopher said, while he looked at his hands.

Oliver sighed. "I know you're aliens. I know you have special . . . skills. Skills that humans don't. Mister Reynolds is fully aware that I know he's the head of the C.I.A.'s Extra-Terrestrial Division." He looked sad. "No one believes me, mind you, but I know the truth."

"They print everything you write," I pointed out.

He shrugged. "They print it because it sells, but my editors don't believe anything I submit. Most of our readers don't either, and the few who do are, for the most part, crackpots, to put it charitably."

"That kind of sucks."

He chuckled. "Yes, it does. Then again, I get to do what I love, and I know the truth. Everyone can call me a crazed conspiracy theorist or whatever the insult of the day is. But knowledge is power."

I'd seen this same expression on Chuckie's face all through school—it was a combination of determination, disappointment, hurt, and defiance. That look on Chuckie's face had always made my heart hurt. It was somewhat unsurprising to discover I didn't care for it on Oliver's face, either.

"Oh, no you don't," Jeff said to me.

"I don't what?"

"You are *not* getting attached to him! Having Mister Joel Oliver here in the limo is one thing. Thinking of him as your friend is another."

"I'm not your enemy, Ambassador Martini."

"Nothing you do helps us," Jeff snapped.

"Oh, on the contrary," Pierre said. "He's helping you far more than you realize."

"I beg your pardon?" Jeff shook his head. "How is what he writes a help?"

Pierre sighed. "Really, it seems so obvious." He looked around. "You lovely people are hiding in plain sight. Mister Joel is considered to be writing fiction by almost everyone. Therefore, if the man who routinely shares that Elvis is still walking amongst us also says that the dear people from American Centaurion are actually aliens living as our neighbors, what will the general populace think?"

"That it's a load of crap." Pierre had a strong point. "In fact, the more MJO insists we're not normal, the more likely it is that someone's going to assume he just feels we insulted him in some way."

"Too much attention isn't good," Jeff protested. "Where there's smoke, there's fire. Too many people insinuating that we're . . . different, and someone's going to decide that maybe we are."

Oliver shook his head. "The government is protecting you, Ambassador. If no one was insinuating that something funny was going on with you, then you might have more cause to worry."

"There were diplomatic plates on some of the cars following us," Len said.

Kyle nodded. "I'm having them run."

"Meaning that not everyone in the government is protecting us, which, I have to add, isn't any kind of a shock."

The sound of a lot of tires screeching echoed through the parking garage. The pod had caught up to us.

"No problem," Jeff said, as he and Christopher prepared to get out of the car. "I'm going to find out exactly who's behind this."

"How?"

He grinned at me. "Well, I'm hoping by beating the crap out of these people, but I'm open to other options."

"I like a man who's willing to experiment with new ideas." Especially in the bedroom, but that wasn't relevant at this precise time.

Jeff chuckled. "I love how you think."

CHAPTER 17

"REMEMBER THEY HAVE GUNS** and a seemingly unlimited supply of bullets," I reminded Jeff before he leaped out of the car.

"We have hyperspeed and an unlimited supply of pissed off," he replied.

I didn't need Christopher to chime in. Jeff was bigger and stronger, but Christopher was nastier, especially in a fight. And both of them had been, like me, feeling tied up and put on a major time out. I almost felt sorry for the guys in the whale pod. Until I thought about what they'd done to our other limo full of people.

"Hurt them. A lot."

"On three," Jeff said to Christopher. He nodded. "Three." They were out of the car, doors nicely closed, before any of us could blink.

"He's not much for patience, is he?" Pierre asked. "Not that I can blame him."

"No, Jeff's not all that patient in these situations." Come to think of it, neither was I. And while I could see bodies flying, there were at least ten cars full of nasty people, and only two of our side involved. "Um, Pierre . . ."

"I shall guard our little princess with my life," he said. "Jimmy shared that you fell more on the active side of the house, darling. Besides, I was at your wedding. I'm sure you're ready to race in there. Just be careful."

"You stay here," I said to Oliver in my strongest mean-person voice, which I hoped was channeling my mother's.

He shrugged. "They're moving too fast for pictures. I'll take whatever ones might be helpful once things are, ah, handled. Until then, I've had a trying afternoon and am taking a nap. So to speak."

"Works for me. Kyle, Len, do what Jeff said, and if there's trouble, get Jamie out of here."

"Will do," Len said.

Kyle grunted. "Let us know if we can help, though. I'd like to kick some ass." He looked back at Jamie. "Sorry."

"She's heard the word already, trust me." I kissed her head. "You be good, Jamie-Kat. Mommy's going to help Daddy."

Who, as I turned back, might indeed need an assist, as there were a lot of guys with semiautomatics firing wildly. A-Cs were fast, Jeff and Christopher were both enhanced, so faster than normal, but still, all it was going to take was one or two random lucky shots and I'd be doing CPR. If we were lucky.

I concentrated, focused on the inner me, and let myself rev for a moment. I had a plan, and I needed to both move at hyperspeed and accurately hit something. I could do either one just fine, but both together wasn't coming easily without an A-C holding onto me. However, Christopher was cornered, Jeff was surrounded, and no one had gotten out of one car, meaning they were the backup or, more likely, the ones in charge.

I considered taking my Glock, but under the circumstances, I wasn't confident I could handle it while running, so I decided to let discretion be the better part of valor. "MJO, please close the door behind me." He nodded; I opened the door, and went for it.

Out of the car and slamming into the one I'd aimed for, almost like a pro. I didn't wait for an invitation—I ripped one of the back doors off. It felt great and didn't hurt at all. Then again, pulling and hitting weren't the same thing.

I looked in to see several people with their jaws hanging open. Three of them had the big-lug look of bodyguards that Kyle carried off a lot better. Two of them, however, were dressed in expensive clothes and looked like they were in charge. I reached in, grabbed both of them by their throats, and pulled them out of the car.

A-Cs were stronger than humans, and I'd inherited that from Jamie, too. I held on and dragged them with me as I ran toward where Jeff and Christopher were. I flung the smaller one to Christopher. "Hang on and use him as a shield."

Dragged the larger one in front of Jeff and held him there. "Keep shooting, hit your bosses. Try to hit or run us over, and we'll just break their necks!" This time, I knew I sounded like my mother. Or

I sounded scary crazy. Either way, the bullets stopped, and everyone backed away.

"Run and I kill them. Move and I kill them. Are we clear?" I waited. No one said anything. "Well? Dudes, you choosing that I kill them and you too?"

The man I was holding cleared his throat. "You told them not to move." He had a slight accent. I couldn't place it, but it didn't sound American in any way. He also didn't sound the way the taxi driver had, disguised voice or not.

"Whatever." He was right, but why give him the satisfaction of agreeing? At least his minions were well behaved and good at following orders to the letter. "Jeff, hold the trash, will you?"

"Sure, baby. Let's see who we have here." He turned my captive around. "No one I know."

"Hang on." I walked at human speeds to Christopher and looked at his captive. "No clue. Hang on again." Trotted to the limo. "MJO? I think we need you. Bring the cameras. Len, Pierre, stay in the car with Jamie. Kyle, come and gather up all the guns. I want them in the trunk of our car."

Oliver and Kyle followed me out of the limo. Kyle started removing weaponry. "You want them tied up?"

"Yes, but we have nothing to do that with." A thought occurred to me. What we needed was a pickup, and not the truck kind. "You know who they are?" I asked Oliver quietly.

"No," he said just as quietly, while he took snaps of every single person. "They're foreigners, and they're likely to use the diplomatic immunity card based on their license plates."

I remembered the lugs in the last car and ran over. They were still sitting there. "Really? Weapons on the ground, butts with the rest of your goon squad, or we kill your bosses."

"Do what the crazy woman says," the guy Jeff was holding called.

His goons dropped a lot of firepower on the ground, then left their limo. I did a fast headcount. Yeah, there was no way we could handle all these people. I took a closer look—none of them were overly impressive in the looks department, meaning they were all likely to be humans. I ran back to our car, dug my phone out, and dialed. She answered immediately. "Mom, are you busy?"

"Only watching a bizarre car chase on the news James insists you didn't start."

"I didn't! They chased us. But that's why I'm calling. We have a lot of bad guys sort of in custody, and I need someone to tell me what to do with them."

"Why did you call me instead of Charles?"

"I think they're involved in whatever's going to go down at the President's Ball, and I figured you'd want to know. Geez, you always complain when I *don't* call you before Chuckie."

"It's just a shock. What's going on?"

Wow. That was a good question. I honestly had no idea. "Well, Mister Joel Oliver thinks they're after me, because they tried to blow us up using Jamie's car seat, but I think they're after him, because they were shooting at all of us, but that was after he was with us. Though I also think there's a lot more going on than we've figured out yet, especially because I don't think the taxis are involved in this part of whatever plan's going down. The police presence in D.C. seems nonexistent. And the traffic around here beyond sucks."

"Someone shot at my daughter and tried to blow my granddaughter up?" I hadn't realized Mom could sound scarier than I'd heard when I'd come in way too late from a date without letting her know. Apparently, she could. "I'll be right there. Call Charles, I want him there, too."

"How do you know where our 'there' is?"

She sighed. "I'm tracking you via the GPS in your cell phone. Charles will track you using the tracking implants Centaurion Division has in all of you. Why would you even feel the need to ask? Other than the fact that you probably didn't remember, I mean." My mother's sarcasm knob went well past eleven.

"I remembered." Sort of. "I'm distracted."

"Yes, I know. I'm used to it. Be there shortly. If we can ever get through this damn traffic."

"Yeah, it wasn't our friend earlier, I can say that. I'd suggest a police escort only I think you'd have to send out to Maryland or Virginia to score any. Possibly to Florida or New York, even."

"Let's deal with the bigger, more pressing issues first, shall we?"

"Okay, love you, Mom, calling Chuckie now."

"Love you, too. Keep all of them where you can see them. Search their cars but be careful in case they're rigged."

"On it." I called Chuckie, had a very similar conversation with him, complete with rage about the continuing danger and insinuations about my lack of focus, and then considered how best to search the cars. Decided I wasn't up to the task, so I traded with Christopher—I held his hostage, he searched the other limos.

Lots of guns and such were found, not much else, including false beards, so I went back to the assumption these guys had nothing to do with the taxis from earlier. By the time Christopher was through and I'd given him back his captive to have and hold, Mom and Chuckie had both arrived. Kevin Lewis was with them. The hotness quotient was now back up to where I liked it.

"I demand diplomatic immunity," the man Jeff was holding declared.

Mom and Chuckie exchanged long-suffering looks. "Let's see your papers," Mom said.

The man Jeff was holding reached into his inner suit pocket and handed Kevin a folio. He nodded and handed it to Mom. "Looks legit."

Mom heaved a sigh. "So, you're from the Republic of Kazakhstan?"

I looked at the men. They didn't really look Central Asian in any way. Then again, that might not mean anything.

"Yes. We demand to be released immediately, and have all our property returned to us."

Mom was muttering under her breath, but she nodded to Jeff and Christopher, who let go—reluctantly. "They tried to kill my wife and child," Jeff said with a growl.

"They have the immunity, we don't have a choice," Chuckie said angrily.

"Stop them!" Kyle shouted as he ran to us. "I ran all the plates. None of these cars are actually diplomatic vehicles."

The Goon Squad turned as one and tried to grab everyone. Kyle slammed into the nearest group, showing that USC really had a great football program. The three men he hit went down, Kyle on top of them.

There was a flurry of activity that included a lot of slamming of bodies and a variety of martial arts. Apparently the Goon Squad hadn't gotten the memo that those working with aliens were highly trained. Mom, Chuckie, and Kevin were all kicking butt and waiting for later to take names. Kyle was slamming body after body to the ground; Jeff and Christopher were taking those bodies and slamming them up against the walls.

However, there were a lot of goons, and our side was quite busy. And the two bad guys clearly in charge were hoofing it for their car.

CHAPTER 18

I DIDN'T HESITATE. I RAN AFTER THEM. At hyperspeed.

The fact that this was a mistake was made quickly clear as I overshot them, their limo, and, in that sense, the parking garage. The only positive was that I didn't hit a wall. I was, however, outside, in front of the exit.

While I caught my breath and tried to determine if I should run back in or not, the decision was made for me, as their limo came barreling down the ramp.

During Operation Drug Addict, a crazed politician had tried to run me down in the middle of the Arizona desert in an Escalade. This seemed remarkably similar, only I wasn't emotionally distraught, and I now had A-C powers.

I jumped out of the way as the limo screeched its way out of the garage. The two escapees were in the front seat, and the driver was aiming for me, but either the missing door caused some sort of wind disturbance, or he was a lot more interested in getting away, because they missed me completely.

However, I wasn't happy with the idea of them getting away. I ran after them and this time caught what I was aiming for. I was through the hole in the car and inside the limo in a split second, and, happily, I didn't just bash out the other side.

I congratulated myself for a moment, then realized, hey, I was now, essentially, in the car with the guys who'd been trying to kill me all afternoon.

The window between the front of the limo and the back was down, and the lack of brilliance of this current plan was reinforced when the one who'd demanded diplomatic immunity pulled a gun from somewhere Kyle and Christopher had missed and aimed it at my head. "Please don't take this personally."

"Excuse me?"

He shrugged. "You're a pretty girl. I don't like killing pretty girls. Or little babies."

"Then why have you been trying to do just that all day?"

"A job is a job."

"Were you in taxis earlier, trying to get us?"

He gave me a small smile. "No. They are . . . amateurs."

"How do you mean?"

He moved the gun nearer to my head. "They didn't want to damage the merchandise."

"Before you pull the trigger," I said quickly, "where the heck are you from? You've got an accent I really can't place." I wanted to keep him talking because I wasn't sure if I had enough speed left to get out of the car without getting hurt or shot. Hurt was better than shot, of course, but not my preferred plan. Of course, my preferred plan had me back in the garage with Jeff right there to at least perform an assist. So much for my plans, preferred or otherwise.

"You heard that woman."

I shook my head. "I don't think you're really from Kazakhstan. I think that was just a really good forgery." Or a way to toss blame onto a country that could easily work as a fall guy, though circumstances suggested I table this line of thought.

He gave me a small smile. "I am from all over."

"I get that. But where did you start out, spend the formative years, and all that jazz?" Keep 'em talking, that was my motto. It was a big reason I was still alive to have a motto.

"Why does it matter?"

"I'd hate to die not knowing."

"Just kill her," the driver snapped. He sounded like he'd grown up next door to wherever the guy with the gun had lived. "We have no time for this. We are behind schedule."

Interestingly enough, I was fairly sure English wasn't either of their first languages, yet they weren't speaking to each other in native tongue. My gift for languages extended only to high school French and a smattering of Spanish, so the likelihood that I'd recognize anything they'd say seemed slim. I wasn't sure if they just didn't want to take the chance or if there was some other reason. Like their reason for having Kazakhstan papers, tabled for later, like when I was out of this car and safe later.

"What, you were supposed to have me offed already? So sorry I've caused your timeline to get screwed up and all."

The gunman shook his head and made a frowny face. "You are not the target."

"You're going to kill me why, then?"

"You are . . . in the way."

"Shut up and kill her," the driver snarled. He was racing us along. The traffic that had been a problem earlier seemed all cleared up, or else he was taking a different route. Unsurprisingly, I heard no sirens. And I didn't want to risk looking away from the man with the gun to see where we were heading or if there might be a cop in silent pursuit.

The gunman nodded. "We are close to the river?"

"Yes. Kill her, toss her body in."

"Why not take me as a hostage?"

The gunman stared at me. "Why would you want that?"

"Better than being dead."

He shook his head again, and I got another shot of the frowny face. "I would like to offer that alternative, but the orders were very clear."

"Orders from whom?"

He cocked the gun. "From the people who want things to run more . . . smoothly."

"I don't get the names of the people who paid you to kill me before I die? What kind of a deal is that?"

"The only kind the people we work for make," the driver snarled.

"I am truly sorry," the gunman said. "Good-bye, Miss Katt."

I could tell by the way the car was moving we were on a bridge. I decided I'd gotten all I was going to. I ducked to the right and slammed myself against the partition separating their side of the car from mine.

The A-C superstrength wasn't as strong in me as it was in Jeff or Christopher, or even Lorraine and Claudia, but it was a lot stronger than humans normally managed. I didn't break through, but I rocked both of them.

The gun went off, the driver shouted, and the car went out of control. The gunman tried to shoot me again, but we were flipping around and he missed. I took the opportunity to kick the gun out of his hand. It went off as it landed, shattering the windshield.

The car hit a railing and, probably due to the lack of a door, caught on something and flipped. The men were shouting in a language I couldn't understand, and I considered screaming but figured I'd save that for later. Especially since I fell out of the limo and headed for the water.

Time seemed to move really slowly. I figured the car was going to land on me, because that was exactly how my luck ran, so I managed to flip myself around and into a dive position, thanking my parents for insisting that I learn how to swim and dive despite living in the middle of the desert.

The limo was reflected in the water, and I could tell I'd been right—it was falling on top of me. I took a deep breath and held it as I hit the water.

CHAPTER 19

THE POTOMAC WAS COLD, WET, AND ICKY. It was also hard when I hit it, but I'd been prepared for that. Sort of.

Track was good for more than running—it had expanded my breathing capacity, so I could hold my breath for a good length of time. Every action movie said the same thing—when something big and nasty was falling on you, get as far down underwater as you can. I swam down as fast as I could.

Despite the movies prepping me for this visually, what I hadn't been prepared for was the impact the limo made when it hit the water. I was close enough that the water's displacement knocked me over. I'd have panicked, but I didn't have much longer until I'd have to breathe. I looked around to figure out which way was up.

Happily, I saw what looked like the bottom of a boat and kicked up toward it. I got around it and hit the surface just as I thought my lungs were going to explode. I looked around and realized what else I hadn't been prepared for: the amount of water traffic. I might no longer be at risk of drowning or being shot, but I was at real risk of being run over by boats.

The limo's swan dive hadn't been missed, and there were more boats congregating and heading toward us. The water got choppier, I got colder, and I became more concerned that I wasn't going to get out of this well.

I tried to remember what to do in cases like this. Not fall in was probably the first rule. Be wearing a life jacket was undoubtedly up there in the top three suggestions. Kick off your shoes was in there somewhere, but I didn't want to lose my Converse if I didn't have to, and they really didn't seem to be weighing me down.

Save the others if you're okay was definitely a rule. Asking myself why I was trying to save the men who'd tried to kill us multiple times over, I swam back toward where the limo had gone in.

I couldn't see anyone, so I took a deep breath and ducked back under the water. I swam down, but it was hard to see. I flailed around and by sheer luck hit what felt like a fender. Dragged myself lower, flailed around again. This time I hit what felt like a human hand. I grabbed and tugged.

Whoever I had didn't move. I tugged harder and felt the body move a bit. But I was almost out of air. I let go and kicked up to the surface. Took another huge breath and went back down.

I found the arm faster, but I wasn't able to really move him. I was also getting colder and tired. I tugged one more time, feeling like my lungs were going to burst. Nothing. I let go, but I had no energy. I kicked up, but wasn't getting any real action from my legs.

As I waited for my life to flash in front of me, I felt an arm go around my waist. Whoever had me was strong and fast, and we bolted to the surface, me gasping like a drowning fish.

"What are you doing?" Jeff asked as he held me up so I could get air without water splashing in my face. "And why are you doing it in the Potomac?"

"Trying to save the guys who tried to kill us. No, I don't have a good answer for why, just think we need to. What are you doing here?"

"Trying to save you. Can you float?"

"Yeah."

"Okay. Then stay here, on the surface." Jeff dove down.

I waited, treading water and enjoying breathing, while more boats came closer. I counted in my head. He was down for a minute, and I was about to dive down again, cold and tired or not, when Jeff's head surfaced. He had the gunman.

"Can you hold him, baby?"

"Yeah." I grabbed the man in the hold lifeguards used, hopefully correctly, as Jeff dove down again.

The air around us started whipping, and I looked up. There was a big helicopter of some kind directly above us. I couldn't tell if it was Coast Guard or Air Force, but its belly was opening up, and some guys in dive gear were lowering down on cables.

Jeff surfaced with the driver in tow. "I don't know if they're still alive," he shouted to me. "I also don't know if we should care. Or why we just risked our lives to save them."

The guys on the cables jumped into the water. What looked like giant baskets were now lowering from the plane. The guys in wetsuits took the two unconscious men. "Be sure they're restrained," I shouted to one.

He nodded and gave me a thumbs up sign. He also winked. I looked closer. It was hard to be sure, but the eyes looked familiar. He and his partner hauled my guy into his basket and rose up with him. The same thing was happening with Jeff's rescue.

Jeff swam over to me and put his arm around my waist. "This is going to be fun to explain."

"How did you get here?"

I got the "duh" look. "Hyperspeed. You've heard of it."

"I mean into the middle of the river."

"I can swim almost as fast as I can run."

"Wow. I didn't know that. You're just all around awesome, aren't you?"

"I do what I can. Our lift's here."

Two more guys lowered down. They had harnesses attached to cables they hooked us into. Then we all rode up in the air. If I ignored the fact that I was freezing cold, had just swum in and swallowed some of the Potomac, and undoubtedly looked beyond awful, it was kind of cool.

We got inside, and the giant chopper closed its belly door. One of the guys in a wetsuit put a blanket around me and one around Jeff. "Thanks for the save."

He pulled his face mask off. "The U.S. Navy lives to serve, Chiefs."

"Jerry!" The rest of the gang pulled their headgear off to reveal the rest of my Top Gun pilots and Tim. "Wow, you guys moved fast."

Tim shrugged. "We're always prepared for it, and Andrews has this equipment ready to go."

"How'd you get to Andrews so fast? Traffic's been backed up for hours."

I got a full complement of "duh" looks. "Gates," Matt Hughes said. I realized he'd been the one who'd winked at me. "You know, that we have everywhere? Especially in bathrooms and military bases?" Alien technology was great for many things, including movement of goods and personnel. The gates looked like airport metal detectors to me, but they moved you hundreds or thousands of miles in seconds. Two years in, they still made me sick to my stomach, but they were effective.

"Oh. Right. Kind of distracted. It's been a busy day. What's the status on the two guys Jeff pulled out of the limo?"

"I think they'll make it," Chip Walker said. "This was fun, Kitty, but I don't know how Imageering's going to cover it all up."

"We have agents at the scene," Tim added. "But I'm not certain if they'll be able to alter all the memories."

Randy and Joe were busy doing CPR on the two gunmen. "One's shot," Randy shared.

"In the shoulder," Joe added. "Kind of a weird angle."

"His buddy shot him instead of me while we were fighting."

"So we saved those murderers why?" Jeff asked me.

"They have information about who hired them to kill us." I thought about it. "You know . . . one of them called me Miss Katt."

"So?"

"So I haven't been Miss Katt for a year. And he said I wasn't the target, that he didn't like killing pretty girls or babies, that I was merely in the way."

"Again, so? I'm wondering why I didn't let them drown. Almost as much as I'm wondering what part of 'stay in the car with our baby' didn't register for you. And nearly as much as I'm wondering why you ran outside and then after those two."

"I didn't want them to get away or you to get hurt." Why share that I'd overshot them unintentionally? Though I had a feeling Jeff knew.

Jeff shook his head. "Only my girl."

"Where's Jamie?"

"Back at the Embassy. The jocks and Pierre are apparently the only ones capable of following any kind of order."

"Are they all okay?"

"Yes. Your newest pal's there, too. Your mother and Reynolds are taking the others into custody, I assume."

"You assume?"

"I had to leave. Something about saving my wife from drowning. I know, I don't have my priorities in order." Jeff's sarcasm knob was right up at eleven again.

I leaned against him. "No argument about your priorities." Blanket or no, my teeth were chattering.

"We need to get her back to the Embassy," Jeff said to Tim as he picked me up and put me on his lap. "She was in the water a lot longer than I was."

"It's just a little hypothermia," I shared in between my teeth clacking.

"It's a lot of hypothermia, and if you weren't enhanced you'd be close to death."

"Superpowers rock." My teeth chattered as an exclamation to each syllable. "And I'm sure the cold'll pass."

"And I'm sure I'm getting you into a bath," Jeff replied. He tucked my blanket and his around me.

"Really?" Maybe this day wasn't going to end up a total waste after all.

Jeff chuckled. "Nice to see your laser focus remains on the priorities."

CHAPTER 20

WE ACTUALLY HAD A HELIPAD on top of the Embassy, but in an effort to be sort of low key, we went to the Georgetown University Medical Center and landed there. Medical personnel arrived with gurneys.

As he was being strapped in, the guy who'd tried to shoot me grabbed my hand. "Why did you save us?"

"My husband saved you."

"I heard. Because you told him to. Why?"

I shrugged. "No idea. Just didn't seem right to let you drown."

"I tried to kill you and your child. More than once."

"Yeah, I know. I don't have a good answer for you."

He stared at me. "My name is Peter." He pronounced it a little strangely, but I was too cold to care.

"Nice to meet you, I guess. I'd rather know who hired you than your name."

Peter grabbed my hand. "I will tell you. Later." He pressed something into my hand. I wasn't so cold that I let on to anyone that he'd done this.

A large number of local law enforcement arrived, shocking me to my core. I hadn't thought there were any cops within a hundred miles, and yet they showed up en masse for what was absolutely a photo op.

The two bad guys were put onto gurneys and hustled off, said law enforcement going with them before I could express my taxpayer's rage about their failure to show up before everything was over.

I managed to get a surreptitious look at what was in my hand—

a memory card like the ones used in a cell phone or digital camera. It was in a plastic case, meaning it was hopefully not ruined by the wet, but I didn't have a lot of hope that we'd get anything off of it.

Tim flashed the diplomatic immunity card before anyone could try to escort us anywhere. Jeff and I went into the hospital, then, with Tim and the flyboys creating some minor confusion, we hypersped out of there and back to the Embassy.

Our rooms were filled with people again or still, I wasn't sure. "Out," Jeff said. "Go to Christopher's side or down to the conference room. We need to get warm and dry."

Amy had Jamie, who appeared to be snoozing in her Snugli carrier. "She's fine," she said as I gave Jamie a closer look. "God, you look like a drowned cat."

"Thanks, I feel like a salmon that got run over swimming upstream against a whole lot of grizzly bears." I looked around. "Where're Mom and Chuckie?"

"Doing something with the prisoners," Christopher said. "Len and Kyle are getting settled in."

"They're going to live here?" Jeff didn't sound happy about this.

Christopher nodded. "Yeah, Angela and Reynolds are both insisting on it. Under the circumstances, we're getting more new residents, too."

"Who?"

"Kevin and his family."

"Awesome! Not that I mind at all, but why?"

"We need more security on staff than just our own people." Christopher grimaced. "I can't argue. These job changes haven't gone smoothly at all."

"I know, I'm a screw-up." I was starting to shiver again. "But I'm also a freezing screw-up. Can we table this for later?"

"Yeah, because you're not the only one having problems, Kitty." Christopher sighed. "We all are. I don't know who's feeling more like a failure, you, Paul, James, or Serene, but I think I can speak for myself and Jeff in saying we're in the running, too."

"Fabulous. Order some uppers while we shower."

Christopher hit me with Glare #5, Amy laughed, and they ushered any stragglers out.

As Jeff and I trotted into our bathroom, I put the memory card into my jewelry box. "New admirer?" Jeff asked, sarcasm knob only at around six.

"No. Peter slipped that to me. I want to examine it later, but I'm hoping it's helpful, as opposed to a tiny bomb that's going to go off the moment we relax."

The com activated. "Chiefs, Commander Reader is suggesting everyone regroup in the morning. Imageering is fully focused on fixing today's incidents, and all available Field teams are needed elsewhere."

Jeff and I looked at each other. "What's going on?" I asked.

"We're having clustered activity, Chief."

"We haven't had that since . . ." Jeff's voice trailed off and his eyes narrowed. "Where is the action, Walter?"

"Paraguay. In the Chaco. Commanders Reader and Crawford are insisting that all Embassy personnel remain here, Chiefs." Walter sounded as though he didn't want to share this news. "Your father is secured, Co-Chief Martini," he added, clearly hoping this news would mean we didn't rage about being under Embassy Arrest.

I decided I was too cold and tired to fight. "Okay, good to know. I assume Mom and Chuckie are going to be all night with the creeps?"

"That appears to be their feeling, yes, Chief."

"Fine, Walter. Thank you."

"Signing off, then, Chiefs."

Jeff shook his head. "I'd be upset about this, but under the circumstances, let's just let James and Tim handle it."

"Works for me. I swear. And I'm proud of you for not racing off to help."

Jeff grunted as we started peeling our clothes off. I didn't despair as I looked at my stained and soggy Aerosmith shirt and Converse—the Elves had salvaged clothes of mine in much worse states than these were.

The Embassy was really like living in the most luxurious penthouse you could imagine, to the third power. So the bathroom was extremely nice. The Elves handled all the cleaning, which was good, since my housekeeping skills remained cheerfully unimpressive.

"Bath or shower?" Jeff asked.

"Both?"

I must have sounded overly hopeful, or he was merely reading my mind, because he got the expression on his face that always reminded me of a big jungle cat about to eat me. I loved that look. Besides, for us, escaping death was sort of like foreplay.

Jeff turned on the tub and, as the water filled up and the bathroom started to steam, he pulled me into his arms. I snuggled in and buried my face in the hair on his chest. "You're not as cold as me."

"I'm bigger."

"Very big."

Jeff chuckled, though it sounded more like a purr. "Glad you think so." He stroked my back, fingers doing a sensuous massage. "You're still shivering."

"I'm cold. Inside and out."

"I'll do my best to warm both." He lifted me up and put me gently into the tub. He joined me, but didn't do anything other than lean back, stretch out, and pull me in between his legs, so I could lean my head on his chest.

"I thought you were going to warm me up inside, too."

"You need to warm up your body first." He sounded worried.

I looked up at him. He looked worried. "I'll be fine."

"I'll have Tito take a look at you later."

"I'm fine."

Jeff kissed the top of my head. "Humor me."

I snuggled my face back into the hair on his chest, between his impressive pecs. "Okay, if you insist."

"I do."

Jeff continued to stroke me, and I let my body relax. I heard water running. "Why are you filling the tub up more?"

He chuckled. "You've been asleep and it's cooled down. For the third time. I think your body's finally feeling normal, that's why you woke up."

I thought about this as he shifted me around into a sitting position. "This is an A-C thing for when you get overcold, isn't it?"

"Yeah. Water isolation." He smiled at my expression. "Which is why we're here, in the tub, together, instead of me sending you over to Dulce to go into a water chamber there."

"I knew I loved you for a lot of reasons."

"Good." Jeff stood up and let the tub drain. "Let's actually clean off now." I considered whether or not to point out that we hadn't had sex while in the tub, but I figured he had his reasons. "I do. We've both got Potomac still on us, at least in our hair."

"That mind reading thing is sometimes freaky."

"Read your emotions. Lust mixed with disappointment is very strong, especially coming from you."

"Humph."

We moved to the shower, and Jeff insisted that we actually cleaned off before we did anything. This was becoming, hands down, the most disappointing bathroom experience of our entire relationship.

"What was in the Potomac that's got you acting like a germaphobe?"

"What isn't in the Potomac's probably a better question." He kissed me, and this was a real kiss, strong, deep, sensuous. I was grinding against him in moments. He pulled away slowly. "I was cold, too."

I thought about it. "You're from an extremely warm planet." Jeff grunted. "And when reptiles get too cold they get really sluggish."

"Thanks for the reptile comparison."

"I'll bet it's apt." I thought about it some more. "Wow, I hate living here even more now."

Jeff snorted. "It takes a lot to make me too cold to make you happy, baby. However . . ."

"Taking a long swim in the freezing cold river did it. Gotcha." I considered all my options. "You want to dry off and then, ah, take a nap?"

Jeff's eyelids drooped, and he got the jungle cat look again. "I want to dry off and go to bed."

CHAPTER 21

WE DRIED OFF QUICKLY. Jeff used hyperspeed; I just hurried it up at human regular. No reason to risk hitting myself or something.

The second my hair was combed out, Jeff's hands were on me, roaming my body, teasing my nipples and squeezing my butt. I was grinding against his leg as his mouth moved to my neck, and I started yowling like a cat in heat.

Jeff lifted me into his arms and wrapped his arms around my back while I wrapped my legs around his waist. "Mmmm, that's what I like." We were in our bedroom, up against a wall, grinding together in a nanosecond. Hyperspeed had great advantages.

His mouth went to do wonderful things to my breasts. From the first time we'd slept together, he'd brought me to orgasm at second base, and he'd continued to never miss a step or an opportunity.

He lifted me, back still against the wall, as his tongue trailed down my stomach. My legs wrapped around his neck as my hands went into his hair, and his tongue went into me.

My hips were bucking as I rubbed against his mouth frantically and he stroked me, inside and out, gently taking me between his teeth, while the fireworks went off behind my eyes and I hit high C.

Jeff kept on until I'd hit all the high notes at least twice, then, with one last nip and lick, trailed his mouth up over my stomach, renewing the relationship with my breasts and neck, as he slid me back down and onto him.

Before we'd become parents, our foreplay could last hours. Now we'd gotten trained to take advantage of available alone time. Not that I minded. Foreplay was great and I loved it, especially the way Jeff did it, but nothing was better than when he was inside me.

I gasped as he entered me, and his head reared back a bit. He had the jungle cat look on his face again. "This is what I've really wanted to do since I picked you up from class." His voice was a low purr, and it made me moan as much as him being inside me did.

He covered my mouth and ravaged my tongue with his, while he slammed into me. I wrapped my limbs around him while I screamed my orgasm into his mouth.

Jeff was a sexual god, and his opinion always seemed to be that it just wasn't good enough unless I had a variety of screaming orgasms. Needless to say, I considered this one of his finer traits. He spun us around and deposited me onto our bed, still moving inside me. I'd have marveled at his skills, but I was too busy yowling my head off.

I managed to take a semiactive role by running my hands over his chest. He had just the right amount of hair to be manly without being a rug, and I wanted my mouth on his pecs. Happily, he knew and leaned closer to me. I attacked, the feel of his chest against my mouth drove me wild and my body writhed against his. "Mmmm, you're such a good bad girl." He drove into me harder and faster, and another climax hit.

He flipped us over while I was still screaming, so he was lying down and I was riding him. His hands stroked and fondled my breasts while he gave me the best ride on a bucking bronco in the world. My wailing was at an all-time high. Fortunately, the Embassy had amazing soundproofing, a contrast to everywhere else we'd lived, so as long as the com wasn't on and the baby was in another room, I could do my thing. I'd never been able to be quiet while even making out with Jeff, let alone doing more. Again, he didn't seem to mind.

He slammed up, and I rocked back, and he exploded inside me at the same time my strongest climax crashed over me. I hit a level where I could shatter crystal, and he roared as our bodies shuddered together. Each throb from him made my orgasm spike, until the room started to spin.

Jeff shifted so I'd fall forward. His hands were still on my breasts, and he moved me gently down until I was lying on top of him, whimpering quietly while the spasms in my body quieted.

He stroked my back and kissed my head. "I love you, baby," he said softly.

I snuggled my face into his neck. "I love you, too, Jeff. I'm sorry

I didn't do what you said and ended up putting us both into the river."

He chuckled as he pulled the covers up and over us. "As long as you're safe, still mine, and in my arms and my bed, I don't really care about anything else. Including you being you and ignoring anything anyone tells you, including me."

"That's my kind of détente."

CHAPTER 22

WE BOTH FELL ASLEEP, which wasn't all that surprising. I woke up a few hours later because my breasts were torpedoes. Did a quick search and retrieved Jamie from Doreen and Irving.

I fed the baby, Jeff did the diaper check and change, and we tucked her into her bassinette, which we put by my side of the bed, just because we were both feeling a little jumpy about exploding cars and river swims. Then we all went back to sleep.

Jamie woke us up a few hours later, we did the feeding routine, and then all collapsed back into bed. I marked swimming in the Potomac as being something we wanted never to do again, either individually or as a family.

The sound of Maroon 5's "Must Get Out" woke us up hours later. One of the nicer things about living in the Embassy was that we continued to avoid the standard A-C Morning Militant Bell Ringing that was so popular with everyone but me. We got to have an actual alarm clock and one of my backup iPods lived there. I had this one continuously tuned to my Hate This Place playlist because, well, why not?

As Maroon 5 shared my sentiments about D.C. and what it was doing to us, we gave Jamie her morning feeding. The music changed to Pink and Steven Tyler singing "Misery." Yeah, I loved it here, I really did.

Once Jamie was burped and resting in her crib, we showered, quickly. These days, our long showers were for when the baby was with someone else or asleep. Once we were clean again, we stayed in our robes while Jeff prepared and we ate breakfast. It was sort of a decadent thing to do, but it made both of us feel more like we were on vacation than relegated to an assignment we both hated.

Jeff made some calls, during which he spent a lot of time grunting. When he finished, I made the standard inquiries. "What's going on?"

He sighed. "The cluster acted just like the one in Paris a few months ago. There were no rage indicators. Based on what happened before, James and Tim knew Reynolds would want to get at least a sample of the superbeings to study." He didn't look happy.

"But they all blew up before our teams could either blow them up ourselves or get a superbeing captive, right?"

"I married the smartest girl in the galaxy. Yes. And there were no signs of outside attack. Just like in Paris."

"So, they were set to self-destruct. We need to find and stop whichever lunatics are behind this supersoldier project."

"If that's what it is."

"I know that's what it is, Jeff. And so do you, if you'll be honest with yourself."

"Maybe. We have something much more pressing to deal with, though, baby. The President's Ball is tomorrow, and barring Reynolds and your mother having extracted something useful out of the prisoners, we're still likely flying blind."

We were interrupted by Walter on the com. "Excuse me, Chiefs, but Mister Katt is here."

"Please ask him to give us a couple of minutes before he comes up, Walter," Jeff said, as he stood up.

"Will do, Chief."

"Why's my dad visiting without calling first?"

"He did call first. He just talked to me yesterday, not you." Jeff started getting dressed. Clean clothes, which included everything we'd been wearing the day before, were in the closet, courtesy of the Elves. I really hoped they didn't hang out and catch our sex life live and in person, but I decided the five-star maid service probably made up for it if they did.

"Oh. What about?" I asked as I rummaged through the closet for an appropriate outfit for today's festivities. I settled for another pair of jeans, a Tom Petty & the Heartbreakers T-shirt, and my Bon Jovi hoodie. I didn't want to risk another piece from my Aerosmith collection, but I still felt the need for some rockin' support.

"Something I think you'll be happy about."

"Why all the mystery?"

Jeff grinned. "I like to keep you guessing." He was, of course, in the standard black suit, white shirt, and black tie combo. You'd separate an A-C from their formal dress and their beloved Armani only if the entire safety of the world depended on it. The Diplomatic Corps were supposed to wear other, regular-type clothes, in order to blend in, but so far, Jeff had managed to make the suit work for everything.

There was a knock at our door. Jeff went to get it, I got Jamie. "Papa Sol's here for a visit, Jamie-Kat!" She did the Happy Baby Dance, which consisted of her sort of bouncing in my arms and making little squealy baby sounds.

I heard what sounded like dog snuffles and cat hisses. Sure enough, we got through the bedroom door and were attacked by a tide of canines. "Dad, why are all the animals here?" I managed to get this out without Duchess, our pit bull, getting her tongue into my mouth, but it took some work on my part.

Dad graciously took Jamie out of my arms. Jeff was otherwise occupied. Dudley, our Great Dane, had his paws on Jeff's shoulders and was giving him a friendly face wash while Dottie, the Dalmatian, had her paws on Jeff's waist, the better for him to pet her while also being mauled by Dudley. Duke, our black Lab, was trying to shove Duchess out of the way so he could monopolize my attention.

"Argh! Sol, a little help?"

"Sure, Jeff. Dogs, sit." My father's command garnered the typical response—the dogs ignored him entirely.

I channeled Mom. "Dogs—SIT!" All four dog butts hit the ground. "That's better. Dad, again, not that it's not great to get a dog bath, and it's still better than being in the Potomac, but what's going on?"

"Jeff didn't tell you?" Dad asked, far too innocently.

"Um, no. Jeff hasn't told me anything. Something about not wanting to ruin a surprise."

"Oh. Um. Well." Dad looked guilty. "Your mother hasn't said anything?"

"No. When I've talked to her, Mom's been busy with all the excitement—"

Jeff cleared his throat in that "shut up, shut up" sort of way. "Yeah, Angela's been tied up, Sol. So why don't you tell Kitty the good news?"

Wonderful, Mom was hiding the fact that she was doing active fieldwork from Dad again, and that probably meant no one had told him about everything that had happened the day before. Plus, he wasn't freaking out and demanding to ensure that Jamie was in one piece, so the likelihood was good that Dad was being protected for his own peace of mind. Wondered how long that would last with the current situation going on and gave it no more than an hour.

"So, what's the news that has you and all the pets here?" A horrible thought flashed through my mind. "Oh, my God, Dad, did they attack you or the house?"

"Did who attack me? The pets? No, of course not. No, they're here so you can take them."

"Excuse me?"

Dad coughed. "Jeff said it wouldn't be a problem."

"We're pet sitting? Where are you guys going?" Where could Mom possibly be planning to go, with us at the terrorism alert level we were at?

Dad chuckled. "We're not taking a trip, kitten. We're just coming here."

"Dad, yesterday was a long, stressful day, and I haven't been up long enough nor ingested enough Coke to be able to catch the most obvious of innuendos. I'm clueless."

He sighed. "Kitten, the Office of the President has been asking your mother for this for a long time. Before you met Jeff she was able to legitimately stay in Arizona. But now that you're here, the President can't see any reason for her not to be as well."

"Mom's here all the time."

"Yeah," Jeff said. "And she's having trouble explaining how she's showing up in less than a minute when someone needs her, when it should take her hours."

My parents had a gate installed in their house. It made a lot of sense, but I could see how the regular use of it could cause Mom, and us, some awkward explanations. "Um, so?"

"And, what with our little Jamie-Kat here," Dad went on, as he kissed her head, "it just seems to make a lot of sense. We're going to be in a no-pets building, and Jeff said you had plenty of space and staff to help."

"Dad, really, what the heck are you talking about?"

Dad smiled at me. "We stayed in Arizona because it was a safer, more normal upbringing for you. But now that you're here, your mother is acquiescing to what the President's people have been asking her to do for years. Your mother and I are moving to D.C."

CHAPTER 23

"**OH, DAD, REALLY? THAT'S SO GREAT!** But what about our house?"

"Oh, we'll still keep it. It's paid off, after all. But, we're going to rent it out to Tim and Alicia." Alicia was Tim's fiancée. They were getting married soon, and Alicia wasn't ready to stop working for the airlines. Living in a regular house made sense for them—Tim was one of the few human males working for us who'd actually chosen to marry a human girl. They were totally exotic for our generation of A-C agents.

"That makes sense. But what about your job? Won't it be the same issue as for Mom, only reversed, if you're going back and forth to ASU all the time?"

"I've taken a sabbatical for this semester, so I can get us settled and see how things go. Professors do it all the time, kitten."

"They usually have more going on than moving cross-country."

"I do. I'm doing a in-depth study of this region with a focus on Washington's secret pathways and underground tunnels, separating fact from fiction."

"Like your own version of *National Treasure*? Sounds interesting." Somewhat, but I wasn't going to tell my dad that I was more interested in using those tunnels to escape Washington rather than study it. "So, when are you moving out here?"

"This week. That way, we can babysit our little Jamie-Kat and see you and Jeff and Amy and Christopher all the time."

I chose not to mention the fact that we saw them all the time already. Gates or not, I wasn't used to being this far away from my parents, and having them close would mean I could run and hide with them if I screwed up too badly.

Because Amy had been one of my besties since high school, and also because her parents were both dead, my parents had stepped in and were covering all the parental duties for her as well. So far, they gave Amy a lot less guilt than they did me, but since Amy's dad had been Operation Confusion's Big Bad, and she'd discovered then that he'd murdered her mother years before, Amy probably needed the slack they cut her.

"We'll be glad to have you guys close. Hopefully the pets will get along with the Poofs."

"I'm sure it won't be any problem," Dad said with utter confidence. I didn't share it, but then again, the Poofs were fully able to take care of themselves, and the cats and dogs had heretofore shown good self-preservation instincts, so I hoped for the best.

"Figure the jocks can walk the dogs when you're not out," Jeff said.

"I think that's kind of below their pay grade, honestly."

He shrugged. "Don't care. Someone's got to do it."

"They like you best, Jeff."

Jeff shot a glare at me almost worthy of Christopher. "I'm sure I'll walk them with you. However, we'll worry about dog walking schedules later."

"I've got it all written down," Dad said, handing Jeff a stuffed folder. "Feeding schedule, exercise, play times. I'm sure you'll do fine. Walter has all the animals' equipment; he'll have it brought up shortly."

Jeff gaped. I was saved from having to make a comment by another knock on the door. I went to get it to find Tito standing there. "Hi, what's up?"

I got the Long-Suffering Doctor look. "You, Jamie, and Jeff are scheduled for tests today."

We were? "Tests? What tests?"

He gave the Long-Suffering Doctor sigh. "The standard tests we do monthly to ensure the three of you are . . . progressing properly."

"Oh, you mean the ones where we make sure we're still more like the X-Men than the Thing?"

"Something like that, yes. I need the three of you in the medical bay. You were supposed to be there fifteen minutes ago."

I managed not to say that Walter hadn't reminded me. Walter might be stuck running my calendar, but this really wasn't his responsibility. "Sorry, my dad arrived with the pets, and it just sort of washed it out of my mind." Not that I wouldn't go for the easy blame lay if I could do it, of course.

"We can't just leave the animals here," Jeff said, making me wonder if he'd comprehended what my dad had told him and he'd apparently agreed to.

"Oh, they'll be fine," Dad said cheerfully. "But if you're worried, just call in some of those nice agents who always escort me to the Bases. They love the pets."

I doubted that very much, seeing as the A-C agents who got stuck with dog and cat duty always seemed like they'd rather be fighting a fugly than dealing with our animals. But I knew enough to keep my yap shut.

Jeff made the call, and four agents who'd clearly drawn the short straws arrived to pet sit. Dad insisted on coming down for the icky tests, so he carried Jamie.

We joined Christopher and Serene, who also had Surcenthumain running through their veins, in Tito's Lab of Horrors. Actually, his setup was nice. His rooms were right next to the infirmary, and he'd made it rather cozy, if you ignored the Mixed Martial Arts and UFC posters that adorned most of the walls. Tito liked to combine his favorite hobby with his life's work, which I couldn't argue with. I liked the posters, but they didn't exactly say "lie back and relax" to most people.

Melanie and Emily were there, as well. "You two really get around. I thought you were still science side." All the Dazzlers were trained in medicine; some were better at it than others, but it was considered a natural part of their education, the way learning a foreign language was for humans.

Melanie laughed. "You know these medical tests are top secret. Who is Doctor Hernandez going to ask to assist him other than us?"

Emily nodded as she took Jamie from me and gave her lots of cuddles. "Besides, our little darling here loves her Aunties Emily and Melanie." She gave her a kiss. "Jamie wants us all ready for the next hybrid babies to come."

Since said babies belonged to Doreen, Lorraine, and Claudia, I couldn't argue. Just as my parents had taken Amy under their wing when she'd lost her family, Melanie and Emily and their husbands had done the same with Doreen. The A-Cs were already one huge, extended family, but several of us were getting closer and more compacted in some interesting ways.

Jamie and I went in first. Blood was taken, orifices were probed, brains were scanned, and reflexes were checked. Because we had two Dazzlers on duty, they did the analysis and such at hyperspeed, meaning we had instant results for Tito to look at and make the Doctor Frowny Face over.

"You're still able to switch from human to enhanced easily," Tito commented. "That's good in some ways, but it means one or the other isn't reflexive, so you'll have the natural reaction most often."

"I think I'm having human reactions that way. Normally, I mean. At least for me."

"Good, and makes sense." He tickled Jamie, then did the same fun stuff with her. "She's really learning fast. She's well beyond what most three month olds should be able to do."

Melanie looked at the results and nodded. "Some of this is standard for A-C babies. But I agree. Her brain functions are still much higher than normal."

I opened my mouth, but Emily beat me to it. "Yes, Kitty, she's fine. So are you. Though neither one of your mutations has stabilized."

"So, what does that mean, exactly? I'm still having trouble controlling the hyperspeed. Will Jamie have that issue?"

"So far, not that we can tell," Melanie said. "Jamie's progressing normally in terms of physical abilities. A little faster in some areas, as we said, but still nothing out of the ordinary."

Emily snorted. "We saw you in Paris, Kitty. You had no trouble at all controlling your speed."

I thought about it. "I was really revved up. ACE said I was under control because I was so enraged. But I thought that was because I was a new mother."

"You're still a new mother," Melanie said with a laugh. "And the maternal instinct doesn't fade away as your child grows."

"It tends to get stronger," Emily added.

Tito looked thoughtful. "The drug works on the id, and our limited knowledge of it shows that it's very rage-related. Every time you're really angry, does your control increase?"

"It's only happened a few times, but yeah. But I don't want to have to be furious twenty-four-seven in order to actually hit what I'm aiming at and not hit all the walls."

"Your control may stabilize when your mutation does," Melanie suggested.

"If I'm still mutating, does that mean instead of crashing into walls I'll go through them?"

Tito shrugged. "We don't know what it means yet, Kitty."

"I know. I'd just like to have better control over my own body."

He looked thoughtful again. "When you were rescuing us in Paris, were you thinking about controlling your powers?"

"No. I was thinking about saving all of you and killing the bad guys."

"When you're having control issues, are you thinking about controlling your powers?"

"I see where you're going with this, and yes, I am." I heaved a sigh. "So, let me guess what you're going to tell me. Unlike what Frankie Goes to Hollywood would suggest, I should relax and just do it, right?"

"Right. So far, it's not hurting you, so I think you're better off allowing your body to react instinctively. Don't dwell on what you can or can't do, don't worry about your control, just let your body and your reflexes do whatever comes naturally."

ACE had said there was a tradeoff to the power real rage gave me, and it was exhaustion. That had been proved true, though I hadn't really talked to anyone else about it, not even Jeff. I decided not to share this tidbit with my medical staff at this precise time. "Okay, whatever you say. And maybe it's just something that's an issue for me."

"I have no idea. We'll question the others about their control, though they're all A-Cs, so it's probably not something they pay attention to the way you have. The five of you are our only test cases for what the Surcenthumain does to A-Cs, humans, or hybrids. The Gowers are our only other living hybrids, and you know we and the C.I.A are studying them closely."

"Naomi and Abigail in particular, yeah, I know. And I also know that five isn't a good test sample."

"No, but it's more than anyone on our side wanted," Melanie said.

"And five is all only as long as no one else ingests it," Emily added. She didn't say, "As Christopher did willingly," but she didn't have to. He appeared to be over both the addiction and withdrawal symptoms, but we had no guess who might still have access to the drug. Chuckie had done his best to round up all there was, but he found new stashes all the time, usually in a raid of some kind.

"We don't know what the five of you can or will do," Melanie added. "Based on the Gowers, those having girls will have babies with stronger powers, but we don't know if that will be true in every case."

"As long as all the babies are healthy and happy, I'll be good with whatever happens."

Jamie and I were ushered out, and Jeff went in next. Serene was on a call, looking worried, so I didn't bother her. From what I picked up, she wasn't happy about whatever she was hearing.

Dad was also on the phone. "Yes, I understand. I'll be there right away." He hung up, came over, and gave me and Jamie both a hug and kiss. "Your mother needs me to take care of something with our new apartment, since she can't get away. You'll be okay, kitten?"

"Sure, Dad. Just routine stuff." I hugged him. "I'll see you later." Dad gave Serene and Christopher both hugs, then he headed off.

Christopher sat down, looking impatient, but not glaring. "You two check out okay?"

"Yep. Tito says I'm still reflexively human."

"Good." He sighed. "In light of what's going on, I think we should postpone our next workout."

I still worked out and trained with Jeff, though my Kung Fu classes were on hold until Jamie was a little older. But Christopher and I did a weekly class in dealing with the effects of becoming mutants, or as I called it in Jeff's hearing, working on our boundaries. I needed someone who could teach me how to be an A-C, or at least cover the parts of it I was now privy to, and Christopher needed someone who didn't make him feel guilty for having willingly shot up.

"No argument here. I'm sure the next two days will be practice enough."

Melanie came out, making the Doctor Frowny Face. "Christopher, we need you."

He and I exchanged the worried glance, but he went in without argument. I tried not to worry about Jeff.

Serene finished her phone call. She gave me a bright smile and opened her mouth as Emily came out, sporting the team look for our medical professionals. "Serene, need you, please."

Serene closed her mouth, nodded, and trotted in. I decided I wasn't going to have good luck against the worry.

I cuddled Jamie, leaned back, and closed my eyes. It was time to go straight to the source. ACE, are you there?

CHAPTER 24

Y ES, KITTY, ACE IS HERE.
   What's going on?
Many things, Kitty, ACE said politely.

I realized that, as per my usual, I hadn't phrased the question correctly. ACE did its best to remain out of the picture unless things were dire and we were unable to handle them. Until that point, questions needed to be specific and pointed, with little weasel room, because if they were vague, ACE got uncomfortable and stressed, which was never good, for Gower if no one else.

I tried again. Why are Jeff, Christopher and Serene in with Tito and the others? I mean aside from routine checkup reasons.

Tito wishes to ensure everyone is healthy and safe.

Is everyone healthy and safe?

Yes. The way ACE said this, there was clearly more to it.

I tried a guess. Is there something new that affects the three of them but doesn't affect me and Jamie?

Yes. ACE sounded pleased by this guess. Score one for me. Tito has identified something that Jeff, Christopher, and Serene have that Kitty does not have.

He'd pointedly left Jamie out of that statement. ACE was always ready and willing to leave big breadcrumbs for me to find, because as long as I guessed right, ACE felt okay confirming. So I did what our benevolent superconsciousness wanted and pondered.

There were any variety of reasons Tito could single out the three of them. But if they were easy, obvious reasons, I'd already know them. I focused on what kinds of tests Tito was running—not what they were, but what they were trying to determine. Genetic mutation.

Did Tito isolate something specific about their genes?

Yes, Kitty.

I resisted asking if I'd pissed ACE off in some way. This was hard for him, and the last thing we wanted was a stressed out super-consciousness that could destroy the world, either on purpose or inadvertently.

Clearly, I needed more specificity. Okay, I might not be up to Chuckie's standards on the math and sciences, and I didn't have a prayer against even the slowest Dazzler out there, but when it came to genetics, I was a Gregor Mendel fangirl of the highest order.

So, what would Tito care about in regard to Jeff, Christopher, and Serene, specifically? That Jamie had whatever seemed likely, since she was Jeff's daughter. But ACE had plainly stated I didn't have this.

I was coming up with nothing, so I opened my eyes and looked at Jamie. She smiled and grabbed my nose. "Oh, you have Mommy's nose! Just like everyone says," I added as Jamie giggled.

"I'm going to take your nose, 'cause it looks just like mine," I said, doing the old "steal your nose" trick that every baby in the world seemed to think was the coolest game on the planet. I pretended to put her nose on my face. "There. Now Mommy has Jamie's nose and Jamie has Mommy's nose."

Jamie gurgled at me and leaned into my chest for a snuggle. I kissed her head. Everyone said she looked just like me, but I still didn't see it. Of course, in hybrid children, human genetics were dominant for external aspects, and A-C genetics dominated the internal workings. The Gowers were a good example, since they all had their mother's beautiful dark skin and Dazzler-worthy good looks. But I could see their father in there, too, in some ways. And, presumably, their grandparents, not that I'd known them.

I jerked. I had indeed known at least one of them, so to speak. I wasn't sure where Ronald Yates, aka Mephistopheles, fit into the overall family tree for the Gowers, but they were Jeff's cousins, and Yates was Jeff and Christopher's grandfather. And, as we'd discovered, Serene's father. And they were the most powerful A-Cs we had. The Gower girls were potentially stronger, per Chuckie, but they were hybrid women. Jeff, Christopher, and Serene were pure A-C.

I closed my eyes again. ACE, has Tito isolated a gene related to Ronald Yates?

Yes, Kitty. ACE sounded so proud of me, I almost blushed. ACE knew Kitty would realize. Kitty thinks right.

Can you tell me more about it?

Some. Tito has identified what makes Jeff, Christopher, and Serene . . . different . . . from other A-Cs.

You mean what makes them stronger in their talents?

Yes. Jamie will have this, too, but it is different for Jamie.

Because I'm her mother?

In a way. ACE sounded evasive again.

Because Jeff was drugged with the Surcenthumain?

Yes. But Jamie is not in danger.

Good to know. Thank you. I knew when to let a dicey topic for ACE die, and, since I could feel ACE being slightly uncomfortable, now was the time. I figured, though, that it couldn't hurt to go for it and see if I could get anything else helpful. I know it's wrong to ask, but can you give me any hint about what's coming at the President's Ball tomorrow night?

Things Kitty is prepared for, as well as things Kitty is not prepared for.

Is there anything I can do to be prepared for whatever it is I'm not prepared for?

ACE was quiet for a few long moments. I almost thought he'd signed off when he spoke again. Kitty should not trust.

Not trust who?

The ones who are not really Kitty's friends.

I rarely trust people who don't like me.

Even Kitty can be fooled. This was true, of course. But Kitty also must trust.

Who should I be trusting?

Those who wish to help Kitty.

Are you saying they aren't the people I think they are, whoever the different theys are you're talking about?

In some cases. Before I could ask for more specifics, ACE spoke again, this time with a lot more urgency. ACE must go. Lorraine and Claudia need ACE's help. With that I felt my mind's connection to ACE evaporate.

CHAPTER 25

MY EYES SNAPPED OPEN. I looked around. Still alone in the infirmary. I got up. "Let's get Daddy and everyone else, Jamie-Kat. I think your fairy godfather ACE needs us to at least provide an assist." She cooed.

I tried to open the door to the examining room. It was locked. This was weird, but I decided I could ponder this or merely knock to gain entry. I knocked.

Tito opened the door. "Kitty, we're in the middle of something."

"Yeah, I realize that. However, the Yates Gene Experiment needs to be put on at least a short hold."

He jerked. "How did you—"

"I'm a good guesser. Look, I think Lorraine and Claudia need us."

He stared at me. "Why? Have they called you?"

"Um, no. But even if they had, I don't have my purse with me." As I thought about it, the last time I'd seen my purse was right before I'd taken a dip in the Potomac. Tried not to worry about its whereabouts. Failed. However, bigger worries were pressing.

"You don't? You feeling all right?"

"Yes, just had a lot going on. Like right now, for instance."

Tito's eyes narrowed. "Did you just talk to ACE?"

"Yes. How'd you guess?"

"I know you by now."

I could see the others starting to crowd around the door. "Look, unless there's an orgy going on—and if so, I want to know why I wasn't invited—I think everyone in the room is going to be better used being wherever the girls are."

Tito opened the door. Everyone was clothed. Jeff and Christopher both were shooting me dirty looks, so I assumed they'd heard my orgy comment. "No one's called us on the com," Christopher said pointedly.

Tito shook his head. "I have the infirmary on lockdown when we do these tests, and that includes incoming and outgoing alerts. That's why I had you turn your cell phones off."

"They're not due to deliver for a couple more weeks," Melanie said, sounding just a little worried. Everyone else looked confused and suspicious.

I couldn't blame them. Of the three of them, I'd really expected Doreen to deliver first. Apparently her baby wanted to go to the President's Ball in warmth, comfort, and style. I looked at Jamie in my arms. She looked back, expectantly, if I was any judge. "I know, but babies come when they want to."

"Kitty's right," Tito said briskly. "Let's get this shut down. We need to save the information, but we can finish later." He, Melanie, and Emily started bustling about, the women at hyperspeed.

"Baby, what's going on?" Jeff's eyes were closed. "I'm not picking up anything from the girls or the flyboys."

I thought about it some more. ACE had sounded stressed. "Jeff, we didn't talk about what . . . happened with me and Jamie during delivery."

Per everyone I'd died on the table and come back. I still didn't remember. However, per ACE, that had happened because Jamie had misunderstood Jeff's fears about my dying in childbirth.

"Right," he said, as he opened his eyes and gave me a stern look. "And we still shouldn't."

"No, I think we should. Because while no one's babies have . . . acted like Jamie did in the womb, that doesn't mean they aren't talented in some way."

"So?" Jeff asked. "You're worried about them handling their powers? We'll take care of that."

I looked around the room. No one here didn't know, except possibly Serene, and she should, all things considered. "Yes, I know you and Christopher can, and should, put blocks in if the babies need them. And, if you're able, you should teach Serene how to do it, too. But that's not what I mean."

Jeff looked confused. So did everyone else. I sighed. "Look, Jamie heard her daddy worrying, and she did something she thought was right that wasn't. All the flyboys were there, and so were the girls. And we haven't told them not to worry about dying in childbirth," I stressed. "And I guarantee you, the human guys are worried about it."

I saw the light dawn in Jeff's eyes. "Oh." He nodded. "Tito, when can you take the infirmary out of lockdown?" He had his Commander voice on.

"It's on a timer," Tito said as he closed things up. "It'll be faster to leave than take it off."

"Then let's go. Oh, and Tito, bring whatever medical supplies make you happy."

He, Melanie, and Emily were all carrying med cases. "You think they aren't in the Science Center?" Emily asked.

"I have no idea where the girls are. I just know that they need an assist from ACE, meaning they likely need the assist from all of us, too."

We took the elevator to the first floor. The gate was actually in the basement, where the elevators didn't go. Aliens were weird. However, taking the elevator instead of the stairs meant Tito wouldn't be barfing his guts out.

We reached the first floor, and, as we were walking past the big kitchen area, I spotted White, rummaging in the refrigerator. "Richard, you doing anything?"

He turned around holding sandwich fixings. "I was going to prepare a snack."

"How'd you like to come along and help us, just in case?"

White stared at me for a long moment, nodded, put the food away, and joined us. "What's going on, Missus Martini? Is it catsuit time?"

"Not that I know of, but never rule it out, Mister White. I think the miracle of birth is on today's docket, but I could be wrong. Whatever it is, however, I think Lorraine and Claudia need us."

"Say no more. Jeffrey, please stop glaring at me. She *is* my partner, after all."

"Huh. I think you want her in a catsuit a little too much."

White chuckled as we reached the basement. Jeff calibrated the gate, which was good. Now that I was enhanced I could actually see the gate. Of course, I couldn't calibrate it. I contemplated the necessity of learning and had to admit it was high. All airport gates recalibrated to the Dome, which was the main gate hub located on the Ancients' original crash site. But I had no idea if the Embassy gate did the same thing. And knowing where I was tossing myself to would probably be a good addition to my assortment of skills.

Jeff ushered everyone through as White took Jamie from me.

"I'll hold onto our Jamie Katherine, since I assume you'll be going through in your usual manner."

"You know it," I replied cheerfully, while Jamie snuggled into White's chest. The gates tended to make me nauseous at best. My preferred way to use them was to have Jeff holding me with my face buried in his neck. "Wise man keeps baby safe from mother's potential vomit."

"Yes, I do know how much you enjoy these trips. Don't dawdle," he reminded us. With that, he walked through.

Jeff grinned as he recalibrated the gate for two full-sized travelers. "I'd love to dawdle, but I think you're too worried to enjoy it."

"Probably. But we can make up for it later."

"Good plan." Jeff swept me up into his arms, I shoved my face into his neck, he walked us through. Three seconds or so of total awful and we stepped out on what I called the Bat Cave level of the Dulce Science Center.

There were A-Cs bustling about doing all sorts of serious, keeping the world safe from the nasty things trying to destroy it stuff. I still didn't know what half the equipment did or what the majority of the many screens of all shapes and sizes showed. But I was happy to be standing here, at the heart of Centaurion Division, where the work everyone did mattered.

Jeff put me down. "Feeling okay, baby?"

I sort of grunted. Not so much, really. The gates remained the bane of my existence.

"Where to, Missus Martini?" White asked. I could tell everyone else was thinking the same question.

"Hang on, still trying not to barf." Thankfully, breakfast had been hours ago. I was cool with the fact it looked like we were going to miss lunch.

I got my stomach under control and realized I had no idea where, in the vastness that was the Science Center, Lorraine and Claudia actually were. Or if they were even in the Science Center.

Jeff got his phone out. "Huh. No missed calls." Everyone else checked their phones, too. The lack of someone trying to reach them was shared.

"Look, call it my feminine intuition. Call one of the flyboys or check with Gladys. Meanwhile, we can head either to medical or to their living quarters."

"They could be in a meeting," Serene said. "I left everyone in one when I came over for Tito's exam."

"Kitty, is this just an exercise in your needing to make us all race around for nothing?" Christopher snapped. "Because right now all I see is business as usual going on. No emergencies."

"Let's discuss this on the way to the elevator banks." I strode off, wondering if I'd misinterpreted ACE's comments. Right now, Christopher seemed right, and if that was the case, I was going to have a whole bunch of really annoyed people on my hands.

Jeff caught up to me. "Baby, are you sure you're just not being jumpy for no reason?" he asked me quietly.

The elevators opened before I could reply, to show Jerry standing there, phone in hand, looking worried. He gaped at us. As he did so, everyone's phones started ringing. "You're here," Jerry managed, as he hung up his phone.

"We are indeed. What's going on?"

"I've been trying to call you. Why aren't you answering your phone?"

"It's in my purse. I think."

Jerry gaped at me. "And you don't have your purse with you?"

"Um, no. Actually, no, I don't."

Jerry stared at me. "Who are you, and what have you done with Kitty?"

"Just put it down to my still adapting with little grace and absolutely no skill to my fabulous new position. Are Lorraine and Claudia okay?"

Jerry blinked. "Yes, I mean, they should be." He looked around. "How did you all know to come over now?"

"A big penguin told me. Look, what's going on?"

Jerry grinned. "The miracle of birth. Times two."

CHAPTER 26

"I KNEW IT!" IT WAS NICE TO BE RIGHT, especially because Christopher had the grace to look chagrined.

"Well, I don't know how," Jerry said. "It just started. We were leaving a meeting, and both Lorraine and Claudia started to feel labor pains." He backed into the elevator, and we followed him. "We do want to hurry."

"Yes," Melanie said, "our babies come fast."

"Like you wouldn't believe," Jerry said under his breath. No one else but me seemed to hear him, possibly because they were all on their respective phones. I felt really out of the loop. However, from what I gathered by shamelessly eavesdropping, everyone was having the same conversation, which was essentially "hurry it up."

The elevator doors opened on the medical floor, and Melanie and Emily disappeared, using the serious Mama Bear Hyperspeed. Tito hung up his phone and ran after them. The rest of us looked at Jerry. "When they say fast, they *mean* fast," he said with feeling.

Christopher grabbed Jerry, Jeff grabbed me, and we all took off after the others. We were there in seconds, which was good, because even by the time we got there, things were hopping.

The girls were in one large room that had two beds and a couple of typical hospital curtains to provide the privacy the girls clearly weren't experiencing—there were a lot of men in there with them. I certainly knew what that felt like—awkward.

"Out!" Tito thundered, right on cue. "Only the fathers."

I took Jamie out of White's arms, grabbed Serene, and walked in. "And us, Tito. Trust me."

He gave me a long look, then nodded. "Fine. Shut the doors will you?"

Serene did as he asked while I stood between the two beds. "You two are really carrying the 'best friends do everything together' thing a little far."

Both girls managed the labor equivalent of a chuckle, which was a gasping semi-yelp. Joe and Randy looked ready to pass out, particularly when they looked at me. Lorraine and Claudia's fathers were there, too. They were functioning as gophers for Tito, Melanie, and Emily. So it was cozy, until their dads looked at me, worried. I was fairly sure why ACE had given me the huge hint earlier.

"The babies are coming a little faster than normal," Tito shared, sounding very calm. "So I need everyone doing what we ask immediately."

"I've called for extra help," Emily shared, not managing to sound as calm as Tito.

"Both babies are breach right now," Melanie added. This remark caused every man in the room other than Tito to go pale.

A number of younger Dazzlers prepped for nursing duty arrived. To a one, they looked grim. Not good. We didn't need every hybrid birth to be a stress test for all involved.

I motioned to Serene and she came over. "Why do you want me in here, Kitty? To see how it's done?" she asked with total innocence. So far as I could tell, Serene didn't do or even recognize sarcasm or irony.

"No. I think we're going to need to, ah, assist." I looked at Jamie. "You know, the best thing for babies when they're being born is to be head down."

"Yow!" Lorraine shouted.

"Good," Tito said. "Head's down."

"Ow!" Claudia yelped.

Tito trotted over to her. "Right, that's what we want." He looked at me. "Keep on doing whatever it is you're doing, Kitty. Seriously."

Serene looked at me and Jamie. "Oh." She nodded and took Jamie's hand in hers. "What are you going to name them?" she asked.

"We don't know if they're boys or girls," Randy shared. "So, per A-C traditions, we'll name them when they come out."

"And you're telling me that in nine months you haven't discussed this, say, once?"

Joe shot a look at Melanie. "No, ma'am." Randy nodded his

agreement. The girls were too busy shouting in pain and doing whatever their mothers, Tito, and the rest of the medical personnel were telling them to do to join in.

"Dudes, seriously, I can tell when you're lying."

Serene looked at me. "I think we need to name them *now*," she said with some urgency. "Or know what their mothers call them."

"We've talked about boy and girl names," Randy allowed.

"Dudes, cough them up."

Before they could, two more people entered the room at hyperspeed. "Are we too late?" Naomi gasped out.

"No," Abigail said in reply. "*Just* in time."

Naomi grabbed Claudia's hand, Abigail grabbed Lorraine's, and they both grabbed Serene. "Keep in contact," Serene said to me, quite calmly.

"Oh, good. Wonder Quintuplets to the rescue again." I wasn't too fazed by this, since the Gower girls and I had done something similar during Operation Confusion, but the expressions on Lorraine and Claudia's fathers' faces were rather priceless.

I could feel the adults sending messages, but they weren't going to me—they were going to Jamie. Who, as near as I could tell, was filtering them to the babies still in the womb in a way they'd comprehend. However, I could also tell Serene was right. The "Hey, you!" approach wasn't working.

"Dudes, names. Like now. Um, they're both boys." At least, so far as I could tell. I was seeing them inside their mothers' stomachs, thanks to the Weird-O-Vision we were sharing in this mental hookup.

"Ross Edward," Joe said quickly. "For both of our dads."

"Sean Zachary," Randy supplied. "Same reasons."

I wouldn't have had to ask which names were from the human side, even if I hadn't known. The A-Cs rarely went for single-syllable names.

Both fathers in the room looked pleased, and they didn't seem upset that they'd landed the middle name slots. Then they looked at their daughters and went right back to looking extremely worried.

Serene nodded and looked at Jamie. "Let's help Ross and Sean get here safely, okay? And make sure their mommies are safe, too."

"Faster is not better," Naomi added gently. "Too slow isn't good either."

"We want just right," Abigail shared.

I curbed a Goldilocks and the Three Bears comment, figuring it wouldn't be met with any form of appreciation from anyone in the room.

"What is 'just right'?" I asked, since I didn't know, and I wasn't sure that Jamie knew, either.

"They know now," Serene said. "Don't worry."

"Push, Claudia," Tito said strongly. "Yours is coming first."

"I *am*," Claudia said, sounding kind of hurt and a lot annoyed.

"Well, push harder," Tito said.

I could hear more information filtering through. Absolutely none of it seemed like real words, other than the baby's names. They weren't images, either. It was a lot of feelings and what I assumed were baby animal senses stuff.

But whatever was really going on, it worked.

"We have Sean," Tito called. He gave the baby to Emily, and spent a few minutes doing something to Claudia. I chose not to look. I hadn't wanted to know when it was me; I really didn't want to know when it was someone else.

Sean was already cleaned and in Claudia's arms by the time Tito was done, since Emily had worked at hyperspeed. The moment he was finished, Tito ran over to Lorraine. "You're up, Ross. Push, Lorraine."

"I am. Hard."

"Push harder than that."

She glared at him but did as requested, and, sure enough, within a matter of moments we had a second baby. Ross was handed off to Melanie while Tito did the same whatever to Lorraine.

We got out of our latest Wonder Quintuplets formation and relaxed. Jamie seemed quite pleased, and I got the impression she was talking to the two new arrivals. But if so, I couldn't access it anymore.

In short order, we had two happy families relaxing and making calls to the other sets of grandparents. Tito made a call and sent agent teams off to get Joe's and Randy's parents.

Since we were already there, we took the opportunity to see the babies first, made the standard comments, and congratulated the parents. As with Jamie, I didn't really see either parent in the babies yet. But I assumed I would. I didn't really care. My two best A-C girlfriends had their healthy baby boys, and they were both okay, with their human husbands both proud and relieved. As far as I was concerned, whatever else happened, this was worth the risks.

Yes, ACE said in my head. Ross and Sean will be worth the risks. Just as Jamie is. And Kitty was.

I was a risk?

Childbirth is always a risk. ACE cannot assist for all, but in some cases, ACE must.

Cases like these?

Yes. Kitty did well.

Only because of you, ACE.

ACE can only do because of Kitty. And for that, ACE might love Kitty most of all.

CHAPTER 27

I FELT ACE HUG MY MIND, which always made me feel warm and loved. Then he broke the connection. I heaved a sigh and got ready to leave so others could come in.

"Kitty," Lorraine said, "thanks."

"Yeah," Claudia chimed in. "You're always there when we need you."

"You're both always there for me." I went to both of them and kissed their foreheads. "That's what friends are for, remember?"

Serene, Jamie, and I left. We were replaced by the rest of Airborne and all of Alpha. Jeff, Christopher, and White stayed outside with us.

"You want to tell us what was really going on?" Jeff asked as Naomi and Abigail joined us.

"Hard to say."

Naomi snorted. "Jeff, Chuck's given you reports on what we can do, I know he has."

Jeff had the grace to look embarrassed. "I haven't read them yet."

I rolled my eyes. "Because they're from Chuckie?"

He sighed. "Actually, no. Because I've been too busy reading everything related to our current mission."

"You need to, ah, test the boys," Abigail said. "I'm not sure what they've got, but they'll need the same protection you two did for Jamie."

Jeff and Christopher exchanged a look. "Does everyone know?" Christopher snapped at me.

"No, just those we've told or who have figured it out. I think you two can come out of the special powers closet by now."

White sighed. "Son, it's a good thing. And let's do as Abigail suggests. Right now." He might be retired, but White still held his authority from when he'd been Pontifex.

The three men went in as Serene, Reader, and Tim came out. "Paul's in there doing Pontifex stuff," Reader shared as he took his goddaughter and gave her a cuddle. He shook his head. "I don't know whether to be relieved or upset about the timing."

"Why either one?"

"As Captains, both Lorraine and Claudia were insisting on going to the President's Ball tomorrow night. Now, there's no way. I want their husbands staying with them, too, and their parents. Which in one sense is great, because now I don't have to worry about them getting hurt or going into labor at a bad time."

"But," Tim said with a sigh, "that reduces Airborne to Matt, Chip, Jerry, and me."

"And cuts down our available A-C agents, too."

Reader nodded. "However, I'd rather have them safely here than quite unsafely there." He rubbed the back of his neck. "Just alters the complexity of who we're stationing where."

"Do we even know enough to station anyone anywhere?"

Tim shrugged. "Sort of. We know we need people inside at the ball, and we have that more than covered. But we need teams on standby, and we don't know where, what they'll really need to be prepared for, nothing."

I considered this. "Guys, we routinely kill superbeings. Why are you all so freaked out?"

Reader sighed. "Girlfriend, it's not the same situation. We're exposed here, in a way none of us have any experience with. One wrong move, and Centaurion Division is shown to everyone to be not of this world. A different wrong move means someone—maybe one, maybe many—dies."

"We're hiding in plain sight even more than we used to," Serene added. "It's making it harder and harder for Imageering to do what we're supposed to in terms of cover-ups."

"You mean I'm making it harder."

Reader made the exasperation sound. "No. Stop trying to shoulder all the blame. This is new for everyone. The former Diplomatic Corps was in place for twenty years, and they were all conversant in what their jobs entailed. We've all had new jobs for about three months."

"Speaking of which," Tim said, "I see Jerry wasn't lying. You don't have your purse with you, and we all know you don't have your phone."

"Geez, sorry. It happens."

"Every time it does, I need to reach you urgently," Tim said flatly. "Let's work on you keeping at least your phone with you at all times going forward."

"Sorry, I'll go find my phone right now."

"No need," Tim said with a grin, as he reached into his pocket and handed me a new cell. "It's programmed with all your settings."

"How?" It looked just like my old one, only it was pristine, with no scratches or anything. I knew it wouldn't look like this for long—none of my phones ever did. With the current situation, I gave it no more than a day before it was at least blemished, if not destroyed.

"The wonders of modern A-C technology," Reader said. "Now that you're equipped with the basics again, try to remember that we still have less than no idea of what's going on, and we need to get a handle on it, and quickly."

Jeff, Christopher, and White joined us while I was getting my phone responsibility lecture. Jeff took Jamie from Reader and snuggled her. "Everything's taken care of."

"What talents did they display?"

Christopher shrugged. "Hard to say. They're more like Jamie than the rest of us, but I don't think they're as powerful."

"Or if they are, it's muted," Jeff said.

"You know, you need to figure out how to pass along the techniques." I ignored Christopher's Glare #1. "Seriously, guys. Serene, Abigail, and Naomi need to know how to do this." I didn't add "just in case," but I could tell Jeff knew I was thinking it.

He sighed. "You're right. But not right now. Mostly," he said as my mouth started to open, "because we haven't had enough time to determine if we actually *can* pass along the abilities or not."

"Oh, fine." We still hadn't found the glowing cube Terry, Christopher's late mother, had used to pass the knowledge of putting in blocks, as well as a wide variety of other things, to Jeff and Christopher when they were young. Without it, if Jeff and Christopher indeed weren't able to pass along how to install blocks, it meant that if we lost one of them, we lost the ability. Forever.

I was distracted from this cheerful line of thought by my new phone ringing.

It wasn't a number I knew. Based on past experience, this was never good. I prepared myself for a death threat, and answered.

CHAPTER 28

"HELLO?"

"Miss Katt?" It was a woman's voice, but I didn't recognize it any more than I had the phone number. I waited for her to start screaming at me. "Hello? Miss Katt?" Huh. No screaming. Scored it one for the win column.

"Possibly. Who's this?"

"This is Nurse Carter from the Georgetown University Medical Center. Is this Miss Katt?" She had a slight accent that sounded Hispanic of some kind to me.

"Ah, yes. I'm fine, thanks for the follow up." Why was everyone calling me Miss Katt all of a sudden? I didn't think Jeff had filed divorce papers, even though I'd probably given him good reason to over the last few months. And even if he had, surely Chuckie, at least, would have mentioned it.

"I beg your pardon? I'm calling about your relative, Peter Kasperoff."

"Who?"

"The man brought in from the crash yesterday, the one where the car went into the river?"

"Oh! Yes. Peter." My would-be assassin had me listed as a relative? "I'm sorry, but why are you calling?"

"You're listed as his next of kin." Next of kin. Wow. I was moving up in the world of the weirdo assassins.

"Um, okay. What's going on with him?"

"I'm sorry to tell you that he's expired."

"Expired? He's out of code?"

"He's passed away."

"You mean he's dead?" He'd been hurt, but he hadn't been the one with a bullet in him, and he'd been well enough to pass me a secret disk before being admitted.

"Yes."

"How did he die?"

"Heart arrest, based on hypothermia."

"Huh. I really thought he'd pull through."

"I'm sorry for your loss. We'd like you to come to the hospital to make arrangements and collect his personal items."

I got the rest of the information, assured Nurse Carter I'd be right over, and hung up. "We need to table the blocks and babies discussion. I think we have bigger issues."

Jeff cocked his head at me. "What's going on?"

"Remember Peter from the river?" Jeff nodded. "Well, he's a deader, and I'm apparently his next of kin. And somehow, he has personal items I need to collect from the hospital."

Jeff stared at me. "You're kidding."

"No, unless this is the medical center's idea of a great practical joke. We need to get back to the Embassy fast." I considered my options and dialed. "Dad, are you done with your apartment thing?"

"Yes, I just finished about five minutes ago."

"Great. Can you please come back to the Embassy and take over the Jamie babysitting gig a little sooner than you might have planned?"

"Sure, kitten. It'll give me a chance to brief Walter on how to take care of the pets."

Lucky Walter. "Great. We'll be back in a couple of minutes."

"You're still in the infirmary?"

"Oh. No, we're not." I brought Dad up to speed on the new births.

"Tell the girls mazel tov for me, kitten. I'll come by to see them when things aren't so tense for you."

"Thanks, Dad, I will." I hung up, trotted into the still packed delivery room, shared Dad's congratulations, told Tito what we were doing, and left.

Serene and the Gower girls opted to stick around in case Claudia or Lorraine needed help. Reader and Tim were still on duty, so they were also staying at Dulce. Reminding myself that our game was afoot in D.C., I grabbed Jeff and headed to the elevator banks, Christopher and White accompanying us.

White went to ensure the infirmary was out of lockdown. We left Christopher in the great room while we fed Jamie. I figured we could be gone a while, so I pumped out another dairy's worth of extra milk, just in case.

My father was waiting for us when we got done. Jamie squealed with joy to see her Papa Sol again so soon. "Where should I watch her?" Dad asked.

"You need me for this?" Christopher asked.

"I don't think so."

"Then come over to our half of the floor, Sol. I think Amy's been needing some time with you or Angela." This was Christopher's code for when Amy was having issues dealing with what had happened three months ago.

Dad nodded. "Certainly. It'll be fun for all of us."

"I have no idea where her diaper bag is." I sucked as a mother sometimes, and this was obviously one of those times.

"Not to worry, kitten. We'll handle it."

Dad, Jamie, and Christopher left. I went to my jewelry box and heaved a sigh of relief—the memory card was still in it.

"I don't think the Operations Team is where our problems lie," Jeff said.

"You really never know." I examined the card. "I'm hoping it didn't get water damage. It looks like a standard memory card for a camera."

Jeff zipped off and was back immediately with a video recorder. He took the memory card and inserted it and hit replay. Nothing.

I sighed. "Oh, well, it was worth a shot."

"I think we want this over to Imageering. This camera isn't high-tech enough, but I'm sure we have equipment that can handle it." Jeff pulled his phone out. "Serene, hi. Yeah, long time no see. I need something extracted from a small camera memory card. It could be nothing, could be dangerous, could have vital information. Great, yes, good. Thanks."

He hung up. "Team will be here immediately." No sooner were the words out of his mouth than there was a knock at the door.

"Glad we can use the gates for most things. If we were waiting for a car, it could be hours."

"You'll get used to the traffic around here, I'm sure."

"I'm not."

We opened the door to find Walter's older brother, William, there, accompanied by Kevin and a couple of the big A-Cs who worked Security. They were standing back like bodyguards.

William was an imageer, and before Operation Confusion had

been teamed with their middle brother, Wayne, who'd been an empath. Wayne had been one of our casualties during the end game of Operation Confusion, and I didn't think William or Walter were over his loss yet. I wasn't, and he wasn't my brother. William had been reassigned to act as Imageering's liaison between Serene and the Embassy, mostly because, as yesterday had amply shown, none of us were shining examples of success in our new roles and William was one of the best imageers we had.

"Hey, Kevin, I thought you were with Mom and Chuckie."

"I was, but your mother sent me back to Dulce this morning to try to help Alpha Team get a handle on the situation."

"You mean the one that's totally out of control?"

Kevin grinned. He had a great smile and amazing teeth. I managed not to drool, but it was always difficult—he had bags of charisma. "Yeah, that situation. The births were a nice break, since we're essentially nowhere. But it sounds like you might have something for us to go on."

I brought them up to speed on how I'd gotten this memory card and that the giver had apparently died from being cold. "Needless to say, I think something fishy's going on."

Kevin nodded. "Under the circumstances, I need to go back with William. We don't want this at any more risk than it's already been. Could be nothing, could tell us who the assassination target is. But I don't like the idea of you two going to the medical center by yourselves."

Jeff grunted. "We can handle ourselves."

William cleared his throat. "Yes, Commanders, you can."

Jeff sighed. "We're not Commanders anymore."

William looked at us. I could tell he was trying not to smile.

"And that's William's well-made point, Jeff." And the one Reader had made to me only a short while earlier. "Alpha Team, the Commanders of the Field, Airborne, they can go handle whatever, and it gets cleaned up fairly easily. The American Centaurion Chief of Mission, on the other hand, can't go off kicking butt at the drop of a shoe." Oh, sure, we'd done that yesterday, but one swim in the Potomac was enough for me for a while.

Jeff ran his hand through his hair. "Good point. Fine, you two head back, be extra cautious, and we'll get some backup." They left, and Jeff shook his head. "I can't believe I'm going to say this, but . . . call Reynolds, and, if he can, have him meet us and the jocks there."

"Will do. And I'm so awed by the personal growth. A freezing swim and a couple of new babies seem to have done you a world of good."

"Don't push it, baby."

"But it's so fun." I called Chuckie. "Dude, you able to tear yourself away from the interrogation of the Goon Squad?"

"Yeah, I am." Chuckie sounded seriously pissed.

"What's wrong?"

"Angela got called into a meeting with the President. No sooner was she gone than another agency took the prisoners."

"You allowed that?"

"I had no choice. They had the right authorization, and they had a lot more backup than I did."

"Well, I guess that works out." I caught him up on the latest. "So, do you need a nap, or can you meet us over at the medical center?"

"No, I'm fine. Angela and I traded off rest time, and I've done more on less sleep. But I'm coming to the Embassy. We'll go over together. At the rate things are going, I don't want the two of you out of my control."

"I think I'll phrase that differently to Jeff."

"Whatever. I'm in my office, I'll be there momentarily." Chuckie had gates in his office and his apartment. They'd saved his life more than once. I'd asked for him to have a gate in his car, but that had been ignored by him and everyone else.

"Great, we'll meet you in the basement, just wait there for us." I hung up, we grabbed our coats, and I looked around. "Where *is* my purse?"

Jeff shook his head. "The jocks were supposed to bring it up from the car. Last night." He pulled out his phone. "Kid, you and the other jock ready for action? Good. Meet us in the basement level, with Kitty's purse. What? Where? Huh. Thanks."

He hung up and looked through our living quarters. "The kid said they brought your purse up here."

I joined him in the hunt. "I don't see it anywhere." I tried not to panic and failed utterly. My purse had my life in it, and its contents had saved my life more than once. I was naked without my purse. It was one thing to not have it with me when I was wandering the Embassy or in a hurry to get to the girls. It was another for it to be completely gone.

Jeff stroked the back of my neck. "We'll find it, baby, don't worry."

"Too late. If it's gone, it was taken by someone inside the Embassy. Or the Elves."

"Who here, Operations Team included, would want your purse? Who besides you could find anything in it anyway?"

A suspicion niggled. "Where's Mister Joel Oliver?"

"You think he took it?"

"I think he'd have an interest in it, yes."

Jeff grunted. "Let's go find him. I'll enjoy beating the crap out of him if he's done anything with your stuff."

"Let's try being nice first. Just for a change of pace." I hit the com's on button. Sometimes I preferred it to shouting. "Walter, where is Mister Joel Oliver?"

"He's with Pierre, Chief. They're in the smaller salon on the second floor. They've been there all morning."

"Great, thanks."

Jeff grabbed my hand and we hypersped there. To find both men kneeling on the floor, the contents of my purse spread out between them. They seemed both intent and rather cheerful; at least they were chatting in a friendly manner while they pawed through all my stuff. The remains of their lunch were on a nearby table. Clearly they'd been settled in here for a while.

"What, and I mean this in the nicest way possible, the hell is going on?" Jeff asked, managing not to snarl or roar.

Pierre looked up at me. "Kitty, Jeff, good of you to join us. I think we've found all the many bugs and tracking devices, but Mister Joel and I can't be sure."

CHAPTER 29

I HEARD A STEP BEHIND US. "What's going on?" Chuckie asked.

"I thought you were meeting us in the basement."

"I was, but standing there like an idiot seemed stupid. So I asked Walter where you were." He walked farther into the room. "Why are the contents of Kitty's purse being rifled by you two?"

"How does he know it's your purse?" Jeff asked me.

"He's seen it for a lot of years. Chuckie, we just got here. No clue."

Pierre sighed and rolled his eyes. "Mister Joel and I discussed it while we were waiting for Jeff to gallantly rescue our fair Kitty—the nasty men with guns were finding you all far too easily."

Oliver nodded. "We searched all of my clothing and equipment last night. I had several tracking devices hidden on me." He pointed to an end table that had a variety of small things that looked like they could be forms of electronic surveillance sitting on it. "The next logical step was your purse and the stroller."

"Which I had the impressive Operations Team retrieve for us," Pierre added. "As well as our little princess' diaper bag."

"You've seen the Elves?"

"Oh, yes. Lovely people. Very dedicated." Pierre clearly approved of the Elves' work ethic.

"Can we focus?" Chuckie asked. Jeff grunted his agreement.

"Is there anything on Jamie's stroller? Or her diaper bag?" I tried not to feel freaked out and failed, based on Jeff rubbing the back of my neck again.

"Christopher searched both for us earlier this morning," Pierre replied. "He said they were clean. He didn't feel up to the challenge your purse presented, though, Kitty."

"Wimp. Why didn't he mention that to us?" I asked Jeff.

He shrugged. "We were all a little busy. Maybe he would have if Tito hadn't been running interesting tests and the girls hadn't delivered."

"What's this?" Pierre asked, echoed by Oliver.

We brought everyone up to speed on the happy arrivals as well as their names, reminded Oliver that he wasn't getting to take pictures or report on this, and told Chuckie we'd fill him in on what Tito was working on when we were all alone, as in, Oliver wasn't around. Chuckie and Oliver both took this in stride, though I could tell Chuckie was getting seriously impatient with the delays.

I took a deep breath. "Okay, so, my purse. What have you found?"

Chuckie went to the end table and examined its contents. He whistled. "You had all of this on you, Oliver?"

"Mister Joel Oliver, I must remind you. And, yes. Most of it was in my camera equipment, but some were in my overcoat."

Jeff pulled out his phone. "Gladys, we need a full Security scan team over at the Embassy. Check the Pontifex's residence and Reynolds' place, too. We've identified a wide variety of surveillance equipment that isn't ours. Thanks, yes. Yes, faster than that."

Jeff's eyes narrowed. "No, I haven't asked him. Are you seriously going to tell me to call James and ask his permission?" Jeff's voice was starting to head to the "rabid dog" growl. "Time's of the essence. No, I'm not going to call Tim or Serene either. Do it, or I'll be happy to remind everyone that I've been sidelined into this crap job for only three months."

He rolled his eyes. "Yes, I realize it's a vital role. Look, if I want a lecture, I can call my mother." He heaved a sigh. "Fine. Thank you *so* much." Jeff hung up and ran his hand through his hair. "I really hate my life sometimes."

Chuckie shrugged. "It's a living. So, is a scan actually going to be run?"

"Yeah. Teams should be here momentarily." No sooner said than several sets of A-Cs arrived, carrying a variety of equipment I didn't want to identify. "Go over the things in this room first," Jeff told them. "Then do the rest of the Embassy. Top to bottom, every room, no matter how small or innocuous."

"Every person should be scanned, too, and all wardrobes," Oliver added.

"What the paparazzo said. Do it all at hyperspeed, make sure the others at the other locations are doing the same." The agents nodded, some pulled out phones, the rest just went to work. Jeff looked at me. "Do we take care of this or the hospital?"

"I think we need to get over there. Nurse Carter called a while ago now."

Chuckie nodded. "If the others were pulled away from my control, I figure there's a good chance whatever your 'relative' left for you is gone now, but the faster we get there, the better chance we have of getting our hands on it, whatever it is."

One of the random A-Cs came over to us. "We've identified everything suspect in this room, sir," he said to Jeff. He looked at me. "The rest of your things should be fine if you want to take them with you, ma'am."

"Super." I trotted over to Pierre and Oliver.

Pierre handed me my purse. "Efficient young men."

"And all drool-worthingly hot, too."

He smiled. "Yes, Jimmy said the perks of working for you would outweigh the dangers. So far, I have to say, it's been a thrilling start to my new career."

"I guess that's one way of putting it."

"I'd like to come with you," Oliver said.

"I don't think Jeff or Chuckie will like that idea."

Oliver shrugged. "A press pass and a big camera can be advantages."

I'd seen the camera work for me already. And, under the circumstances, safety in numbers seemed like a good plan. Plus, that meant Oliver couldn't wander through any more of the Embassy than he likely already had. "Works for me. Pierre, can you manage things here?"

"Can, have, and will, darling. Carry on, and enjoy yourselves."

Oliver and I joined Jeff and Chuckie as Len and Kyle entered the room. "Why is he coming with us?" Jeff asked.

"He wants to, and he might help."

Chuckie rubbed his forehead. "Unreal. Fine, yes, why not bring Mister Joel Oliver along?"

"We can discuss his intelligence while we're heading to the medical center."

"I'm refraining from comment," Chuckie said dryly. He looked at Len and Kyle. "Have they been searched yet?"

The boys looked shocked, as though they were being accused of treason. Jeff motioned to an A-C, who zipped over and did the whole search and scan thing. "They're clean, sir." He did the same for Jeff, Chuckie, Oliver, and Pierre. "All good, sir."

"Why wouldn't we be?" Len asked.

"We've been infiltrated," Jeff snapped. "Kitty's purse was loaded with bugs, our investigative reporter here was loaded, too."

"You think we did that?" Kyle asked, looking both stricken and angry. Len was stone-faced, but his eyes were flashing. The boys weren't liking this accusation at all.

Chuckie examined them. "No," he said finally. I relaxed, Jeff grumbled, the boys looked relieved and still hurt. "But right now, we can't be sure."

I thought about yesterday's fun-filled timeline. "If I was bugged, it wasn't by the boys. They haven't been around long enough. Same with MJO, they weren't around him long enough to bug anything. And he and Pierre found all of his bugs last night."

"Plenty of time if you're good enough," Chuckie said.

I shook my head. "They aren't that good yet."

"Thanks a lot," Kyle muttered.

"What's going on?" Len asked.

"We'll fill you in on the way to the limo," Jeff said firmly.

Before we could leave, the melodious tones of the front doorbell rang out. "Are we expecting company?"

"Not that I know of," Jeff said.

"I haven't had time to finalize calendars, but no, Walter didn't inform me of such," Pierre said, as he dashed off, presumably to get the door.

"All of you," Jeff said to the agents, "get the place cleaned up and make sure it looks human, top speed. Get the bugs over to Dulce, pronto. I want all the intelligence on them as fast as possible. *Our* fast, not human fast."

I blinked and the bugs all disappeared and things were put into place. The agents were nowhere to be seen. "Hyperspeed rocks."

Pierre stuck his head in. "There's quite a large a group of gentlemen and ladies to see you, Ambassadors. And you, too, Mister Reynolds. They wouldn't take no or come back once you've scheduled an appointment for an answer, either."

We all looked at each other. "What's going on?" Jeff asked.

"No idea," Chuckie said. "But I think we'd better go find out."

CHAPTER 30

"I'VE PUT THEM INTO THE SMALL PARLOR on the first floor," Pierre said. "It's the most businesslike room closest to the front door. I did my best to ensure they saw as little of the Embassy as possible."

"Thanks, Pierre, good job." Jeff jerked his head at me and Chuckie. "Let's go and see who's dropped in for a visit. Jocks and reporters stay here." They all looked disappointed, but didn't argue.

"How the hell does anyone know I'm here?" Chuckie asked quietly as we walked down the hall.

"You're here a lot."

"Tell me about it," Jeff muttered as we reached the stairs and headed down.

We entered the room to find it packed with people. I knew some of them—Esteban Cantu, Madeline Cartwright, and Vincent Armstrong. Cantu was a rather handsome Latin man who was the head of the C.I.A.'s Antiterrorism unit. A unit that didn't report in to the P.T.C.U. in any way. Armstrong was the senior senator from Florida and looked the part. And Cartwright was their Pentagon liaison.

There had been a fourth to their little cabal, John Cooper, from the C.I.A. He'd been one of the ones in charge of Operation Confusion. Happily, he was long dead now—Chuckie had taken him out after he'd tried to kill us all several different times.

I suspected the three of them still wanted to get rid of Chuckie and us so they could take over Centaurion Division, but so far we had no real proof. They were also on several committees that dealt with South America, national security, and anti-American activities, meaning they interacted with Centaurion Division and the C.I.A.'s ET division frequently. However, normally we dealt with them at Langley.

"Reynolds," Cantu said with a hearty smile. "I figured we'd find you here."

"Cantu. What can I do for you?" Chuckie asked, voice clipped. They pointedly didn't shake hands.

"Oh, I think it might be what we can do for you," Armstrong said. "Madeline, why don't you make the introductions?" There were six more people, three men, three women, all dressed according to the latest fashions from Intimidation Weekly. They all had the "look," too. We were in a room full of political animals.

Cartwright was an older woman, with short hair and cat's-eye glasses, and she always dressed severely. It was like she was trying to channel Lotte Lenya in *From Russia With Love*, only the American version. Of the original four and now three of them, though, I liked Cartwright the best, which was a classic example of damning with faint praise.

She managed a fleeting smile. "Ambassadors. How things have changed in the last few months, haven't they? Especially for you, Missus Martini."

"Pretty much completely, yes," I said cheerfully. Why let them know we weren't enjoying our new jobs?

"How's your daughter?" she inquired.

"Doing great. I'll force baby pictures on you later. But we're late for a meeting, since we had no idea you were stopping by, so could we get to why you're all here?"

"Absolutely. Please allow me to introduce Senator Lydia Montgomery, Miz Lillian Culver, Mister Guy Gadoire, and Representative Edmund Brewer. I'm sure you know Marion Villanova, the Chief Aide to the Secretary of State, and Secretary of Transportation Langston Whitmore."

"Only from TV." I hadn't met any of these people in person yet, but I knew their respective spouses quite well. Lydia Montgomery was Eugene's wife, Lillian Culver claimed dear Abner as her husband, Guy Gadoire was Vance Beaumont's main man, and Edmund Brewer was Nathalie's vintner husband. Marion Villanova and Langston Whitmore were the ones playing pretend with Leslie Manning and Bryce Taylor.

Whitmore gave me a beaming smile. "I believe you're in the Washington Wife class with my personal assistant, Bryce, aren't you, Missus Martini?"

"Ambassador Martini," Chuckie corrected. "American Centaurion recognizes two Chiefs of Mission."

"Of course, my apologies," Whitmore said. "Is there a formal apology method your people prefer?"

"Oh, Langston," Villanova said, "the first word in their country's name is American. Stop acting like they wear feathers or something." He chuckled in a way that I knew was supposed to be boyishly contrite while she smiled apologetically. "You have a lovely Embassy." Considering Whitmore technically outranked Villanova, I thought this was an interesting little piece of theater.

"Thank you." I tried to channel Pierre. "We do our best."

"My friend Leslie says you're quite the life of the party in class."

"Oh, yeah, that's me all right." Either Leslie had lied like a wet rug, for reasons I couldn't fathom, Villanova was being sweetly snide, or she was trying to put a nice spin on things. I tabled my decision on this for later.

The youngest woman stepped forward. "You must be Kitty," she said, extending her hand. She was the first one to do so. "I'm Lydia."

We shook paws. "Eugene's told me so much about you! Nice to finally meet you." She looked like Eugene—average. There was nothing wrong with that, but I could see a little more why this transition was hard on him—they'd really been regular folks before Lydia had gone into politics.

"I agree. Eugene speaks so highly of you, I was hoping we'd have time to meet before now."

"Me too. Better late than never, though, right?"

Representative Brewer shook hands with all of us, marking him as the only one in the room who might possibly have been raised right, though I was willing to cut Lydia some slack. He looked exactly like I'd expect a winery-owner-turned-politician to look. He also looked like your quintessential Californian—tall, tan, laid-back, and confident.

"My wife, Nathalie, says she can't wait to see your ensemble tomorrow night," he shared as he got to me. "She expects it to be spectacular."

"Does she? I guess I'd better make sure it is, then. How's the wine business?"

"Good! I have wonderful people in place, running things. Allows me to focus on my constituents. Let me know if you'd like me to send a case over. Our Chardonnay is particularly fantastic."

"Thank you, but it's against our religion to drink."

"You're Mormons?"

Why this was always the first question was beyond me. More people than Mormons didn't drink. "No. American Centaurion has its own religion. But thank you for the offer. If we were allowed to drink, I'm sure we'd love it."

Lillian Culver was one of those women who, when you first looked at her, seemed really stunningly attractive—not Dazzler-level, but still hot for a human. But the longer you looked at her, the more you realized she was all bones and angles, and the moment you realized this, you also saw that she wasn't really all that attractive. If you looked a little while longer, you started to wonder if she ate meals, and how big her head really was in proportion to her body.

Culver hit me with a wide smile, and I mean wide. She looked like she was auditioning to play the Joker in drag. It was sort of attractive but mostly horrifying, and also somewhat hypnotic. "My Abner's described you perfectly."

I jerked myself out of my almost stupefied study of her looks and back to the present moment. "Really? I'm sort of amazed that all of your spouses and friends are interested enough in me to talk about me outside of class, let alone to all of you."

"Oh, don't be so modest," Brewer said. "You're one of the youngest ambassadors on the Row, maybe *the* youngest. And I think you're the highest-ranking politician in the class, therefore."

Social climbing. Well, there were worse reasons for these people to come calling. I was pretty sure they all had those worse reasons in mind, though.

Gadoire had saved himself for last. The men got hearty handshakes. I, on the other hand, got a sweeping bow and the back of my hand kissed. He didn't do it very well, and I resisted the urge to ask for a moist towelette.

"Madame Ambassador, it's truly an honor. My Vance says your wit and charm makes everyone around you laugh all day long." He spoke in a French accent I was 99% sure was faked.

I had to censor the first ten responses that came to mind. "Does he? How sweet," was all I could manage that wouldn't fall on the snide or sarcastic side of the house. I was certain, however, that if I was around Gadoire for too long, I'd certainly be laughing all day long. Or washing my hands constantly. Or both.

Chuckie and Jeff both looked as if they were controlling their gag reflexes. "Cantu, while this is very pleasant, I'm wondering why it couldn't wait until the President's Ball tomorrow night."

Chuckie's tone was very light. "The ambassadors have a tight schedule today, and you're disrupting it."

The entire gang put expressions of dismay and chagrin on their faces. I didn't buy it for a New York minute. Culver's expression mirrored the Joker's when he was pretending he was sad that he'd killed one of the Robins or put Batgirl in a wheelchair. It was official—this woman creeped me the hell out.

Culver took the lead. "I'm so sorry. Blame me, Mister Reynolds. We wanted a chance to talk to the ambassadors. American Centaurion is very influential in circles that affect us, and we just wanted to be sure we could start off on the right foot. We're also here for you, any of you, should you need help navigating these new waters."

I was sure the nine sharks in front of us would be more than happy to help us swim right into their maws. But I didn't say that. "What influence are you hoping we'll exert for you?" Hey, it was a lot better than calling them all Great Whites or something or, in Culver's case, calling her Joker Jaws. To her face.

Joker Jaws waved her hand in that "it's no big deal" way. Pierre did it a lot better. "There are certain . . . programs moving forward that represent the next evolution in protection of individuals and municipalities. We'd like to have American Centaurion's support for these—in terms of defense, your little principality carries a great deal of sway."

"In return," Brewer said, "we'd of course look closely at any issues American Centaurion might be having and do our best to . . . smooth them over."

"Would you?" Jeff asked. I could tell he was controlling himself from tossing them onto the street. We were saved by the bell. "Who's here now?" Jeff asked.

"I'm not expecting anyone."

"We were expecting to be gone by now," Chuckie added meaningfully. I couldn't blame him. I wanted to have been gone at least fifteen minutes ago.

"Oh, that'll be Zachary," Cartwright said. "He had to travel separately from the rest of us." She smiled at me. "The traffic's been so terrible that we all carpooled."

I managed not to ask how Cartwright, who worked at the Pentagon, was in a carpool with any of these people. The answer was obvious—they'd been plotting somewhere together before storming our particular castle.

Instead, I took an educated guess as to who our straggler was.

"You mean Senator Zachary Kramer?" Also known as Marcia Kramer's husband. Fabulous. With him joining us, the only spouse missing from this little group was Jack Ryan's wife, Pia. I wasn't disappointed that she wasn't along—we were at Marx Brothers occupancy in the room as it was. Of course, for all I knew, Pia Ryan was on her way and just stuck in traffic.

"Yes, indeed," a man's voice boomed out. Sure enough, Pierre was ushering in a man about White's age. He resembled Armstrong and most of the other congressmen I'd met—he was well dressed, well coiffed, and exuded chummy confidence. "So sorry I'm late, all. Had to drop Marcia off at a friend's place. What have I missed?"

"Oh, we'd just shared our little request," Culver said quickly.

"Great." Kramer seemed pleased. "So, what's your answer?"

Both Jeff and I opened our mouths. But before we could speak, Pierre dashed in. "Ambassadors, I'm *so* sorry to interrupt, but you're already terribly late. You know how the king gets when you keep him waiting. As your Majordomo, I'm going to have to insist you both leave immediately."

CHAPTER 31

JEFF AND I SNAPPED OUR MOUTHS SHUT. The rest of the room looked as though they'd been goosed or had just eaten spoiled chum, depending. Chuckie looked as though he wanted to make Pierre his top operative.

Jeff recovered quickest. "Thank you, Pierre. You're right." He gave everyone a charming smile. "Thanks so much for dropping by. Please, next time, set up an appointment so we can really spend some quality time together."

"Madeline, perhaps you could organize that and coordinate with the Embassy Majordomo," Chuckie said pointedly. Cartwright's eyes narrowed—an interesting look behind her cat's-eye glasses— but she nodded and managed her standard fleeting smile.

Jeff took my arm and jerked his head at Chuckie. He nodded to the others. "We all need to get going. Pierre will see you out."

The three of us left the room in a reasonably stately manner and continued it to the stairs. Then Jeff grabbed Chuckie and zipped us back up to the room where Oliver and the boys were. It was a short trip, so Chuckie only gagged for a second or two.

"I want you two jocks ensuring the ten people who just came in leave immediately. Shove them physically if they aren't doing what Pierre wants, which is getting the hell out of our Embassy."

Len and Kyle took off. "What was that all about?" Oliver asked. We gave him the fast, confusing rundown. He nodded sagely. "Ah."

"Ah?"

"Sorry. You're too new. This is a tight-knit group. The politicians are in the lobbyists' pockets. For those not in the know, American Centaurion has the reputation of being very well placed politically, in terms of both national and international defense. Obviously, for those in the know, you're a key group."

"Yeah, everyone wants to make us the War Division."

Oliver nodded. "Understandable. Deplorable," he added quickly as Jeff glared at him, "but understandable."

"So Lydia's already on Culver and Gadoire's payrolls?" This was disappointing. I liked Eugene and I didn't want to hate his wife.

"Maybe not," Oliver said. "She's new. However, they're a hugely influential group. If she wants to rise up in the Washington hierarchy, they're a good set to join. One of them is related to the head of Titan Security, too."

"Really? Which one?" I figured it couldn't be Madeline Cartwright—not only did she seem just too boring for this level of intrigue, she was a Pentagon employee, and I knew their background checks rivaled Chuckie's.

Oliver shook his head. "I don't know, can't find the information. The records have been cleaned, so to speak."

"How do you clean off records of your relatives?"

"Change their names, steal and delete all the birth records, replace them with new ones." Chuckie shrugged. "We do it all the time with witness protection. I didn't know Titan had this direct a Washington connection, though."

"They've taken great pains to hide it," Oliver said. "I only know from piecing together little bits of information here and there, found over time and while I was doing my exposé on the situation with the police department. So far, it hasn't been enough to even write an article about, let alone take to someone like you."

"Take it to me now," Chuckie said. "I don't like discovering a conspiracy theory I know nothing about."

"Losing a perfect track record?"

He shot me a glare. "No. But part of my job is to determine which of the theories and rumors are true. Like the supersoldier project that came out of nowhere. I don't like being blindsided. Titan's got a lot of clout—I need to know who or what they're connected to, and discovering who they have hidden in our government would be an intelligent place to start."

"As far as I can tell, this was put in place decades ago," Oliver said.

"That's some serious long-term planning."

"Our enemies tend to fall on that side of the house," Chuckie reminded me. "And I consider Titan to be among our enemies." He shook his head. "They've been investigated. Senator McMillan has certainly had a number of background checks run on Titan's board of directors and chief officers. They focused on Titan because they won the local protection contract, but they've done the same with all the other security companies bidding on government contracts."

"Go Arizona." McMillan was our senior senator, and my sorority roommate, Caroline, worked for him now. "We rock the suspicious."

"And yet they've found nothing actionable against Titan," Chuckie pointed out.

"Are we safe in assuming they want to kill all of us and make Centaurion the War Division, or do we think they just want all the money and power in the world?"

"Yes." Chuckie shook his head. "And yes, I know that was an either-or question. Always assume they're out to get you. It may sound paranoid, but it keeps you alive."

Jeff ran his hand through his hair. "What a great mindset to live with."

Chuckie shrugged. "Look back at the last few years and call me overcautious."

"What bothers me most is what's bothered me since Operation Confusion—that there are conspiracies and plans going on that you and my mom know nothing about. And we don't know if Titan's part of an older plot we didn't know anything about before but at least have an inkling of now, or if it's part of a brand-new plan to kill the people we care about and take over. Or something else entirely."

Jeff, Chuckie, and I shared the "we're doomed" look.

"Ah, well," Oliver said in a tone of voice clearly intended to cheer us up. "I'm sure it'll all come out eventually. The truth always does."

"Does it?" Jeff didn't sound happy. "Because if that's the case, that means we're going to be exposed somewhere along the line."

The boys returned before any of the rest of us could make a sarcastic comment about Oliver's optimism or reassure Jeff that we'd remain hiding in plain sight without issue. Of course, it might just have been me who had to hold back the fact that the truth very often never came out because it was too busy being beaten to a pulp and rearranged into something "more palatable." Yeah, I'd picked up a few things in the short time we'd been here. Which was why I was less worried about us being discovered than Jeff was.

"Pierre had them all leaving, but we made sure they didn't dawdle," Len shared.

"Good, then let's get out of here. Our appointment with the 'king' is overdue."

"What?" Kyle asked. "We're seeing a king?"

"Not so much, no."

The six of us trotted off, me, Oliver, and Chuckie bringing the boys up to speed. We got into one of the limos that didn't have a car seat in it. Jeff and I sat in the back, Chuckie and Oliver faced us, Len had the wheel, Kyle had shotgun. Not the team I was used to, but we were a team nonetheless.

"How do you keep all these people straight?" Kyle asked as we finished our Weirdness Wrap-Up.

"Unwillingly."

"And is there really a king?"

"Yes," Jeff said. "Only he's on Alpha Four."

"So," Len said, getting us back on topic, "whoever bugged Mister Joel Oliver, they had plenty of time and opportunity, right? Because he doesn't live in a secured building, at least, not like you do."

"Right."

"But who bugged Kitty?" Kyle asked. "Because from what you all said, there were a lot of different bugs in her purse."

"But nothing in the baby's things," I added.

"The baby would be presumed to be with her mother," Oliver suggested.

"Not all the time."

"So they aren't after Jamie," Chuckie said.

"Good," Jeff growled. "Not that it stopped them from trying to kill her."

"Is it the same people, though? I mean, we never have just one plan going on."

Chuckie sighed. "Good point. Let's assume we have multiple actions against us active. It'll make us more alert."

"Maybe whoever bugged Kitty didn't have access to Jamie's diaper bag," Kyle suggested.

Jeff's phone rang before we could comment. "Hi, Gladys. Really. Really? Huh." He looked at me and Oliver. "Good initiative, those teams. Good. Really. Thanks, Gladys. Yeah, we'll sleep better. If, you know, we ever get to sleep again."

He hung up and looked at Chuckie. "They searched your home and office, the Embassy, the Pontifex's residence, Kitty's parents' home as well as their new place, and Mister Joel Oliver's trashed apartment. Gladys had each Centaurion Base run through a full scan set, too. The only bugs found were the ones in the Embassy—those that were on his clothes and equipment and in Kitty's purse. Between the two, there were over a dozen different pieces of tracking equipment. They're running comparisons now, but it's a good guess they won't all be from the same group, organization, or country."

We all let that sit on the air for a while. I could see Chuckie's conspiracy wheels turning. I could also tell they weren't settling on anything key.

"So, I guess the big questions are, why are Mister Joel Oliver and I so very popular, and how did we get so many bugs on us both, in, I'd have to guess, such a short period of time?"

"Succinctly put." Chuckie looked as if he might have gotten something. "Martini, you said there were around a dozen pieces of tracking software between Kitty and Mister Joel Oliver?"

"Yes." Jeff's phone beeped. "Test results are back. We've identified matches between what was in Kitty's purse and what was on our reporter here. Seven matching sets, so we can safely assume there are seven different groups who were bugging them. Huh."

"What?"

"There's one that was only in your purse, baby. Doesn't match at all with the others."

"So there's one person out there only following me, instead of me and MJO? I feel so special."

"Seven sets . . ." Chuckie's voice trailed off. I knew his expression; the wheels were turning. "That fits."

I thought about the past hour and made the leap. "You think the people who visited us unexpectedly were the ones who bugged me?"

"Yeah, because there were seven of them in addition to Cantu, Armstrong, and Cartwright. And there was no real reason for them to make the first lobbying and bribery steps today."

"Unless they know someone's gonna die at the President's Ball."

"I'm more concerned about Kitty being spied on in her Washington Wife class," Jeff said, looking and sounding worried.

"Eugene wouldn't bug me." I considered whether it was a good time to suggest I not attend the class anymore. Thought about it and figured I'd be told I had to go to perform counterespionage and decided not to get into that resulting discussion.

Jeff nodded. "I don't get anything threatening or dangerous from him."

"He wouldn't have to bug you to get information about where

you were going," Chuckie said. "You'd tell him, as long as he asked in a way that made sense."

"Or he's not involved."

"Possible." Chuckie didn't sound convinced either way. "However, the other six that dropped by all have significant others in class with you, don't they?"

"Oh, snap. Yeah, and that explains why they called me and Eugene over yesterday morning—to plant their bugs. My purse was shoved under the middle of the table, and I wasn't paying any attention to it because I was so focused on the return-to-high school situation. So they all could and probably did drop something in." I thought about it. "I'll bet the seventh bug was planted by Jack Ryan. His wife works for the C.I.A."

"Not in my division, and her division's not read in on American Centaurion. Which means her spying on you makes sense."

"So they showed up today because we'd found their bugs?" Jeff asked.

Chuckie nodded. "Sounds right to me."

Jeff made a call. "Yeah, me again. Please have the agents sweep the lower floors of the Embassy for bugs. Yes, again. Trust me, they're going to find some." He waited a few moments. "Right. How many? Really? Great. No, not at this moment. Thank you." He hung up, looking angry.

"Well?" Chuckie asked.

"More bugs planted. Ten of them, in fact."

"So, we'll neutralize those and prepare ourselves for more impromptu visits. That covers the really obvious. But I haven't been around Cantu, Armstrong, or Cartwright for them to bug me. So who does the nonmatching bug that's only on me belong to?"

Chuckie said. "No idea. I have another question, though. What is it everyone who bugged both of you wants to know, and do they know it already or not?"

CHAPTER 32

"THAT'S TWO QUESTIONS, REALLY," I pointed out.

"Oh, pardon me, Miss No Exaggeration Allowed," Chuckie replied with a grin.

"Missus," Jeff snapped.

"Boys, don't start. And we can't really answer your questions yet, Chuckie, though my guess is no, or we wouldn't have been visited by The Gang of Ten." But it did remind me of a small, but I felt important, point. "Why did Peter call me Miss Katt?"

"Isn't his name Pierre?" Kyle asked.

"Yes, but I'm talking about a different Peter. This one is one of the ones who tried to kill us all day yesterday."

"No idea," Chuckie said. "Hopefully Serene's team will find something on that memory card."

"Think our visitors and Peter are connected?"

"Maybe," Chuckie allowed. "But if so, the bigger questions would be which one of them is behind the assassination attempt, and who do they want to kill?"

"I hate it when you ask the hard questions. Over and over again."

"Give me a hard answer and make all our lives easier."

"When the light dawns for me, you'll be the first to know."

Traffic was a lot calmer than the day before, and we made it to the Georgetown University Medical Center in decent time. I checked my watch. Jeff had given it to me for my birthday—it was top of the line, extremely waterproof, and all the other bad things proof, so it was still working. Nurse Carter had called me about an hour and thirty minutes ago. I hoped we hadn't taken too long to get here.

We parked and had the "do we leave the limo unattended or not" argument. Chuckie and Jeff wanted Len and Kyle to stay with the limo. I didn't want to separate our group. Jeff compromised, called Reader, and a set of A-C agents came to do parking garage duty.

The six of us trooped in and found Nurse Carter without too much trouble. She was middle-aged, seemed in pretty good physical shape, and, as her voice had indicated, looked Hispanic, though I couldn't say if she was Mexican, Cuban, or something else. She was also quite brisk.

After I showed my ID and explained that Katt was my maiden name, thankfully shown on my driver's license, which read Katt Martini, she managed a fleeting smile. Apparently it was *the* smile for middle-aged women in Washington. "Well, Miss Katt, thank you for coming down so quickly." She looked at the men with me. "Oh, were those other men really your employees? If so, I'm sorry, we can't break protocol."

"Employees?"

"The men who came by about an hour ago. They said you'd asked them to claim your uncle's things, but we have strict rules here. They weren't on the list, I'd already contacted you, and you are the one who has to claim the deceased's belongings."

I'd moved from Peter's random friends and family list up to niece status in less than two hours. I wondered if I stalled a bit if I'd end up his wife or daughter. "I didn't send anyone." I looked up at Chuckie, who shook his head. "No one should have come here other than me."

"Then, I wonder who they were?" she said absently, as she went into a locked room at the nurse's station. She came out with a clipboard. "Come with me, please."

"What did the men who tried to get my uncle's things look like?" I asked her as we walked briskly along to the elevators.

"Like businessmen, like your friends," she indicated Chuckie and the boys, not Jeff or Oliver. She looked at me sharply. "Why would someone try to claim your uncle's things illegally?"

Since he wasn't actually my uncle, technically I was claiming illegally. But apparently Peter had wanted me to so claim, so it was, therefore, legal. My small moral quandary over, I checked her expression. She looked suspicious. This probably wasn't good. "Huh. I have no idea. Maybe they were my uncle's rivals."

"Oh. Business or politics?"

We were in D.C., it wasn't an insightful question so much as covering the likely bases. "Both, I think." The elevator arrived, and we got in and headed for the basement level.

"Well, we certainly don't want to cause an international incident here." Nurse Carter gave a nervous titter. "Trust me, we ensured your uncle's things were protected. His personal items are in the vault."

"The medical center has a vault?"

"Absolutely. We get many dignitaries here. We don't want anyone . . . untoward . . . taking advantage of them while they're ill or injured."

Interesting. So Nurse Carter was used to shadowy people trying to snag other people's property. "These other men, they didn't have any paperwork that would have given them clearance, did they?"

"You mean like a warrant? No. I would have contacted you if that had been the case."

"How did you get anything of my uncle's in the first place?"

"Oh, every patient's belongings are bagged and tagged when they arrive. He requested his things be sent to the vault, after asking that we be sure to notify his next of kin of his predicament."

So Peter had been aware of the kind of security the medical center had. "Do all the area hospitals work the same way?"

"Of course." The doors opened, and we trailed Nurse Carter as she wound her way through the rat maze of corridors. They weren't too brightly lit—not dim but not really typical medical bright white light, either. Presumably because there weren't patients down here. We ended up at a room with a Security kiosk in front of it.

The guard reminded me of our A-C Security teams. Not that he was gorgeous, far from it. But he was big and had that totally bored yet totally alert at the same time thing going on.

He and Nurse Carter exchanged some sign and countersign stuff that seemed amazingly complex for a hospital, then he allowed her inside. I started to follow, and he put his hand up. "Only the nurse."

She looked at me. "Miss Katt can come in. The gentlemen need to wait outside."

"I'd like to go with my wife," Jeff said. He sounded worried. And annoyed that she was still calling me Miss. I was accepting that, for whatever reason, a wedding ring, driver's license with my married name on it, and my husband and/or baby with me weren't convincing some people that I was marriageable material.

"She'll be fine," Nurse Carter said reassuringly. "If she gets emotional, I'll get her right back out to you."

I knew Jeff wasn't worried about my sobbing over my "uncle's" things. I figured he didn't like the idea of us separating this way. I couldn't blame him. Then again, if this was how they did things at the D.C. hospitals, making a fuss would draw a lot of unwanted attention.

"I'll be fine." I squeezed Jeff's hand and followed Nurse Carter into the vault.

The door closed behind us, sounding very loud and very emphatic. The lighting was fairly dim, like the rest of the floor. Apparently they liked to keep it creepy in their basement. How Stephen King of them.

With that cheery thought in my mind, I followed Nurse Carter to the back of the vault, where there was a bank of what looked like safety deposit boxes. She inserted a key into one, opened it, pulled out a bunch of stuff in a long tray, and put it down on the table nearby.

"Now," she said, as she turned around, took a nasty looking handgun out of the tray, and pointed it at me, "why don't you tell me what the hell is going on?"

CHAPTER 33

THIS WAS SO TYPICAL FOR MY LUCK that I didn't even comment on it. "I have no freaking idea. Who the hell are you? And why the elaborate ruse to get me down here?"

Her eyes narrowed. "It's not a ruse. Why did the Dingo put you as his next of kin?"

"The Dingo?" I'd heard some amazing nicknames by now, but this one was in the running for World's Worst for sure.

She shrugged. "It's his name in the business."

"What business, the assassin business? You guys have a union or something?"

"Yes, the assassin business, and I'm not in it."

"Right. That's why you have the big gun pointed at me."

"I don't like taking chances."

"So, you moonlight in nursing and kill people at the same time? That's convenient."

"I haven't killed anybody. Today," she added, apparently for truthfulness.

"Great. I haven't either. I'm willing to start with you, though, if you don't get that gun out of my face." This was bluster on my part. Hyperspeed did nothing for you if the bullet caught you, and she was close enough that I wasn't sure I could get out of the way in time.

"Why did the Dingo put you as next of kin?"

"Again, I have no freaking idea. I don't make up these plans. I just get caught up in them and have to figure them out before everyone I care about gets killed. Why do you know him as the Dingo and who the hell are you?"

She studied me. "I'm with a . . . secret organization."

"Wow, me too. What's the freaking name of your secret organization?"

"What's the name of yours?"

"Oh, for God's sake." I had to figure Jeff had picked up what was going on by now. "My husband's going to break down that door in a moment, and then you're going to have a lot more to worry about than secret handshakes and tricky passwords."

I looked at the stuff in the tray. None of it looked familiar. None of it looked waterlogged, either. "How the hell did Peter or the Dingo or whoever the hell he was give you all that stuff, and, more importantly, how is it that none of it looks like it took a swim in the Potomac earlier?"

"These things were with him when we checked him in. He didn't say they weren't his. And he was quite specific that he only had one living relative in town. So why are you listed as his next of kin?"

"I'm assuming because we saved his life."

"Why? You're working with him?"

"No. You know, my husband asked me that, too, why I wanted to save his life. So did everyone else. I can't tell you why, I just didn't think it was right to let him and the other dude who spent all day trying to kill me drown. Not, I have to mention, that I have a problem killing the big bad fuglies, at least under most circumstances."

"What other 'dude'?"

"The other guy who came in with Peter the Dingo Dog Man. There were two of them, both admitted. I saw them get strapped onto the gurneys myself."

"Shit."

"Excuse me?"

"There was only one admitted. That means they took the other one."

"Who is 'they'?"

"Our enemies."

"When you say 'our,' do you mean enemies of yours and your secret organization's, enemies of mine, or enemies of both of us?"

"Yes."

"I'm really considering the benefits of just hating your guts right now."

Nurse Carter cracked a smile. "I can understand that."

I decided to just go for it. "Look, is this about the assassination attempt that's going to happen at the President's Ball?"

She stared at me. "What? What are you talking about?" She seemed genuinely confused. It so figured.

"Oh, great. So, since you seem unaware of that, let's just identify what the hell plan you're working on, for, or against, shall we? Just so I can sort of keep it straight."

She blinked. "What are you talking about?"

"That's exactly what I'm asking you. Let me speak slower—what the hell is going on, and why are you still pointing a gun at me?"

Nurse Carter seemed to reach a decision. "I'm with the Paraguay Secret Police. I'm investigating dangerous alien activity in our country. We've traced the ones in charge back to people in your government."

"When you say 'my' government, which one do you mean?"

"How many governments do you work for?"

"Technically? Um, I'm honestly not sure. The lines get blurred and all that."

She stared at me. "You *are* Angela Katt's daughter, aren't you?"

"I might be."

"Are you insinuating that your mother works for more than one government?" Her eyes narrowed again. "Is she still Mossad?"

"Not to my knowledge, but I think it's once in, you always get to go to the alumni dinners sort of thing. But, no, my mother works for the President of the United States."

"But you don't?"

"No. I mean, I'm not against the President, or the U.S. Or anything like that." She relaxed a tiny bit. I decided to go for it. "I work for American Centaurion. I mean, that's why I'm one of their head diplomats."

"You're what?"

Why was this a surprise? We weren't exactly flying under the radar these past few months. "Are you the worst informed member of covert ops in history? Why are you asking me this?"

"You're listed as a senator's aide."

"Well, I have no idea where or how, but I've never assisted any senator with much of anything." Oh, sure, Jeff and I had eliminated Leventhal Reid at the end of Operation Drug Addict, but he'd been a member of the House of Representatives.

Nurse Carter reached into a pocket and pulled out a picture. She looked at it. "This isn't you," she said, somewhat accusingly.

"No idea whose mug shot you're looking at, but I'm not going to apologize for it not being me."

The guys chose this moment to finally breach the door. "Don't come any closer or I'll shoot her," Nurse Carter shouted, as Jeff used the super hyperspeed and got the gun away from her, while the human guys raced up and surrounded me.

"Geez, what took you guys so long?"

"We had to knock out the security guard and it took Reynolds a while to crack their vault."

"I didn't have any decent equipment on me," Chuckie said by way of apology.

"Whatever. I have no idea what's going on, and good luck to all of you in getting a straight answer out of Nurse Carter here."

"Take her picture," Chuckie said to Oliver, who complied.

"My government will not pay for me to be returned," she said.

"We're not planning to ransom you, but a little cooperation in the form of you explaining what the hell you think is going on wouldn't go amiss."

Nurse Carter looked around. "Not here."

"Well, if not here, then why the hell did you ask me questions here in the first place?" My phone chose this time to ring. I grabbed it. "Hello?"

"Kit-Kat! You tied up, sis?"

"Hey, Caro Syrup! How's my girl?"

Caroline sighed. "I'm stranded at the stupid airport. We got rerouted three times, my ride bailed on me, I can't raise anyone at his Embassy, and everyone else has left already. There are no cabs or limos around, God alone knows why. The Metro is having issues, something to do with street construction screwing it up, but no trains have been able to come in or out for hours. We just got back from South America, I'm wiped out, and I was hoping you could maybe do your sister a solid and come pick me up?"

I got a funny feeling and grabbed the picture out of Nurse Carter's hand. Sure enough, while the girl in it wasn't me, I knew her really well. In fact, I was talking to her. She wasn't my real sister, of course. But considering how garbled Nurse Carter's intel seemed to be, perhaps the confusion was understandable.

"Caro, did you just, in fact, get back from Paraguay?"

"You know I'm not supposed to confirm or deny, Kit-Kat."

"Work with me on this one."

"Yes. Can you come get me?"

"Yeah, we'll be there soon. Really soon. And, Caro—do me a huge favor?"

"Sure, what?"

"Don't let anyone get you other than me, and if someone other than me tries to even talk to you, call me immediately while you run screaming toward the most security people you can find."

CHAPTER 34

"UH, WHAT'S GOING ON?" CAROLINE SOUNDED** only slightly freaked. She'd been working in Washington for well over a year now, after all.

"Highest level security breaches. You're in danger. You need to trust me."

"Always have, always do."

"Chuckie and I will be coming for you. Stay around security, stay around a lot of people, call me if anyone comes near you. Which airport are you at?"

"National."

"This means nothing to me."

She managed a laugh. "The Ronald Reagan Washington National Airport. In Arlington."

"That means something, thanks. Be there in a flash." I hung up. "We need to move, fast. Bring Nurse Carter and all of Peter the Dingo Dog's stuff along. I think we have yet another kidnap-murder combo to foil."

Len and Kyle took everything from the tray. "Is there anything else?" Len asked.

I looked at Nurse Carter. "Is there?"

"No."

"Jeff?"

"She's not lying, at least as far as I can tell."

Chuckie produced handcuffs from somewhere about his person and cuffed her. "Let's go. Why do you think Caroline's in danger?"

Since Caroline was not only my sorority roommate but also my closest girlfriend from college, it meant, of course, that Chuckie knew her well. He'd recommended her for the job with Senator McMillan. As a matter of fact, so had my mother.

"Nurse Carter, why did you think the girl in this picture was Angela Katt's daughter?"

"She recommended her for the position, recommended very highly."

"My mother's never recommended me for anything," I mentioned to Jeff as we raced along. "Neither have you," I added to Chuckie.

"You didn't need it," he said as we got the elevator.

"Right." I looked back at Nurse Carter. "That's it? My mom recommends someone and that makes her me?"

"No. She's the sister of the wife of the American Centaurion Ambassador. That would make her Angela Katt's daughter."

"No, not really. That would make her Angela Katt's daughter's sorority sister. Jeff, we need to get to the National airport in Arlington like five minutes ago. We'll need a car there, too, but I don't think we have time to drive there."

Jeff pulled his phone and made a call—to Reader, as far as I could tell. I was busy examining the photo. It showed Caroline and a large group of people, all grouped around a tent. I wasn't certain, but the scenery looked like what I remembered seeing of the Chaco, when I'd watched a twelve-superbeing formation try to take on a lot of A-Cs.

Memory shared that the C.I.A. had been on the scene and had tried to keep us from destroying the superbeings. I handed the photo to Chuckie. "I think some of your brothers and sisters are making a play." Like me, Chuckie was an only child.

He, of course, knew what I meant. "This was taken in Paraguay." He shook Nurse Carter. "Why are you people spying on American politicians?"

"We're trying to determine who's in charge of the project," she said angrily.

"What project?" Chuckie's voice was hard.

She snorted. "The one that hires our poorest people and then, when they never come home, claims they've never heard of them. The one that turns people into inhuman monsters."

Jeff hung up as we reached the elevator banks. "Alpha Team's going to meet us at National. We have a floater gate marking on our limo."

"Jeff, remember, right before Operation Drug Addict, there was a big superbeing cluster in the Chaco?"

Jeff winced. "I hate your nicknames for operations. Especially that one."

"Whatever. Do you remember?"

"Yes. The C.I.A. was on the scene; they wanted our people to let those superbeings survive. Argentina sent in stinger missiles at my request and blew them up." He sighed. "The cluster was just like the one we had in Paris a few months ago. Just like the one in the Chaco, again, this morning. Only we didn't blow the cluster up either of those times, they self-destructed. So, yes, I know where you're going with this, baby."

"Right. I don't think that project's been stopped." I looked up at Chuckie. "My take on Senator McMillan is that he's a good man. What's your take?"

"He is a good man. He's also unafraid to speak out against things he thinks are wrong." Chuckie's eyes narrowed. "The man behind Caroline—is he familiar to you?"

I took the photo back and gave the man Chuckie pointed out a closer inspection. He was wearing sunglasses and had what looked like a couple of weeks' worth of facial hair. But he was very familiar. So was the man standing behind him. "That's my 'Uncle' Peter, and the guy with him is the other guy we fished out of the Potomac."

Jeff cursed quietly. "I knew we should have let them drown."

"No, I think Peter had a change of heart somehow. That's why he listed me as his family." And why he'd slipped me the memory card, though I didn't think I wanted to mention that around Nurse Carter. "Per our 'nurse' here, the other guy never got checked into the hospital, so whoever's running this had him picked up."

"How would that be?" Chuckie asked. "There were supposed to be Centaurion teams assigned to the prisoners."

"There weren't any operatives around other than Airborne when we reached the Medical Center. Peter and his crony got handed off to local law enforcement, of which there was a tonnage. Assume some or all of them were undercover bad guys."

"Makes sense." Jeff sent a text. "But why not grab both of them?"

"I'm concerned about what happened to the teams that were supposed to be covering this," Chuckie said.

Jeff's phone beeped and he sighed. "Per Serene, when our teams arrived at the hospital, they were told the prisoners were in police custody, so they headed back."

"Figures. I'm really more concerned with how Peter died. He wasn't in bad shape, not bad enough to die."

"I think he was murdered," Nurse Carter said. "My cover requires me to actually perform my nursing duties. I couldn't stay with him the entire time, and I had to go home when my shift was over because no one needed me to cover for them, and hanging around would have raised suspicions."

"Maybe they realized he was switching sides, or at least not willing to off me anymore."

"They might have realized we found the bugs," Oliver suggested. "Or he was killed because he failed to kill you and ended up on the local news."

"That doesn't explain where the other guy went to, or how."

"Where's the body?" Chuckie asked as the elevator showed it was just reaching the second floor.

"The morgue," Nurse Carter replied. "It's on this level."

"We don't have the time. Caro's in danger."

Chuckie looked torn. "We'll do it, sir," Len offered. Kyle nodded.

"You'll need me to identify and get the body," Nurse Carter mentioned.

Chuckie shook his head. "They're too new."

"I'll go with them," Oliver said.

"No offense," Chuckie said, "but you're not trained to stop an operative."

Jeff growled. "I cannot believe I'm going to say this. I'll stay with the jocks. Kitty told Caroline you'd be with her, not me."

Chuckie and I both gaped at him. "Seriously?" I asked finally. "You're actually okay with letting me and Chuckie go off on this mission together? Without you?"

The elevator finally arrived. Jeff nodded as the doors opened. "Yeah. Because you won't be alone. James sent over some backup for us."

Michael Gower stepped out. "Hey everyone. James said I needed to get here pronto and be ready to kick some serious ass. What's going on?"

CHAPTER 35

MICHAEL WAS A SLIGHTLY SMALLER VERSION of his older brother—big, black, bald and, like every other A-C, beautiful. He was also a major player. It had bothered me a lot when we'd first met. Now, I just looked at it the way I looked at Chuckie being the Conspiracy King—part of what made him who he was.

"Good," Chuckie said. "Martini, check on the teams who were in charge of this botched hospital transfer. We need to know if they were fooled or if one or more of them are traitors."

Jeff looked like he wanted to argue, but the logic of this directive was too much for him. "Yeah, we'll get that taken care of." He stared at Michael. "You know, Michael could stay here . . ."

"He's not trained either," Chuckie pointed out.

Jeff sighed. "True enough."

Michael grinned. "I'll take care of Kitty, Jeff, I promise."

Jeff grunted, and I kissed him good-bye. "Be careful."

He hugged me. "You, too, baby." He gave Chuckie a glare. "If anything happens to her . . ."

Chuckie rolled his eyes. "I'd better be dead first. Yeah, yeah, as if that isn't my mindset already?"

"Which team should I go with?" Oliver asked.

"Stay here," Chuckie said. "Take pictures of anything that seems remotely relevant, odd, interesting, you know the drill."

Oliver nodded. "My cameras and investigative skills will be fully focused."

"Let's go," I said to Michael as I grabbed his hand and Chuckie's. "We'll explain on the way. And let's use the stairs, because these are the slowest elevators in the world."

I let Michael control all the hyperspeed. Doubling the effect was hard as hell on a human, and I didn't want Chuckie puking his guts out if we could help it. Michael, who worked with a lot of humans, seemed more willing to go easy on it. Then again, it might be that he didn't have any jealousy or dominance issues with Chuckie.

Whatever the reason, we made it to the limo quickly, and Chuckie had to gag for only about half a minute before we could take the gate.

Floater gates were harder to create and maintain, but they usually allowed more than one person to go through easily. Now that I had the A-C powers, I could actually see the gate as a real thing, as opposed to a weird, almost invisible shimmering. The A-C agents who'd come to guard the limo were still there. We had them stay, because I didn't want Jeff in a rigged car any more than he wanted me in one.

I kept a hold on Michael and Chuckie as we stepped through the gate. It had been a long, exciting, exertion-filled couple of days already, and my body really hated going through gates when I was fully rested and relaxed. I managed not to barf my guts out, but only because it was a really short trip, as gate transfers went, and I had a death grip on their hands.

We exited, as was totally par for the A-C course, in a men's bathroom. Not in a stall, for once, but still, right there, in the bathroom. The joys of floater gates were without number. Amazingly enough, there was no one at a urinal, though most of the stalls seemed occupied. Doing my best to ignore the sounds, smells, and my own nausea, I dragged both men out, fast.

I hadn't had the brains to ask Caroline where in the airport she actually was, but fortunately, that's what phones were for. I called her while Michael called Reader to find out where Alpha Team was.

"Caro, you okay?"

"Yeah, Kit-Kat, I am. Right now. But, I think there are men watching me."

"Fabulous. Where are you at?"

"Main Security desk for Terminal B. Feeling naked, exposed, and freaked out."

"I always knew you were smart." I thought about it. "You're not at Baggage Claim?"

"No, they're moving everyone up once they get their luggage, since there's absolutely no ground transportation coming into National right now."

I gave Chuckie and Michael Caroline's location; Michael passed it along while Chuckie headed us for the right area.

As we trotted along I hooked my purse over my neck and then took a good look around. No police. At all. Not that I expected a ton of cops in the airport, but if National was cut off, an officer of the law or two hanging around wouldn't be a shocker, if only to ensure no one panicked or to control panic should it start.

While there were no cops, there were absolutely a lot of men around who didn't seem to have any luggage. I could see the little plastic earphones so popular with the Matrix movies and covert operatives.

"Chuckie, are any of these your guys by any chance?"

"No. Figure they look at me as a roadblock or an adversary, not an ally."

"So it's business as usual."

"Pretty much. Where the hell is Alpha Team?"

"Meeting us," Michael said.

Airborne apparently wasn't coming, which made sense since half of the team were new parents and the other half were busy being new uncles. Besides, none of them were A-Cs, and under the circumstances, A-Cs and their hyperspeed were what I wanted.

Serene hadn't been allowed to make an appearance at any active scenes for a few weeks now. It dawned on me that this meant that Alpha Team, therefore, consisted of Reader, Tim, and, since I was here, me. Meaning we had only two people with A-C talents with us, and only one of us was going to be able to ensure that we escaped, as opposed to slammed into walls.

We spotted Caroline before I could share this aloud. She, like the majority of my sorority sisters, was small, fair, and pretty. I could see how someone who didn't really know us could potentially mistake us for sisters, though it was a stretch.

She had a rolling bag, a duffel, and a backpack, and she looked worried and exhausted. Not good. She was actively chatting with the people behind the security counter, which was smart. She saw me and Chuckie, and her expression went to relief.

I ran to her and gave her a hug. "You okay?"

"Yeah. Really freaked out. Security says there are no limos or taxis they can reach."

"That means there are more innocent bystanders around for us to be distracted trying to protect," Chuckie said quietly as he joined us and gave Caroline a hug.

"Chuck, God, am I glad to see you and Kit-Kat. What the hell's going on?"

"Tell you later. Kitty, what's your plan?"

Caroline stared at him. "Kit-Kat's in charge?"

"More often than anyone likes," he said with a grin. "We'll brief you later. Kitty?"

I grabbed Michael. "Michael Gower, Caroline Chase. Michael, Caroline's your responsibility. If you have to, you leave us to get her back to the Embassy safely."

"Got it." Michael gave Caroline his wide, "you so hot, babe" smile that he gave to every female between 18 and 110. "Nice to meet you."

"At least I'll die happy," Caroline said with a laugh as Michael slung her duffel over his shoulder, took her rolling bag in one hand, and her hand in his other.

"Stay with us as long as you can." I looked around and finally spotted Reader and Tim. They weren't alone. Gower was with them, and so was White. "Awesome, my partner's here!" I shook my head as they reached us. "Paul, you shouldn't be out here."

He shrugged. "The Pontifex is part of Alpha Team."

"No argument, I'm glad you're here, even though it puts you in danger." I was. The number of A-Cs had increased to a more acceptable ratio.

"Where is Jeffrey?" White asked.

"Handling another part of this fun operation. Where's Christopher?" I was sort of surprised he hadn't found a way to come along somehow.

"He's handling things at the Embassy," White said.

"There are things to handle?"

White nodded. "Sadly, yes. We'll fill you in once we're all back together." He gave me a small smile. "Catsuit time again, Missus Martini?"

After a couple of days of everyone calling me Miss Katt, it was a refreshing change. "It is indeed, Mister White." I did fast intros for Caroline and then took stock again of our position. "I may be crazy, but it looks like we could just walk out of here."

"You are crazy," Tim said, "and we can't. We got in via gates. We were late meeting up with you because we scanned the perimeter."

"Any police officers about?"

"No." Tim sighed. "There are a lot of unfriendlies, though."

Reader nodded. "They're ready for us and clearly ready to take a lot of hostages. All ground transportation into this airport has mysteriously stopped or vanished, but there's no terrorism alert."

Caroline stared at him. "Oh, my God! I know you! You did that Calvin Klein ad that caused so much controversy a few years ago."

Reader flashed the cover-boy grin. "It's always nice to be recognized."

She laughed. "We had that framed and hanging up in our rec room at the sorority."

Gower looked at me. "How much did you have to do with that?"

I managed not to blush. "Perhaps a little. I think we have other, more pressing, matters."

"Like survival," Chuckie said. "Why don't we just use a gate to get out of here?"

"Wow, aren't you Mister Logical?"

"Yeah, I am. Let's move to a bathroom and get quietly and safely home. I realize you haven't tried that at all these past couple of days, but I really recommend it as a good plan." Chuckie had a sarcasm knob, too.

"Which bathroom has the gate in it?" I asked Reader.

"The one we came through. The one they sent you to doesn't."

He started off in the direction they'd come from, and we followed in a rather tight group. We got about fifty yards, and Reader stopped walking. "I think Reynolds' plan is offline."

The bathroom was clearly marked. There were also a lot of mean, nasty-looking men wearing the little plastic earbud things standing around it. That, in and of itself, wouldn't have been the problem. The problem was the guy doing free balloon animals. He was undoubtedly there to draw a crowd, and a crowd he had. Families, some younger folks, even some of your standard business travelers were there. Free was powerful, there was nothing to do, and the guy was running good, engaging patter.

Chuckie cursed quietly. "Okay, so Plan A and Plan B are completely out. Should we call for a floater gate right here?"

"Can't do the crowd control," Gower said. "Richard and Michael don't have implants. Mine was removed when I became Pontifex."

"Implants?" Caroline asked. "I'm confused."

"There are gases natural to Earth that many from American Centaurion can manipulate to create mass hallucinations," I said quickly, while I pondered our limited options. "Used only for crowd control in danger situations. Like this one."

"Ah. I've picked up that American Centaurion isn't . . . normal."

"Oh, in some ways we're very normal," White said genially. "In others, we are quite different, yes."

"Who did you pick that up from?" Chuckie asked Caroline. "And how is it that you came in from Paraguay but are here, instead of Dulles or, as would make sense, considering the people on the plane, Andrews?"

"Now is probably not the time," I pointed out.

"Until we have at least Plans C through G in place, sure it is."

Caroline sighed. "They only allowed the politicians to get off at Andrews. The rest of us had to stay on the plane and disembark here. It's part of our security process—they make us do this practically every time; supposedly it helps us fly under the radar. Sometimes they drop us off first and then take the pols to Andrews. Sometimes we all get off here. Occasionally we all get off at Andrews. Why we have to go through all this rigmarole I don't know, but the senator gave up on trying to win that battle months ago."

"Where's everyone else who was with you?" Chuckie asked, sounding tense.

She shrugged. "They left. They all had their cars here. I thought I had a ride, which is why I didn't go along with one of them."

"And what's made you suspicious of American Centaurion?" He still sounded tense. And ready to read Caroline her rights if her answer was wrong.

Caroline rolled her eyes. "Chuck, because of things *you* told me in school. I pretty much figure everyone's hiding something here and no one's what they seem to be or say they are. It means I'm right, or at least not too surprised, most of the time."

"Oh. Well. Yeah." Chuckie cleared his throat. "Good viewpoint. Carry on."

She laughed and patted his cheek. "Same old Chuck. Thank God."

I was done running through options. "I know what to do."

"And what, exactly, is that?" Reader asked.

I shrugged. "I'm going with what's worked every time before."

White smiled at me. "The crazy, Missus Martini?"

"You know it."

CHAPTER 36

❝I'M GOING TO HATE THIS, AREN'T I?" Chuckie asked.

"Most likely." I dug my iPod and headphones out. "James, what's our status for a limo?"

"Ready to send from the Dome on my order." The Dome Gate was the main gate hub for the entire world, housed in New Mexico, on the original alien crash site. The Ancients' ship's fuel had an impressive afterlife, and it powered the Dome. Most large transfers, like cars, tanks, or planes, went through the Dome. But a gate was a gate, and that meant we could have a car here fast.

"Great. Alter the order. Send a fleet of limos. Have them showing up as soon as possible. Every one needs a Field team in it, ready to defend or attack. Or possibly just drive people to their destinations."

"What the hell are you planning, girlfriend?"

"I'm going to remove the innocent bystanders and divide the bad guys' focus. Someone went to a hell of a lot of trouble to strand this airport, so let's do our best to block their goals. Chop, chop, time's a-wastin'. We need at least a hundred limos." There were a lot of people in the airport. "Anyone who doesn't get passengers needs to help create chaos for the bad guys."

Reader sighed as he pulled out his phone. "I can't believe I'm doing this."

"Paul, as soon as Richard and I get rolling, I want you to use your most effective, diplomatic touch and make sure the security people share that the good folks from American Centaurion have discovered the plight of those stranded at National and are providing limos free of charge for all travelers."

"Why are we doing that?" Gower asked.

"Like a good neighbor, Alpha Centauri is there, remember? Just channel it to our being Good Samaritans, and make it work. As soon as the limos show up, have the Field teams with them do the mind control stuff. I'm going to assume it won't work on our enemies, but hope springs eternal, so tell them to give it a try anyway."

Gower nodded and pulled out his phone, presumably to score some Pontifex-level Field support. White had never rolled without a lot of backup; I wasn't excited to see Gower still acting like he was the Head of Recruitment instead of the religious leader of the entire Earth A-C population. Then again, Christopher had mentioned we were all having trouble adjusting. Then also again, Gower had ACE riding shotgun in his consciousness. Which begged a question.

Gower hung up, so I asked said beggar. "Paul, what's ACE's status right now?"

"He's uncomfortable, but hasn't asked to talk to you. Which," Gower added with a sigh, "usually means ACE approves of whatever it is you have planned."

"ACE is the best."

"ACE?" Caroline asked.

"Later, Caro. Like when we're all somewhere a lot safer than here. We'll do the whole high-level debrief then."

"Kitty, your massive limo invasion might get some of the bystanders out of the way, but even if it removes all of them, we still have a world of hurt eyeballing us," Tim pointed out.

"Mister White and I are going to create a diversion. You all are going to ensure that Chuckie and Caroline get out of here safely. Whether that means you get into the bathroom or take one of the many limos coming, I don't care."

"I care," Chuckie said. "We want to take a gate. I've had enough of our people being delayed, shot at, and driven off the road." Caroline's eyes widened, and she looked, if possible, even more worried than she had been.

Reader nodded. "Great, thanks Gladys." He hung up. "Reynolds, we're going to get a floater gate. It'll show once Kitty rolls her diversion. Whatever it's going to be."

"Kitty, I want to know what your plan is," Chuckie said, in his "won't take no for an answer" voice I knew so well. "And I want to know before you roll it."

I considered my options and tuned my iPod to my Hate This Place playlist. It was getting a lot of use. I scrolled through to Fall

Out Boy's "I Don't Care." By now, I didn't care what anyone thought or wanted. I was sick and tired of being trapped in this crazy town with all these crazy people who were, once again, trying to kill everyone I cared about.

"Richard and I are going to engage the gaggle of goons waiting for us by the bathroom with a gate. Should we successfully get into the bathroom, we're going to use the gate in it to get home."

"And what are you going to do when, as is so much more likely, you don't get into that bathroom?" Chuckie asked, clearly voicing everyone else's concern.

I sighed. "We're going to lure them away from you all and the floater gate. Once you're all off the premises, I guarantee you they'll leave the limos and travelers alone and go after me and Richard."

"Then what?" Tim asked.

White shrugged. "Then we kick butt and take names."

"You are such a natural, Mister White."

"Kitty, that sounds really dangerous," Caroline said nervously. "Isn't your husband going to have a fit?"

"He'll have kittens," Reader said with a snicker. It was nice to see that his ability to be the comic relief wasn't waning, despite his promotion to head man.

"He's used to me. Caro, look, don't panic. Just do what the boys say. Boys, be good, get back to the Embassy."

"And be ready to pull your butt out of the fire," Chuckie added. "Right?"

"Of course right." I didn't expect to need it, but then again, it never hurt to have Plan Z in place, too. "Ready, Mister White?"

"Ready whenever you are, Missus Martini."

"Awesome. Then let's go be the New Avengers again and cause some mayhem."

CHAPTER 37

WHITE AND I STEPPED US AWAY from our group and toward the latest Goon Squad. Yes, what I wanted was right by them and the bathroom, but it was too close. I wandered us off, casually, searching for another option.

"Mister White, when you were Pontifex, you seemed to have an unlimited supply of whatever kind of cash you might need."

"True enough, Missus Martini. What of it?"

"Do you still have that? Sort of like former presidents still have Secret Service details? Still on you and in active use?"

"I do indeed. Again, what of it?"

"I'm shocked you can't guess. Must be three months of us doing absolutely nothing interesting making you rusty." Happily, I spotted an option in the vicinity, within sight and sound of the Goons and everyone else. It was also located by an elevator and an escalator. It was the best we were going to get, so that meant it was perfect. I wanted the many innocents going in a direction away from the Goons, after all.

"My shame knows no bounds. But I still have no idea why my having money would help in this instance. I doubt these men are bribable, at least, not in this situation."

"Pull your wallet out, and get ready to follow my lead." While he did as requested, I put in my headphones, and hit play. I grabbed White's free hand and started off. "Rick, honey, I'd like you to become a crazed philanthropist when I say go. Got it?"

"I do, Kathy, I do." Nice to know he remembered our undercover nicknames from Operation Confusion. I was all over nostalgia for that—we'd kicked butt big time.

We went to the ATM machine I'd spotted. It was one of the ones that wasn't actually attached to any bank and also charged an outrageous transaction fee. Good. No one was going to feel a twinge of guilt, particularly me.

Fall Out Boy were sharing their disdain for others' opinions, and I was revved. Now was as good a time as any. "Ready?" I asked softly. White nodded. "Then here we go." I took a deep breath and screamed. "Oh, my GOD! It's raining money!"

White used hyperspeed and started spraying money out. I grabbed a chunk of bills and did the same, still squealing my head off.

Unsurprisingly, it worked.

People came running from all over the terminal as we sprayed the money in the direction away from the Goon Squad. As they arrived, many squealed along with me and called to their friends and relatives. Others tried to jostle for position. A couple of airport employees actually tried to protect the money. It was chaos, but chaos that was centered far enough away that the Goon Squad would have to leave position to regain a hostage opportunity.

I looked around. Some of the Goons were heading toward the rest of our group. However, I saw a shimmering and watched as the rest of our team disappeared through the floater gate, using hyperspeed. Absolutely no one noticed, other than possibly some of the Goon Squad, at least the ones who slammed into the Security Desk as the gate disappeared.

Not all the Goons were busy explaining why they'd lunged at the desk, though—some were looking like they really wanted in on the money grab. I had no guess as to what the balloon man had been paid, but he'd dropped a balloon mid-giraffe and raced over along with everyone else.

White did something to the cash machine, and it actually began spewing money, too. "Great thinking."

He nodded. "I can now comprehend the plan, and part two has to be the two of us running in the opposite direction."

"I love having the best of the best as my partner. Ready?"

"Yes, the machine shows no signs of slowing." He threw some more money, a big roll, up high and the money fell like big, greenish snowflakes. The entire terminal was filled with people grabbing the cash. We were also getting jostled. Time to go.

I grabbed his hand and we shoved through the crowd. I smiled sweetly at the Goon Squad and we ran for the escalator heading down. We didn't stand there, we ran down the steps, but at human speeds.

We reached the bottom, and I looked back. I didn't have time for a full head count, but it looked as if the majority if not all of the Goons were after us. So far, so very good.

White yanked me, hard, and ran us back up on the up escalator. "Why are we going back up?"

"More of them coming," he replied shortly. I looked behind us. He wasn't kidding. While I'd been checking out the first Squadron of Goons, another plethora had shown up on the lower level.

We crested the top, and I saw a sign for the elevated Metro station. I dragged White along, and we raced up the escalators, Miss Li's "Bourgeois Shangri-La" on my personal soundtrack. I agreed with her—we really did need to get away.

"Why the Metro? I was under the impression the trains weren't running."

"Right. So we can have the Goon Squadron chase us there, and no one's in danger."

"Other than us."

"Well, that was the point, right?"

"I though the point was everyone escaping unharmed."

"Oh, ye of little faith." We ran, pursued by a lot of goons. We were only dodging them because White was controlling when we used a burst of hyperspeed and when we just ran at human normal. "You're really good at altering our speed."

"I've been doing this for decades, Missus Martini. You've been learning for three months. There are some things I'll naturally be more expert at. This is one of them."

"No complaints here." There were no trains in the station and no other travelers, either. I looked around. There were, however, more goons than I could count. "Did we seriously just get roles in *The Matrix Really Reloaded* or something?"

"No. We're just popular."

"Well, at least they're not shooting at us."

"True enough. Possibly because we're trapped."

This was sort of true. We couldn't make it back into the airport because every doorway was blocked by a lot of goon bods. However, that hadn't been my plan anyway.

I jumped onto the tracks, pulling White along. "Which way heads us back toward the Embassy?"

"I believe this one," he said as we took off at human normal. The platform was raised, and neither one of us wanted to risk falling off.

The sun was starting to set, and I realized the day had really gone by quickly—something to be said for your best friends giving birth combined with a lot of intrigue. It also meant we had even fewer hours to figure out what was going on. However, this wasn't my exact concern at the moment, so I decided to table those worries for later, like when we were back at the Embassy.

We kept running, the sound of Clutch's "Electric Worry" revving me so that I didn't feel all sprinted out. Despite years of track training, which said that runners who looked behind them lost their races, I turned around. "No one's following us."

We both slowed down to a decent jog. "Are we still alone?" White asked a few minutes later.

I checked again. "Yeah, we are."

"Does that mean we can stop running now?"

We both heard the sound at the same time.

"Um. No. I think that means we want to run as fast as humanly possible. And by humanly, I really mean alienly, at the best hyperspeed either one of us can manage."

The headlight confirmed to our eyes what our ears had already picked up. The Metro was running again.

CHAPTER 38

NOT ONLY WAS THE TRAIN HEADING RIGHT FOR US, but it was going a lot faster than I figured it should be if it planned to stop for passengers. Then again, I had a feeling the only passengers planned were me and White, and if we became train hood ornaments, that was undoubtedly in the bad guys' playbook under the "happy outcomes to troublesome problems" header.

"Back or forward?" White asked.

"Rock or hard place, you mean." We were still up in the air and it was too far to jump off the tracks and have a hope of landing safely. We also had no time to make the decision. "Jumper" by Third Eye Blind came on my iPod and, along with it, an idea. Worked for me. I did what I'd been doing for the past couple of years. I went for the crazy.

I took off, dragging White with me, heading right for the train. The jump was going to require split second timing as well as a sincere hope that White was up for it. "Do you trust me?" I shouted as we raced toward the train racing right back at us.

"Yes."

"Then jump as high as you can right now!"

We jumped. Our momentum allowed us some lift, but clearly Michael wasn't the only A-C who could jump, because White was the reason we actually landed on the top of the train instead of into its windshield.

"Don't stop!" he shouted, as we continued to run along the top of the train. He didn't have to tell me why—the station had a roof, and we'd be slammed into it if we didn't keep on running in the opposite direction.

"Just like Paris," I called as we sailed over the gaps between cars.

"Let's hope not."

We reached the end of the train fast. Neither one of us hesitated. We jumped off. White pulled me into his arms midair and managed a good wrap and cover. We landed, on his shoulder, I was pretty sure, and rolled.

Once we rolled to a stop I staggered to my feet. "You okay?"

White nodded. "Somewhat."

I reached down and helped him up. "You look a little worse for wear."

"You're not a party yourself, Missus Martini."

"Let's get out of here."

"I agree." White cleared his throat. "Are you, ah, able to manage the hyperspeed?"

"I think so." I took a closer look. "Richard, you're bleeding."

"I am. I'll heal faster than you would have."

"You're holding yourself funny, too."

"I believe my shoulder is dislocated, and I imagine I'll need a stitch or two. Now isn't the time to dwell on my injuries, which are relatively minor, albeit unpleasant. I'll be fine, however, I used quite a bit of energy on that jump."

"Gotcha. If you can, please God, steer, I've got the hyperjuice. At least for a few miles."

"I believe a few is all we'll need."

We took off again. I was tired, too, so I was going at the slow version of hyperspeed, which always sounded like an oxymoron but really existed. We were still going fast, but someone with sharp eyes could have spotted us as blurry images.

White's steering ensured I didn't run us off the tracks. After a short while we were even with the ground, and we got off the tracks. Just in time, as another train barreled past, right after its homicidal brother.

I had no idea where we were, but White seemed to, so we ran along the street, passing cars as if they were standing still. If it wasn't for the fact that I knew he was hurt, I would have possibly enjoyed this. As it was, I wanted to get home, and by home I really meant either my parents' house in Arizona or the Dulce Science Center in New Mexico. Sadly, neither was an option.

We crossed the river. "Oh, look. The Potomac. Let's not go swimming."

"No argument from me, Missus Martini."

We were decently far away from the airport when I felt us slowing down. I was a sprinter, and while I'd spent time on distance, both when I ran track and since joining up with Centaurion Division, I only had so much gas in the tank on the best days. This was absolutely not one of the best days.

We were at a walk in a matter of moments. "I'm sorry, I can't run anymore."

White nodded. "I'm fine with a rest."

I spotted a big parking lot nearby as Go West's "The King of Wishful Thinking" came on my iPod. We walked through it, slowly, stopping several times to rest. The sun set fully. The lighting in this part of the parking lot wasn't impressive. It figured we'd have to stop for a rest in the Creepshow Parking Lot.

"I think we're by a mall." Though there weren't a lot of cars. Then again, for all I knew, whatever had kept the taxis away from National had kept customers away from the mall, too. I looked around but couldn't spot so much as a security golf cart, let alone a police car.

"Good. I hope."

I dropped my iPod back into my purse and dug my phone out. Jeff answered on the first ring. "Where are you?"

"We aren't sure. At a mall near the airport. Richard got hurt."

"WHAT?" Jeff's bellow was always impressive.

White took the phone from me. "Hello, Jeffrey." I could hear Jeff shouting. He sounded beyond freaked. White sighed. "Jeffrey, I'm not the Pontifex anymore. Yes, actually, that does mean that I'm able to risk life and limb. No, she's not hurt, or if she is, she hasn't mentioned it."

"Fine here. You blocked the impact." Apparently Jeff heard me, because I could hear him asking what impact I was talking about. He was merely yelling, not bellowing. "Tell him to stop scaring the baby."

"Your wife would like me to pass along the gentle suggestion that you're likely distressing your child. Ah, well, then, feel free to keep on shouting at me." I couldn't hear Jeff anymore. White was trying not to laugh. "Yes, apology accepted. I understand. It's been a trying couple of days. I believe Kathy was calling for us to get a lift." White gave up and laughed. "Yes, we're undercover again. Not really, if you catch my meaning, however. Yes, thank you. Good."

He handed the phone back to me. "Jeffrey would like to speak to you while they send a team to fetch us."

I dutifully took my phone back. "It wasn't my fault."

"It's never your fault. How badly is he hurt?"

"I don't know. He thinks his shoulder's dislocated, and I see blood, but not a lot. We had to jump off the train tracks."

I could hear Jeff take a deep breath. "Fine. I'm going to get all of this from you once we have you both back and secured."

"Who's coming to get us?"

"People we can trust."

"You're staying at the Embassy, right?"

"Yes. Not that I'm happy about it, let me add, but Reynolds and your mother have both thrown high-level security temper tantrums and are now both insisting that once one of the team returns, he or she isn't allowed out again."

"I guess there were a lot of us running around these past couple of days."

"You in particular. Anyway, sit tight, baby. Your ride will be there shortly."

I was going to ask again who was coming to get us when I heard what sounded like a muted sprinkler system. "Who's coming for us in a chopper? C.I.A. that we like, C.I.A. that we don't like, someone from our team, or an assassin?"

Jeff cursed impressively. "Figure it's an assassin. None of us sent a chopper."

"Okay, hanging up, love you, gotta run. For real. Someone find us and fast." I flung my phone back into my purse, grabbed White's hand, and took off.

"I thought you said you were run out," he said as we headed for one of the buildings.

"It's amazing how people coming to shoot us from the air gives me that ability to go on."

We rounded a corner and were greeted by the sight of a lot of goons. I couldn't be sure if they were the same squad from the airport, but they had the same look, and they certainly had the same earpieces.

"We're officially in a Matrix movie, Mister White. And I'd like to go for popcorn and a Coke."

"Well, we could take in a movie, Missus Martini, but I'm not sure we can do that without endangering everyone inside."

White leaned up against the building. This wasn't a good sign. "Richard, how badly are you hurt? I want the truth, not a reassuring statement."

"I've been better."

I looked around. We were essentially surrounded. I could possibly push myself and get us . . . somewhere. But I was lost around here still, and White seemed to be in need of, at minimum, a lie-down and some pain meds. Stitches and God knew what else were probably going to be a necessity as well.

The goons were moving casually. I wasn't sure why. Maybe they didn't think we'd seen them since we weren't running away. Either that, or, as was more likely, we were completely surrounded, and they could conserve their energy.

"I'm feeling very Alamo-ish again."

"Again?"

"Had that feeling during Operation Fugly. Having it again now."

On cue, White winced at the name. "I shudder to discover what you're going to name this initiative, Missus Martini."

I was about to say that my main goal was to have us survive to be able to name it anything other than Operation Rest In Peace when I saw goon bodies fly. I blinked, and then the last person I'd expected was in front of us.

CHAPTER 39

"I HOPE YOU TWO ARE DONE playing around," Christopher snapped. I was treated to Patented Glare #2. His father got Glare #5. Christopher was a glaring *artist*.

Of course, as I thought about it—while Christopher flung his father's good arm over his shoulder, wrapped his arm around White's waist, and grabbed my hand—it made total sense. He'd been ready to do something similar during Operation Confusion, after all, and had been restrained by my mother, Chuckie, Jeff, and Gower. And Jeff had Jamie to consider and protect. Plus Christopher was as tired of not kicking butt as the rest of us.

"Hang on," he said. Then he took off, at the fastest hyperspeed I'd ever experienced.

We barreled through the bad guys as if they weren't even there. Everything seemed to be standing still, other than my stomach, which shared that I might be enhanced, but this speed was beyond my new limits.

I didn't pass out or barf, but only because it was over fast. We stopped. Sadly, we weren't at the Embassy. We were, however, no longer surrounded by bad guys, so this was a great location as far as I was concerned.

"How'd you find us?" I managed to gasp out, in between retching.

I got Glare #3. Wow, he was really pulling out all the stops to impress. I was sort of sorry Amy was missing this show. I was sure she'd find it hot.

"I'm enhanced, remember? I can see you if I want to. Jeff shouted that my father was hurt, I looked, saw what was wrong and where you were, and left."

"Against a direct order?"

Christopher shrugged. "I was moving too fast to pay attention."

"You mean you were far enough away from Mom or Chuckie that they couldn't grab you."

He grinned. "Something like that, yeah."

"When did my mom get there?"

"Right after Reynolds called her and told her what was going on and what you and my father were doing." He shook his head. "Dad, you shouldn't have gone with James."

White rolled his eyes. "Yes, son, that's exactly what I need right now. A lecture."

"No, you need your shoulder put back in and a couple of stitches."

"Why aren't we at the Embassy? Or anywhere else I'd consider safe?" I looked around. "Where are we?" We were in a doorway near a street corner as near as I could tell. There were cars and stoplights, so street corner somewhere seemed likely. Trees were blocking the street signs, so I had no clue, not that my seeing the street names would have likely told me anything anyway.

"We're on the way home. I could tell you both needed a break from the speed," Christopher said. "We're stopped here just so you two can normalize. Then we're moving again. So try to stop gagging."

"Sorry I'm the delay."

White shook his head. "Son, we're both feeling chagrined and apologetic. Stop snarling."

"That wasn't snarling, Richard. I've seen him snarl. Trust me, it's nastier."

"I feel so guilty," Christopher said, in a tone that indicated quite the opposite. "Dad, clench your teeth."

White did as ordered, and Christopher did some move that, clearly, put White's dislocated shoulder back in. White shouted, then nodded. "Thank you, son." He put his good arm around Christopher and hugged him tightly. "We both appreciate being alive."

Christopher pulled me in for a group hug in a few moments. This was an A-C thing, and I never minded it. I leaned my head against Christopher's shoulder. Not nearly as comfy as Reader's but it'd do in a pinch.

"What now?" I asked finally.

"Now we get home. I don't know if you two are bugged or what, but according to James, the guys after you at the airport are all run off or detained."

"Meaning the large number of men who almost got us this time are new additions to the fold. Wonderful. I don't know who could have bugged us, since we were declared clean before we left the Embassy."

"Reynolds could have," Christopher offered.

"No way in the world." This time I was the one snarling. "I'm officially sick and beyond tired of you and Jeff treating Chuckie like crap or like he's our enemy. I'll walk home alone, too, if I have to hear any more of it from you. Richard came with James and Tim, by the way. They also on your suspect list?"

Christopher sighed. "Fine. I wasn't actually accusing him. And I'm certainly not accusing James or Tim, either. I was pointing out that you haven't been alone since you left the Embassy."

"Let's get back to the Embassy," White said soothingly. "We'll worry about it then."

I looked around. My vision was also enhanced, and I could see a lot farther than I'd been able to before, as well as see well in the dark. And what I saw looked a lot like another Goon Squad on the ground and a helicopter in the air. I looked in the other direction. There were three taxis cruising by. Two of them had clearly been in a fender bender.

"Okay, I'm not mad at you anymore, Christopher."

"Why not?"

"Because they're finding us somehow." I pointed as the goons got closer and the taxis all pulled illegal U-turns. Unsurprisingly, there were no cops nearby.

Christopher put his father's arm over his shoulder again, grabbed White's waist and my hand, and we were off, again at the fastest speeds ever.

This time, we stopped on the steps of the Embassy. I gagged my way to the front door, preferring to toss the cookies inside, where it appeared to be somewhat safer.

We got inside to find Tito waiting for us with a gurney. "I've had medical support brought over from Dulce," he told us.

"Why?" I asked as I helped White get onto the gurney. Unlike every other man I worked with, he didn't whine about it. Meaning he was either really hurt or more mature about things. I voted for both.

"No one wants our forces divided if at all possible."

"Well, we had a phalanx of bad guys after us, so we might want to be prepped for a siege."

Dazzlers appeared on the scene. Sadly, none of them were Dazzlers I knew well, but Tito used these gals frequently. They started fussing around White immediately.

"Pontifex White needs immediate attention," one of them shared with Tito.

"Former Pontifex," White reminded gently. The girl blushed and nodded. "I'm sure it's not as dire as all that."

Tito eyed him critically. "Christopher? I know you looked at him internally. Diagnosis?"

"Muscle tear that's already repairing, but he does need stitches. Heavy bruising, but nothing broken. I put his shoulder back in."

"Now you've gotten the former Pontifex all banged up." Tito shook his head. "Wasn't Paris enough fun for the two of you?"

"No, we've been bored," White replied. "Truly, I'd prefer my lectures after you patch me up."

Tito and his Dazzler assistants took White off to the medical portion of the Embassy. It wasn't as snazzy as what the Science Center had, or even up to what the other bases had, but it was still impressive by human standards.

"You going with your dad?"

Christopher shook his head. "I can monitor him without being in the room."

"Your new talents never cease to amaze me. Or creep me out."

He managed a chuckle. "Nice to know. Let's join the others and see how bad our situation is."

"It's us. I figure we've been at DEFCON Worse for hours if not days."

Christopher sighed. "I hate it when I think you're right. And I definitely think you're right."

CHAPTER 40

WE HEADED FOR THE MAIN MEETING ROOM, which was on the second floor. The Embassy had two elevators, on opposite sides of the building. We took the one that didn't have White and his medical entourage in it.

It was nice to be in an elevator with Christopher and not feel we were being illicit. Enough time had passed and more than enough had happened that we didn't have to act like opposing magnets.

On the other hand, I could tell the adrenaline high that had kept me going was wearing off. I was about to crash, and potentially crash big time. My emotions felt jumbled beyond belief, and I realized that if one person so much as mildly snapped at me, I was going to lose it in a big, embarrassing way.

The elevator doors opened, and before I could blink, someone had picked me up in his arms. Jeff had moved at the really fast hyperspeed, but if I were in sensory deprivation, I'd still know the feel of him holding me.

I buried my face in his neck, wrapped my legs around his waist and my arms around his shoulders, and heaved a shuddering sigh.

"It's okay, baby," he said softly. "I'm here." I whimpered, and he kissed my head. "No one's going to yell at you, or even tease you."

"I'll leave you two alone," Christopher said.

"Thanks. And thanks for getting them."

"They can't neuter us, no matter how hard they try."

Jeff laughed softly. "And God knows, sometimes it feels like everyone's trying. Tell the others what I said when I left still stands."

"Will do." I felt a third hand on my back and figured it was Christopher's. "It's okay, Kitty. My dad will be fine; everyone else is safe, at least currently. We'll figure it out and fix it, just like we always do."

I nodded. He patted my back, then the hand left, and I heard footsteps going away from us.

"If you want to cry, baby, we're alone and we'll be left alone."

I sort of did but sort of didn't. I took a deep breath, let it out slowly, and shook my head. "No. I'd rather not look like a red balloon for the next couple of hours."

Jeff chuckled. "Even when you're crying, you're the sexiest girl in the galaxy."

I snorted. "Wow, you're a great liar, all of a sudden."

"Nope, it's true."

I snuggled more tightly against him. "I love you."

"I love you, too, baby. It'll be okay. I promise. We'll figure out what the hell's going on, stop it, and bring a world of hurt to our enemies. Just like always."

We stood there for a while. I didn't try to figure out how long. I just let myself relax, let myself remember that nothing could hurt me when he was holding me, let my body shudder, my emotions calm, and my mind center.

After a while, I found I was wondering if we could sneak off and have sex before we went to powwow with everyone else. Meaning I was feeling normal again.

Jeff picked it up, of course. "As much as I love your current idea, I don't think we can spare the time."

"I'd suggest a quickie, but I agree with you." I took another deep breath and pulled my face out of his neck. "So, let's figure out what's going on and kick bad guy butt, so we can get back to doing the really important stuff." Hey, I considered orgasms to be vitally important to my well-being.

Jeff grinned and kissed me. It was strong and sensuous, and his lips and tongue owned mine, just like always. The world seemed to be shifting back where it belonged.

He ended our kiss slowly, then let my body slide down his until I was standing. Jeff kept his arm around my shoulders and I kept mine around his waist as we walked slowly to the conference room.

Then we walked past it. "Where are we going?"

"We have so many people here, we're actually meeting in the ballroom."

"Wow. I say again, if they really want to get rid of us, all they have to do is bomb the Embassy right now, and we're no longer anyone's problem."

I'd said this in the ballroom doorway, and apparently I wasn't using my Inside Voice, because I was heard.

Chuckie, in particular, had caught this, and he nodded. "I agree. Which begs an interesting question."

"And that is?"

"If American Centaurion is the actual target, why aren't we dead in a pile of rubble right now?"

I pondered this while Jeff and I found our seats. I had no idea where we'd gotten them, but there were a lot of long tables set up in a big U formation. Almost everyone who was anyone in Centaurion Division was here, though we were missing the new parents and their nearest and dearest. My mother and Kevin Lewis were also in attendance, as were Nurse Carter and Caroline. It looked just the way our living room had yesterday—really crowded—only everyone had a seat, and we looked a lot more official. Or like we were in a Corporate America Training Session.

"Maybe, despite all the evidence, we're not the targets," I offered as I dumped my purse on the floor at my feet.

"If so, I'd like to know who is," Chuckie said. "Desperately."

"I'd like to know how they were finding Kitty and my father so easily," Christopher said. "Since all the bugs on Kitty were removed."

I thought about it. "Whoever's in charge has some serious pull with the transportation in this area."

"So?" Christopher snapped. I saw Jeff flash him a warning look. "I mean, what does that have to do with how they're finding you?" Christopher asked, far more nicely than I figured he felt.

"There are traffic cameras all over the place, right?"

Chuckie nodded. "I see where you're going, and yes, that makes sense. White, you said you stopped and they found you, correct?"

"Correct."

"We were at a corner with a stoplight," I added.

"Then traffic cameras would have spotted you, especially if they were monitoring for people to appear out of thin air." Chuckie looked grim. "It takes real pull to do what's been done and not show up on my radar or Angela's."

My mom nodded, looking as grim as Chuckie. "I think we're looking at either a government agency like the C.I.A., Homeland Security, or the F.B.I, or we're looking at a very high-level politician."

"The President?" I asked.

"I hope not," Mom said.

Chuckie shook his head. "It's out of character." I saw Mom relax. It was nice to know I wasn't the only one who considered Chuckie's theories to be sound. "However, we have a couple of other Cabinet members who I wouldn't put it past."

"Any politician with the right pull could manage it," Kevin said, from behind Mom. "Bribery and blackmail work most of the time, and power's a strong motivator."

"We have two who made the pilgrimage here earlier today, Villanova and Whitmore."

"What were the Chief Aide to the Secretary of State and the Secretary of Transportation doing here?" Mom asked in her bordering-on-enraged tone.

As we brought the rest of the room up to speed on our visit from the Cabal of Evil, Tito came in, White with him. He looked fine. A-Cs worked and healed fast. Tim spoke quietly to them, presumably bringing them up to speed on the nowhere we were with things.

"Think it's either one of them?" Kevin asked Mom.

"Could be. But we'll need a hell of a lot of hard evidence to convince the President."

Despite our lack of information, I could feel ideas starting to form in my mind. Scoring a Subway Party Platter was on the list—I hadn't eaten in what seemed like forever, albeit it was only this morning, however many hours ago that had really been.

"What's the possibility of eating while we think?"

Pierre waved his hand. "Already handled, darling. Sustenance coming in from Dulce, under armed guard. Should be here shortly."

"You're a god, Pierre. So, how far have you guys gotten on everything while Richard and I were running around?"

"Not far," Chuckie said. "There were some . . . issues at the Embassy while we were gone."

That's right, White had said Christopher was handling something. I looked at him. "What happened?" I looked around again. Two people in particular were missing. "Where are Dad and Jamie?"

CHAPTER 41

"**S**AFE," MOM REPLIED. I FELT MY BODY RELAX. "They're at the Pontifex's residence."

"Why?"

"In addition to everything else," Christopher shared, "we had a gas leak scare at the Irish Embassy, right after you left for the hospital. Everyone within a five-block radius was being advised to leave the premises, just in case. We cleared all personnel just to be safe. Once we got the all-clear, it seemed wiser to leave nonessential personnel there for the time being."

Kevin nodded. "Denise and our kids are over there, too. Along with some P.T.C.U. operatives, three Centaurion Division agent teams, Naomi and Abigail, and Gladys."

"Gladys is helping babysit Jamie, Raymond, and Rachel? What have I missed?" The Lewis kids tended toward the angelic side of the house, and my dad and Denise should have been plenty to take care of Jamie. With Naomi and Abigail along, that should have meant Jamie was the happiest of little campers, not in need of the overall Head of Security to keep her in line.

I was treated to Glare #2. "I didn't want to discover the gas leak was a fake to make us lower our guard, particularly the guard on Jamie," Christopher snapped.

"Fine, fine, no argument, just curious." Another thought occurred. "You cleared out Walter?" I wondered how much of a fight he'd put up about leaving his post and figured a lot.

"Not so much." Christopher's expression told me it had indeed been a big, stressful argument. "Walter insisted on staying with the people from the gas company. Gladys agreed." A fight Christopher had lost. We all loved losing, so I didn't have to guess about his opinion on this outcome, though him switching to Glare #4 was something of a clue.

"Well, he's dedicated." Walter, at least, was doing a great job. One whole person in our Embassy had transitioned without major incident. We probably should award Walter a medal.

"I also had to field a lot of questions from most of our Embassy neighbors, the people working on the gas leak, and anyone else who could call or come by." Christopher clearly hadn't enjoyed this, if his tone and expression were any indication. Or he'd just eaten a lemon. It was interesting to see this look combined with Glare #5.

"Why? Did everyone really get to see me taking a dip in the Potomac?"

"Both of us, actually," Jeff said.

Serene nodded. "Yes, I'm sorry, Kitty. We couldn't hide it, there were too many witnesses."

"Oh, well. Maybe it'll make all our Embassy neighbors hate us a little less. Or at least feel sorry enough to forgive us for whatever else we'll screw up next." I looked at Nurse Carter. "But enough of that. I've spent well over a year and a half watching Paraguay pop up again and again and being told, every time I ask, that it's on a need to know and I don't."

"It is classified, and you're not cleared for it," Mom said with a resigned sigh.

"I've spent the past two days with people trying to kill me and all manner of weird going on. Frankly, if anyone deserves to know what the hell is going on with Paraguay, it's me." I stood up. "However, fine and dandy, you all don't want to tell me, for whatever reason. So, no worries. Instead of you telling me, I'll tell you. You can correct me when I'm wrong, but I'm pretty sure I'm right."

Mom leaned her head on her hand. "Go to town, kitten." I recognized the expression on her face. I decided not to share that, as far as I could tell, my mother was testing me. Again. Oh, well, she liked to ensure the skills were kept up to snuff. And this way, she could legitimately say that neither she, Kevin, nor Chuckie had told me anything.

I looked at Nurse Carter. "You're supposedly Paraguay Secret Police." She nodded. "And you're investigating what's happening to your poorest citizens." Another nod. "And yet, your intel runs from extremely sketchy to downright wrong, you're working as a real nurse, and you didn't kill me or anyone else when you had the chance."

She looked uncomfortable. "What are you driving at?"

"You're no more Secret Police than I am." Reader coughed. "Okay, scratch that. I'm more Secret Police than you are. What I really think you are is someone who lost a loved one to the supersoldier program I freaking know some lunatic's running in the middle of the Chaco."

Her mouth dropped open, but she snapped it shut. "You're wrong."

Chuckie was trying not to laugh. Mom had an expression I was really used to on her face—her "you're so busted, but please, do continue to dig your hole deeper" look. It was one of her classics, honed to perfection throughout the years.

"What you are is someone who has some skills and followed some leads, and you're in way, way over your head. Your government isn't going to ask for you back, because your government isn't aware that you're here undercover doing the work they aren't interested in doing. Your government is either trying to handle this on their own or, very possibly, approves of the supersoldier plan and is using *Aliens* as a blueprint."

"That was a good movie," Tim commented. "But the monsters weren't controllable. What would make anyone think a superbeing could be controlled?"

"I have one word for you: Mephistopheles. I also point to yesterday's odd superbeing cluster right there in the Chaco again and say trust me on this one. So, Nurse Carter, what's your take? Is your government fully behind the idea of Aliens: The Next Generation?"

"Not everyone in the government," she said quietly.

"Just like here. How nice, we have something in common. So, since you knew who he was, what's the story on my 'uncle,' Peter the Dingo Dog?"

"Dingo Dog?" Mom stared at me, then her head snapped toward Nurse Carter. "Are you saying that the man who tried to kill Kitty was the Dingo?"

Nurse Carter nodded. "Yes."

"Just who is the Dingo? I mean, I've heard some wacky names in my time, but his takes the prize."

"He's an assassin," Mom said.

"Him trying to kill me all day yesterday, and telling me he was hired to do so, were sort of a tip-off for that one, Mom. I meant, why does he have that particular nickname, and why are you so much more freaked now than you were before you heard his name? Oh, and either he was faking his voice or he's not from Australia."

Mom heaved a sigh. "He's not. No one is sure where he's originally from. We have no pictures of him. Peter Kasperoff might not
be his real name, but most sources say he's from the former Eastern
Bloc somewhere, most likely KGB trained. He got the nickname
because he's like a vicious wild dog."

"A loyal dog," Nurse Carter added.

"A loyal dog you knew, accurately, when you don't have any of
your other facts really straight. So, what's your connection to the
Dingo?"

Nurse Carter shook her head. "There is a dossier on him. I was
able to read it before—" She stopped herself and slammed her
mouth shut.

"Look, either we're all friends here or we're going to have to
lock you away. Right now, whoever you want avenged or whatever
wrongs you want to right, we're probably your best hope for achiev-
ing that. So spill it."

Chuckie cleared his throat. "Right now, you're in deep trouble.
Prove yourself helpful, and I can make all those troubles disappear.
Refuse to cooperate, and I'll have to show you that the C.I.A. really
is staffed with the nastiest people on the planet."

I didn't actually think Chuckie was going to take Nurse Carter
away to torture her in unspeakable ways, but from the way she
blanched, it was clear she did. She nodded slowly. "He killed the
doctor at my hospital who asked too many questions."

"You witnessed this?" Chuckie asked.

"Yes."

"Then how is it you're alive? I mean, he told me he didn't like
to kill pretty girls or babies, and you're not barking, but if you could
identify him, why let you live?"

Nurse Carter swallowed and looked down. "When the first gunshots came, I and two other nurses, we hid with the dead bodies in
our morgue. He and his partner killed everyone. They didn't find us.
The authorities said it was terrorists. But we heard them, before we
hid ourselves, when they were talking to Doctor Rijos. They wanted
information he had on the . . . project. He refused to tell them where
it was. So they . . . they killed everyone."

"So no one could pass the information along," Chuckie said.
"Thorough and effective, albeit overkill. And sloppy."

"Sloppy?" Christopher asked.

"Three women escaped," Chuckie said calmly. "If you're supposed to kill everyone, not checking the morgue is sloppy work."

"You do that kind of work?" Nurse Carter asked, sounding suspicious and afraid.

"No," Mom answered. "Our jobs are to stop people from doing that kind of work."

"And," I reminded everyone, "we now have less than a day to do it."

CHAPTER 42

CHUCKIE SMILED AT ME. "Oh, I'd like Nurse Carter here to explain how she survived, however."

"I just did," she said.

Chuckie shook his head. "I've read the file on the Dingo. He isn't sloppy. Leaving not one, not two, but three nurses alive by not checking the morgue is sloppy. I guarantee he checked. So either you're lying, or you're his accomplice and you're here to infiltrate us."

She looked like she was going to argue. Chuckie shook his head again. "I'm a very patient man. You've used up all the patience I'm willing to spare. Tell us the truth, the whole truth, or so help me God, I'll make you wish the Dingo *had* killed you."

His expression was calm, but his eyes were icy. She took the hint. "His partner was injured, badly, by some local police who were there when they started killing everyone. When they found us hiding, I offered to help him. We patched him up, and they let us go."

"Why?" Mom asked. "That seems kind, but stupid."

"I don't know. He . . . he said it cleared his debt."

"That makes sense." Everyone looked at me. "Oh, come on! This is why he passed information to me and made me his next of kin. We'd saved his life, and his partner's life, after they'd tried to kill us. He couldn't let me live, right, because we had the upper hand. But he could give me what he knew I wanted, which was who hired them and who they were going after. Speaking of which, any progress?"

"It was heavily encrypted," Serene said. "But we broke it and

completed the decipher just before I needed to come over here."
She didn't look happy. She did, however, look a lot less like, as
Reader put it, our Ditz in Residence and a lot more like one of
Centaurion Division's key personnel. It was nice to see that the
promotion had been good for her. So another one of us was blos-
soming in their new role, even under pressure; it was a small vic-
tory, but I was willing to take it.

"And?"

Serene shook her head. "One sentence: The quick brown fox
jumps over the lazy dog."

There was dead silence. "That was it?" Chuckie asked finally,
clearly voicing everyone else's thoughts.

"The disk was corrupted, most likely from the water, but so far
as we can determine, there was only that one sentence on it." Serene
clearly felt she was failing at her job. There was far too much of that
going around right now.

"What the hell does that mean?" Jeff asked.

Mom's brow was furrowed. "It's the first line they teach you
when you're learning to type. At least, it was. Who knows how you
learn these days."

"It's still used, Mom. I learned it." The A-Cs and half of the
humans looked really confused. It was easy to tell who was a self-
taught typist in the room and who wasn't, not that I thought this was
going to help us in even the smallest way. "It's a pangram—it uses
every letter of the alphabet. You type it so you learn where every
letter is on the keyboard."

"We intercepted a typing tutorial?" Reader sounded less than
thrilled.

"It was handed to me, and the Dingo Dog didn't want anyone
else to know I had it."

"Maybe he gave it to you to confuse you," Kevin suggested.

"No," Tim said. "If that were his goal, he could have just told
Kitty whatever he wanted. I was in the helicopter, and we were
watching. I never saw him pass that to her, so he did it so no one
else would know." Hughes, Walker, and Jerry all nodded their
agreement.

"So that means it's a message." Chuckie sounded as though he
was heading for a migraine. I hated that, because it always indicated we were clueless, and I *really* hated that.

Something else was bugging me. "Serene, you said this line was
encrypted?"

"Yes. A very complex encryption. It also had to be translated."

"Excuse me?"

She shrugged. "The original sentence was in Russian, written in Cyrillic. We had to have Moscow Base do translations."

"And you're sure those were a hundred percent correct?" Christopher asked.

Serene nodded. "Yes, it was checked and verified at least ten times. Mostly because no one at Moscow Base could believe this was the entire message."

"It means something to someone. And it was important enough to encrypt. Or else the Dingo Dog really feels learning to type is a high-priority assignment." I sighed. "Well, at least we know something. And that he's loyal. Or weird. Or both." Probably both. "He also said that he wasn't one of the guys in the taxis, and since he was already 'dead' when I saw them last, he was likely telling the truth."

"Did he give you anything on them?" Chuckie asked.

"He said they were amateurs and didn't want to harm the merchandise." I saw a lot of stressed out expressions. "I know. That doesn't really give us much help at all."

"This is the most information we've had, girlfriend," Reader reminded me. "But we're no closer."

"Maybe we are. I heard Peter and his partner talking—well, shouting—in a foreign tongue right before we went into the Potomac. I guarantee that wherever Peter's from, his partner is from there, too. Considering Serene just said this fab message came out in Russian, let's figure this confirms Mom's intel that they're from somewhere in the former Soviet Bloc."

"We couldn't determine country of origin," Serene said. "We tried, in case we were translating incorrectly. But the sentence is too short to show any kind of regional inflection."

"And it's an American sentence, which would mask it even more."

Serene looked down. "I'm sorry. I'm better with explosives. Maybe . . . maybe Christopher should take a look. In case I've . . . missed something." I saw the confidence she'd been showing only minutes earlier start to fade away. I didn't want that to happen, but I had no idea what to do or say, especially if Christopher agreed with her.

I looked over just in time to see Jeff shake his head almost imperceptibly at Christopher. "No," Christopher said quickly. "You're doing a great job, Serene. This transition's been hard on everyone. But I don't think I'd get more out of this than you and the entire Imageering team have."

Serene looked up and gave him a brave little smile, but she did look a bit more like she had earlier. I decided giving Serene a Girl Power lecture, suggesting we just call it a day and deal with whatever tomorrow night, or asking that we all get our old jobs back would probably be tactless, stupid, and useless, respectively. We needed to think, ergo, I needed to talk.

I forged on. "Based on everything we know, Peter and his partner are either related or bestest buds, or maybe the only two survivors from their village. But Peter cares enough about his partner to have let Nurse Carter live. We saved both of them, remember." Which reminded me. "Jeff, what's the story on Peter's body?"

"It was gone when we got there." Jeff sounded angry and worried. "Nurse Carter opened every freezer, no Dingo. Or his partner, but we knew that already, since he never made it inside."

"No." Tim shook his head. "He made it inside. All of Airborne was there, we watched. The agent teams assigned might have been turned away by what they thought were D.C. cops, but I guarantee both prisoners were checked into the hospital." The three flyboys nodded their agreement again.

"Only one prisoner came in," Nurse Carter stated for the official record. "Believe me, I looked for the Dingo's partner. I never found him, and I would recognize him. All the records I saw indicated one prisoner, only, as well."

I looked at Chuckie. "So we can be absolutely positive the C.I.A. is involved."

CHAPTER 43

CHUCKIE GAVE ME A LONG LOOK. "Not that I'm arguing, but how do you figure? Right now, it could be any of the Alphabet Agencies."

"True, but we both know this sounds more like the C.I.A.'s style. Don't they have that death drug?"

"That's the movies."

"*You* were the one who told me about the death drug, when we were in high school, and *you* said it was real."

"Maybe I was misinformed."

"Right." I stared him down. He stared back. I narrowed my eyes. He tried not to laugh. This earned a quiet growl from Jeff. "Time's wasting," I said finally.

Chuckie sighed. "True enough. Yes, we have such a drug, and yes, field agents use it on a somewhat frequent basis, and yes, I'm *not* supposed to acknowledge that we have it, let alone to a room full of people. Happy?"

"Relieved. Would have hated to have your perfect conspiracy record blemished."

"Near perfect," he correct.

"Right, you were wrong about where Hoffa was buried. Where *is*—"

"*If* you could go on with the situation at hand," Mom snapped.

"Fine, fine. So, the C.I.A. took the Dingo Dog's partner and altered the records so it appears that he was never there. He was hurt but not that badly, so I think we can safely assume he's alive. The question is, did they use the death drug on the Dingo, or did they kill him for real and just remove his body to tidy up?"

"No idea," Jeff said.

"I did check him, and he seemed legitimately dead," Nurse Carter said.

Chuckie shook his head. "If they did use the drug, it's incredibly effective. No insult to your skills as a nurse intended, but it's unlikely you'd have realized it was a fake unless you knew the exact signs to look for."

"And I don't," Nurse Carter admitted. "So we don't know if he was really dead or not."

Len nodded. "We all searched, and Mister Joel Oliver took a lot of pictures, but there was no way to verify if they took a real dead body or a live one."

"All the other bodies were there," Kyle added. "Only his was missing."

"Okay, so we're at a semi-dead end until we go through what he left for me as next of kin and figure out what the message means. So, time to get some other information. Mom, Chuckie, the super-soldier project—it's clearly being run out of Paraguay. I know what happened yesterday is a part of it. But is the superbeing formation we had in Paris a scant three months ago part of it, or is it a different set of lunatics trying to create the ultimate killing machines?"

Chuckie looked at Mom. Mom gave him the "oh what the hell" sign. He looked back to me. "Based on information we gained during the infiltration—"

"You mean Operation Confusion, right?"

Everyone I could see *other* than Chuckie winced. He just laughed. "Yes, that one. Anyway, based on what we were able to ferret out, there is a program, but whether or not Paris was merely part of it or is another initiative, we don't know yet. Someone very high up in the government is in charge."

"How high?"

"So high we can't actually get many details. Any time any team goes to Paraguay to investigate, the locations we've identified as having the project are wiped clean."

I looked at Caroline. "That's what your senator's doing down there all the time, isn't it? His committees are trying to catch these people, or at least a trace of them."

She nodded. "So far, just as Chuck said, nothing."

I remembered something. "Chuckie, what happened to the picture we took from Nurse Carter?"

"I have it here." He pulled it out of his inner suit pocket. "Is now the time?"

"Yes, it is."

Chuckie nodded, turned in his chair so he was looking directly at Caroline, shot Jeff a look that, to me, clearly said "monitor emotions" and put the picture down in front of her. "Who are the people in this photo?" His tone was very friendly.

Caroline looked at it. "Well, that's most, though not all, of the team on the last few missions to Paraguay."

"Who are the men behind you?" Chuckie kept his tone friendly. "I recognize most of the others, but we need to identify anyone who might be in danger."

"The one nearest to me is my friend Pete." She looked up at me. "He was the one who was supposed to pick me up from the airport. I still don't know why he hasn't answered his phone."

I managed not to say anything I knew Chuckie didn't want me to. "Who's the dude next to Pete?"

"His cousin, Vic."

"As in Victor?" Chuckie asked. She nodded. "What are their last names?"

"Keller."

"How long have you and Pete been dating?" Chuckie asked.

"Oh, we're not. Not really." Caroline sighed. "He's older than me, by a lot. I know he likes me, but I'm not sure that I want to date someone in his line of work."

"What is his line of work?" Chuckie asked. I was amazed at how calm and conversational he sounded.

"He and Vic work for Titan."

"That's the large security firm that contracts with the government, right, Titan Security?" Chuckie asked, still sounding as though they were catching up on friends from college.

"Yeah. I know it's supposed to make you feel more secure if your guy's always packing heat, but it sort of freaks me out. I mean, we need it when we're down in Paraguay. There's lots going on, and having Pete and Vic with us keeps everyone safe."

"Is that how you met him?" I asked. "Because he was assigned to your protection detail?"

"Yeah. Titan has the contract to cover us when we're in South America. The senator and I have gone down so often that Titan assigned a permanent team to us."

"Has he been to your apartment?"

Caroline blushed. "Yes, but not for anything illicit. He's taken me out several times, and he always picks me up at home."

My memory nudged. "You said he was with an Embassy. How

can he be working for Titan and be attached to an Embassy at the same time?"

"Vic's wife is part of the diplomatic mission from Paraguay. Pete and Vic are really close, so they both house with the Embassy. They got some special approval to do that, I don't know from where. But Senator McMillan said it looked legit."

"So he checked their credentials?" Chuckie asked.

Caroline nodded. "He doesn't like them, I don't think. I know he doesn't like that Pete's taken me out. Though he does his best to hide it." She sighed. "Pete's supposedly my date for the President's Ball tomorrow. Not that I have any idea if that's still on, either the date or the Ball." She laughed half-heartedly. "Or if you're even going to let me leave your Embassy."

Chuckie looked at Jeff. "She's clean," Jeff said. "Telling the truth as she knows it." Chuckie nodded like he wasn't surprised, which, all scary things considered, was a relief.

"Why would I lie to you about anything?" Caroline asked, sounding completely shocked. "Kit-Kat's one of my best friends, and so is Chuck. You guys saved me from whatever's going on." She looked at me. "What *is* going on?"

"Caro, the President's Ball is still on. You, however, are only going under full guard."

"Why? Not that I'm complaining, not after this afternoon, but I'm confused."

"You didn't ask who took this picture or where we got it from," Chuckie said.

She shrugged. "I figured you'd gotten it from Esteban. I know you work with him frequently; he's mentioned it because he knows we're friends."

"Esteban Cantu?" Chuckie asked. "As in the head of the C.I.A.'s Antiterrorism unit?"

"Yeah. You *do* know him, right, Chuck?" Caroline sounded worried.

"Oh, I know him all right." Chuckie looked at me. "Well, now we know."

"Now we know what?" Christopher asked.

I sighed. "Now we know who's in charge of Operation Assassination."

CHAPTER 44

ON CUE, EVERYONE WINCED, except Chuckie, who was too busy thinking, and Caroline, who looked as if she were considering making confusion an art form. I couldn't blame her.

I was thinking, too, of course. So I kept on talking. "So, Caro, didn't it seem weird to you that Pete has an odd accent?"

"No. He sounds like everyone else from Paraguay." She jerked. "Wait a minute, how did you know he had an accent?"

"Well, I could say I guessed, but I've actually met him. And we didn't get that picture from Esteban Cantu. We got it from Nurse Carter here."

Caroline looked at her. "I've never seen her before. How did she get our picture?"

"Doctor Rijos had it in his file," Nurse Carter said. "I put it in my purse. The Dingo did not search us."

"We don't have a Doctor Rijos attached to our mission," Caroline said.

"Nope, you probably don't." I looked at Michael. "Be prepared. She's normally fairly cool under pressure but . . ."

He nodded. "Happy to help." I was sure he was. Michael was clearly doing his best to stake his claim on Caroline early.

"What are you expecting me to freak about, Kit-Kat? I think I've handled everything pretty damn well."

"You have." I took a deep breath. "Caro, here's the thing. Your sorta boyfriend?" She nodded. "He's the guy we were talking about before. Peter Kasperoff, aka the Dingo. As in, the dude who tried to off me in several ways yesterday, assisted by his cousin, Surly Vic.

They're now presumed dead or back under C.I.A. and Titan Security control."

She stared at me. She stared some more. No one spoke. Caroline stared some more. She finally opened her mouth. "You're saying that the people who were hired to protect us, and that us includes a number of prominent and influential politicians, are actually assassins?"

"Pretty much."

"And I was going to go to the President's Ball with an infamous assassin?"

"You got it."

She looked around. "And no one in this room seems overly surprised."

"We're kind of used to it. Welcome to My Super Secret Life, where people try to kill us on a regular basis, and we thwart bad-guy schemes for breakfast. We're almost like a reality show, only without the alcohol and hot tubs."

Her mouth went to a straight line. "I need someone to check on Senator McMillan and his wife, right now!" I was so proud. She was going to save the freak out I knew would be coming for later. That was my Caro Syrup.

"Already on it," Mom said approvingly. Apparently, Caroline was her favorite daughter. My memory nudged me again, harder.

"Caro, Peter seemed to be under the impression you were my sister."

"I am."

"I mean real, as in blood, not as in sorority. Any guess as to why?"

She grimaced. "Not really. I mean, I have our sorority composite picture up and he's asked about it." She blinked. "Oh."

"Oh?"

"He asked me about you. He point-blank asked me if my sister was attached to American Centaurion. I said yes, because you are. I didn't say you weren't my real sister. I didn't say that you *were*, either, but I guess he assumed."

"Or he was having a joke."

Chuckie's head snapped to me. "Explain that."

I rolled my eyes. "Peter the Dingo Dog seems like a very interesting person. He clearly has a strong attachment to his cousin." Like Jeff and Christopher had, but I didn't think they'd appreciate me making that comparison out loud. "To the point that he'll do things against his best interests if it's for someone he perceives as having done either of them a true service."

"Fine, but the joke?" Chuckie seemed rather intent.

"Why are you haranguing her on this point?" Jeff asked, sounding protective.

Chuckie made the exasperation sound. "She's making profiling statements. We have a good file on the Dingo, but not good enough. We have three people in this room who have all interacted with him and lived. One of those people has shown an amazing ability to think like the people we're trying to stop. Now, can Kitty answer my damn question?"

"Fine, fine," Jeff muttered.

I leaned down. "I'm fine now," I whispered to him. "You can relax." I heard his stomach grumble. "And hopefully food will be here soon."

As I said this, agents appeared with a full spread. A buffet table was set up and everyone filed through to get food. I looked at the food. I looked again. "Um, what's all this?" There was nothing on the buffet I could recognize as edible.

"National specialties," Pierre said, as he fussed around the display and sent some of the agents off for things he felt were missing.

"What nation?"

"Your neighbors'." Pierre shook his head. "We need to blend a tad more effectively, darling, and your kitchen staff is, what, actually several thousand miles away? Today that was a blessing, but otherwise we need a better system for entertaining. However, until such time as we can achieve it, I want us all getting used to eating the foods of those countries near and dear to us."

"By near and dear you mean on our block?"

"That and the surrounding neighborhoods. The Gas Leak District, so to speak."

I felt I should recognize *something* on this table, but so far, every dish was a mystery. I wanted to ask what everything was, but I could tell Chuckie wasn't happy with the delay, so I made sure to stand next to him in the food line and instead of asking him to tell me what I was eating, I took one for the team. "You want me to give you my joke theory now or wait?"

"Now. We don't have time to wait."

I heard Reader groan. His view was that the moment I gave my theories, we had no time to eat. But since the main action was set for tomorrow night, I figured we could risk it. "Works for me. Okay,

Peter called me Miss Katt. I know he knew I was married. He was calling me Miss Katt for a reason, and I think it's because he's seen my picture at Caroline's place and has thought of me, therefore, as Katherine Katt."

"Kitty," Caroline, who was with us, clearly intending to stay as near to Chuckie as possible, said as she loaded some food onto her plate without grimace or hesitation. "I have the fancy-shmancy composite picture, the big one. It has everyone's names, nicknames, and pledge names on it. He commented on you being called Kitty Katt. He thought it was funny."

"So he was in Caro's apartment basically casing her life. Great. And cats have nine lives, and he'd been trying to kill me all day and I'd evaded it. I think he was getting a triple, at least, out of the joke."

Chuckie nodded slowly. "That kind of word play, especially the layers of it, indicates a high intelligence."

"Maybe more than one kind of intelligence."

Chuckie raised his eyebrow. "How do you mean?"

"Maybe Peter the Dingo Dog knows that I've foiled some other assassination attempts."

"Extra layers to the nine lives joke. I can see it. We need to have Caroline's apartment searched and watched."

"I agree. What the heck is that?"

"Pasta of some kind," Jeff said as he put an extra helping of the supposed pasta onto his plate. "We already assigned teams to Caroline's place, Reynolds."

"It doesn't look like pasta."

"It looks better than that tapeworm dish Alexander said was a delicacy from 'home.' Anyway, we sent teams to check it out," Jeff said, piling what might have been squid, might have been octopus, or might have been really thick weeds onto his plate.

"What are they searching for?" Mister Joel Oliver said as he cheerfully shoved in with us.

"None of your business," Jeff growled.

Caroline looked at Oliver. "I know you. Mister Joel Oliver, right? The investigative reporter?"

Oliver nodded. "I don't believe I've had the pleasure of meeting you in person, Miss Chase."

"You haven't. I've seen your picture and byline. The senator reads every article you write."

I looked up at Chuckie. "He knows, doesn't he? And by knows, I mean knows everything."

Chuckie nodded. "He's from Arizona. The higher-level politicians with Centaurion bases in their states know some to all about what's going on."

Caroline cleared her throat. "What, really, *is* going on?"

I looked at my plate while I pondered how to answer her question. I had a tiny bit of everything on it. No worries, if anything actually tasted better than vile, I could go back for seconds. "I wish something normal, like steak or macaroni and cheese, was going on," I muttered.

"Kit-Kat, I'd really like an answer."

I looked up at Jeff and Chuckie. They both had resigned looks on their faces. Oliver cleared his throat. "May I?"

"Yes," Chuckie said quickly. I almost asked why, then it dawned on me that if Oliver gave away classified information, Chuckie could say he was wrong, but if I did it, it would be kind of damning. Besides, maybe he'd break it to her gently.

Oliver smiled. "Miss Chase, about half the people, or more, in this room are originally from one of the planets in the Alpha Centauri system, or their parents were. Honestly, most in the room are Earth-born, and all born here are considered American citizens with all the rights and privileges thereof. American Centaurion is the name given to the several tens of thousands of alien refugees who now live among us."

Or, you know, he could just blurt it all out and let the chips fall where they may.

CHAPTER 45

CAROLINE STARED AT ME. "You married a space alien?" she asked finally.

I gave her a bright smile. "Jeff was born on Earth. He's a legal U.S. resident with all the rights thereof. And he's a prince." Hey, it had mattered to my other sorority sisters.

Caroline shook her head. "You never change."

"I didn't date aliens before!"

"Or royalty. However, if there was a way to work in the bizarre naturally, you were always our go-to girl." Caroline took a long look at Jeff, then slowly turned around and scanned the room. "Chuck?" she said finally.

"Yes?"

"You're not an alien, right?"

"Correct."

"And neither is Kit-Kat, right?"

"Right." Chuckie shot me a worried glance. I checked Jeff's expression. He was trying not to laugh.

Caroline's eyes narrowed. "But Michael is, isn't he?"

"Yes." I gave up and gave in. "You want me to point out the, ah, American Centaurions from the regular U.S. citizens?"

She shook her head. "Nope."

I was kind of shocked. "Why not?"

Caroline grinned. "Jelly Bean and Twix told me about your wedding, and they mentioned how incredibly good-looking your husband's entire extended family was. I think I can spot them on my own."

"I think my feelings should be hurt," Chuckie said with a laugh.

Caroline shook her head. "Oh, no, Chuck. Don't feel like that at all. You're still considered our sorority's most eligible bachelor." Chuckie looked shocked and slightly embarrassed. Caroline, however, was still scanning the room. "The model, James. Is he an alien?"

"Nope, merely good-looking enough to pass."

"His boyfriend is, though, right? And that's Michael's older brother?"

"Yes. You're handling this really well." Better than Amy had, as I thought about it, and Amy had heard all of Chuckie's theories at least as much as Caroline had.

Caroline grinned. "I work in D.C. You're crazy if you think this is the most bizarre thing going on around here." She laughed at my expression. "Unlike your friends from high school, or even most of our sisters, I not only listened to Chuck's theories, I never discounted them. It's part of how I got the job with the senator."

"Because you're a conspiracy theorist?"

She snorted. "No, silly. Because Chuck's always right. You took him seriously, so I took him seriously. And it helped a lot. I sounded like I was already an insider when I interviewed."

Jeff groaned. "Great. Another one who thinks you walk on water."

Chuckie laughed. "It makes a refreshing change."

Caroline shrugged. "Let's eat and figure out how to stop these creeps from hurting anyone else."

"I like where your head's at." Went back to our seats. I put my plate down and decided I could wait a bit before diving in.

I went to Mom first. "Do we have enough to take Cantu in for questioning?"

She shook her head. "Hardly. That Caroline thinks he took the picture with people only you and a completely unreliable source say shows the Dingo in it is even less concrete information than what you normally come up with. Charles and I need hard, solid proof before we move against Cantu or anyone else politically connected. Without it we might as well quit before they fire us."

"I didn't think spies got fired."

"True. We get burned. Or killed. I'd like to avoid both choices."

"No argument here."

"Go eat the dinner you whined for."

"Yes, Mom."

I contemplated my plate and decided I could wait just a little longer. I trotted over to Chuckie instead, reached into his pocket, and pulled out the picture. "Since everyone knows, other than Nurse Carter, who likely suspects, let's save ourselves a lot of pain." I handed the picture to Christopher. "Time to show off the skills."

He sighed. "Can I eat first? I'm hungry."

"You can't eat and paw a picture at the same time?"

"I can. However, I'd prefer to do it on a full stomach. The speed I had to go to get you and my father to safety demands rest and fuel."

"Wimp." Though, he was eating the food, so clearly, he was a braver cuisine enthusiast than I was.

I sat down and gingerly tried my food. Most of it was actually pretty good, but from the way everyone else was chowing down, you'd have thought they were either starving, international gourmands, or ate these foods every day. I voted for starving. I was, which was why I was overcoming my current food fear.

Michael and Chuckie were quietly explaining some things to Caroline, and everyone else was chatting about whatever while they ate. I wanted to think, but that meant talk, and my mother was in the room. I didn't want the "don't talk with your mouth full" lecture again, and certainly not with this many witnesses present.

So I forced myself to try to untangle what was going on while trying not to look at what I was putting into my mouth. This, of course, meant that, instead of focusing on the problem at hand, my mind was merrily wandering all over the place.

"Caro doesn't have a date for the President's Ball anymore."

Jeff snorted quietly. "I'm sure Michael will be more than happy to stand in."

This appeared to be true, since Michael clearly had the charm turned up to eleven. "Okay, great, so that's good. But should she go?"

"Yes," Christopher said. "Because if she doesn't, it could indicate that we're onto their plan. Whatever it is."

"I think Len and Kyle should go, too."

"Why?" Jeff asked. "Besides, they don't have dates."

I snorted. "I'm sure they can both head over to either Dulce or NASA Base and find at least a dozen A-C girls, each, who'd be willing to take one for the team and go to the President's Ball with two cute human guys of eligible age."

"Stop matchmaking."

"I'm not. At all. But I think we want as much of our team as possible there, because I have a feeling we're not going to stop the whatever from happening, at least until such time as we're physically on-site."

"Let's keep trying anyway," Christopher said. "Just for laughs."

"Kitty, Pierre says that we have dress fittings tomorrow morning," Amy shared.

"Can't wait."

"He also says that he's ordered up something for your friend Caroline, too, since she's now part of our strike force." Amy was clearly acting as the Pierre Translator. I assumed he was too well-mannered to shout at me the way everyone else usually did. I didn't expect this nicety to last, of course.

"Excellent. Maybe we'll all match or something."

"I don't see why you're being snippy," Amy said, sounding hurt. "Pierre wants to be good at his job."

"I'll bet cash money that Pierre is always good at any job Pierre wants to do. He was James' go-to guy during our wedding."

"Caroline wasn't in your wedding either, right?" Amy asked, voice carefully neutral.

"Nope, like you and Sheila, unable to make it due to my fab planning skills."

"Ah. That's too bad."

"Yeah, well, I look at it as another close friend who missed my wedding race and the embarrassment thereof and count it in the win column. The President's Ball should be nostalgic, though. We'll be all dressed up and likely running for our lives."

I saw Jeff pass a sign to Christopher, who turned to Amy. "You'll look great, don't worry. And I'll be there to protect you." This set them off on a little nuzzlefest, which I didn't begrudge them. Though they definitely kept it at the G-rated level, presumably because Christopher's dad and my mom were nearby.

Jeff nudged me and leaned down. "She's jealous," he whispered in my ear.

My mother was indeed in the room, as were many others, so I did my best to focus and not start rubbing up against him. "Why? What'd I do this time?" I whispered.

Jeff chuckled. "You didn't do anything. And she's not jealous of you so much as she's jealous of Caroline's relationship with you and with Reynolds."

"Amy still hates Chuckie. Why would she care that Caro likes him?"

He sighed. "It's complicated, but I think it's because Caroline actually thinks as highly of Reynolds as you do, and he clearly likes her, and he's just as clearly never liked Amy. The three of you are all friends, college friends, with a very different history and dynamic than she has with you, or Reynolds, for that matter."

"Well, Amy could take a clue on that, you know."

"Let's adjourn this meeting of the Reynolds Fan Club before it really gets going, okay? Just telling you so you'll understand if Amy's acting strangely toward you or Caroline."

"Is Caro jealous?"

"No. She's worried, tired, stressed, angry, confused, and relieved that you, Reynolds, and your mother are here. And she's definitely interested in Michael." He sounded a little worried when he mentioned the Michael interest. "But she's not jealous."

"Don't worry. Caro can handle a player. She's not really into the idea of finding Mister Right and settling down. She's not against it, but it's not something she's concerned about. Her motto's always been, when it happens, it'll happen."

"Huh. Kind of like yours."

"I suppose." I leaned up and kissed his cheek. "I just hope she finds someone as wonderful as I did."

Jeff smiled and looked extremely pleased. He opened his mouth, but before he could say anything we were interrupted by a really loud sound.

It was a sound I was somewhat familiar with, even though I'd never heard it in an A-C facility before—the sound of a fire alarm.

CHAPTER 46

JEFF STOOD UP. **"EVERYONE,** evacuation procedures!"

We had evacuation procedures? Apparently we did, since everyone other than me and Caroline seemed to know what was going on, and everyone including Caroline leaped up in what seemed like an orderly fashion. A-Cs grabbed the humans near them, and everyone headed toward the exits.

Jeff took my hand; I grabbed my purse and stood up. We took a couple of steps, but something was bothering me. I pulled my hand out of his. I sniffed. I smelled no smoke. I listened. I heard no crackling between the blares of the alarms. I looked around, saw no smoke.

"Why are you suddenly not willing to hold my hand?" Jeff asked.

I shook my head. "I don't smell smoke. We're in the middle of some kind of operation. I don't like the coincidence."

"There was a gas leak earlier," Jeff reminded me.

"Yeah." The alarms were still clamoring, so I didn't figure I could hear Walter through the intercom. I took Jeff's hand, but this time I dragged him along as I ran for the stairs. We headed up to the third floor and Walter's rooms.

I breathed a sigh of relief—he was still in there. "Chiefs, shouldn't you be evacuating?"

"Maybe. Walt, did you trigger the fire alarm?"

He gave me the "you so crazy" look. "No, Chief. The alarms go off automatically."

"But there's no smoke, no smell of smoke, all our food was prepared in Dulce, and I wasn't cooking, so I doubt someone forgot to turn the stoves off."

Walter looked doubtful, but Jeff was listening. "Walter, turn off the alarms, please." He did so, and Jeff listened more closely. "I don't hear anything out of the ordinary."

"Not all fires will show immediately to our senses, Chiefs," Walter said. "Besides, it could be in the basement or one of the top floors. I don't think it's good for you two to be at risk."

"You weren't exactly running off," I pointed out.

"No, but my job is to be the last man to leave, in the case of any emergencies."

"Let's get out of here and figure it out once we're sure the building is secure," Jeff said.

"No. Something's wrong with all of this."

Jeff gave me a long look. "Feminine intuition?"

"I think so. I mean, there's been a lot of extra 'just one of those things' going on, like roadwork and a gas leak scare. Suddenly out of nowhere we have fire alarms going off? When we're in what would have to be the best maintained Embassy in the world?"

Jeff nodded. "Fine. Walter, start scans and have Dulce scan us as well. You stay here," he said to me. "I'm going to check the Embassy."

"Don't go alone."

Jeff kissed me. "Want you to stay with Walter." With that, he was gone.

I decided not to spend the time muttering about how my spouse didn't listen to me in a danger situation, mostly because Jeff could probably do that rant better than I could. Instead I chose to try to figure out what was going on.

Walter was engrossed and intent, so I did my best not to bother him. Which meant I could think or look around. It was me, so I looked around while thinking, to score the double, at least in my own mind.

Walter's Mini Command Center was attached to his living quarters—similarly to how the nursery was set up in our apartment. It made it easier to understand how he, and Gladys, ever got any sleep—there were monitors, switches, microphones, and all sorts of impressive-looking apparatus all over the place.

Walter sat in a reasonably comfy chair at what I figured was the main console, in part because it was big and impressive and in part because it said "Main Console" on it. There was a small cot next to this, though I could see a real bedroom in the other part of his suite. The real bedroom had a smaller set of switches and monitors and such.

There were a variety of voices talking. Walter seemed to follow them all as he flipped switches, turned knobs, wrote things down, and replied back. He was doing it all at hyperspeed, not that I could blame him.

"We need to make sure the Pontifex's residence is secure." My baby and father were there; I didn't want them running into the street for no reason other than to potentially get kidnapped.

"Pontifex's residence is secure," Gladys' voice came over one of the feeds.

"Is everyone who was there secure, as in, inside and not getting snatched off the streets or something?"

Gladys sighed, and she put a lot of sarcasm into something that in reality had no syllables. "Yes, all personnel are inside, safe, and secured. I'm physically there, Co-Chief Martini."

Oh. Right. She was. And per everyone Gladys was not only talented but extremely formidable. I'd still never met her in person. I still didn't want to. Somehow, I felt that knowing what she looked like would either ruin my impression of her or scare the crap out of me. I was fairly certain Gladys could take me. She might even be able to take my mom. Maybe not me and Mom together though. So we had that going for us.

Someone over at the Dulce Science Center was confirming that they weren't picking up anything untoward going on in the Embassy, which pulled me back into the moment. "My scans don't show anything either, Chief," Walter added. "Including how the alarm was tripped."

"Confirmed by all bases," Gladys chimed in. "No sign of how the alarm was triggered or by whom."

"By someone working against us," Chuckie said from behind me.

I turned. He looked pissed and stressed. "What's wrong? And why are you back inside? Did Jeff get you?"

"No. I realized you and Martini weren't out with the rest of us standing on the sidewalk. It dawned on me that I'd reacted without thinking, I saw nothing looking, smelling, or sounding dangerous within the Embassy, so I came back in to see what was going on."

"What is going on?"

Christopher arrived, Glare #1 going like there was no tomorrow and he really wanted to ensure it was his legacy to future generations. "You were right, Reynolds. I can't find it anywhere."

"You couldn't find what?"

"I found nothing," Jeff said as he joined us. "There's not one thing out of place in the entire Embassy."

"Oh, there's something out of place," Christopher snarled.

"I didn't check the hidden level." Jeff's eyes narrowed. "The stress from the two of you is off the charts. Should I check that area just in case?"

"Don't bother," Chuckie said, jaws clenched. "They already got what they came for. And we're once again screwed."

"And," Christopher added, "this time, it's all my fault."

CHAPTER 47

WE ALL STARED AT CHRISTOPHER for a long moment. "That was nicely dramatic. You want to share what the two of you are talking about?"

Christopher nodded. "The picture Nurse Carter had is gone. And I never read it. So we have no more information on the Dingo, his cousin, or anyone else." He looked down. "I should have read it when you wanted me to, Kitty."

I managed to refrain from saying something really obvious like "you didn't pick it up before racing out?" because that was clearly a given. Besides, Christopher's expression and body language said he was already beating himself up far more than I could ever manage.

Jeff nudged me. I got the clue. "It's okay, Christopher. We're used to working with less. I should have let Chuckie hold onto it until you were ready."

"Enough of the pity party," Chuckie said firmly. "Mistakes happen. So the fire alarm was tripped to get us out and let them grab the picture, presumably before White or another imageer could read it. Though I still have no idea how they know what we're doing or saying."

"Guess we're lucky they let us finish eating."

Jeff grunted. "A full stomach's nice. Catching these assassins would be better."

"Why are we assuming it's the Dingo Dog and/or Surly Vic?" I looked at Walter. "How many people supposedly from the gas company were here earlier?"

"Three, Chief."

"Huh."

"Kitty, why are you saying supposedly?" Christopher asked. "They had all the proper identification."

"You know, I really need to get all of you to a few movies or at least watching TV shows that were made in this century. One of the easiest disguises out there is to pretend to be a workman with one of the utility companies. No one wants to question too much if they're worried their building's going to blow sky high."

Chuckie nodded. "They were alone in the building?"

"No, sir, Mister Reynolds," Walter said. "I stayed with them the entire time. They tried to separate, to check things more quickly, but I wouldn't allow it."

"Good man. There were three of them, though, Walt. Was there ever a time when one of them was out of your sight, even if it was for a really short time?"

Walter's brow furrowed. "I don't know if we'd call it out of my sight, but when we were all in the ballroom, they were each in different parts of the room. I did keep my eyes on them, though."

"But three is hard to watch, and while you're looking at one, you can't look at the others." I looked up at Chuckie. "So they planted bugs, at least. And this was after we'd scanned everything and found all those bugs in my purse and on Mister Joel Oliver. I'll bet we haven't scanned for bugs since."

Walter looked chagrined. "No, Chief, I haven't." Christopher hypersped off.

"No worries, Walt. Of all of us, you're the only one who's actually not screwing up."

Christopher returned. "Found them, at least I think I have. I left them in place."

"Good," Chuckie said. "We'll check them in a moment. Walter, can you describe the men who were here?"

"I can do better than that, Mister Reynolds." Walter turned back to his main console, fiddled with some knobs, flicked some switches, typed something into his computer keyboard, and suddenly we had video.

"You video tape us?" Maybe it was some weird A-C thing, but I didn't like it. The former Diplomatic Corps had liked doing that a little too much.

"No, Chief. But we have video at every entrance to the building. It's standard practice for all Embassies, not just ours."

"Just the entrances?" Chuckie asked, sounding mildly worried. "Nothing more?"

"Why wouldn't that be plenty?"

Chuckie gave me the "duh" look. "Because most Embassies have video feeds on all their general areas. And this one should, too."

Walter looked uncomfortable. "Ah, well . . ."

Jeff sighed. "My order, Reynolds. After what was found in that secret lab, I didn't want any of us being spied on."

Chuckie gave Jeff a look I could only think of as disgusted and long-suffering. "You live to make everyone's jobs harder, don't you? Mine in particular."

"It seemed like a good idea at the time." Jeff wasn't snapping or snarling, but his eyes were narrowed.

"So, as opposed to ensuring the safety of this Embassy and everyone in it, you chose to remove one of the standard security elements every building in this city has installed, simply because video feeds were used against us a few months ago, and you didn't bother to put any other kind of backup in place?" Chuckie sounded both angry and resigned. I had a feeling the migraine was trying to show up and join the party.

"Boys, don't start."

Jeff shook his head. "I hate saying it, but Reynolds is right. And, frankly, I should have run that decision by James and Tim—and you," he added to Chuckie. "So, this one's my screw-up. Walter, turn all the video feeds for all the public areas back on, please."

While Walter quickly complied, I stared at the pictures our doorway cameras had caught. "Those guys aren't Peter the Dingo Dog or Surly Vic. But they look familiar." I considered. "Can someone get everyone else back inside, and get Len, Kyle, and Mister Joel Oliver in here, please?"

"I'll get them," Jeff said. "You two check out and dismantle those bugs," he added to Chuckie and Christopher.

The three of them trotted off. "I'm sorry about the bugs, Chief," Walter said quietly.

"Walt, they didn't get to do whatever else they'd planned only because you refused to leave this Embassy unattended. I'm not joking, you're the only one of us who's actually doing a good job."

He perked up a little. "Thanks, Chief. You're not doing as badly as you think you are, you know."

"Ha. I'm betting I'm doing worse than I think I am. But you know, we do persevere, right?"

"That's the spirit," Oliver said as he and the boys joined us. "I'll be happy to give you some pointers about how to survive in this town."

"Later. I'll take your course. It can't be worse than The Washington Wife class."

"How is Darcy?"

I looked at him. He looked sincerely interested. "You're kidding me. You know her?"

"Quite well." Oliver shot me a small smile. "I imagine you're driving her crazy. Carry on; it's good for her. Now, what did you need from me and the young gentlemen?"

Kyle pointed at the screen. "Those guys look familiar. But I don't know why."

"I do," Len said. "They were driving the cabs that were after us yesterday."

CHAPTER 48

"YEAH, THAT'S WHAT I THOUGHT. But they're not wearing their fake beards."

"Too obvious for the situation," Oliver said.

"True, they were pretty lame."

"But I agree," Oliver went on. "That one was the one who spoke to you." He pointed at one of the men on the video.

"He was the one in charge," Walter confirmed.

"Do the videos capture sound, too?"

Walter shook his head. "There's too much interference under most circumstances. We need different cameras installed if we want to capture sound, too. At least sound we can distinguish as more than a cacophony."

"Great. Well, at least we have something, and faces are probably more important than voices right now. Let's blow these up and get Mom's and Chuckie's people on the whole recognition database thingies." I looked at the images as Walter did the picture captures and size increases. "These guys don't look anything like the Dingo Dog or Surly Vic."

"We know they're not the same people," Kyle said patiently.

"No, I mean they don't look like they come from the same part of the world. Can someone get Nurse Carter in here?"

I heard a sigh behind me and turned just in time to see Jeff zip off. He was back momentarily, Nurse Carter in tow. She gagged a little from the hyperspeed and was then positioned in front of the monitors. We were back to *Night at the Opera* status. I took heart—the last time we'd had a ton of our own people shoved into a smaller room, we'd figured out what was going on.

I gave her the fast high-level "we've been infiltrated and are being bugged downstairs" recap. "So, we're hoping you can identify our intruders."

Nurse Carter stared at the pictures. "I don't know them," she said finally.

So much for that idea—even the Marx Brothers were letting the team down. I tried another guess. "Do you think they could be your countrymen?"

She nodded slowly. "It's possible."

"How probable?" Chuckie asked as he and Christopher shoved into the room.

"I'm really not sure." Nurse Carter shook her head. "I'm sorry." She turned around. "So, what are you going to do with me?"

"Keep you here, with us, under guard," Chuckie answered without missing a beat. Jeff and Christopher both nodded.

Either Nurse Carter was already aware that if the three of them were in agreement, arguing was fruitless or she didn't mind sticking around. "Good. I would prefer to be here, I think."

"Why so?"

She smiled at me. "After what's been going on, I believe you're working for the same goals I am. And under the circumstances, I don't want to be left alone to be murdered by whoever's trying to kill people."

I saw Chuckie nudge Jeff, who grunted. "Like with Caroline, telling the truth as she knows it, and not picking up anything negative toward any of us." He looked at Walter. "Have all bases scan us again."

"And our neighbors, if they can."

Everyone looked at me. "Why?" Christopher asked finally.

I rolled my eyes. "Really? I'm the only one here who's ever heard of high-powered surveillance equipment? Really, Chuckie?"

He sighed. "Good point."

"I've heard of it," Christopher snapped. "I just don't get what you're going for, having us use it to spy on our neighbors."

"Dude, seriously, has Tito given you any tests to ensure your brain wasn't affected negatively by the Surcenthumain? Every Embassy around us was infiltrated in some way today. I'm betting none of them had their version of Walter hanging around, because no human can run fast enough to escape if the place goes boom. So, they could have put in any amount of surveillance, trained on *us*, and our neighbors would be none the wiser. I want Chuckie to look for what's looking at us. I'm not trying to see what the Irish and Romanians wear under their kilts."

"They don't wear kilts," Christopher snapped.

"I know. Figure of speech, okay?"

"Sorry, just having trouble keeping up with the Kittyisms."

I decided to end our spat. We were only having it because everyone was freaked out and upset. "Look, let's just get the good cameras in here and going so we can all relax. About that, if nothing else."

Chuckie sighed. "I have to agree. Martini, are you actually equipped for this?"

Jeff nodded. "I'm sure we are. Dulce or NASA Base should have something on hand that will work. However, we've just moved into Alpha Team territory." He rubbed his forehead. "Let's go downstairs and see what James wants to do."

"Wait." Everyone looked at me. "Walter, what do our video feeds show? They were running, right, when the fire alarms went off?"

"Yes, Chief." He fiddled with some knobs and the picture changed. I saw everyone other than me, Jeff, and Walter go out the front door. Then the film went dark. "What the—" Walter fiddled with some more knobs and flipped some switches. Still all we saw was blackness.

"Was our equipment tampered with?" Jeff asked, voice taut.

"Possible," Walter said, still intent and fiddling. "Switching to see the feeds on the other external locations." They were black, too. One moment boring nothing going on, the next, they went dark.

A thought occurred. "Walt, fast forward the feeds." He did as requested. Suddenly there were pictures again. "How many cameras did we have on before Jeff had you turn them all back on?"

"Just three, Chief. The one for the front door, the one for the side, where we take out the trash and get deliveries, and the one for the underground garage."

I sighed. "There are three of them. It wouldn't take a lot to toss something over the cameras covering the side and the garage, right?"

"How would they knock out the camera at the front door?" Chuckie asked.

I pondered. "They didn't come in from the front, that's where all of you were. They came in from the side or underground. One of them turned off the front camera feed, just in case. They probably put dark cloth over the other cameras—they were in here, casing the place, after all. I'm sure they looked for and found all the various cameras' plugs."

"They went into every room, Chief," Walter confirmed. "They said they had to be sure each room didn't contain a leak. And you can leave the cameras running while blacking out the pictures, so the offline alert wouldn't be triggered."

"Yeah, they might be lame with their taxi driving, but they knew what they were doing inside. So they flipped the fire alarm switch in some way and trotted in here without a problem because they already knew their way around. After all, Walter wasn't watching the cameras, was he? He was trying to figure out where the supposed fire was. He wasn't looking for someone to try to come in when, during a fire alarm, everyone wants to go out."

"That's true, Chief." Walter sounded dejected. "I never checked the video feeds."

"Not your fault. You acted just as they expected, meaning normally. Besides, Jeff had you turn most of the cameras off, so I'll wager you're not a big fan of watching them, because you know it makes us feel uncomfortable."

Walter blushed, so I knew I'd hit that one on the head. "We haven't had a need before, Chief."

"There's a need now," Chuckie said. "But Kitty's theory makes sense. The garage has more security, so assume they came in and left through the side. It would be fairly easy to block that camera, which we need to remedy, by the way."

"Will do," Walter said quickly. "I'll get expanded lenses onto all the cameras tomorrow, Mister Reynolds."

Chuckie nodded. "Good, but for all we know, they blocked it earlier in the day, and we just didn't notice, though they could have just as easily worn dark clothing and ski masks to cover the cameras right before they triggered the alarm. They got what they were looking for, turned the front camera back on, left through the side entrance and removed whatever they'd put on the camera there, went to the garage entrance, removed whatever was covering that camera, and walked on down the street."

Jeff sighed. "Let's go share the latest news with Alpha Team."

"Why?" Christopher asked morosely.

Jeff chuckled mirthlessly. "I don't want to be greedy. Let's share the misery with our friends and family."

CHAPTER 49

WE LEFT WALTER AND TROOPED to the elevator. Why make the humans sick for no reason? We'd undoubtedly have a reason shortly.

There were a number of agents zipping through our facility. "We figured if they could plant bugs in the ballroom, there was a chance for elsewhere," Tim said as we joined him, Reader, Gower, and Serene, all of whom looked tense and alert but fully in charge. At least someone was.

"There was a chance for more than bugs," I said. "We're really batting a thousand right now on getting fooled, scammed, and ripped off."

We shared the wonderful news that we'd lost the picture and had been far too easily broken into while all of us were essentially on the premises while I wondered if the Suicide Hotline made house calls.

The four of them took this in better stride than some of us had. "Mistakes happen," Reader said as we finished our tale of woeful inadequacy.

"Find anything else?" Jeff asked.

Reader shook his head. "Not so far, but they're not done."

William joined us. "Commanders, Chiefs, no other bugs found on premises. We also checked for things of a more dangerous nature. Nothing."

Everyone looked relieved, but the ol' feminine intuition felt twitchy. "Why go through all of this merely to take the picture Nurse Carter had? Even if Christopher had read it, it's not as though he'd have gotten 'current hideout' out of it."

"Serene might have," Reader said quietly.

"True, but that presumes they know us really well. I get how they knew we had the picture. Chuckie interrogated Caroline, and she was talking about it while we were sitting in the room with all the bugs. But to remove us all from the building to steal one little snapshot seems like overkill."

"It was incriminating evidence," Chuckie said. "Proof Titan has assassins on the payroll and around some of our most influential politicians."

Nurse Carter and I looked at each other. "Where did you put the things the Dingo left for you to claim?" she asked me.

"No freaking idea, but I'll bet that stuff's gone, too."

Reader swore under his breath while Gower zipped off. He was back quickly, empty-handed. "We had the things Jeff brought back from the hospital in the conference room. All gone."

"So anything the Dingo wanted you to get is gone," Chuckie said, migraine clearly arriving at any second. "Do you remember what it was?" he asked Nurse Carter.

"A wallet, a man's personal care kit, a small Bible, and a manila envelope. We're not allowed to look into anything that's going into lockup, and two hospital personnel as well as Security put the patient's belongings away, so I didn't get to look inside anything."

"I can't believe the Dingo Dog carried a Bible with him. He kills people for a living."

"The personal care kit could have held explosives, a disassembled gun, poisons . . . anything." By the way Chuckie rubbed his forehead, I knew the migraine had made its grand entrance. "For all we know, the envelope contained the name of the assassination target."

"I doubt it."

Everyone looked at me. "Want to explain that?" Christopher asked.

"Look, we were all in the freaking Potomac. Jeff pulled the two bodies out, but he didn't pull their damn car out of the river. And even if he had, you and Kyle searched all those limos."

"True. We didn't find anything like what was just described. Not," Christopher added with a sigh, "that we couldn't have missed them. I wasn't looking for paperwork or men's toiletry kits. I was looking for guns and ammo."

I didn't share with him that he hadn't found all the guns, either. Why make it worse? "Fine. So, seriously, nothing Nurse Carter had waiting for me in that hospital vault was wet or looked as if it had so much as been in the same vicinity as a bottle of Dasani. So the Dingo got this from somewhere or someone after he left Tim's control but before he got to Nurse Carter."

Chuckie looked like he'd fought the migraine off for a minute. "So he was given those things by the same people who took his partner away."

"I think that's a legitimate logic leap, yeah. But instead of doing with them whatever he was supposed to, he instead had Nurse Carter lock them up." I looked at her, and my brain kicked, hard. "Wait a damn minute. You know him and he knows you. And that means he knew who he was handing this stuff to."

"*If* he handed it to her," Chuckie said, in that silky yet deadly way he'd clearly learned from working at the C.I.A.

She looked like she was going to argue, but perhaps all of us glaring at her convinced her it would be futile. Instead her shoulders slumped, and she nodded. "He recognized me. He told me these things had to go to you, to list you as his niece, that it mattered greatly, and that it would matter greatly to me."

"And yet you didn't look inside any of it?"

"I wanted to, believe me. But I couldn't, there were too many witnesses. The Dingo was very . . . cautious when he spoke to me. I know he realized who I was. I believe it's why he trusted me."

"No reason why we should, however," Chuckie said. "Since you conveniently forgot to tell us about this."

"I thought it was self-evident."

"No, that's the right to life, liberty, and the pursuit of happiness. Usually when we're trying to stop a major disaster, we like to share all our information with each other."

Nurse Carter's eyes flashed. "Look, I don't know you people! Half of you *aren't* people, either, not as I'd think of them, are you? You supposedly arrested me, but I haven't had my rights read, haven't had a phone call, haven't had my crimes explained."

"I don't have to do any of that," Chuckie said, voice still dangerous. "You're under arrest because you're a potential terrorist and you threatened an ambassador's life. You don't get any of the niceties local law enforcement's forced to use. You get to prove you're not a threat or you get a cell in an underground vault. Period."

"As if you're not going to put me into that cell anyway? For all I knew when you took me, you were going to kill me. You could still be part of the conspiracy I'm here trying to stop, or worse, really related to the Dingo and be the ones planning to finish whatever job he was assigned to. So I don't know why you think I'm a bad person for not stating the obvious once I'd told you about my experiences with the Dingo."

"Because we explained that you tell us the truth or you go to the cell," Tim said. "We're trying to stop an assassination, and we don't know the target. You're not helping us at all. I say lock her up."

"I'm willing to agree," Christopher said. Everyone nodded.

I looked at Jeff. His eyes were narrowed. "What are you getting?"

"Aside from the fact that Nurse Carter here is desperately trying to hide her emotions from me? Terror. Pure, unadulterated terror. She's more afraid of everyone in this room than she ever was when discussing the Dingo."

"Does that make her our enemy?" Chuckie asked.

Len cleared his throat. "Ah, sir?"

"Yes?" every man other than Kyle said this in unison. I managed not to laugh, but it took effort. I noted that, terrified or not, Nurse Carter found this funny, too.

"We fingerprinted her, remember? You had her prints run."

Chuckie nodded. "Results aren't back yet."

Kyle held up his PDA. "Back now, sir. This is Magdalena Rijos-Carter, R.N. She has dual citizenship in the U.S. and Paraguay. No outstanding warrants, no police record. On file because her husband was in the Air Force and to obtain citizenship."

Len looked at his phone, where he clearly had the same info Kyle did. "Her husband died during a training maneuver." Len looked up. "In the New Mexican desert. Several years ago."

I decided to take the leap. "So, her husband died fighting a superbeing, right?"

Len nodded. "From what this says, or rather, the way it doesn't say anything, yes, I think so. He was given a hero's funeral."

"And your brother was murdered in front of you." I shook my head. "You knew about American Centaurion and didn't come to us for help?"

"I only knew my husband worked high security missions. He never said what he did. I wouldn't have believed him if he told me. Not until . . ."

"Until your brother found out about the supersoldier project in the Chaco?" She nodded. "Who did you lose to that project?"

She looked down. "Our son. He was doing work with some of the indigent, and . . ." She looked up and there were tears in her eyes. "They took out the entire village. From what we were able to gather, some were infected with whatever it is that makes them turn into monsters. And they killed the others. I . . . don't know if our son was one of the monsters or not. Or if he's still possibly alive."

"When did this happen?"

"About a year and a half ago."

Right when we'd handled the clustered formation in the Chaco, before Operation Drug Addict got underway.

Jeff cleared his throat. "Your son isn't alive. If he was turned into a superbeing, he was destroyed. I gave the order and watched it happen."

Nurse Carter looked at him. "Thank you," she said finally.

"Why are you thanking him?" Christopher asked quietly.

"Because now I know. For certain, that there can be no hope, but also that there can be no more horror."

I looked back at Jeff. "What do you think?"

"What I thought before. Reynolds, she's not our enemy. Not sure what to do with her, but the underground prison isn't the right choice."

"She's not our friend, either," Chuckie pointed out.

Nurse Carter shrugged. "As the saying goes, the enemy of my enemy is my friend. I want these people stopped. If I can help you keep the Dingo's target from being killed, I will. Especially if it means you can stop my enemies from murdering someone else's brilliant, loving brother, or taking anyone else's beloved son and murdering him in the way I know he died."

I patted her shoulder. "We're doing our best. Today, our best is none too good, but, you know, we sometimes manage to pull out a miracle."

"We need that miracle, girlfriend," Reader said with a sigh. "Because we've lost whatever clues we had and are, pretty much, back to square one. And time's running out."

CHAPTER 50

"OKAY, SO, LET'S GET BACK to where we were before we finally got Nurse Carter's full info. Let me ask, though, did you work with the taxi drivers, helping them get in here?"

"Absolutely not," she said firmly. "I wanted that information more than you do."

"Where did you get the gun you had in the security deposit box?"

She shrugged. "It was the Dingo's. He told me it was water-logged when he slipped it to me, but I figured you wouldn't know that, and I was hoping I wouldn't have to pull the trigger."

"It worked. I had no clue it was his gun." And said gun had been in front of my face only the day before, too. It figured. As Jeff liked to point out, I had fabulous attention to detail, just not usually the details most people cared about.

"The relevant question is, does this mean the three enterprising taxi drivers are working with the Dingo and company?" Chuckie asked. "Or are they working their own angle?"

Tim shook his head. "There's always more than one thing going on."

"I think another question should be were the taxi drivers the only ones who broke in this evening," Reader said.

"We have no way of knowing, since the cameras were tampered with."

Len cleared his throat. "The guys in the taxis seemed a lot less . . . effective than the ones who blew up the limo and put us into that car chase."

"And Kitty into the Potomac," Reader added, while shooting me the cover-boy grin. "But yeah," he said, smile gone, "I'll give you that our other limo was destroyed."

"They had a lot of firepower."

"The limo was blown up, though," Reader said shortly. "They shot out the tires, shot out the windows, and tossed in an explosive."

"Who saw it happen?" Chuckie asked.

"What? Why?" Reader sounded almost as snappish as Jeff normally did when talking to Chuckie.

"Because we still don't know who bugged Kitty or how," Chuckie replied. "And, as Kitty just pointed out, if they were taking the picture to avoid White or Serene reading it, then they know us very well. And infiltration is always a risk in any operation, especially this one."

"I hated my last driver. Not that I want to speak ill of the dead. If we really think he's dead."

Reader, Tim, and Christopher were all on their phones. Jeff didn't look convinced. "I didn't pick up anything treacherous from any of your drivers, and I check for it."

I sighed. "Jeff, there are liars in the A-C community. It's a skill, and it's a well-hidden one."

"I know you've told me about it. I just don't believe it," he said.

"Christopher can block you."

"He's enhanced. Serene can probably block me, too. But I don't really buy it with our regular people."

"Camilla is our shining example. I wonder if we should bring her over?" Camilla had been, thankfully, a double agent during Operation Confusion. Without her, and her ability to lie, we'd all likely be dead or enslaved by Ronaldo Al Dejahl.

I liked her, though she wasn't someone anyone hung out with. A-Cs who were truly able to lie convincingly were extremely rare, trained in secret, and pretty much could be considered the Jedi Monks of the A-C population. They had their own clubhouse somewhere, but the rest of us never got to go there. Most A-Cs didn't know the clubhouse existed. Jeff's father, Alfred, had, but Jeff hadn't. Which was an interesting point to ponder, only not right now.

"She's on assignment," Chuckie said.

"Huh? What assignment?" I was never told anything even before I'd moved into the Embassy, and it was worse these days.

"She's doing something very delicate," Chuckie said. "It's approved at the highest levels."

"Seriously?"

"Yes. And nothing you do or say is going to get the information out of me. However, I'm with you—it's fairly easy for a human to lie to an empath if they know what to focus on."

"Huh." Jeff shot Chuckie a dirty look. "Not that anyone can tell with you." Chuckie laughed.

"Boys . . ."

"Not starting," Jeff said quickly. "But do you really think we had a car full of traitors following you?" He sounded a little freaked out, a little angry, and a lot protective.

"No. I think we had one guy, maybe two, whoever the humans were. I think, once the gunfire started, they shot the A-Cs in the car, rolled down the windows, jumped out of the car and into one of the many other limo options surrounding us, while their cronies tossed a bomb into the limo and blew up any sign of internal foul play."

"Glass in the limos is bulletproof," Reader acknowledged as he hung up. "All the metal's reinforced, too."

"So even if you're slow on the laser shield button, you should have time to hit it, right?"

He nodded. "Right. And there were two humans in the car, the one who'd driven you to your Washington Wife class and the one you'd had before him who also hadn't worked out."

"One human was driving and I remember that the other one took shotgun. Meaning they were the ones who had the best access to said laser shield button, as well as every other doohickey in the car."

"So, maybe Kitty didn't like them not because they hadn't gone through a danger situation with her, but because she picked up something wrong they were doing," Len suggested.

"Or maybe it was both," Tim said, closing his phone. "But I just checked on the teams James and I sent out to reclaim our agents' bodies. They found six A-C bodies."

"Oh, let me play! Let me play! No humans, right?"

Tim nodded. "Forensics is looking to see if they can tell if the blast was internal and where it was centered. Not sure they'll get much, it was pretty big."

"Okay, no worries, 'cause I think we're right unless they find something that completely contradicts this theory. Let's get back to the bigger worries. Jeff, I know you monitor emotions, but what if someone has an empathic shield up? Could you tell?"

He shrugged. "No idea, baby. At all."

"So are you sure you're reading people correctly?" Chuckie asked, pointedly looking at Nurse Carter.

"Yes, because I'm getting plenty of emotions from her." Jeff looked thoughtful. "Usually humans and A-Cs feel more than one emotion at any time. Terror usually wins out and holds the emotional stage alone, but otherwise, and sometimes even when terrified, we all have more going on than just one emotion."

"So maybe you can sort of monitor for someone exhibiting only a single emotion."

Jeff nodded. "The way you try to think about something benign when you don't want me to know you're upset, lusting after someone other than me, or angry with me."

Damn. The whole focusing on flowers thing didn't work? This fooling the superempath stuff was clearly not my forté.

Jeff grinned at me. "It's okay, baby. I usually ignore you when you want me to. I figure it's only polite."

"Humph. But anyway, clearly it would take someone with a lot of training, like Camilla had, someone having the Surcenthumain assist, or some kind of device that would block an empath without raising their internal flags."

Chuckie nodded slowly. "Your former Diplomatic Corps had, what, over twenty years to have people working on this? It would be doable in that time if you had empaths to use as test subjects."

"Which they did." I shuddered. The memory of what had been done to our agents and hybrids before we'd caught on always lurked on the edge of my mind, waiting to jump out and scare the crap out of me while also making me sick to my stomach and enraged.

William cleared his throat. "Ah, Commanders, Chiefs? Do you need me for anything else?"

"Sorry," Jeff said quietly. "Why don't you get the rest of the teams back to Dulce?"

William gave him a quick smile. "Happy to."

"Stop in and see Walter before you go," I suggested. "He's doing a great job, but I don't think he believes us when we tell him so."

William chuckled. "I'm sure he doesn't, but thanks, Chief, I will."

We waited until William was out of earshot. "Okay, I feel stupid and thoughtless for bringing that up in front of him."

Jeff shook his head. "He understands. We lose people all the time, including people we love. It's part of our jobs and always has been. William understands more than most. He's our best imageer right now, after Christopher and Serene."

"Then ensure he's guarded," Chuckie said. "Because we don't know much, but we do know that there's already been too much killing, and there's bound to be more before this is through. And as of now, every Centaurion agent needs to be considered a target."

CHAPTER 51

"YOU'RE A TARGET, TOO," I MENTIONED. "In fact, I think you need to be under whatever guard everyone else is, Chuckie. My parents, too."

"We already have Centaurion and ETD guards with your parents, in addition to P.T.C.U. ones. I'll be fine. Use the personnel for other people."

"Ha. Last big operation we had you were only fine by seconds. For all we know, you're only here tonight because you and Mom were up all night doing interrogations and so were safe. But I'll give you an option. You stay here in one of the empty guest rooms, I'll let the personnel go elsewhere." Jeff opened his mouth. "Do *not* start."

Jeff sighed. "I'm not. I agree with you. I think Reynolds should stay here until this is over."

Everyone, not just Chuckie and I, heck, even Nurse Carter, stared at him. "You okay?" Christopher managed to ask.

Jeff rolled his eyes. "Kitty's right. Someone's trying to kill God alone knows who. Reynolds likes to act like he's invulnerable, but he's not. And I don't want to have to deal with the hysterics my wife will go through if you're hurt or killed," he added to Chuckie.

"Thanks, I think." Chuckie sounded dazed. "Really? You want me here? Without extra threats or a pack of Dobermans outside my door?"

I put my hand on Jeff's forehead. "No fever."

Jeff gave all of us a dirty look, me in particular. "You ask me to behave in a mature fashion, but the moment I do . . ."

"Just happily shocked, that's all," I said quickly. "Let me applaud the grown-up moment. Chuckie, take some agents with you when you go to get your stuff. And before you start arguing, Mister Joel Oliver is staying here too. Look at it as you riding herd on him, okay?"

Chuckie sighed. "Fine. Let's get that over with before the next confusing yet deadly thing happens."

"And," Oliver said, "remember that you, we hope, still have things to get."

"Good point." Chuckie grinned. "They're mostly new things I had to get in the last three months, so I'll stop arguing."

"Great, hurry it up, though," Reader said. "We still need to work on determining what's going on. Before whatever it is happens and all we can do is clean up or bury the dead."

Cheerful pronouncements of doom over, we fretted some more about things we couldn't control, got more useless information that merely confirmed things were dire, and speculated on whether Chuckie's place would be toasted before or after he got there.

In the midst of the useless fretting, my phone rang. I stepped away from the group while I dug it out and looked at who was calling. "Bernie! Hi, what's up?"

"Hey, Kitty! I heard there was some kind of gas leak scare around where I think you live. You guys okay?"

"Yeah, we're fine. It was a false alarm."

"Oh, thank goodness. Hey, I was wondering if you wanted to do a play date sometime. I know you have the big shebang tomorrow night, but maybe in the day beforehand?"

I really wanted to say yes. Bernie was normal, and her son was normal, and wouldn't it be nice for me and Jamie to just go hang out and pretend to be normal? But duty was calling, loudly, and this was, I reminded myself, why I'd lost touch with most of my friends over the past two years.

"I can't." I didn't have to fake the regret in my voice. "There's too much we have to do before we go to the ball. But hopefully sometime next week. Maybe after Mommy and Me." If, you know, we survived tomorrow night.

"Okay, well, have fun. I spent dinner last night and tonight whining to Raul about how you get to go and we don't." She laughed. "He said he has another friend going, and he's going to see if he has a spare invitation. I doubt it'll happen, but I have a nice dress on hand, just in case."

"It'd be great to see you there!" It would. Not that I necessarily wanted yet another person in whatever danger was going on, though the idea that Bernie was the Dingo's target seemed as unlikely as me winning the Miss Universe pageant. But I figured their chances of actually getting to go were slim to none, so I could be excited safely. "I really hope Raul swings it."

"Me too, like you wouldn't believe. Well, I'll let you go. See you tomorrow, maybe, and next week for sure!"

"Plan on it!" I hung up and heaved a sigh as I dropped my phone back into my purse. Being married to Jeff and saving the world on a regular basis had seemed worth the sacrifices three months ago. Now, being married to Jeff still rocked, but the sacrifices didn't seem as worthwhile by a long shot.

My phone rang again. I pulled it out. Not a number I knew. Hoped another "relative" hadn't "died" and answered. "Hello?"

"Is this Kitty Martini?" The voice was familiar, but I wasn't sure why.

"Yes. Who's this?"

"It's Leslie Manning. I wanted to . . . apologize for how everyone was yesterday morning."

It had been so long ago in terms of experience, I'd almost forgotten about Kitty and Eugene's High School Reunion moment. "Yeah, thanks. We're used to it."

"Look . . . I want . . ." Her voice trailed off.

I waited. Nothing. "Yes? Leslie, is there something you needed?"

"Yes." I realized she was crying. "I need help."

"Why the hell are you calling *me*?"

"Because you're not my friend."

"Excuse me?"

She sniffled. "It's complicated, okay? Like everything else in this town. You're still fighting it, trying not to fit in. And I think I need someone who cares more about being a real person than being a Washington player. You stick up for Eugene when, if you cut him dead, I promise you, Abner would pull you into the group because he thinks you're cute. He thinks he could make you his little pet. I know you'd kick him in the balls before he ever got a chance to try it."

"Got that right. Leslie, really, what's this about?"

I heard a voice in the background. "I can't tell you right now." Her voice dropped to just above a whisper. "Tomorrow, okay? At the ball. I'll find you and find a way, okay? Please?"

"Um, sure. That sounds good. Try to find me before I overturn the punch bowl or something, though."

She laughed. "I will. Kitty . . . thank you. See you tomorrow."

She hung up before I could say there was no reason for thanks—I hadn't done or promised to do anything other than speak to her tomorrow night.

My phone rang again. Again a number I didn't know. As I answered, it occurred to me that I had no idea how Leslie had scored my phone number. "Hello, is this Ambassador Martini?"

"Yes." This voice I recognized. It was good ol' Jack Ryan. "What's up, Jack?"

"Don't go to the ball tomorrow night."

"Right. Hilarious. I may die laughing."

"No," he said urgently. "You might die."

CHAPTER 52

I CONSIDERED HOW TO REPLY to this statement of potential fact. Saying "Right you are, and you, too!" indicated more knowledge of current clandestine events than I wanted Ryan to know.

However, playing stupid was always sure to work in some ways, so I went for it. "Oh, come on. What, Abner decided I have to die because I won't play your little high school games?"

"No. Look, I'm not supposed to be saying this to anyone. I already warned the others. I know we're not friends, and I'm not interested in being your friend, either. But I know you, and I know that something bad's going to happen at the ball tomorrow. So, I'm telling you, as a fellow classmate, not to go."

"Why do you care?"

"I don't want someone I know to die horrifically, okay? Is there a problem?"

"No, not with that mindset." Ryan's wife was in the C.I.A. If she'd leaked something to him she could lose her job. "Jack, how did you hear this information?"

"I eavesdropped on a conversation of Pia's."

"Why are you eavesdropping on your wife?"

"I thought she was cheating on me."

I could understand why she'd want to, but I managed to keep that statement to myself. "That was sort of low."

"Yeah, I'm sure it was. She's not cheating, so there's that."

"So glad to hear it."

"But she was saying that they expected some kind of action tomorrow at Planet Hollywood."

"Um, that's a defunct restaurant chain, isn't it?"

He sighed, rather condescendingly. "That's the code name for the President's Ball."

"How do you know?" He was silent. "Jack, how do you *know*?"

He sighed. "I looked through her Blackberry and found the reference."

"Again because you thought she was cheating?"

"Yes."

"She works for the freaking C.I.A. Why is her being secretive some kind of shocker alert to you?"

"Look, I don't ask about your relationship with your husband! Besides, that's not why I called. Don't go tomorrow night, okay? I'm trying to protect you. You'd think you'd be a little grateful."

He had a point. "Thanks, Jack. I appreciate the head's up. You called everyone in class?"

"And Missus Lockwood. Well, I haven't called Eugene yet. But he's next."

Nice to see where Eugene and I rated on the Danger Warning List. But then again, it hadn't occurred to me to even think about warning any of them to stay away from the ball, in part because I knew it would leak classified information, but also because I hadn't thought about any of them since before my limo exploded.

"Okay, I'll do my best."

"Good. See you next week. I hope." He hung up, presumably to call Eugene and freak him out next. I mentally kicked myself. I hadn't asked Jack how he'd gotten my number either.

I wondered if Leslie had called me because Ryan had called her, or if she was calling about something else entirely. If she'd gotten Ryan's warning, she certainly hadn't acted like it when we'd spoken. In fact, just the opposite. She clearly expected and wanted me to be at the ball. This opened up a whole new set of questions I would have asked myself, only my phone rang again.

"What am I, the switchboard for *American Idol*?" I looked at the number before I answered. "Hi Eugene."

"Kitty, I just got the strangest call from Jack. I didn't know he had my phone number."

"Ditto and ditto, dude. You're calling me sooner than I'd have expected, though. He just called me a couple minutes ago."

"As if I wanted to chat with him for one moment longer than necessary? There's no way Lydia can miss the President's Ball. Do you think Jack's actually got real information, or do you think he's trying to scare us away?"

That was one of the questions Leslie's call had raised for me, but I didn't have a good answer. "I don't know." I also had the realistic moral quandary that Ryan had apparently been able to get over, namely, if you know something horrible is going to happen, do you warn people or do you shut the hell up?

Chuckie returned as I was contemplating this. I looked at him. He'd been working in the C.I.A. for a long time. My parents had been working in clandestine and covert ops for a lot longer. And I hadn't found out about any of it until I'd absolutely had to—when my life was actually in danger, when I was actually involved.

Reality said that Chuckie had longed to tell me . . . and hadn't because his job required that he didn't. I'd wanted to tell him, too, when I'd joined Centaurion Division. But I hadn't known he had the clearance for me to share the information at the time, so I'd lied and told him nothing.

"I think it'll be okay," I lied. "You can't ask Lydia to commit career suicide based on a phone call from a guy we know hates us."

Eugene sighed. "Okay, good. She's so excited about going, I can't imagine the fight we'd have if I tried to suggest we should be elsewhere."

"Yeah, I'm sure. Just relax, have a nice night together, and remember to tell her she looks great a lot tomorrow before you get there."

He laughed. "I will. Thanks, Kitty. See you tomorrow night. Hopefully one of us won't blow the place sky high."

"From your mouth to God's ears, dude."

We hung up before I thought to ask if Lydia had mentioned dropping by my Embassy today or ask about her taste in friends and associates. Oh, well. I counted to thirty. My phone rang again. Why not? Apparently everyone in the world wanted to talk to me tonight. "Hello?"

"Kitty?"

"Yes. Who's this?"

"It's Bryce."

Oh, goody. The tool was calling me now. "What do you want? By the way, how the hell did you get my phone number?"

"Darcy gave everyone a roster on the first day of class. You got one, too, I'm sure."

I probably had. I'd hated class from Day One, and I hadn't looked at a single thing that woman had handed out. "Oh. Okay. Why are you calling?"

"Jack called with some whacked out conspiracy theory. Did he call you?"

"Yeah, and Eugene. Jack said he'd called everyone."

Bryce heaved a sigh. "Look, I think he's delusional. He's been worried that Pia's been cheating on him for weeks. I think it's gotten to him. I know he's been drinking. Once he called me, and I took a minute to think about it, it was clear he's just doing this for attention."

"What if he's right?"

Bryce snorted. It was on the Lockwood Snort Scale of Gentlemanly and Discreet of course, but it was still a snort. "Please. He's undoubtedly sloshed. I just figured I'd call and let you know that the rest of us aren't in on this, it's not some ridiculous high school type prank to get you or Eugene to stay away."

"Good thing, because we're both going. We can't exactly back out."

"Good." Bryce sounded relieved. "And, you know, sorry about how we acted yesterday. We were just playing with you."

"I'm sure." I knew they were playing with us. Like cats played with mice. I, however, was more cat-qualified than they were, so the hell with their little intimidation plan. "Anyway, yes, we're going, bummer about Jack, thanks for calling."

"You're welcome. See you tomorrow?"

"You bet." We hung up. "But not if I see you first, Bryce."

CHAPTER 53

I PUT MY PHONE BACK into my purse, waiting for it to ring again at any moment. Didn't. Amazing.

I rejoined everyone. "Chuckie, is the code name for the President's Ball 'Planet Hollywood'?"

He nodded. "Why?"

I shared my unique series of phone calls, leaving out the normal call with Bernie, since it wasn't relevant. "I'm trying to figure out if Jack just shared real high-level information or not."

"Sounds like he did." Chuckie seemed less concerned with this than I'd have expected.

"You're not worried?"

He shrugged. "It's not as if he told you anything specific. It's pretty standard to assume that something bad will be attempted at an event like this. For all we know, it's her division being careful. And if they actually know more than we do, which I doubt, he doesn't know it, so it's only the barest of leaks."

"Because no one is going to miss this event," Reader said. "It's the talk of the town. Paul can't take two steps outside the Pontifex's residence without someone asking if he's going to be at the ball."

Gower nodded. "I'm sure your friend's call won't stop your other friends from attending, Kitty."

"Dude, where in my explanation did I make it sound like most of these people are my friends? Classmates, yes. Friends, no. Only Eugene. We're not in with the Washington Wife In Crowd, trust me."

"I don't think you need to worry, Kitty," Chuckie said. "This leak, such as it is, isn't enough to warrant anyone panicking, though after this is done, I may have a word with his wife and explain that her husband is snooping around. If she doesn't already know."

"Meaning she could be feeding him false information to keep him happy," Tim said.

"True enough," Reader agreed. "But I'm with Reynolds. This isn't a high enough priority to warrant any more of our time."

The conversation went back to the other higher priority problems. After a few minutes, it was clear that while high-level meetings had to continue, Jeff and I weren't adding all that much. I was tired, and the torpedoes were suggesting that baby feeding rather than psychopathic mind-melding would be in my best interests. Jeff and I went up to our apartment while Mom went with a few dozen A-Cs to get Dad and Jamie.

We got into our rooms, and I noticed something missing. A lot of somethings. "Where are all the Poofs?"

"I'd assume they're with Jamie and your father." Jeff shrugged. "You know they go wherever they want to."

Someone knocked, and I heard Jamie's Papa Sol and Nana Angela are the BEST Grandparents in the WORLD squeal-giggle combo. I also heard snuffling, yipping, and hissing. Jeff opened the door, and the tide of canines blew in, dragging A-C agents behind them, followed by the agents carrying the deluxe cat carriers. Mom, Dad, and Jamie came in, more A-Cs behind them.

"Wow, it's a party." I took my child, who demanded kisses from both Mom and Dad before letting go of Mom's shirt.

Mom gave Jamie a tickle. "She was angelic as usual. So unlike you in that one way."

"Hilarious." Dad opened the cat carriers, and all three cats exited from one. All the Poofs exited from the other. "Dad, why were all the pets and Poofs with you?"

He gave me a shocked and affronted look. "There was a potential gas leak. You didn't think I'd leave any of the animals in danger, did you?"

"No, Dad, no," I said quickly, lest the "they are our family members, too" lecture begin. "Just didn't think about it."

Dad nodded. "I understand, kitten. There's been a lot going on." He looked into our bedroom. "Jeff, where are the dog beds?"

Jeff coughed. "In the other room. The big dayroom," he added hopefully.

Dad's expression went from pleasant to stern instantly. "The dogs are used to sleeping with us. They're excellent protection, too."

"I don't really want the animals in the same room as Jamie," Jeff said.

"We had cats and dogs before Kitty was born, and they were always in our rooms." Dad shook his head. "You have the Poofs in the room with you."

"They're different," Jeff said, clearly grasping for any port in this storm.

Dad shot him the Evil Parent Eye. "Jeff, when you agreed to take the pets, we went over sleeping arrangements."

"Oh, Dad, relax. You know they'll be in our room within a matter of minutes, no matter where Jeff put the dog beds." In my experience, the dogs merely dragged their beds to where they wanted to sleep and then refused to budge.

"Where are you planning to have the cats sleep?" Dad asked, voice like ice.

"With us," Jeff said quickly. "I'm just worried that the Poofs might, ah, get territorial and hurt the dogs. Or the cats."

"Oh, don't worry about that," Dad said, all signs of annoyance gone. "They got along wonderfully while we were over at Paul and James' residence." He pointed into our room again.

Sure enough, Candy and Kane were both on the larger Poof Condo already, surrounded by Poofs, all snoozing as if they'd lived here together forever. Sugarfoot was grooming himself and also the three Poofs hanging out in the middle of the bed with him. Clearly the Poofs and the cats were getting along just fine.

I heard some snarly sounds, took a look over my shoulder, and sure enough, the dogs were all dragging their beds down the hall. Duchess gave me an extra wag as she pulled her bed into our room. Dudley shot Jeff a betrayed look as he followed her. Dottie dropped her bed on Jeff's feet, indicating clearly that the rest of the job was his. Duke, never one to pass on a good idea, did the same.

Jeff heaved a sigh. "No problem. Our room's big enough." He picked the beds up and arranged them in a row along the side that didn't have the Poof Condos and the door to Jamie's room on it. The dogs took this opportunity to wash his face. "Gah. I'm cleaning up. Kitty, are you ready to feed Jamie?" I could tell he was praying my answer would be yes.

"Yes."

Jeff shot me a grateful look. "Great, be right there." He trotted into our bathroom.

"Mom, are you sure Dad should go tomorrow?"

Mom nodded. "It'll raise suspicions if my husband isn't with me for this. The President's clear on what your father does and what your father knows." Mom shot me a look, so I was pretty sure the President also knew what Dad didn't know, meaning the President knew more than me, but that was always a given.

"Okay, if you're sure." I realized my tone didn't indicate I was sure, because my father hugged me.

"I'll be fine, kitten."

"But, who's going to watch Jamie if we're all at the President's Ball?"

"Gladys," Mom replied. "Believe me, she's excellent."

"With babysitting or protection?"

"Both." The way Mom said it, clearly Gladys had her Mossad Stamp of Approval. "And Denise Lewis will be with her."

"Why doesn't Denise get to go to the President's Ball when Dad's going?"

"Kevin's not attending, at least, not as a guest. And Denise doesn't actually want to go."

"I don't want to go, either."

Mom laughed. "I'm sure. But you'll be fine, kitten."

"My Washington Wife teacher told me to disavow all knowledge of the class while I'm there." I figured it would be better if she heard that coming from me.

Mom's eyes narrowed. "Well, I'm sure Missus Lockwood has her reasons."

"You know her?"

"Yes. I'm not a fan." Mom kissed my cheek. "She's not my kind of woman. There's more than one way to handle things, kitten. Your ways seem to work, so don't let that stuck-up, condescending, uppity woman with the most overinflated ego based on doing the least amount of actual meaningful work bother you."

"Don't hold back, tell me how you really feel about her."

Mom snorted. "Be happy I'll be too busy tomorrow night to spend any time with her, or else she'd get an earful, if not my fist in her face."

I hugged her. "Thanks, Mom."

She hugged me back, but not the bear hug, since I was holding Jamie. "Any time, kitten. No one disavows knowledge of my daughter and gets a pass from me. They might get shot, sent to Guantanamo, or merely cut dead, but they don't get to insult my child, and my parenting skills, in that way and get off without some form of pain."

I hugged her again. "I love you, Mom."

"I love you, too. You'll be fine tomorrow, kitten. Just do what you do best, and don't let the people who'd never have the courage to face what you do on a regular basis get you down."

"Turkey opinions shall be avoided, I promise."

Mom kissed my cheek. "That's my girl."

CHAPTER 54

MY PARENTS LEFT, AND JEFF AND I settled in to take care of Jamie. The dogs only tried to help a few times. Jeff found this unsanitary and freaky, but Jamie didn't seem to mind at all. Me, I'd grown up with dogs shoving their noses into anything I was doing, so no biggie from my side of the lounger.

Feeding, bathing, and the rest of the nightly routine over, we put Jamie to bed. She was just starting to transition from bassinette to crib. Some nights she wanted to be in the bassinette, others she wanted the space. Tonight was a crib night, presumably because she had extra Poof companions. Poofs on guard duty were not an issue.

We tucked her in with her half of the baby monitor, closed the nursery door, got into our nightclothes, made sure our half of the baby monitor was securely on the nightstand, and snuggled under the covers. I'd gotten used to the sleepy purring sounds the Poofs made, and the cats were similar. The dogs were louder, but it was a comfy sound, four dogs snoring, dreaming, scratching.

"Why weren't the animals more upset about being left by your parents?" Jeff asked as he turned off the light on the nightstand. Since we were in a "human" building, so to speak, we actually had windows and got to turn the lights on and off. I'd gotten used to the night light glow, but since we kept a night light on in the nursery, I made do.

"They're my pets, too. And they adore you. I'm sure the dogs and cats are looking at this as a cool vacation. We'll know if they start to get homesick." I'd been homesick for three months, so I was sure I'd recognize it in the pets should it overtake them.

Jeff hugged me. "I know you don't like it here. And nothing that's happened these past couple of days has helped."

"Getting Len, Kyle, and Pierre here has. Just haven't had any time to enjoy them being here, really. And I don't feel like we're doing anything useful or helpful anymore. We used to matter. Now, I don't know."

He sighed. "I do know what you mean, baby. I sometimes wonder if Richard was insane when he suggested this."

"I know. I miss kicking butt."

"You kicked some yesterday and today."

"Not really. You did a lot more of that than I did."

"Not really. And not effectively."

This was getting morose. I decided a conversation switch was probably in our best interests. "I made a new friend. At least, I think so."

"Yeah? Who?"

"One of the moms in my Mommy and Me class. Her son is a couple of months older than Jamie. She's an adjunct at Georgetown, and her husband is a law professor."

"Does she know what you do?"

"Yeah, she knows I'm an ambassador. She didn't seem overawed by it. Or like she was being friendly to suck up. She seemed like . . . me, really."

Jeff hugged me. "Good. So you have a friend in each of those classes. That's great."

"Mommy and Me is a lot more fun than the Washington Wife class. And I doubt anyone in it is going to try to kill me, or anyone else, either."

"You never know. You're the one who likes to point out how the cops don't like to go to domestic disputes."

I laughed. "True. Bernie's call was the only one I enjoyed."

"Bernie?" He didn't sound happy. "I thought you said it was another mother."

"Whoa there, big fella. Rein in the needless jealousy. Her name is Bernice. Her nickname is Bernie. Her husband's name is Raul."

"Ah, okay. What's their last name?"

"You know, I didn't get it."

"Oh, well, doesn't matter. What was she calling for?"

"To make a play date for her son and Jamie."

"Sounds nice. When are you going?"

"No idea. She was hoping we could go tomorrow. I said no because, well, frankly, who the hell knows what's going to happen tomorrow, especially after what's happened the last two days?"

"Yeah." Jeff sighed. "I'm sorry."

"It's okay."

"No, it's not. You're unhappy, and you finally have someone who made you feel normal and happy, and our jobs are preventing you from getting to do normal mother things."

"Not really. I mean, our current job almost begs me to do the normal mother things so we fit in here. It's our old jobs, which we both miss more than I know we want to admit to each other, that are causing the issue."

"Yeah. Maybe we should leave it for the others to handle. And I just don't mean tonight. I mean in general."

"Maybe." I thought about Mom's parting admonition. "I don't want people to die just because you and I are trying too hard to fit in or gracefully stepping aside while others take over our roles. We're not exiting CEOs of a corporation. We're part of the team that protects this world on a regular basis."

Jeff chuckled. "Thanks for the pep talk, baby." One of the dogs started having a noisy dream, and Jeff jumped.

"You going to be okay with all the animals sleeping in the room with us?"

"I think so." Jeff cleared his throat. "How, ah . . . how do they react when you're . . ."

"Having sex?"

"Yeah."

I snuggled next to him and nuzzled his neck. "Well, honestly, there's only one way to find out."

"Very true," Jeff purred as he pulled me closer to him. This was definitely a better conversation. "And let me mention again that I love how you focus on the priorities."

"It's a gift and a skill."

CHAPTER 55

JEFF PULLED MY TOP OFF WITH ONE HAND while his other stroked my breasts. He moved his mouth to my neck, and I moaned. He nibbled, and I moaned louder. The soundproofing in the Embassy truly lived up to its hype—we'd never woken Jamie once, and considering I was sometimes shattering crystal, it was the one good thing about living here.

"Mmmm," he said against my neck. "Last night was too long ago." He bit my neck, and I yowled my agreement while my hips started bucking. Jeff stopped the lovely things his hands and mouth were doing. "What was that?"

"Um, me?"

He looked over his shoulder. "Ah, no. We have company. Interested company."

I sat up. Sure enough, Duchess was at the side of the bed. "Good girl, back to bed." She gave a doggy sigh and went back to her bed. She settled in, but she was watching. "Stay. Good girl." I lay back and pulled Jeff onto me. "We're good."

We started back up, I yowled happily, Jeff stopped. "We are not alone."

I looked around. The three cats were all awake, watching. I sat up. Duchess was still in her bed, radiating long-suffering good dogness. The other three dogs, however, were covering the "watching from the side of the bed" portion of the festivities.

"All dogs, back to bed!" I got three more dog sighs, but they did as they were told. "Stay! I mean it." I lay back down. "Ignore the cats and they'll get bored."

"Really? You're used to this?"

"Yeah. Trust me, I know my parents still do the deed. I think they're interested because it's us, and it's all new, in that sense."

Jeff looked around. "I'm not really used to an audience."

"They're dogs and cats. We do it in front of the Poofs all the time."

"The Poofs have the decency not to look, or at least not to let me know they're looking."

I looked closely at his expression. Sure enough, he was embarrassed and freaked out. And, sadly, no longer even close to being in the moment.

I pondered my options. It wasn't as though this was the first time I'd ever been in this situation. I rolled out of bed and went to the pantry in the kitchen. "Deluxe dog biscuits, large size, flavored for preference." I opened the pantry. Sure enough, the Elves had the pantry covered as well as the refrigerator. There was a large box of biscuits sitting on the shelf. "You guys rock. Whoever you are."

Went back into the bedroom, tossed four biscuits each to the dogs, grabbed the parent side of the baby monitor, and jerked my head at Jeff. "Come with me, quickly."

Jeff hypersped out of the room, and I shut the door, leaving the dogs munching happily. I put the box back and the monitor on the counter. "Okay, now, let's relax while they eat. They'll all settle down with us out of the room."

"You're sure they won't bark and wake the baby?"

"I'm positive." If the soundproofing here ensured my cat-in-heat yowling didn't wake the baby, it was unlikely the dogs were going to manage it. "Okay, I'm going to get a Coke, then we're going to go to the living room, sit on the couch, and relax." And, hopefully, reenact pleasant times from the Lair.

"Okay." Jeff didn't sound convinced. I decided not to focus on that. We'd managed to get past my freaking out about waking Jamie during sex. We just needed to get past his freaking out about dogs and cats being around. We could do that, right? I stretched while I tried not to worry. I opened the fridge and bent over to grab a Coke.

Before my hand closed around the can Jeff was up against me rubbing in a very pleasant, interesting, and insistent manner. "Mmmmm, do that again," he growled.

"Do what again? Bend over? Stretch? Get a soda?"

He picked me up and flipped me so my legs went around his waist. "All of the above."

Well, this had been my plan, so I wasn't going to argue. I stretched and bent back, so I could close the refrigerator door. Why

waste the electricity? Besides, we didn't need the light—windows
or no, there were night lights all over the place. I passed on the
soda. I planned to have my mouth otherwise occupied.

Earth-friendly actions over, I straightened up to find Jeff definitely purring, with the "jungle cat about to eat me" look on his
face. I loved that look. He buried his face in my breasts, and we
reenacted the first orgasm he'd ever given me. I was all over this
kind of nostalgia.

I'd sort of figured we'd head to the living room and a couch, but
Jeff had other ideas. Still ravaging my breasts and squeezing my
butt while I ground against him and did my best to get his T-shirt
off, he took us into the formal dining room. He flung a chair aside
and laid me back onto the table, so my behind was at the edge.

Before I'd met Jeff I'd had a fantasy about being ravaged on a
conference table. Since meeting him I'd had that one fulfilled more
than once. But it never got old, and a big dining room table resembled a conference table in more ways than one.

Jeff had his shirt and my pajama bottoms off now, though he was
still in his. He grabbed my wrists and held them up over my head.
"I've heard you're unhappy with your current job. I think you need
to apply for a new position."

"What sort of work experience are you looking for?" I was managing to talk only because he didn't have me completely insane
from desire. I didn't figure speech was going to remain in my rep-
ertoire long.

He gave me a slow smile as he slid the fingers of his free hand
over my neck, playing with the spots he knew make me incoherent.
"I like to train up. Show you how we do things around here." His
fingers stroked my breasts and gently rubbed my nipples.

I gave up on speech. Moaning was taking all of my vocal capacity. Jeff's mouth followed his hand. As his tongue curled around my
breasts, I gave up and let the yowling begin.

He trailed his tongue down as he let go of my wrists and slid his
hands to my thighs. As his mouth went between my legs, he spread
them wide. My yowling hit High C. Still keeping my legs wide, he
gently flipped me over. I grabbed the sides of the table as he nipped
my behind and went back to making me hit all the high notes.

I lost track of time, and orgasms, until Jeff's tongue trailed up
my back. He bit the back of my neck as he entered me and all I
could do was gasp and moan as his body's weight held me captive
while he pounded inside me.

"That's right," he growled in my ear. "Let's see if you can handle the pressure this job entails." He lifted his body off mine, slid his hands under me, cupped my breasts, and lifted, so my body was curved. I let go of the table and pulled my arms in, so I was resting my head on my forearms.

"Good," Jeff purred. "Now, let's see if you remember the rest of this important process."

I managed to make some inarticulate sounds that tried to indicate I not only remembered but thought of it fondly. I wrapped my legs around and under his butt, or, as I thought of it, moved my feet into position to help his amazingly perfect thruster engines put the pedal to the metal.

He spread one hand so it still supported me but allowed his thumb and little finger to play with my breasts, while his other hand slid over my stomach and down, to stroke me in alternate time to his thrusts, while I squeezed my legs in time with him, until I wanted to go insane from the feelings both inside and out.

This was one of the variations of the Alpha Centaurion Love Knot, and, as I'd discovered early and appreciated immensely, it was amazingly efficient at making me want to pass out from pleasure. It took very little time before an incredible orgasm hit. As it did so, Jeff pulled me up so my body was fully against his now.

In between shrieking his name, I grabbed the back of his head, while he bit down on my neck and, hands still doing their amazing job, pressed me down onto him harder, while he exploded inside me.

Jeff might have had an issue yesterday with recovery from swimming in the Potomac, but he was in his standard fine form now. As my legs unhooked, he turned me around, bodies still shuddering from climax, so I could wrap my legs and arms around him while he held and squeezed my butt and stayed inside me, getting ready for Round Two.

This time, he did head us to the couch. I wasn't empathic, and I couldn't read minds, but experience told me that since we'd done a variation, Jeff wanted to ensure I still loved the original.

Sure enough, he laid me on the couch and flipped my legs up to his shoulders, keeping my arms inside his, against my body. I locked my feet around his neck, grabbed those thrusters, and we went to town.

He was deep inside me this way, and I loved it. It was intense, almost frantic, him slamming into me, with me pulling him in even deeper the only movement I could make, every thrust feeling deeper and better than the last.

He'd just climaxed, so it took a while for him to build back up, but this was more than fine with me. I was busy yowling like a cat in heat while he growled because it was so intense that he couldn't talk, either. My orgasm started and, in this position, it just kept on going and going and going. The Love Knot ensured an Energizer Bunny climax, every time.

Jeff's body shuddered and then he roared as he erupted into me, and I climaxed so hard I could barely breathe.

My legs went weak, and he let them fall around his hips while he wrapped his arms around me and kissed me deeply. I usually couldn't talk immediately after this kind of sexual experience, and tonight was no exception. The beauty of being with an empath, however, was that I could instead allow all the feelings of love, lust, and gratification wash over me and know he understood and appreciated them all.

After a few minutes, Jeff nuzzled my ear. "Nice interviewing skills. You're hired."

I laughed. "Can't wait to start. I already love the benefits package."

CHAPTER 56

JEFF STOOD UP, CRADLED ME in his arms, and headed us for the bedroom, stopping only to grab the baby monitor.

The dogs and cats appeared asleep and uninterested, which hardly mattered, since I was blissfully exhausted. Jeff slid us under the covers.

"We're naked."

He chuckled. "Jamie won't care. We'll worry about clothes when we get up to feed her."

"O-kay." I wrapped around him, snuggled my face into his pecs, and went to sleep.

The sound of The All-American Rejects' "Gives You Hell" woke us, not Jamie. We got up quickly, found our nightclothes and put them back on, and checked on her. She was awake, playing with her Poof, several other Poofs standing guard.

"She didn't wake up for a feeding." I tried not to worry about this.

"She's fine," Jeff said as he picked her up and gave her a kiss. "Babies do sleep through the night, you know."

"Is she off schedule?"

He sighed. "I don't think we have a schedule to compare her to, baby. We'll mention it next week, when Tito does our tests again, if she sleeps through the night again."

I thought about what we were saying. More to the point, I thought about the fact that we were saying it in front of Jamie. "Not that there's anything wrong with sleeping through the night *or* waking up to have a feeding."

Jeff caught on. "Right. Jamie should do what's best for her health."

Our potentially unhelpful attempts to ensure our child didn't think we either did or didn't want her to sleep through the night over, we did the morning routine, which was nice, then tried to mentally prep for whatever this day was going to hold, which wasn't.

Potential assassinations aside, Jeff actually had ambassador-type work to do. Sadly, Lockwood was right—Jeff might think of me as the Co-Chief of Mission and Walter might use the title, but when it came down to the paperwork, at least, Jeff was the only one who mattered.

Then again, I didn't like paperwork. And we now had four dogs that needed walking. Of course, we also had lunatics after us, or possibly after us. I checked and verified that our outfits for tonight weren't in Pierre's hands so fittings would be later, confirmed that Caroline was still sleeping, made sure the new parents and babies were doing well, and got a "no thanks anyway" from Amy. Then I rounded up the boys.

They arrived at my door looking ready for action. I could tell they were both packing heat. "Dog walking time," I announced cheerfully.

Len and Kyle both stared at me for a long moment. "Are we driving?" Kyle asked finally.

"Um, no. While the dogs would be all for a cool ride in a limo and the idea of a dog park has certain charm until you, you know, think about it in regard to our dogs, the term 'walk the dog' refers to just that. Taking the dog and letting it walk. And do its business. In this case, letting all four of them do their business."

I could tell from their expressions that when Len and Kyle had envisioned working for the C.I.A., never had the idea of being on dog walking duty occurred to them. I felt for them. When I'd killed my first superbeing, I hadn't envisioned doing what I did now, either. Live and learn fast was my motto, of course.

"Come on, guys. I have to push the stroller. You're both big dudes. You should be able to handle the dogs without issue."

"It's their issue we don't want to handle," Len mentioned.

"It's a crap job, I'll give you that." Snickering to myself, I got the dogs' leashes on, handed Dudley and Duke to Kyle and Dottie and Duchess to Len, then got Jamie bundled up for the great outdoors.

Diaper bag hooked on one handle-hook and my purse hooked

onto the other, random Poofs along for the ride, we headed for the elevator. The dogs tried to pull the boys the way they did with whichever A-C had them; but though A-Cs might be stronger, football players were apparently better at dog handling, at least my two were. Both boys had the dogs minding by the time we reached the front of the Embassy.

Navigating the steps was an issue, or would have been if White hadn't joined us. "Need a helping hand, Missus Martini?"

"I never say no. You want to come for a walk with us, Richard?" It was a safe bet—he had his coat on.

"Frankly, I'd love to." He held the door for all of us, then helped me get Jamie's stroller down the stairs. Enhanced or not, her stroller had so many bells, whistles, and A-C gadgets on it that I couldn't lift it safely by myself, especially not with her in it.

We went over to Sheridan Circle Park first because it was close and the dogs really needed the stop. Len and Kyle remained underwhelmed by their dog duties, but they only complained a little bit. Dog necessities completed, I contemplated where to go next. It was a nice day, and we'd been out for only five minutes—seemed sort of a waste to just go back to the Embassy.

"Any suggested destination, Richard?"

He gave me a small smile. "I'm sure you're not aware of it, but we're fairly close to the Embassy of Paraguay."

"What a great destination idea!" It was particularly great because I knew without asking that Jeff, Chuckie, Reader, and everyone else would forbid us to go. Under the circumstances, I let the accurate mention of my lack of awareness slide. "Lead the way, Mister White."

We started at a slow stroll, Len and the girl dogs in front of us, Kyle and the boy dogs bringing up the rear, White walking next to me. It was rather pleasant.

The one positive I had to give this area was that the buildings were, for the most part, beautiful. They tended toward old and stately, with lots of mature and well-maintained foliage. The streets were loaded with trees, and there was a lot of grass. It was much greener than I was used to, coming from the beiges, browns, and reds of the desert.

One of the things no one had mentioned to me until I'd lived at the Embassy over a month was that it was actually disguised to look as old as everything else around it. It gave the feeling of having been here for a couple of centuries, as opposed to a few decades. Our Embassy wasn't the most astounding, architecturewise, but it absolutely fit in with its surroundings and achieved the whole "looking smaller outside than inside" thing, though everyone insisted it was just good design, not cloaking or any other mysterious visual effect.

"What's the word, Richard? Did anyone make any progress on any damn thing last night or this morning?"

"Sadly, no. Other than our Concierge Majordomo, who's planned the Embassy's social calendar for the next several months, presuming we all survive tonight."

I wasn't sure if I should feel happy nothing had progressed without my help or worried. Settled for both. "Pierre's a god."

"Truly. He's also ordered all the equipment needed for the school and day care center."

I ran that sentence over again in my mind. Wasn't computing. "Excuse me?"

White chuckled. "Denise Lewis wants to have something to do to pass the time, since she had to give up her job to relocate here. And our children don't go to regular schools." This I knew to be true; they were all schooled within the A-C community.

"Denise wants to teach and run a day care center?"

"The Lewises will be living on premises, and Kevin will have the title of Defense Attaché. Because she has a teaching degree and also has children living with us, Denise has graciously requested to be in charge of the day care center and school. For the Embassy personnel and for those in Alpha and Airborne who might prefer to have their children schooled here as well."

"Can I take my classes from Denise, too?"

"Sadly, no." White said this with a straight face, but I could tell he wanted to laugh. Hey, it was worth a shot.

It didn't take us too long to reach our destination. The building the Paraguay Diplomatic Mission was housed in was one of the more boring and nondescript ones—not ugly, just not trying to shout "look at me!" like some of the others. Our Embassy wasn't wearing glitter and fringe, but it was a lot snazzier looking.

"You sure we should be here?" Len asked. "They tried to kill us all two days ago."

"No. Assassins tried to kill us. Sure, they're associated with this diplomatic mission, but that doesn't mean everyone else here is out to get us, or even knows what's going on."

We all stared. The dogs got bored and sat down, heaving doggy sighs. "Looks like a building," Kyle offered.

"I don't see anything overly suspicious," I had to admit. "Should we go in?"

"I doubt that would be wise, Missus Martini. However . . ." White stepped away from me and wandered toward the side of the building. He was blocked from view from most of the street when he went to hyperspeed, zipped around the building, and stopped right where he'd taken off from. It was as if he'd never left. He shook his head, turned around, and came back.

"See anything good?"

"Nothing we can use. All the curtains are drawn."

"Is that normal?"

"We keep our curtains drawn," White reminded me.

"Yeah, 'cause we're not normal." I pondered my options. I really wanted to go into this Embassy. However, I had Jamie with me, and while I could legitimately get into trouble when I was alone, I didn't think it said Mother of the Year to drag my baby into potentially hostile territory.

"Remember, we walk in, we're on their land," Len said, apparently because he'd read my mind.

"Fine." I sighed. "Well, let's head on back then. At least I know where this building is now."

"Actually, let's head up a little farther," White suggested. "We can look at other Embassies."

"Gotcha. We're not casing Paraguay's Embassy; we're comparing architectural designs. Wise move, Mister White."

"I do my best."

I got Jamie out of the stroller and carried her. She might as well get to enjoy the architecture, too. After all, it was never too early to start learning, apparently.

We got back into formation, White pushing the stroller, and walked on. No one talked—we were all thinking. At least, I knew I was, and I assumed White was. The boys might have been thinking, or they might have been contemplating their letters of resignation, I couldn't be positive.

We reached a major intersection, crossed the street, and started walking back on the other side. Passed the Paraguayan Embassy— still a whole lot of nothing going on, especially from a distance. This walk was boring, at least by my standards, though the dogs were living it up in the sniffing, snuffling, and peeing on random trees departments.

However, as walks went, it was a nice one, sauntering up and down part of what was nicknamed Embassy Row. I wasn't expecting to see anyone I knew, since I didn't really know our neighbors well. We hadn't had a lot of bonding time during the one disastrous party we'd thrown.

So it took me a couple of seconds to realize someone was calling my name as she came running out of the Croatian Embassy.

CHAPTER 57

"KITTY!" MARCIA KRAMER RACED OVER, dragging Nathalie Gagnon-Brewer behind her. "What are you doing here?"

I stared at her for a long moment. "I'm an ambassador. We live in this neighborhood. I'm taking a walk, what does it look like I'm doing? What are *you* doing here?"

"Visiting friends."

"You two have friends in the Croatian diplomatic mission?" I found it hard to believe either one of them had friends outside of the Washington Wife class. The idea that anyone else could stand them just seemed too unreal.

"We have friends all over," Marcia said with a sniff. Her sniff was returned by all four dogs, who were busy sniffing the two new arrivals with interest. Marcia tried to shove them away surreptitiously, but our dogs were pros at avoiding anything but the most strenuous of hints.

Nathalie hadn't looked up from her iPhone. Apparently she was deep into another Angry Birds session and couldn't tear herself away, people in front of her and dog noses in her crotch or no. "Bonjour," she said absently.

"Nice to see you. See you tonight." I tried to walk on.

"Is this your baby?" Marcia asked as she sidestepped Dottie only to walk right into Dudley, who, after finishing his sniffing extravaganza, had pointedly moved himself between Marcia and me.

I wanted desperately to say we'd found the child held in my arms, who everyone in the world said looked exactly like me, in a basket on the Embassy steps, but I managed to rein myself in. Aunt Emily would have been proud. "Yes." Tried to walk on again.

"She's so cute," Marcia said.

"Thank you."

"Can I hold her?"

I stared at her. "No." Duchess growled softly. I had no idea if she was reacting to my feelings or not, but my dogs, like Jeff, were pretty in tune with my emotions, Duchess in particular.

She looked shocked. "Why not?"

"I don't pass my three-month-old daughter around to anyone and everyone."

"Oh, new mother thing. I get it." She looked at White and gave him what I could only think of as a coy smile. "Is this your husband? He's even more handsome than I've heard."

White resembled Timothy Dalton, and he was an A-C, so he was a good example of how to look amazingly hot when you were over fifty. However, my husband he was not. Having met him, I knew Marcia's husband was around White's age, though, so I could see how she'd be confused.

White smiled. "No, I'm her husband's uncle. Richard White. And you are?"

"Marcia Kramer. My husband is Senator Zachary Kramer, from Illinois." She put out her hand.

White took it and did the whole gallant thing, which included hand kissing. Unsurprisingly, he did it better than Gadoire had the other day, but it was still nauseating, though it might just have been making me ill because I couldn't stand Marcia. I managed not to gag, but it took real effort. The dogs didn't try to butt in, which was something of a shock, but I took the small victories whenever they showed up.

"And you, Mademoiselle?" White said to Nathalie.

She managed to drag herself away from her phone. "I'm a Madame."

Since White seemed intent on being polite, I broke down. "Nathalie Gagnon-Brewer, Richard White."

"Pleased to make your acquaintance," she said, offering her hand. White did the whole gallant thing again while I contemplated flowers, not to hide from Jeff but to keep from barfing. Maybe I'd have thought this was old world charming if I didn't have the far too recent memory of Gadoire slobbering on my hand to turn my stomach.

They finished, and Nathalie seemed to notice Len and Kyle for the first time. They both got appraising looks. "And who are your young men?" She shot me a sly smile. "You take the French ideas for both sides of the marriage, oui?"

It took me a bit to realize she was insinuating that Len and Kyle were my boy toys. It had apparently taken the boys less time. They were both busily petting the dogs, who were quite willing to act as distractions; Kyle's face was already red.

"Um, not so much, no. Great seeing you both. Dogs need to go do what dogs do on a walk. Would hate for them to do it here in front of your friend's Embassy."

"Oh, they won't care," Marcia said, with a casual wave of her hand toward the Croatians. I knew we'd mind, so I was pretty sure they would, too. I wanted to ask her just who she thought would say it was okay for someone else's dog to poop on their friends' property anyway. Particularly four large dogs. Particularly Dudley. No one wants a Great Dane to relieve itself anywhere in their general vicinity. The boys could already attest to that.

"I'd care." Tried to walk on again.

"Did you hear about Jack?" Marcia asked.

"He called last night, yeah. We're all still going to the President's Ball anyway, despite Jack's warning."

"Oh, I didn't mean about that." Marcia put her hand on my arm. Duchess did the low growl thing again, but Marcia either didn't hear it or wasn't worried about being ripped to shreds by my dogs. I wondered if she actually thought I liked her while Len got Duchess back under control. "Poor Jack, he killed himself this morning."

I stopped trying to walk on. "Excuse me?" My body felt cold.

She nodded. "Hung himself. It's so sad. Abner thinks it's because Pia found out he'd been snooping on her. They had a huge fight, and she went to a friend's house for the night. Poor Abner."

"Poor Abner? Jack's the one who's dead!"

Marcia shook her head. "Abner found Jack. He was worried about him after Bryce confirmed that Jack had called everyone from class to warn them to stay away from the ball. Abner's a mess."

"I'll bet he's going to make the ball anyway, though, isn't he?"

She gave me a dirty look. "He has no choice. Lillian needs to attend, so her husband has to attend with her."

"So sad," Nathalie said, back to Angry Birds, since the boys were still petting the dogs as if they were going for the Best Dog Walker of the Year Award. "Poor Pia."

"Why does no one but me think it's Jack we should be feeling sorry for? If you were all his friends and you thought he was delusional last night, why didn't someone go over and see him *then*, as opposed to this morning when it was too late?"

Marcia patted my arm, then took her hand away. "Like Bryce says, if someone's determined to kill himself, there's nothing anyone else can do to stop him."

"Are you kidding me? Of course there are things someone else can do!"

White put his arm around my waist. "Kathy, I think we need to move on. Mourn at home, dear."

Nathalie looked up, gave us a sharp look, then smiled again. "Ah. Pardon my confusion. Don't let us detain you any longer." She nudged Marcia. "They're on a time limit."

Great. I'd moved from an affair with the boys to an affair with my husband's uncle. Or an affair with all three of them. I had no clear idea how Nathalie actually thought, after all, but it was obvious her mind went straight to "affair" no matter what the circumstances.

"Oh!" Marcia blushed, proving she was also one with the "affair" mindset. "I'm sorry we slowed you down. Anyway, I figured you'd want to know about Jack. See you this evening."

"Yes, bye. Take care. Or whatever." I let White lead me off. Len showed restraint and didn't run down the street, though I got the impression he wanted to. "Okay, Rick, honey, I get that you wanted us to get away. But you know they now firmly believe I'm having an affair with you."

"Good," he said as he moved us along, still keeping a hold of me. "It will keep them off balance, and I believe that will be important."

"Why so?"

"Because those women were lying."

CHAPTER 58

"WELL, THEY BOTH CAN'T STAND ME, and color me totally shocked and impressed that any A-C can spot a human lying, but what do you mean? Do you think Jack isn't dead?"

"I'm sure whoever they said was dead is no longer with us on the mortal plane," White said as we walked down the street. "However, they weren't in the Croatian Embassy. They were in the doorway when we came by, but they weren't inside."

"You're sure?"

"Positive." Apparently he felt we were far enough away, because he stopped walking and pretended to fiddle with the stroller. "Gentlemen, your thoughts?"

"I agree," Kyle said. "I saw them in the doorway as we approached the property. The door wasn't open at any time."

"I saw them when we were on the other side of the street," Len said. "They were walking on the street and went into the doorway. But they didn't go into the building at that time."

"So, why did they hide in the doorway? So they could jump out at me?"

"To share that your other friend had died?" White asked.

"They aren't my friends, and neither is—was, he. Len, can you pull up the information on the death? Jack Ryan, owns a car dealership in Silver Spring, married to Pia Ryan, who works for the C.I.A."

Len made Duchess and Dottie sit, then got busy on his PDA while I pondered. Something felt weirder than normal. As I thought about it, neither woman had mentioned that their spouses had stopped by my Embassy the day before. Of course, it was possible they didn't know. I wouldn't share my business with them, and maybe their husbands felt the same. Or maybe they had another reason to talk to us. "Think they're involved in the stuff with Paraguay?"

"I believe it's possible," White said. "I'd say they're involved in something, and it's likely to be illicit."

"So why hide in the doorway of another Embassy?"

"Lookout?" Kyle offered, while Dudley and Duke stared intently behind us.

"That makes sense, actually. Len, anything yet?"

"Just coming through. Listed as a suicide. Because his wife works for the Agency, it's being treated as a possible homicide."

I thought about it. "You know, Jack didn't sound either drunk or delusional when he called me last night."

"I can't speak to the inebriation," White said, "but if he was warning you, he wouldn't sound delusional to you, since we, in fact, know something bad is going to happen tonight."

"Yes, but there's a difference between loony conspiracy theorists and the ones who know what they're talking about. And, trust me, they sound different."

"True. You did spend many formative years with Mister Reynolds."

"Exactly. So, let's take the leap and say that Jack didn't kill himself, but instead he was murdered. Why kill him?"

"Because he'd leaked information," Len said without missing a beat.

"Chuckie wasn't worried about it. If the Conspiracy King doesn't worry about a leak, I'd guess no one else does."

"Well, it wasn't a leak out of our division," Kyle offered. "Mister Reynolds might have worried if it had been."

I stared at him. "He leaked C.I.A. information. And it was out of *someone's* division. Maybe that someone wasn't happy that people were being told to stay away from the President's Ball."

"Specific people," Len suggested.

"Yeah, maybe, because while Jack said he'd called everyone in class and the instructor, it didn't sound like he'd called anyone else. He might not know anyone else who's going to the ball other than his wife's coworkers. And Eugene and I were dead last on his to-call list, so I think he might have said something if he'd called other people before his Washington Wife classmates."

"Do you have a roster of your classmates?" White asked.

"Apparently I do somewhere. We can look for it when we're

back. Did anyone pay attention to where Marcia and Nathalie went after we left them?"

Kyle nodded. "Our sunglasses have mirroring inside, on the outer parts of the lenses."

"You have rearview mirrored sunglasses? Really?"

He shrugged. "The C.I.A. has all the cool toys. Anyway, they watched us, then they walked off in the other direction."

"They went out of range once we'd stopped again," Len added.

"Why are the dogs still staring back there, then?"

Len shrugged. "Dogs have better senses of hearing and smell than we do. Do you want us to go back and follow them?"

I tried to sight along the same way Duchess was looking, since she was the best trained of the four dogs. As I did so, I saw that she was actually looking across the street. I could just see the Paraguayan Embassy in the distance, but that wasn't what my dog was watching.

She was watching a man I recognized. I'd been seeing him a lot recently. "Why is Malcolm Buchanan hanging out down the street?"

The men with me all turned. Either Buchanan noticed or he had seen enough of whatever he was watching, because he wandered off in the opposite direction.

"Who's he?" Len asked, sounding suspicious and willing to make Jeff proud in the defending my honor category.

"Yet another person from my Washington Wife class. Not one of the jerks. At least, as far as I know."

"I believe he was watching you," White said.

"I saw him earlier," Len admitted. "But he didn't seem interested in us."

"Before." This was now the third time I'd spotted Buchanan somewhere just hanging around.

"He was watching you," Len said. "I just thought it was because he thought you were hot." Len seemed to realize what he'd said, because he matched Kyle in the turning red department.

While Len busied himself with being embarrassed, I wondered if it was time for a restraining order, but dismissed the idea as a little too flattering toward myself. If Buchanan was following me, I had to figure it wasn't to see if I wanted to have an illicit affair. "I honestly don't think he's after me like that." I didn't. There was too much going on, and Buchanan had now been identified as likely being involved in it in some way.

"Do you want to follow him?" Kyle asked. He didn't sound like he thought this was a great plan, but he'd be willing if I was all for it.

Part of me did, but I honestly didn't have any guess about what we'd find out. And with Jamie along, it didn't sound wise. Plus, if I sent the boys without me, Jeff would have a conniption fit if he ever found out, and I was fairly sure he'd find out. And if they spotted both Buchanan and the women, and they weren't together, then the boys would likely split up, and that meant they could be in danger.

"No. This is yet more weird to add to the almost nothing we have to work on."

"True," White said, as we all started walking again. "However, we have another person dead, before the main event."

"And there would have been more dead, too, if Mister Joel Oliver hadn't been around and we hadn't worked really well as a team yesterday."

The conversation died down as we strolled along. I wondered if anyone else from the Washington Wife class was going to call me or leap out from the bushes to share some more weirdness. While I waited for the next round of strange and unusual, I pondered everything, but doing it silently meant I was getting nothing other than the strong feeling that Ryan had been murdered.

I hadn't liked him at all, and he hadn't liked me, either. But he'd still called to warn me, and I knew he'd been warning me about real danger, even if the others he'd contacted didn't. And now he was dead, and it didn't seem like any of his so-called friends really cared.

Why I cared I couldn't say. But I did. We'd lost six agents and now Jack Ryan, and I had no idea if the events were connected, but my gut said they were. My mother believed in listening to the gut.

Sadly, my gut had no concrete information to share, like who was behind this, who the real assassination target was, or what we could do to stop it. My gut was totally letting the rest of me down, but there was nothing I could do about it.

My brain suggested I run my mouth, as opposed to continuing on in silence, which clearly wasn't working for me. But I didn't really want to chat about the nothing we'd gleaned so far from this excursion, mostly because we were going to have to rehash it the moment we got back to the Embassy.

Of course, we could always talk about something else. I went for continuing our prior conversation. "Did Jeff and Christopher go to school at the Embassy, Richard?"

He took this out-of-the-blue question in stride. "In a sense. They were the only children here when Theresa was our Head Diplomat.

She handled their schooling." This I knew to be true in more ways than one. "Once she . . . passed away, the boys were schooled at East Base."

We reached Sheridan Circle and crossed into the park to give the dogs one last chance. "You know, I hadn't thought about day care or anything for Jamie." Yet another one in the Good Mother Fail column. "I didn't think she'd need it this young."

White coughed delicately. "Your penchant for running off into danger isn't exactly a secret."

"Hey, I didn't go into the Paraguayan Embassy. Either time."

"Yet."

"Fine, fine. But it's not like I'd have raced in there, even if something exciting had happened when were nearby, not with Jamie along."

"No one believes that, Missus Martini, Pierre least of all. Yesterday was all it took for Pierre to declare that the day care center needed to be put into operation immediately."

"Can't argue with the logic." Dog duties done, we crossed the street. Because of how the circle crosswalks worked, we ended up in front of Ireland's Embassy, with another street to cross to get home. I looked down Massachusetts Avenue and heaved a sigh. "Especially since we have unfriendly company. Again."

CHAPTER 59

L **EN SPOTTED WHAT I HAD**—three taxis heading for us.
Three very familiar taxis.

He stopped walking at the corner by an open area between
buildings, presumably so we'd have an exit strategy. We were close
enough to home to make it if we ran, but under the circumstances,
crossing the street didn't seem wise. White and I moved closer to
him, and Kyle did the same, still flanking us.

I contemplated my options and put Jamie back into the
stroller. Once she was in, I lowered the sun shield completely, so
no one could see her. "Poofies, be on small and quiet guard duty.
Protect Jamie." Poof purrs and tiny growls assured me that the
Poofs were on top of things. I also kept my finger over the laser
shield button.

"Let's buddy up to the stroller, just in case," I suggested, as I
pulled Len a little closer. White did the same with Kyle. Good,
ready for anything they'd want to throw at us—literally, I hoped.

The three taxis drove around the circle and pulled up to the curb
next to us. "You folks need a ride?" the driver of the first taxi asked.
He was disguised as he'd been the day before—poorly. I still
couldn't tell what country he might originally be from, including if
it was this one.

The boys had made the dogs sit, but all four of them were sniffing like mad.

"Seriously? You're trying this tactic again, after it worked *so*
well for you yesterday? Oh, by the way, give me back the picture
and the rest of the things you stole."

He grinned at me. "Finders keepers." He had good teeth, which tended to indicate an affluent country of origin. Or at least an affluent upbringing.

I did a quick check. The other taxis were behind his, idling, with their drivers behind the wheels, no firearms in evidence. If this was a kidnap attempt, it was a really low-key one.

I wasn't particularly worried, not the way I'd been the day before, and not just because we had more, and better, backup than yesterday, or because we were less than a block from our Embassy. I just wasn't getting any indicators that it was time for fight *or* flight. "What's going on?"

"We're hoping you can tell us."

"Who is 'us'?" I could see Len out of the corner of my eye—both girl dogs were on their feet and straining at their leads. Checked Kyle out of the other corner—same with the boy dogs. All four seemed quite intent, though they weren't barking or growling.

"We're friends."

"Right. Friends don't kidnap each other."

"That depends." He cocked his head. "If you'd come with us yesterday, you wouldn't have ended up in the river."

"I like swimming. And I'm sure I'd have ended up somewhere else unpleasant."

"Unpleasant is in the eye of the beholder." He checked his rearview mirror. "Some of what you have to do is very unpleasant. Many of those you consider friends are considered by others to be unpleasant. But you still trust them. And you should trust us, too."

"Why would you think I'd trust you at all? Especially since I have no idea who 'you' are, whether it's just the three of you on some bizarre crusade or if there's a whole bunch of you out there, or what you actually hope to achieve with any of this, other than stalling us from getting around the block."

He shook his head. "Just because you refuse our offers of help doesn't mean we're your enemies."

"It also doesn't mean you're our friends. Why are you protecting the Dingo?"

He rolled his eyes as he checked his rearview mirror again. "We're not. We're not the ones who took him. We're trying to protect *you*. Why do you think we arrived before?"

"You mean after the bomb two days ago before, when you chased us, or last night before, when you also chased us?"

"Both. You needed us, we arrived. Just because you didn't take advantage of our services doesn't mean we're not here to help you."

"Why are you here now? Nothing's going on."

"There's always something going on. You know that. Besides, you'll enjoy the ride, trust me."

"Fine. You want us to become bestest buds? Start with sharing your names. And your affiliation."

Dudley started it. He growled, low, deep, long, and nasty. Duke followed suit, then the girl dogs joined in. Dottie started the barking, but it took almost no time for the others to add in. They were barking at the taxi and the ones behind it, as near as I could tell, and it was taking all the strength the boys had to keep them under a semblance of control. These weren't friendly barks—these were Enemy Alert barks.

The reason for my dogs' reactions raised its head. There was a German shepherd in the backseat. It bared its teeth at my dogs, who shared that they were perfectly willing to take him or her on, best two out of three.

I checked the other cars. I could see dog ears in the taxi behind us, and I heard the sound of other dogs barking, so I assumed each cab had a dog of some kind in it.

"What the hell is going on and who the hell are you?" I shouted over the din.

The taxi behind him honked. He grinned. "Call me Ishmael," he called. "And I'm affiliated with Rapid Response Taxi Service." With that he gunned it, and the taxis headed off, each one with a German Shepherd leaning out a window, barking and snarling right back at my dogs.

All of a sudden, Dottie's bark changed. She spun and started the Happy, Happy, Joy, Joy bark. The others caught on and did the same. I recognized this greeting.

I turned around to see whose arrival had signaled to the Three Stooges that it was time to go and to my dogs that it was time to calm down. I was sort of unsurprised to see that it was Chuckie.

CHAPTER 60

CHUCKIE WAS ALONE, WHICH DID SURPRISE ME. "What the hell is going on?" he asked as he got nearer to us.

"Where's Jeff?"

"Back at the Embassy, being the ambassador. The one who doesn't get to run off at top speed any time he feels like it." He patted the dogs, and they calmed down. The dogs loved Chuckie. Not as much as they loved Jeff, of course. I didn't think they actually loved me, Mom, or Dad as much as they loved Jeff. But Chuckie was definitely up there on my dogs' Top Ten List of People We Love the Mostest.

"I don't buy it."

Chuckie sighed. "I was alerted by your dogs barking their heads off."

"How could you have heard them? I know they were loud as hell, but the soundproofing in the Embassy is amazingly good."

He mumbled something.

"Come again?"

Chuckie sighed. "Fluffy and some of the other Poofs started acting stressed and were throwing themselves at a window. Since we know they can somehow travel wherever they want in a way no one understands, it was pretty clear they wanted us to see something. Your husband and I went to look and saw your dogs going nuts. Martini monitored your emotions. You weren't scared; you were annoyed. We checked the surveillance cameras; I didn't think it was a good idea to have a bunch of A-Cs race up out of nowhere. So, I came, since that's part of my job. Now, I ask again, what the hell just happened?"

"You tell us." I brought Chuckie up to speed on the taxi situation. I deftly left out the fact that we'd walked up and down the street, or that we'd run into Marcia and Nathalie, let alone that we'd spotted Buchanan doing the Nonchalant Dude on Observation Duty routine. I'd save that for later. "Ishmael might be some sort of clue, but to me, he's Moe, and the other two are Larry and Curly."

"Did you pick up anything?" Chuckie asked White and the boys.

Len nodded. "They were watching for who was going to come out of the Embassy, all three of them, the two who weren't talking to us in particular."

"They only watched the Embassy," Kyle added. "They didn't look around."

White looked pensive. He was also looking around carefully.

"What's up, Mister White?"

"I'm trying to figure out why they came right now."

"Want to explain that?"

He nodded slowly. "The two times you've seen them, you'd just gone through a dangerous situation and were, for all intents and purposes, out in the open. The only other interaction we've had with them was when they created the gas leak to plant surveillance in the Embassy."

"Correctamundo. And I see your point. Why did they drop by now? Nothing's blown up, at least that I know of, and we're not being pursued, so why show up when all we're doing is walking the dogs?"

Chuckie's eyes narrowed. "We're not done scanning the neighborhood, but this would indicate that they knew you were out. And that means you're right—they installed surveillance somewhere we haven't found and neutralized." He cursed under his breath. "Every Embassy in this area could be compromised."

"Maybe. They were insisting they weren't part of the big plan. They also said they were trying to protect us from the Dingo."

"No," Len said. "He said they were trying to protect *you*."

"I assume he meant the inclusive 'you.'"

"I don't think he did. He was only talking to you. He didn't look at any of us, not even Mister White. Only you. And you were the only one of us here who ended up in the Potomac, and he didn't say anything about how we'd have been spared worrying about you or anything like that."

"So I have a fan club? Lucky me."

Len looked at Kyle. "What about the other two?"

Kyle shook his head. "Like I said, they were watching the Embassy, pretty much exclusively."

"So I have a fan club of one, and his pals tag along. Still not thrilled."

"No one got anything else?" Chuckie asked, clearly hoping one of us had managed a bit more.

"Ishmael didn't sound like he had an accent." Hey, it wasn't much, but it was something.

"Does that mean you think he's American or that you think he's good at disguising his voice?"

"No clue, sorry."

"Their license plates were caked with mud," Kyle said, "so I couldn't get the numbers."

"Figures." Chuckie heaved a sigh. "Well, at least they didn't attack you."

"No. Though with the dogs they had along, it was a possibility. But I'm pretty sure our dogs could have won." Though I wasn't positive. The three German Shepherds had been darned big, and all my dogs tended more toward the lover, not the fighter, side of the house.

"Let's hope we don't have to find out," Chuckie said. "Anything else? At all?"

Len looked a little uncomfortable. He took a deep breath. "We went by several other Embassies on our walk. Specifically, the Paraguayan Embassy. Twice, once from each side of the street."

Chuckie gave me and White a long look. "Which one of you suggested that?" He didn't sound happy.

White shrugged. "I did. We found nothing of interest."

"The curtains were all closed," I added. "Not that I know personally because I stayed on the street with Jamie, the dogs, and the boys."

Chuckie raised his eyebrow. "Really?"

"Yes," White said. "I did a quick check at hyperspeed. All curtains closed, no real sounds coming from inside. However, that means nothing—I'm sure their soundproofing is excellent."

"See? I'm not an idiot, Chuckie."

"Yeah? I've heard those kinds of protests from you before. They always come right before you do something even more dangerous than you've insisted you won't do."

"Well, we did get some other information, too."

Chuckie's eyebrow rose again. "Really? What? And just when did you plan to share?" He didn't sound pleased. At all.

"It's that Jack Ryan supposedly offed himself, and as for when, when we were home." I gave him what we'd gotten from Marcia and Nathalie. "They didn't mention that their husbands had dropped by yesterday, either."

Chuckie shook his head slowly. "I'd assume that visit wasn't on anyone's books, and I doubt any of those who came to see us told their significant others about it. Most of what they do ends up being classified. I can't stand any of them, but the ones with high-level clearances have them for a reason. I'm with you, though, on Ryan's 'suicide.' The timing's just a little too convenient."

"You think the C.I.A. took him out because he leaked about the President's Ball?"

"Possible, but no one believed him."

"Well, someone did, because I really don't think Mister Jack 'I know Tom Clancy had me in mind when he created the character' Ryan was the suicidal type."

"There was also someone watching Kitty," Len added. "A man from her Washington Wife class."

Chuckie gave me the hairy eyeball. "Really. And when were you going to share *this* tidbit? Never, later on this afternoon, or when we're all running for our lives?"

I refrained from calling Len a narc, but it took effort. Then again, Chuckie had hired him and Kyle specifically, and, as he'd be the first to remind me, the people protecting you have a right to share when you've been a tad free with the risks.

"Geez, dude. Home. I was planning to tell you, Jeff, James, Tim, and whoever else when we got home, which, if the Stooges hadn't shown up, would have been about ten minutes ago."

"Right. Does your husband buy it when you toss this B.S. at him?

I shot my best withering glare at him, to which Chuckie responded with his Dead Man's Stare that was, frankly, a lot more intimidating than I'd ever let him know. "Scoff all you want, Secret Agent Man. I was telling the truth."

"Sure you were. So, who's your latest stalker?"

"Malcolm Buchanan. He's sort of a loner, but, unlike ninety-nine percent of the class, he's never been nasty to me. However, I've never seen him around outside of class before these last couple of days."

"He following you because he thinks you're hot?" Chuckie asked, as if this could be the likely reason.

"Could be. Len thought so," Kyle said, while Len gave him a

dirty look. At least neither one of them was blushing. "I can't say I'd argue with the theory, either."

"Oh, please."

Chuckie shrugged. "You're the one who tends to be clueless about this sort of thing. I, on the other hand, spent half a lifetime watching men pine for you."

Since Chuckie had been, as far as I knew, the only one so pining, I didn't want to continue this conversation. I was enjoying not feeling guilty every day for not realizing he'd been in love with me. It was never a line of thought that made Jeff happy in any way, either. Plus, there was too much weird going on.

"Flattering as it is that all of you seem to think I'm a femme fatale, trust me, I really think he must be involved somehow."

White cleared his throat. "I think we need to pay attention to other matters."

I thanked God for the conversation shift as the rest of us looked where he was, at the Romanian Embassy, which was across the street from ours. It was big and blocky, nicely done, but nothing ornate, not one of the "look at me" Embassies. It was, however, sparkling clean, which, since it was bright white all over, was pretty impressive.

However, White wasn't observing the building's architecture. There was someone standing at a window on the second floor. Standing there, watching us. And, now that we were all looking, whoever it was waved and made the "come here" sign.

"Interesting. I think someone wants a visit."

"No," Chuckie said flatly.

"It's Romania, not Paraguay. I doubt they're still harboring a grudge over that party." The person was waving more insistently now. I couldn't tell if it was a man or a woman. "Is the waver wearing gloves?"

"Yes." Chuckie sounded impressed with me. I wondered if this meant he'd let the walk to the Paraguayan Embassy and my slowness to share slide. It was unlikely, of course, but a girl could dream. "That's why we can see the hands well, but not the face. I think he or she is taking care to be hard to see."

"But Richard saw them."

"Yes. I remind you that A-Cs have enhanced eyesight. I truly believe whoever's up there wants to speak with us."

"So why doesn't whoever it is come out?" Kyle asked.

"Maybe he can't," Len said. "Or . . . maybe he's afraid of being spotted."

I decided I'd had enough standing around wondering. We were across the street from the Embassy, and at least three of the men with me were packing heat. Plus, I had four big dogs and an assortment of Stealth Poofs.

I shoved the stroller toward the front door. A little faster than I'd intended, but fortunately White was able to catch up and grab me before I slammed us into the building.

This meant, of course, that Chuckie and the boys had no choice but to follow us. Which was good, because I didn't even have to knock. The door opened the moment we reached it.

There was no one there.

CHAPTER 61

"HELLO?" I WASN'T CROSSING the threshold until I knew we weren't heading into the Romanian House of Horrors.

A young woman's head peeped around the door. I realized she was behind it. "Please come in, Ambassador."

It was such a shock to hear someone, anyone, refer to me as an actual ambassador that I gaped for a moment. Recovered quickly. "Thanks. Don't let the stroller roll over your toes—it's heavy."

She smiled. "Not to worry." She looked at the dogs. "Could you, perhaps, take your pets around to the back?"

"No," Chuckie said. "Get the dogs back home," he told Len and Kyle. "Advise the ambassador that we're visiting neighbors."

The boys shot worried looks at me, but they nodded and headed to our Embassy. The young woman looked a little disappointed for a moment, then put a welcoming smile back on.

We trooped in. It was nice inside. A big mahogany visitor's desk dominated the entry room, with a staircase curving up behind it, very Turn of a Couple of Centuries Ago—though I didn't spend a lot of time looking around. I was fairly sure Chuckie was handling that part of the festivities.

Once the door closed behind us, the girl bobbed her head. "The Ambassadress would like to speak with you. If you'll wait a moment, I'll fetch her."

She trotted upstairs while we all exchanged the standard "what's going on?" looks.

"You know her?" Chuckie asked.

"No." I got Jamie out of the stroller. She had her Poof in her hands, and I decided that was probably smart. It looked like a stuffed animal, after all, and that way, if needed, her Poof could activate without issue. "Harlie, Poofikins, into Kitty's purse. Other Poofies, guard Richard, Chuckie, and the stroller." Poofs disappeared into male pockets as I put the diaper bag where Jamie and the Poofs had been and put my purse over my shoulder. "Chuckie, Fluffy's with you, right?"

"Right," he mumbled. Jeff always acted like this about the Poofs, too, which cracked me up. I refrained from singing "Macho Man." Out loud. It was playing in my head, though.

White, unsurprisingly, had no issue with a couple of Poofs. "I don't recognize the young lady, either. She wasn't one of the guests at the . . . party."

"Amy's not here. We can call it a fiasco."

"Then how does she know you?" Chuckie wasn't going to let this one go. "Oh, and let me mention—you just lost whatever points you'd made by not going into Paraguay's Embassy. We're now on Romanian soil, meaning that we're subject to their laws and there's not one damn thing I can do about it."

"Not to worry, Mister Reynolds," a woman's voice said from above us. "You are guests of Romania, not prisoners. And not enemies."

We all looked up. The young woman was helping an older lady. She was older than Mom but not as old as my Nana, at least as I judged it.

She smiled at us. "We are alone; just Adriana and I are here right now."

"I'm afraid you have the better of us, Madame," White said with extreme courtliness.

She smiled again. "I do, do I not? I am Olga Dalca, wife of Andrei, who is our ambassador." I opened my mouth to introduce ourselves, but she waved her hand. "No, no. I know who you are, Ambassador Katt-Martini, and your Mister Reynolds. And Former Pontifex White, I know you as well. Your two young men are new, are they not? The ones who took your handsome animals back home? I believe their names are Leonard Parker and Kyle Constantine, is that correct?"

"Yes," Chuckie said, clearly unhappy she knew this information. I realized that, until this moment, I hadn't known either one of their last names, or that Len was his nickname. I felt out of the loop, which was pretty much my par for every course. "I confess to failing to remember meeting you, however, Ambassadress."

"Oh, you have not met me, Mister Reynolds. Not until today." Olga sighed. "I would come down to greet you properly but . . .

perhaps you would come up instead? I would very much like to see your child."

I had Poofs on me, and she didn't look or sound dangerous. I also figured the stroller would take care of itself. I trotted up the steps, White and Chuckie following me.

"This is Jamie, our Junior Ambassadress," I said as I reached the second floor and realized why Olga hadn't wanted to come down. There was a wheelchair behind her—Adriana was literally holding her up. The gloves on her hands had to have been custom-made; they were extremely fancy, dove-colored and dainty—but they were workout gloves like the ones I'd seen wheelchair athletes use. "Please, don't feel you have to stand on our account."

Olga smiled warmly. "Thank you. I would have asked your young men to assist me, but since they did not accompany you, that was not an option. Besides, it's nicer up here." She sat back down with a sigh. "Adriana, please bring our guests something to drink, they look thirsty." Adriana headed downstairs while Olga turned her wheelchair around, then rolled down the hall. "Please bring the beautiful baby here, to the sunlight."

I followed her along a short hallway. She was right—this floor was lovely, decorated in what I took to be Old Romanian Treasures and Trinkets style. But it was warm, comfy, and not at all what you'd expect from the outside.

We went into a room that was clearly a study, with what I realized was the window we'd seen her at. There were actually two windows in the room, near each other, one with a view of our Embassy and one with a view onto the Circle. Both were floor to ceiling, and there were handicapped railings around them, which explained how she'd been able to stand and signal to us.

Chuckie prevented me from going to the windows. He went instead, to each one, and checked out the surrounding buildings.

"Chuckie, really."

Olga chuckled. "He is cautious, and this is wise. We are safe here, at least so I believe, but better to be sure." She was turned sideways to the window that faced our Embassy. She reached for Jamie. "May I?"

She wasn't Marcia Kramer—I handed Jamie to her. Jamie studied her for a few moments, then grabbed her nose. Olga laughed. "Oh, she is adorable. How old?"

"Three months."

"So advanced." Olga said this quite calmly. I felt some suspicions starting to wriggle.

"I suppose. She's our first, so I wouldn't know," I lied.

Olga looked at me. "I see you are cautious, too. This is also wise."

White cleared his throat. "Ah, Madame? I believe you wanted us to visit, and I have to assume it wasn't just to meet the baby."

"Oh, but of course it was," Olga said, giving us a very wide-eyed, innocent look. "At least, that is what I will say, and you will be able to say it, too, since it is true."

"What are you afraid of?" I asked.

"Or who?" Chuckie added.

Olga shrugged, gently jiggling Jamie and making goo-goo faces at her, while Jamie giggled. "Afraid? I am not afraid so much. For myself, at least. For others? For them I am quite afraid."

"Why tell us about it?"

She looked up at me. "Because you are the only ones who can stop it."

CHAPTER 62

"STOP WHAT?" CHUCKIE ASKED, voice carefully neutral. "There are a lot of 'its' going on right now," I added. I doubted I'd achieved the same neutrality in my tone, but I wasn't Mr. C.I.A., so I cut myself a break on that one.

Olga looked out the window. "I like it here. The medical care is very good. I would not be doing so well if I were back home."

"What are you suffering from?" White asked. He didn't sound impatient or anything. I figured I'd been going to all those classes for something, and if Olga wanted to extend the visit by getting around to the pertinent facts slowly, so be it. Diplomacy was going to be my middle name, at least for as long as I could manage it.

"Multiple Sclerosis. I can move without the chair less and less these days." She sighed and looked back to us. "Therefore, I have a different view about many things." She kissed Jamie on the head. "Because I sit here most days and watch the world outside, I see things. Many things."

"Things of interest to us?" Chuckie asked.

"Oh, I'm sure." She smiled and looked back out the window. "I know American Centaurion is . . . different. Sometimes I take pictures, so my Andrei can tell me who it is I'm seeing." She chuckled. "He said your little party was quite the event. I would have enjoyed it greatly when I was younger."

"It was a disaster, but I'm really glad you're not holding a grudge."

She laughed. "Oh, my dear, we all make mistakes. You're all so young. You'll learn." She gave White a conspiratorial smile. "As those of us who have lived longer already know."

"I'd appreciate learning what it is you want to tell us," Chuckie said politely while White chuckled. "We're on a schedule of a sort."

"Oh, yes. The President's Ball. I won't be attending."

"It's handicapped accessible."

Olga looked up at me. "Yes, it is. And the President sent a personal message, asking me to consider attending, especially under the circumstances."

"Circumstances?"

"Our president is coming for the event. That is why only Adriana and I are here right now. The rest of our mission is with him on a tour of the city. He would like me to attend as well. But it's hard to escape if you're in a wheelchair. And I cannot be certain an Alpha Centaurion will be near enough to me when disaster strikes."

I looked at Chuckie. "Does everyone in the world know?"

He shot me the "shut up, shut up" look. "I'm sorry, Ambassadress. I think you meant American Centaurion."

Olga was clearly too well-bred to roll her eyes, but I was pretty sure she wanted to. "Mister Reynolds, please. Let us drop the pretense. As I said, it's only Adriana and myself here. We know, she and I. Only we two. Andrei suspects, I believe, but it's difficult to believe. Unless you spend your days watching."

"What conclusions have you drawn?" White asked.

She shrugged. "You're here to protect and serve. Most of you, anyway. I know you must feel you're not doing well right now."

"The Party from Hell was a tip-off, yeah."

She shook her head. "You were genuinely trying. Andrei told me how devastated everyone seemed when things went . . . awry. I understand there were tears."

"Doreen's very pregnant, and Amy was really expecting better results." Hey, I'd managed not to burst into tears in front of people. I'd saved that for when I was alone with Jeff. I was a good wife and ambassador that way.

"I can tell you truthfully that the people who had your mission before you would have thrown a perfect gathering."

"Great, good to know."

I got the Severe Mother Look. Wow, I hadn't realized my mom hadn't made that one up on her own. "Their party would have been perfect. And only some would have been invited—only those whose influence they were courting."

"Our new Concierge Majordomo says we didn't invite enough people."

She nodded. "Perhaps not. But your oversight was based on location and being very new here. No one was left off the list as an intentional slight. Your invitation did say 'our nearest neighbors,' did it not?"

"Yes. Amy did a nice job with those. She did them by hand." Why I was trying to get any kind of kudos for the fiasco I couldn't say, but you're supposed to support your best friends' efforts.

"They were lovely. Please let her know I have preserved ours in a memory book."

"Will do." I didn't want to ask if it was the Nice Handwriting memory book or the We're Still Laughing At THIS memory book.

"However, your predecessors would never have invited most of the countries you did. And for those who were so lucky as to receive an invitation? No real emotions would have been expressed. No caring. They put on good faces, but they were not good people."

Well, events had certainly proved that to be true. "That sort of sounds like D.C. in a nutshell."

"No. As you will find, many are here to do the best they can. We don't all agree, but most of us do try to do what is best."

"Best is in the eye of the beholder," Chuckie mentioned.

"True." Olga chuckled. "However, I can assure you, those you replaced were not working for anyone's interests but their own."

She was right, of course. I was curious how she'd figured it out, though, since the former Diplomatic Corps had fooled most of the A-C community for years. "What makes you say that?"

"I met them. They were not pleasant because Romania was not of interest to them. We had nothing they wanted. And refused to perhaps give them things they might want in the future. We were not of . . . like mind."

I could feel the hair on the back of my neck stand up. "What countries *were* they friendly and of like mind with?"

"Oh, all the majors. They had a particularly strong fondness for France."

"Yeah, we sure know that."

"They were also quite friendly with the South American countries." She made eye contact with me. "Especially Paraguay."

CHAPTER 63

I COULD FEEL CHUCKIE PRAYING that I'd keep my mouth shut. But as far as we knew, we had a world of hurt heading toward us, and we knew nothing. Olga, who apparently spent her days looking out of two windows, seemed to know a lot more than we did.

"Paraguay's been coming up a lot recently." I felt that was a noncommittal enough statement that Chuckie might not strangle me for it later.

"I'm sure it has been. It is quite pivotal for certain things."

"What things do you mean, Madame?" White asked.

"So sad about the police force," Olga said with a sigh. "I am not certain the correct decision was made."

"You mean to put Titan Security in charge, or to lay off what seems like half the police force?"

"Either." Olga smiled at Jamie. "So sad, to be willing to disavow your loved one, just for the sake of politics."

"You mean the head of Titan, right? Someone influential is his son or daughter or something?" Per Oliver, anyway. Of course, also per Oliver, there wasn't enough evidence to make an educated guess as to who said relative might be.

Olga kissed Jamie's fingertips, which earned her the I Love YOU baby giggles. "What do you know of Titan?"

"What *should* we know?" Chuckie countered.

"Have you met him, the man in charge?"

"No." I looked at Chuckie, who shook his head. "Really? You've never met him?"

"No need." He looked at the desk. There was a newspaper on it.

Chuckie picked it up, flipped to the business section, and handed it to me. "He's always in there somewhere these days."

"Wow, just like Ronald Yates used to be." Of course, Yates had owned the media outlet, and this man didn't actually look like Yates. But I could see the resemblance in his expression, which said he was taking over whether anyone else liked it or not.

He looked around sixty, plus or minus, and appeared trim. Nothing exceptional about Mr. Antony Marling really, other than that he headed the top private security firm in the U.S. and, per the article, possibly the world. "Huh. He's a French expat."

"He and his wife both have very interesting names, don't you think?" Olga asked.

I scanned the article. He was "in" with the Pentagon as well as some others—Madeline Cartwright was credited with the "one of our most trusted suppliers" line. She really knew all the best dudes.

After the Pentagon's little "we love Titan" paragraph and a typical "wonderful suppliers and people" quote from Cartwright, I found the wife's name. Cybele Siler Marling, who had also been, per this article, "a weapons genius in her own right," had died years before. Twins, a boy and a girl, were mentioned but not named. According to the article, they'd died when his wife had.

"Um, yeah. Interesting. Hers especially. Very French. Or something. So, his wife and kids are supposedly dead." I looked over at Olga. "Any guess as to which one of them is really alive and working as a politician in Washington?"

Olga shook her head. "The only other thing I know of Mister Marling is that he is very fond of visiting France and Paraguay. And that he might have children the press is not aware of in both of those countries and here. Or he might not."

Maybe he was more like Yates than I'd first thought. "So it could be anyone. Or no one at all. Great." Story of our lives these days.

"You may keep the paper," Olga said graciously.

"Um, thanks. I think." I folded it up and shoved it into my purse. "So, Paraguay, France, Titan . . . is there a connection we should be making?"

"The men in the taxis," Olga said, looking at me, "what did they tell you?"

I held back the sigh I wanted to heave as Olga sent us off onto yet another tangent. "That they were friends and we should trust them and go for a ride somewhere. Oh, and the driver said his name was Ishmael."

She nodded. "Didn't something strike you as odd about what they did?"

"Everything they've done and said so far has struck me as odd. This isn't our first encounter with them."

"I see." She looked, quite pointedly, at Chuckie, who was really doing a good job of not looking impatient with Olga's pussyfooting around.

My brain kicked. "They left when Chuckie came." I looked back at Olga. "That's what you mean, isn't it?"

"Yes. Your new young men have firearms on their persons, do they not? So the drivers would not have run because your Mister Reynolds was coming with a gun." I didn't even ask how she knew Chuckie and the boys were packing heat. Either she could see the outline or she was making an extremely educated guess.

She looked at me expectantly. Great, another mother-type testing me. I wondered if my mom had sent a memo out or something asking anyone who ran across me to really make me work for it before giving me any necessary information.

But, since I *was* my mother's daughter, I was trained to actually think when the test questions appeared out of nowhere in the middle of dire circumstances.

I considered what Olga had and hadn't said. It was clear to me that she knew a lot, if not everything, about what was going on. But she didn't want to come out and say whatever. So she was protecting herself, which made sense. However, she wanted us to know, so she was likely dropping hints we were missing.

I looked at Chuckie again. She seemed to feel he was key. He looked back at me. "Chess?" he asked rather hopefully.

"Probably. It always is. But I can't be sure if we're playing one game with one really sneaky opponent or speed chess with a whole lot of lesser players. And I have no idea what pieces are where, let alone who either side's king really is."

Sure, the current working hypothesis had Esteban Cantu as the head of Operation Assassination, but that didn't mean he actually *was*—he could be working for the real big bad fugly, and, based on all the very high-level things that were going on, most of which seemed above Cantu's pay grade, it was likely we hadn't identified that person yet. So, until we knew who that was, we had no idea of what was happening on our opponents' chessboards. And we still had less than no idea of who our side's king was.

I was proud of myself for thinking of all of this silently, and I knew without asking that Chuckie was the happiest man in the world that I'd so managed. But basically, all I'd done was confirm for myself that we were still pretty much nowhere. Go me.

I sighed. "Len and Kyle didn't get much more than we did, but should we have them come over?"

Olga coughed discreetly. "Oh, I'm sure the new young men would enjoy Adriana's company and she theirs. But I'm sure they're too new to matter in this discussion."

She was using the word "new" an awful lot, and it seemed quite intentional. I looked back at Chuckie. Silence wasn't working for me. "Why would Len and Kyle being new matter to the Three Stooges?"

"No idea," he said. "They didn't recognize the drivers . . ." He stopped talking and looked at Olga. "But the drivers recognized me, didn't they?"

She gave him a small smile. "They did seem to leave the moment you were in the doorway of the American Centaurion Embassy."

My brain decided to kick in. "They recognized Chuckie, and clearly not as the international playboy he is."

"He pretends to be," Olga corrected gently.

"Right, whatever." I took the logic leap. "So, they left not because they knew who Chuckie was but because—"

"I'd know who they were," he finished for me. "Len and Kyle are too new to know all the various terrorists out there . . ." Chuckie looked at Olga closely. "But that's not what you're insinuating. The drivers know me because we work together in some way."

She smiled. "See? I knew you would know."

"So they're C.I.A.? They honestly don't seem . . . sneaky enough. I mean, they've been sneaky and able to get past us, sad as it is to admit, but they just don't seem up to the level of what I'm used to from the C.I.A." I jerked. "They were in here yesterday, weren't they?"

"Oh, yes," Olga said calmly. "Adriana did not leave them alone, and she and I refused to leave the building, even though there was the possibility of a dangerous gas leak." The way she said it, it was clear that Olga, at least, hadn't been even remotely concerned that the gas leak might be real.

"Did they plant bugs?"

"Of course they did." Olga smiled at the expressions on our faces. "However, we do know how to find and remove them. They were in what I would call the standard places. All were focused on your Embassy," she added casually.

Chuckie's eyes narrowed. "I had operatives come in here last night."

"You did. They were very polite. We allowed them to search, of course. It would not do for us to allow just anyone to know that we are able to spot and disable surveillance equipment. They might ask what I did before I married Andrei."

"You were some kind of special ops or KGB or something, weren't you?" If my mother had been Mossad before she and Dad got married, why not Olga?

She laughed. "How would an old lady in a wheelchair have ever been a part of the KGB? Really, such a silly question." Of course, she winked at me as she said this.

"Right, gotcha, Comrade." She laughed again. "Okay, so, Chuckie, what did your teams think of the surveillance stuff they've found so far?"

"It's as Comrade Ambassadress said: They were in all the standard places. My teams searched in all the nonstandard places, but they were clean." He cocked his head at me. "You don't think they're C.I.A., do you?"

"I don't know. But it wouldn't surprise me if they were F.B.I. or Homeland Security or something. Do you know?" I asked Olga.

She shrugged. "I believe I do. However, my assumptions are not the same as yours."

I groaned. "Are we still being bugged or something, and you don't want anyone to think you've willingly helped us?" Olga was about to answer when Adriana came into the room with a rolling cart that had a pitcher of lemonade and several glasses, along with some little cakes and cookies.

Adriana poured and handed glasses around. I could tell Chuckie wanted to do some sort of poison test on everything, though he took a glass politely. "There's no alcohol in this, correct?" he asked pointedly, as White took his glass.

Olga and Adriana exchanged an amused look. "No, Mister Reynolds," Adriana said. "We wouldn't want to cause any of our Alpha Centaurion neighbors distress."

"And I don't believe we are still being bugged, no," Olga said to me. She looked at Chuckie. "A part of you must be wondering if you should have asked to bring your dogs inside instead of sending the young men to take them safely home."

I thought about this. They weren't Chuckie's dogs, and she most certainly knew that. "Dogs . . ." I took my glass and decided to go for it. I took a drink. "Tart. Very nice."

"Dogs?" Chuckie asked, as he and White took the Lemonade Nestea Plunge and had a sip. None of us convulsed and dropped to the floor. I took a cookie.

"There were dogs in each taxi. Big German Shepherds. Who the hell drives around with big dogs in their cars? I mean, while they're trying to do dangerous or clandestine work? Other than K-9 cops, I mean."

Chuckie and I looked at each other, then back at Olga, who had the pleased look of a kindergarten teacher whose prize pupils had just managed to finger-paint an acceptable-looking flower. I had the feeling Olga was teaching the very slow kindergarteners today, but hey, at least we were catching up and catching on.

"Oh, please no," Chuckie said. "We've got undercover local LEOs involved, too? Can this get any worse?"

She shrugged. "Things are going on in their city that they need to protect the citizens from, aren't they?"

"They'd be the only cops around who are doing anything, at least in my limited experience from the past couple of days."

Chuckie's eyes narrowed. "But there are no undercover K-9 divisions here."

"Those dogs were impressive specimens, so I can believe they're trained. Cop trained or not, though, I can't say. We didn't interact with them enough. Thank God."

Olga shrugged again. "I don't believe they are your enemies."

"So why are they after me, then?" I asked, after I finished the cookie. I grabbed a little cake.

"I presume they believe you to be in danger," White said as he sipped his drink. "Or to have information they need or want. Delicious beverage, ladies."

"Or both," Olga said. "And thank you, Mister White, Adriana makes wonderful refreshments, doesn't she? Thank you, Adriana. I believe you'll be needed downstairs." As she said this, Jamie, who was still sitting in Olga's lap, looked toward the Embassy and cooed expectantly.

Adriana trotted off. I heard the doorbell ring.

"Chuckie, why don't you want local law enforcement involved?"

"Because they get in our way, cause delays we probably can't afford, and generally muck up the works."

"They occasionally stop crimes and catch criminals, too," I

reminded him while I snagged another little cake and filled up my glass. "Though not actually in this city. At least so far as my experiences show." I had my suspicions, so I filled up another glass, too.

"Yes, but this is a huge international incident, meaning it's not within their jurisdiction, though they'll spend a lot of time trying to convince us otherwise."

"So far, they haven't done anything like that."

"Yeah? Then why have they been around so much? If," Chuckie added with a sideways glance at Olga, "we aren't being fed a different line of misdirection."

There was a soft knock, and Adriana put her head into the room. "I'm sorry Ambassadress, but there are other visitors."

Chuckie moved so he was in front of me and Olga. I could tell by the way he was standing that he was ready to pull his gun. Adriana stepped aside, and someone walked in carrying a big basket wrapped in cellophane and tied with a huge ribbon. The basket was quite large, Adriana wasn't all that tall, whoever was carrying it was, and he also clearly wanted to avoid hitting her with it, because he held it up high.

This meant we couldn't see his head. Chuckie's hand was moving for his gun when the basket lowered, revealing Jeff's face. Chuckie relaxed while Jamie made the Daddy's Here! squeal.

Jeff nodded to him. "Thanks. The jocks are downstairs. Guarding the stroller." The way he said it, I assumed the boys were also checking the stroller for any potential bugs and such.

"Good. Next time, lower the basket sooner, please." Chuckie stepped aside. "Ambassadress Dalca, please allow me to introduce Ambassador Martini."

She smiled. "Call me Olga."

"I'm Jeff. Ambassadress, this is, ah, a little something we wanted to bring over to apologize for the party."

She laughed as Jamie bounced expectantly on her lap. "You mean, this is a good ruse to get you over here without suspicion, because you know your wife, your child, your uncle, and your friend are here with me, and you do not know why."

Jeff gaped at her for a moment. "Close enough, yeah. But we do mean it about the gift." He put the basket down on the floor at her feet, picked Jamie up, and cuddled her. She made Happiest Baby in the World sounds, which earned her several Daddy Kisses.

Jeff looked around again as I handed him his lemonade. "Thanks, baby. So, you've told her?"

Chuckie shot Jeff the "shut up, shut up" look. "No," he said quickly. "The Ambassadress was just about to finally share her thoughts about Paraguay with us." She hadn't been, but apparently Chuckie was hoping this broad hint would do the trick.

Instead, Olga reached down and opened the basket—and gasped.

CHAPTER 64

"OH MY!" OLGA SAID, STARING at the basket and its contents.

I looked into the basket, just in case whoever had put this together hadn't been Pierre, and therefore hadn't done it right. Nothing looked overwhelmingly familiar, the packaging on everything
was in a language I couldn't read, and it was all arranged beautifully. I relaxed.

"Romanian specialties," Olga said, clearly pleased. "We cannot
find any of these things in America." She looked up and gave us a
very fond look. "I appreciate your agents picking these things up
for me, in between their killings of what I believe you call superbeings and protecting us in other, more mundane ways."

While the men looked uncomfortable, I tried to figure out how
Olga knew as much as she did, former KGB agent or not. A
thought occurred. "You read the *World Weekly News*, don't you,
Olga?"

"Oh, yes. The reporter, Mister Joel Oliver, he's quite the inves-
tigator."

Jeff grunted. "You all still think he helps us?"

"Oh, he does," Olga said. "You must understand—I believe him
because I observe. Most don't, not even those whose jobs are in
surveillance. They have other things to do, to think about." She
gestured to the chair. "I . . . not so much."

White cleared his throat. "Ah, Madame, I believe we would all
relax a bit more if you were to share with us the information you've
gleaned. In a more straightforward manner, since we all know lives
are at stake." I was impressed and really wanted to know why White

hadn't nominated himself as our Chief of Mission, since he was clearly the best we had right now with the diplomatic touch.

She beamed at him. "You're quite good. I do understand why those who had your mission prior were so determined to eliminate you." Olga looked back to Jeff. "However, we were actually discussing the gentlemen in the taxis."

"What were the conclusions?" Jeff asked.

I brought him up to date with the semblance of what we thought we might know. "So, we're still guessing about who they actually are. And Chuckie really wants to know what's going on with Paraguay." So did I, of course.

"You really think they're law enforcement of some kind?" Jeff didn't look convinced. "They don't really dress like it from what you've all said."

"You're used to Chuckie and guys from the big agencies, who always wear suits. Some people do go undercover, and they do it by not looking exactly like their counterparts. You know, like *Serpico* and every other cop show on TV. The way Richard and I did in Paris."

Jeff grunted. "Let's not reminisce."

"Please," Chuckie said strongly, still shooting us the "shut up, shut up" look. I didn't know why—Olga seemed to be the most informed person in town, so it wasn't like we were fooling her.

"Fine. Let's talk Paraguay."

Olga nodded. "There are some very . . . unsavory things going on there."

"How unsavory, and how involved is the Paraguayan government?"

Olga shrugged. "It's like your government—some are involved and some are not."

"Do you feel like naming names?" Chuckie asked.

"Absolutely not," Olga said calmly. "For me to accuse anyone of wrongdoing would be . . . undiplomatic."

"Fantastic." Chuckie took a long swig of lemonade. "So, I assume you'd somehow like us to play twenty questions and pray we can figure it all out before more people die."

"More people?" Olga asked. She actually sounded surprised, which both shocked and interested me.

I nodded. "We lost six of our agents, and someone I know supposedly committed suicide last night or this morning. And, yes, I think they're related, but we have no ideas of how, or even why, let alone who's actually in danger."

"Is that all?" Olga asked.

I looked at Chuckie. The migraine was clearly riding shotgun. Checked out Jeff. He had the "here we go again" look on his face I was used to. Turned to White. "What are your thoughts?"

"I believe we have an ally who would like to be very sure before she shares her information," White said. I noted that both Jeff and Chuckie looked resigned.

"Works for me. Olga, there are also international assassins involved, who've tried to kill me more than once. The taxi guys who are apparently local undercover cops are adding into the mix, though we don't know why or what their game really is. We've had three whole phalanxes of extras from the Matrix movies chasing us. I think we have at least one, maybe two, maybe more, supersoldier projects going on, at least one of which is running wild in Paraguay. The Potomac's cold and gross. And the traffic in this city is nobody's friend."

She laughed. "That is very true." She leaned forward. "As to what you just told me, remember that politics is like a very convoluted ball of yarn. You pull the string, and sometimes what unravels is not what you expect."

I nodded. "To quote the immortal Buckaroo Banzai, remember . . . no matter where you go . . . there you are."

She blinked. "Excuse me?"

"I have more sage sayings I can pull up, if we're going for Washington Name That Useless Tune or something. However, pulling yarn, while a folksy euphemism, isn't helping us with this current situation any more than Buckaroo's wisdom. Hard facts, even if they're tiny, would be so much more useful." I looked at my watch. "Because we have, based on Mister Watch here, less than eight hours before the President's Ball starts, and we have no idea who's marked for death or not. Please, let's do Chuckie's blood pressure a favor and cut to the chase."

Olga smiled. "Your mother tends to prefer to cut to the chase, as you say, as well."

"I knew you'd know my mom, because that's just how it goes for me. So, are you two bitter enemies, frenemies, or compadres?"

"Oh, we are quite friendly now. I find your mother to be an exceptional woman. You are very much like her."

"Awesome. Then, let's pretend it's Mom asking, shall we?"

Olga laughed. "As you wish."

"Super. Who's the damn target?"

She shook her head. "I don't know. I just know that something very bad will be happening tonight."

"Awesome. Is Titan Security involved?"

"I'm sure they are."

"Excellent. Head man is in the know?"

"Mister Marling would be in the know, yes."

"Cool. Is he working with someone in a position of governmental power or is he cowboying it?"

"It's difficult to be certain, but I'd assume he is not executing a complex set of plans without some sort of assistance."

"Booyah. What agencies might be working with Titan on this little assassination plan?"

She laughed. "The C.I.A., of course. Not your division," she said to Chuckie. "I'm sure several others as well, but they would be . . . secondary."

"Fabulous. What's going on with Paraguay?"

"Exactly what you think. There is a dangerous project being run down there. And while the danger at the President's Ball is more imminent, the project endangers everyone."

"Everyone who?" Chuckie asked.

Olga looked somewhat surprised by the question. "Everyone in the world."

CHAPTER 65

"WOULD YOU MIND EXPLAINING THAT?" Chuckie asked.

"Certainly." Olga shook her head. "Killing one person, even a few persons, is nothing compared to the creation of creatures that are chaotic killing machines and close to impossible to kill."

"How the hell have they found a parasite to infect anyone recently? We took down the ozone shield on Alpha Four. The few superbeings that still manage to show up and form on Earth our agents destroy. That should mean we wiped out and continue to wipe out all their potential new recruits."

Olga shrugged. "Allies shift and change, do they not?"

"Are you insinuating Alpha Four's sold us out?" Jeff asked, eyes narrowed.

Olga looked across the street at our Embassy. Then she looked back at me. "Not really."

"It's the freaking former Diplomatic Corps, Jeff. They were in Yates' pocket. For all we know, they knew he was Mephistopheles."

Chuckie nodded slowly. "If that was the case, and I agree that it seems likely, then Mephistopheles could have actually had something, maybe much, to do with this."

"Dude, I'm betting he started it. It would be just like him. For all we know, Mephistopheles might have been able to control the specially created supersoldiers, too, or at least figured he could, based on them being created in his heinous image." I wondered if they'd all have his same icky breath, then realized that of course they would. All the in-control fuglies had stunk up the joint, so there was no reason to assume their sorta-progeny would have had breath mints added during their creation.

Olga nodded. "You must destroy the project. There are indeed several, but the one in Paraguay is the closest to success."

"That's why Titan's down there, and that's why they had Caro and everyone being watched. They're not protecting our congressional fact-finding team, they're protecting the supersoldier project."

"Then why try to kill you?" Jeff asked.

I looked at Olga. "Because we get in the way. All the time."

"And you get in the way the most," Chuckie said. "You were Enemy Number One per the last major operation."

"But they wanted Jamie last time," Jeff said, as he cuddled her protectively. "The assassins would have killed her, too."

"So we have different groups with different goals. You know, like always."

"Is it always?" Chuckie asked.

"Often enough. Though, yeah, we usually have one lunatic mastermind per operation. But the Puppet Masters always seem to throw lots of different crap at us, just to keep it fresh and exciting." I was going to say more, but my phone rang. Mercifully, it wasn't an unknown number. I stepped away so that I was by the window that faced the Circle and the others could continue our Discussion of Doom. "Hey, James, what's up?"

"Girlfriend, answer these questions for me, would you? Why did Pierre send six teams to Romania on a 'mission of vital importance'? Where the hell are you, Jeff, Richard, and Reynolds? And why are your dogs sitting on my feet?"

"The dogs love you, we're across the street with the Romanian Ambassadress, and Pierre is doing his job. He's the only one adapting with poise and competence, which may be why you're confused. Maybe we can make him the Chief of Mission."

"I wish. I don't want to even ask why you're all over there. I just want to request that you come back soon and have some actual intelligence to report when you do."

"You miss me?"

"Always, babe. However, I'm really missing information, a game plan, or a hope of averting domestic and international tragedy."

"You were a lot more fun when you weren't the Head of the Field."

"I'm designing the posters for 'Give Us Back Our Old Jobs Week.' However, that won't happen if we have nothing. Like we do right now."

"Working on it."

"With Romania?"

"You'd be surprised."

"Always am. Time, it's of the essence."

"Gotcha, Mister Main Man. We'll be home soon. Soonish. Pronto."

I heard voices in the background. "Oh, and Tim says that Walter says that Pierre says that Amy says that some guy named Vance came by to see you. When he found out you weren't here, he didn't stay."

"Why was Vance around, and why was Amy answering the door?"

"No idea. I've been in what we call War Room discussions, mostly discussing how we're all going to fail and die, most likely in a few hours. It's amazingly unfun to tell our friends in the P.T.C.U. about our lack of results."

"Be home soon, just have to stop by a park and score some uppers, 'cause boy, does it sound like we all need them."

"Sounds good, but you don't need to score for everyone. Lack of information just seems to make your mother more determined to kick butt."

"I'm not surprised."

"I'm not either, girlfriend. I know where you get it from." I heard more voices. "Kevin told me to tell you that he's viewing this like being down at halftime during the Super Bowl, so I think he's prepping a 'go team' speech. Paul says he's looking on the bright side of life, too. And Tim says he's not willing to give up having his own driver."

"Nice to know. I'll score extra uppers just in case you and Serene bring the others around to our way of thinking."

"Come home first and take your dogs with you to the park. They're really demanding a lot of attention."

"Rub their tummies. They like that."

"Trust me, babe, I know. Everyone knows. To the point where I tried to assign some teams to dog petting duty, but your hounds wouldn't go for it."

"They're selective."

"So am I. I select that we solve our mystery crisis."

"Demanding, aren't you?"

"Will demanding help?"

"Who knows?"

"Not me, girlfriend. Not me."

We hung up, and I turned back to everyone. All of whom were staring at me. "Uppers? Really?" Jeff asked, like he'd believe it.

"We may need them." I opened my mouth to ask if they'd gotten any more intel out of Olga while I was engaged in witty banter with Reader, but I saw something out of the corner of my eye and turned back to the window instead. There was someone standing on the sidewalk, waving at me.

"What is this, Weird Reverse Day?" I looked closely. Somewhat unsurprisingly, it was Vance. I half-waved back. He increased his waving from "hey, pay attention to me" up to "me, me, look at me" with some "my price is right, come on down" added in. I looked over my shoulder, just in case. There was no one else he could be sort of spotting from the street. I pointed to myself as Vance did more over-the-top gestures to indicate that I was the absolute object of his focus.

"New boyfriend?" Jeff asked, jealousy meter only around a five on the scale.

"Only if pigs are flying, trust me." I considered my options. "Why isn't he just coming to the front door?"

Olga turned her chair and looked out. "Ah. Because we would not allow him in."

"Not that I'm complaining about your good judgment, but why not?"

"His husband is not friendly to us."

"Why not?"

"I honestly have no idea. Perhaps because we don't, as I believe the Americans like to say, buy his bullshit."

"I really like her," I said to Jeff. "Look, stay up here. I want to go see what my not-at-all-dear friend Vance wants so much that he's sullied himself to drop by our Embassies." My purse was still over my neck. I checked: Poofikins and Harlie were in it. Good, ready for the next level of whatever weird action was going on.

"I'm going with you," Jeff said.

"No. I don't want Jamie around him, exposed, or in the slightest amount of danger if we can help it. And before you start, accept that I'll win this particular argument."

"Fine. Then take Reynolds."

Chuckie shook his head. "Not a good idea. I'm not sure what he knows, and I'd prefer to keep a semblance of my cover intact." He smiled at Olga. "At least, outside this room."

She laughed while White finished his lemonade. "That leaves

me, Jeffrey. Other classmates already believe Kathy and I are an item."

"Too true, Rick, honey. Let's go make some magic happen."

Jeff groaned. "Not this again. You love to torture me, don't you?"

I leaned up and kissed his cheek. "Yes, because you punish me so well for it."

CHAPTER 66

WHITE AND I TROTTED DOWNSTAIRS. The boys were indeed guarding the stroller, while drinking lemonade and chatting it up with Adriana. I couldn't blame them—she was a cute girl. She seemed thrilled with the attention. I had to figure she was—if Olga felt confined by the chair, what would Adriana feel like, confined because of her employer?

Our errand was explained. "You want us to come with you?" Len asked.

Part of me wanted to say yes. Then I looked at Adriana's expression. Nothing but her eyes showed how much she wanted the boys to stay, but her eyes were pleading for it. "No, but pick a window and be ready to run out if weird taxis or other dangers appear."

The boys nodded, and the look in Adriana's eyes changed to relief. She led them to a window where they'd have a good view of the street.

We left the three of them stationed on Lower Level Lookout and went outside. "Plans, Missus Martini?"

"Gonna wing it, Mister White. You know, like always."

"You do work well off the cuff."

"I do my best work when I have no idea of what's going on, you mean." I glanced up. Yes, Jeff and Chuckie were on Upper Level Lookout. We were good.

"Any guess as to what your latest non-friend wants?" White asked as we headed for the sidewalk.

"Not a clue. I guarantee it'll be weird, though. That seems to be today's theme."

We stopped speaking as Vance raced over to us. "Took you forever to notice me," he snapped, as he looked over his shoulder.

"Most people trying to get my attention knock, ring the doorbell, call, or similar, Vance. So sorry I wasn't watching for you trying to take flight on the sidewalk."

He turned back to give me a dirty look. "I couldn't risk going onto Romanian soil."

"Yeah, 'cause they don't like you."

He jerked. "They confirmed that?"

I was really glad Chuckie had stayed upstairs. Why give him more reasons to want to strangle me? "No, I just assumed because they're lovely people with class and manners that you weren't their type."

"Hilarious." He looked at White. "Speaking of manners, were you ever planning to introduce me to your husband?"

"Not really, since he's not here. This is my uncle by marriage, Richard White. Richard, this is Vance Beaumont. He's married to Guy Gadoire, who's a tobacco lobbyist."

"Ah, one of the Dealers of Death," White said genially. "It's a pleasure."

Vance rolled his eyes. "There are worse things than tobacco." He gave White an appraising look. "Nice to see that you've got someone to occupy your time while your husband's working."

I didn't rise to it. White seemed to feel us appearing to be having an affair was a good cover. Whether he had a brilliant reason for this or just enjoyed torturing Jeff on occasion, I couldn't guess. "Whatever. How did you know where I was?"

"I'd been by, your house girl said you were out walking your dogs, I saw two guys who looked like bodyguards leave the Romanian Embassy walking four dogs. They took them across the street and went into your Embassy. I looked around to see if you were in one of the Embassies here. You were, I spotted you, couldn't go in, and so I signaled you."

I wondered if I should share that Amy was the second-highest-ranking female in our Embassy at the moment, or if I should just save it for the President's Ball later on tonight. Saving it would have a certain satisfaction to it, as long as I warned Amy first. Without the warning, she'd knee Vance in the balls faster than he could blink.

"Gotcha. So, what's going on, and why are you sharing it with me?"

"Do you know about Jack?"

"Yes, he offed himself, presumably not with cigarettes, so you're off the hook on that one. You coming to tell me how distraught you are when you couldn't have been bothered to be there for him when he might have needed you, or just coming to ensure that I know the news?"

"Neither." Vance stepped closer. "Look, can we get out of the street?"

"Why not come into the Romanian Embassy with us?"

He gave me a dirty look. "I'm not here because I like you."

"Thank goodness we've cleared *that* up. Why are you here?"

"I need your help."

Leslie had called last night for the same reason. Why the people in my Washington Wife class felt I was their go-to girl for assistance was beyond me. "Why? And why me?"

"Why you? Because you're not a real insider."

"Gee, thanks for the flattery. It's not really your forté, is it?"

Vance glared at me. "You haven't been here long enough to have made all the compromises and alliances that would prevent you from helping me. And the why is that I need help."

"Fine, I'll bite. What's going on, and why do you think I'm going to care?"

"I think Jack was murdered."

So did I, but I wasn't sure I should say so. I went for the smooth and noncommittal response. "Oh?"

Vance nodded. "And I'm pretty sure I'm next."

I managed to refrain from saying that I hoped he was right. Reality said that, loathsome or not, I didn't want Vance murdered. "Why so?"

"Because I know what Jack figured out."

"And that is?"

"He's right, there's going to be an assassination attempt tonight."

"At the President's Ball?"

"Yes."

"Why there?"

Vance shrugged. "Because it can't be canceled. So the target will have to attend."

"Do you know who the target is?"

Vance nodded and opened his mouth as White slammed into me, taking us both to the ground. So I didn't actually see the bullets hit.

CHAPTER 67

I HEARD THE BULLETS HIT, HOWEVER. Along with Vance screaming his head off. The sound of screeching tires was also pretty loud.

Things happened fast, as White rolled us into the street to avoid a stream of bullets. As my perspective went over and over, I saw Vance run into the Romanian Embassy, as Len and Kyle ran out, which coincided with a taxi pulling up next to us.

"Get in!" the driver shouted.

White grabbed me and flung us both inside. We landed on the floor, him still on top of me. Well, we landed on something big and furry that was lying on the floor.

The car burned rubber and drove off. The animal under me scrambled to get out of the literal dog pile. I chose to assist as fast as I could. The dog jumped onto the backseat as I got to my knees and risked a look around. The boys were running after us, guns out. Malcolm Buchanan was on the scene, also running toward us, but from Sheridan Circle Park. Unsurprisingly, he also had a gun out. It wasn't a sniper rifle, however.

As the taxi flung itself into the Circle, I could just see Chuckie in the distance, coming out of the Romanian Embassy at a dead run. I assumed he'd had to physically restrain Jeff, for which I was thankful. Jamie was going to be a lot safer on Romanian soil right now, as opposed to out in the street where bullets were flying.

Bullets were still being sent toward us, confirming White and I were the targets, not Vance. Said bullets weren't coming from my guys or Buchanan, which meant whoever was trying to kill us was somewhere above ground level.

"Get down!" the driver shoved at us, as he flung the car into a jerky serpentine pattern. White grabbed me and pulled me back down to the floor. The dog that I'd landed on flattened on the rear seat. "Are either of you hit?" the driver asked.

"Hi Moe, how's it going? Curly and Larry along for this ride?" I hadn't seen the other taxis during my short perusal of the chaos.

"I believe our driver said his name was Ishmael," White said. "And I wasn't hit with bullets. Missus Martini?"

"Not leaking either. Thanks for the save, Mister White." I felt something cold and wet shove against the back of my neck. "Dude, call your Cujo off, will you?"

"Prince isn't going to hurt you."

I shifted so I could look Prince in his furry face. I was rewarded with a slobbery face wash. Happily, he wasn't holding a grudge for our impromptu MMA match. "Thanks for that, Prince." I petted his head while I searched through my purse for an acceptable dog treat.

Found a pack of teething biscuits. Jamie wasn't really ready for them yet, but I'd been advised to have some around just in case. I gave one to Prince, who apparently felt it was a taste sensation. He finished quickly, gave me another doggy kiss, and rolled over so I could rub his tummy. I so rubbed. Make friends with the big dogs, that was my motto. "So, Ishmoe, what the hell's going on?"

"Ishmoe? What the hell?"

"Why do you care what I call you? You haven't told me your real name, so any name's as good as another. I ask again, where are the rest of the Three Stooges?"

He actually laughed. "I get it now. They're trying to find the person or persons shooting at you." We were still driving fast, but the zigzagging had stopped. "So, what's going on?"

"I asked you first."

"Look, someone's trying to kill you. Again. Tell me what's going on so I can help you."

"Tell us your real name first. And who you work for." We slowed down and came to a stop. I got back up on my knees. We were at a stoplight, and no bullets seemed headed toward us. Prince rolled onto his paws and shoved his head at me. I made with the pets, then shoved Prince over and sat my butt down on the backseat, helping White up and onto the seat next to me.

"I work for people trying to protect you. And my name isn't important." The light changed, and we drove forward, at a normal rate of speed.

"I know your name isn't important. I also know it's not Ishmael or, as much as you all resemble the Three Stooges, Moe. I want to know your damn name. Or should I be talking to Prince here instead?"

Prince hopped onto the floor, the better to get right in between us. He shoved his head at White, who wisely gave him vigorous pets.

While we were doing this, I heard what I was pretty sure was a police band radio. There was a discussion of shots being fired in the Sheridan Circle area, along with voiced concerns that the limited police force available wasn't able to get there in time.

There was something bothering me about all of this, and it was a different bother than everything else. Ishmael didn't seem dangerous. Prince was, clearly, a big softie, if him crawling up so he was now lying on both my and White's lap to better get petting was any indication.

Olga somehow felt they were K-9 cops. But even if *Turner and Hooch* or all the *K-9* movies were accurate representations of working with police dogs—which I highly doubted—what was truly missing from this experience was a police badge. Prince had nothing on him to identify him as part of a K-9 unit. And by now, if Ishmael were really a cop, a badge should have been flashed, if only to set our minds at ease.

I studied the back of Ishmael's head. His hair was neatly trimmed. The beard was clearly false. He was driving with his left hand on the top of the steering wheel, while he fiddled with his radio without looking at it.

His radio crackled. "Whale One, do you copy?"

He grabbed the microphone. It looked just like the ones in all the cop shows and movies. "Whale One here. Catfish and company safe. Repeat, Catfish and company safe."

"Orcas got away," a third voice shared. "Other fishermen out in the water caused disruption."

"Roger that. Whale One out." He switched the radio to another band, still not looking at it.

Olga's beliefs gelled with things Oliver had told me only a couple of days ago. I dug out my phone and pulled up the Internet, took a stab and did a specific name search. Happily, A-C phones were top of the line with about 100 Gs to everyone else's 3, 4, or 5. I had what I was looking for in moments. Sure damn enough.

I showed it to White. "Huh. Interesting, Missus Martini."

I decided to take the leap. "So, Officer Melville, your parents were of a literary turn of mind, I see. Can I call you Herman, or are you really attached to Ishmael for everyday conversations?"

He jerked the steering wheel so hard that Prince lost his balance and rolled onto the floor. "What . . . what are you talking about?"

"Dude, you weren't that hard to find." I studied my phone. "The entire K-9 division was let go due to budget cuts. You were all allowed to keep your dogs, presumably because your Chief of Police wasn't thrilled with this. There were only twelve of you." I looked up. "The other teams are working what parts of the city?"

"You're way off base, lady," Ishmael said as Prince righted himself and shoved his head between us so we could each scratch behind an ear. We complied.

"You know, I can get why you're not much for Herman, it's sort of old-fashioned. But Ishmael is worse, in that sense. Maybe I'll just call you Officer Moe. And I'm not off base at all. I'm actually Catfish, and I know it. No idea what you've named everyone else with me in your hunt for whoever the hell Moby Dick is, but I can recognize my code name when I hear it. I do appreciate the timely save, though."

"I was in the area."

"Right. You and the rest of the fishing expedition were lurking around. You've been in my area every day for the past few days. Why? And why all the elaborate taxi ruse stuff?"

"Really, I'm just a gypsy cab driver who likes to help out the good citizens of Washington, D.C."

"And I'm actually Mata Hari, I've just aged really freaking well. Look, why all this ridiculous subterfuge? Especially since you appear to be on the side of truth, justice, and the American Way."

Ishmael opened his mouth, but White beat him to it. "Really, time is of the essence. Please stop your attempts to lie to us and tell us the truth. We might, in return, be willing to trust you and perhaps even share pertinent information."

Our driver considered for a few moments, while the radio crackled and people shared the unsurprising news that, now that an officer of the law had arrived at Sheridan Circle, there were no signs of any gunmen or any other form of disturbance. He heaved a sigh. "Yes, fine. And please continue to call me Ishmael."

I snorted a laugh. "Why?"

He gave me a pained look. "It's my code name. Look, we've been remaining incognito because we didn't want to get into it with your friends."

"You mean you don't want the C.I.A. aware that you're trampling onto their turf because instead of fighting with you, they'll merely arrest you?"

"What do you mean?" he asked, far too casually.

"I mean that you don't own a badge anymore. None of your unit does. So, in the olden days, if you'd crossed into Federal territory, you'd get chewed out, but your Chief or Captain could still cover for you. Now? Now you're a private citizen. And the Feds aren't nice to interfering taxi drivers who have no legal authority to detain prisoners or kidnap ambassadors or anything."

"I can't confirm or deny your accusations."

"Officer Moe, seriously, if you actually want to help us bring down Titan Security, you're going to have to give us some assistance, starting with information."

This time, Ishmael slammed on the brakes and pulled over so fast Prince wasn't the only one losing balance. White and I righted ourselves, and I helped Prince back up onto the seat.

Ishmael turned around, a shocked look on his face. "How did you know?"

I looked straight at him. "Well, we don't let just anyone in on the secret, but the truth is . . . I'm psychic."

CHAPTER 68

ISHMAEL GAPED AT ME. **"REALLY?"**

"Seriously, you really have to ask? No!" I waved my phone at him. "It's all here, matter of public and *World Weekly News* record. Titan has the main contract to provide security to the parts of D.C. deprived of officers of the law. This city's the test case before Titan and the rest of the big security companies go into a major battle to get protection contracts throughout the U.S., and then Europe and the Middle East. What I want to know is—what the hell is your plan? Because I get a lot of flack for *my* plans, but at least mine have some coherency."

He stared at me for a long few seconds. Then he sighed. "Our plan is simple. To do what we agreed to do—protect and serve."

"Why have I been your main protection focus?"

Ishmael gave me the "duh" look. "Because you've been targeted by assassins. And those assassins were hired by Titan Security."

"How did you know that?" White asked.

"Her limo blew up. She was chased by a lot of men. And someone just tried to shoot you."

"Good points. But you showing up on the scene, every time, seems a little too coincidental. Especially the first time."

"We're good."

"Officer Moe, you were on the scene far too quickly. No one's that good." At least, no one human.

"We had a tip something was going down."

"A tip from whom? The only tipster who seems remotely accurate right now is Mister Joel Oliver, and I don't think you're on his call list."

When I said Oliver's name, Ishmael's eyes shifted a little. Living with A-Cs for the past two years had really honed my ability to spot the poor liars. He hadn't said anything, and I hadn't asked a question, but he was acting shifty. Light dawned. "You really were in the right place at the right time. Because you weren't following me, were you. *You* were who was following Mister Joel Oliver. To protect him, right?"

He looked ready to argue, so I hit him with Mom's intimidating stare. It worked. "Right," Ishmael said with a sigh. "He's in danger, because he found out and wrote the truth. He might write for a complete rag, but when it comes to what happened with the police department, he was completely on the money."

I pondered some more while hoping he didn't believe everything Oliver wrote. Because I had the impression Ishmael currently thought we were regular people, and I really wanted someone, anyone, to buy that we were "just folks." At this point, it would make a refreshing change.

"The three of you who've been tailing me, you weren't the ones he spotted, were you? It was some of your fellow K-9s, right?"

"Right. We all honestly work as cab drivers. Have to make money somehow, and it allows us the mobility we're used to while also letting us blend in. We tend to stagger driving shifts, though. When we're not driving, we'll patrol on foot, if we have a good tip about things going down."

I shook my head. "Twelve of you policing a town this size isn't a drop in the bucket."

"Better us than Titan," he snarled. "They aren't in it for the protection. At least, not the kind we mean. They're worse than the Mob, and deadlier."

"Dude, on your side. Just pointing out that you're all sort of sounding like modern day Don Quixotes."

Before anyone else could make a comment, my phone rang. Prince helped me dig it out and helped himself to another teething biscuit as a reward for a job well done.

"Hi, Jeff, we're fine."

"Thanks for calling to let me know." His sarcasm knob was already at eleven.

"We were kind of busy until now."

"Yeah, I know, I picked that up. You're back to annoyed with some feelings of satisfaction and sympathy, which is why I called."

"Thanks for waiting. I probably couldn't have answered the phone any sooner. Is everyone else okay? You and Jamie in particular?"

"Yes. I have a headache, but everyone's fine. No one shot at the jocks or Reynolds. Only you."

"I feel all special. Why do you have a headache?"

"Reynolds did something to my neck to keep me immobile when the bullets started flying. I haven't killed him yet for it. But I want to."

"Chuckie uses the Vulcan Nerve Pinch when he has to. It's his job. And he did it to protect you and Jamie."

"Right, right. I knew without asking that you'd be taking his side on this one. Huh?" I heard voices in the background. "Oh, yeah. Everyone would like to know what the hell is going on."

"I'm not sure I can summarize easily."

"No problem. We're coming to you. Just stay put."

I covered the phone. "Officer Moe, we have a request to stay here." He shook his head. "Too exposed."

"Well, what do you suggest, then? Richard and I are happy to get out and wait for my husband, who's coming to get us."

He sighed. "We'll head somewhere safer." He put the car in gear and headed us off.

"Where are we going?"

"I'll tell you once we get there. If your husband can find you here, he can find you there, too."

"Thanks for the cryptic non-assist." I went back to Jeff. "Sorry, our sort of protector feels we're too exposed here. He's heading for higher ground or some such. Think you can still follow us?"

"I'm assuming you're asking that so you don't give away intelligence."

"Indeed." I waited. Nothing. "No 'atta girls' or something?"

"Atta girl." He didn't say it with enough enthusiasm, but I decided to let it pass. The headache was probably dampening his spirits.

"So, what happened once I left. How's Olga?"

"Cool as a Romanian cucumber. She says we have a beautiful baby, she thanks you for visiting, and hopes you'll visit again soon. Want to explain that?"

"Not right now."

"Again, I'm not surprised. By the way, we have several taxis following us."

"You're in a limo?"

"Yes. Two of them. Alpha Team's coming along, because they're so happy that you and our retired Pontifex were shot at in front of our own Embassy."

"Great. I'd like to point out again that this wasn't my fault. What happened to Vance? He said he knew who tonight's target was."

"Did he? We got nothing out of him. He tried cowering behind the jocks, which didn't work well. We left him with your mother, sobbing his guts out."

"I hope Mom's clear that I don't like him."

"Trust me. She took one look at him and asked him why he thought acting like an immature asshole was the right way to behave in a civilized society. He started crying then."

"I am *so* sorry I'm missing that."

"Yeah, well, I read him, and he's a wimp."

"Jeff, I could have told you that without . . . um . . . you know."

"You're so good with subterfuge."

"Blah, blah, blah. I'm getting off. Call if you can't find us."

"I will. Be careful, baby."

"Always."

"Right. It still amazes me that, after all this time, you think you can fool me."

We hung up, and I paid more attention to where we were going. It looked vaguely familiar.

Ishmael was on his police radio again, talking to his cronies. I got the impression he was calling the full Dirty Dozen in for a pow-wow.

My phone rang again. "Hello?"

"Kitty, darling, when will you be gracing our Embassy again with your delightful presence?"

"No clue, Pierre. Why?"

"Fitting time, dearest. We'll take care of the rest of our bevy of beauties first, but you, as the ambassador, must look perfect."

"I'll do my best to get back soon. Oh, and Pierre, please make sure the dress will be something I can run in."

"Trust me, darling. I do know you."

We hung up as Ishmael turned us down a familiar street. I took a look at where I was pretty sure he was heading us. "Are you freaking kidding me?"

CHAPTER 69

WE PULLED INTO THE SAME PARKING GARAGE Jeff had had us head into only yesterday. "What is this, Secret Meeting Central? Where's the employees' lounge and the conference room?"

Ishmael parked on the same level I'd been on with the Dingo and all his cronies the day before. I spotted a few bullet casings that had been missed by the cleanup team and sent Reader a text about it. No one was going to accuse me of not paying attention this time.

Ishmael sighed. "It's under construction, only the construction's on hold because of budget cuts. The foundation's considered somewhat unstable, though it's safe enough as long as there aren't hundreds of cars parked here. So no one comes around."

"I'll bet. So, is there a posted schedule? And, if so, whose supposedly clandestine meeting are we interrupting? Homeland Security? C.I.A.? Keystone Kops?" Reader's text reply was, charitably, snippy. I snipped back. "Huh?" I realized Ishmael had said something I'd missed.

"I *said* that this is a safe location. We meet here all the time."

"Huh. I wonder who else does. And who else knows you do."

"We're secure," he snapped as two limos, followed by five taxis, arrived and parked. We all got out. I desperately wanted to make a Spy vs. Spy joke, but even in this company, perhaps especially in this company, I figured it would go over badly.

Jeff pointedly walked over and moved me and White away from Ishmael. "We're fine," I said quietly.

"I prefer you closer to me, for a variety of reasons."

"No complaints from me. Where's Jamie?"

"With Denise, at our new day care center." He sounded resigned. "I can't argue with the need, and Jamie adores her, so I think it'll be fine. Your parents are at the Embassy in case of problems. Christopher's there, too . . . just in case." He didn't have to say just in case for what—at the rate we were going, the likelihood that someone would try to take over the Embassy this afternoon seemed at least probable.

"Good, though I think the people responsible for all the crap with the Embassy are here in the parking garage with us. Why did you choose this location yesterday?"

"It's big, empty, and no one comes in this area. Isn't that why you had the taxi guy come here?"

"No, I didn't direct him. He came here on his own. He says they come here all the time."

"Huh." Jeff didn't seem to think this was too big a deal. "I wasn't trying to be exclusive with the location, baby. It was just close and convenient."

Kevin was along for this ride, and he flashed the P.T.C.U. badge. "Let's remember, gentlemen, that you're meeting with a Federal agent and act accordingly." Ishmael and his gang all nodded.

"Richard," Reader said, "I'd like you in the limo with Paul." He didn't make it sound like a request.

White sighed. "Fun while it lasted, Missus Martini. I'm complying, James, no need to look so distressed." White got into the limo with Gower, though he left the door open so they could both see and hear what was going on.

Chuckie took a long look at Ishmael. "I want all the disguises off, and I want them off now." His tone clearly indicated arguing would be a bad idea. Reader and Tim were flanking him, and the looks on their faces shared that they agreed with Chuckie and would be happy to help him kick some serious K-9 butt if said order was ignored.

Ishmael nodded, and he and the others removed their rather lame disguises. Once off, they all looked like regular guys in their twenties and thirties. I could see the cop in all of them, though. There was something about the way they stood, the aura of authority they radiated, not to mention the cop haircuts.

I noted all the dogs were sniffing intently. I looked where they were focused—it was the area where I'd spotted the bullet casings.

Chuckie looked long and hard at Ishmael and a few of the others. "Do you know why they were avoiding you?" I asked.

He nodded, as he pointed to Ishmael and the ones I identified as

Curly and Larry. "They were part of the police team that came to my apartment a few months ago when it was . . . ransacked." I presumed he meant when it was trashed during Operation Confusion, but I kept that to myself.

"We were sent there," Ishmael said.

"Why were K-9 units at an attempted robbery?" Jeff asked quickly, presumably because he didn't think I was smart enough to not give things away.

Ishmael shrugged. "We'd gotten a tip that it was a drug deal gone bad."

Chuckie nodded. "Typical frame setup." He gave me a pointed look. "It didn't work." I got the hint. I was to shut up and not share why I thought it hadn't worked. It was an easy guess—Chuckie, likely with assistance from the Gower girls, had found and removed anything planted before any local law enforcement had shown up.

"Yeah, well, the hell you caused us for that made it pretty clear we were close to blowing your cover." Ishmael didn't sound too sorry about that. Prince was straining at his lead, but Ishmael held him pretty firmly.

"Illegal search and seizure isn't good for anyone's record," Chuckie replied. "You might want to remember that."

"We'll take a memo," Ishmael said in a bored tone of voice.

"Do that," Kevin said pleasantly. "Kidnapping's not on the list of things good little boys do, either."

While they were doing the typical male posturing that seemed to activate whenever one alpha male was in proximity to another, I counted heads. Len and Kyle were leaning against the limo with the current and former Pontifexes in it, and Jerry, Hughes, and Walker were leaning against the second limo. Each limo had its doors open on the sides facing us. All of the men looked very ready to rumble. Counting me, that meant we had nine on our side, eleven if White and Gower got into any fight we might have, which I knew both of them would.

There had been two men and two dogs per taxi. It wasn't complicated math. So we were evenly matched, if I didn't count Prince and the rest of his pack. Only, that was wrong. "Officer Moe, where's your twelfth man and beast?" I asked as Prince yanked hard and pulled out of Ishmael's grasp. He made a beeline for where I'd spotted the casings and started sniffing around.

Prince started barking his head off. Ishmael ran to his dog, and I followed. I spotted something other than bullet casings. Blood. And lots of it.

CHAPTER 70

THE OTHER DOGS JOINED PRINCE, and everyone crowded around us. "Stop shoving, you're going to ruin evidence," Ishmael shouted.

Everyone backed off, the K-9 cops dragging their dogs away. Prince whined, loudly, then threw back his head and howled. The other dogs joined in.

"We have two officers down," I told Kevin and Chuckie once the men had quieted their dogs. "One human, one canine."

"We'll need to run tests to see whose blood this is, Kitty," Kevin said.

I shook my head and pointed to the dogs. "They already know. You think they were just doing the dog version of a twenty-one gun salute for a stranger?" I looked at Ishmael. "You've been too obvious. Someone spotted you following me and Mister Joel Oliver and decided to thin your herd."

Ishmael and the rest of his guys looked ill. "He wanted to look for clues to what you were doing here yesterday," the one I thought of as Larry said.

The rest of them started talking, and it was clear they were all freaked, upset, and ready to hit something. Ishmael tried to get them under control, but the dogs weren't the only ones not listening to commands.

"Shut UP!" Jeff bellowed. Everyone, man and beast, got very silent very quickly. No one bellowed like my husband. Once his voice had stopped echoing, Jeff looked around, eyes narrowed. "I feel for your loss. But right now, there's a number of bad things going on, and if you're not going to become part of the solution, then we're going to arrest you all and let the guys in charge of taking people to Guantanamo sort you out."

Ishmael's squad nodded and pulled themselves together. I wasn't sure how much human speak the dogs understood, but they were all clear that the Leader of the Pack had just laid down the law, and none of them wanted to challenge for dominance. Eleven dogs were sitting at attention, ears alert, ready for action or for doggie treats, depending.

Kevin and Chuckie took down the pertinent information while Reader and Tim called for some agent teams. No reason to involve the D.C. police—apparently the only ones who could make it on time to a crime scene had been laid off and were here with us.

I spent the time handing out teething biscuit doggie treats and pets, which earned me a lot of dog kisses. Ensure the big dogs love you, that was my motto. I discreetly used a baby wipe to clean off the dog slobber.

"So, you want to tell us what's going on now?" Jeff asked once our teams showed up, all in limos. The A-Cs got out and started doing their thing. The human drivers stayed in the cars. I resisted the impulse to have Jeff and Chuckie do some sort of lie detector test on them—if we couldn't trust the majority of our human agents, we were screwed anyway. However, I found myself hoping Ishmael was right and that the garage wasn't going to find a dozen vehicles to be too much for it.

Ishmael and I brought everyone up to speed. "So, you're all no longer law enforcement," Kevin said when we were done. "You're just vigilantes."

Ishmael shot him a dirty look. "Not my fault we got cut." He glared at Chuckie. "One too many complaints will do that for you."

Chuckie shook his head. "Neither I nor anyone in my agency caused your team to be cut." He had his Conspiracy Hat on, I could tell. "When cutting units, I'd think one of the last any force would cut would be K-9, if only for the dogs' drug-sniffing ability."

"Yeah, well, that wasn't the opinion of the higher-ups," Ishmael said angrily.

"What were you working on around the time you all got the pink slips?" I asked.

"The usual stuff, running down drug tips, handling some aspects of search and seizure. Nothing extraordinary. His case was the oddest," Ishmael jerked his head at Chuckie.

"Did you take anything from Chuckie's place and enter it into evidence?"

The entire squad shook their heads. The one I was thinking of as Curly cocked his head at me. "You think we found something somewhere that made us targets?"

"Yeah, I really do." I pondered some more. "Were you sent to any high-profile places? Like the White House?"

"I know where you're going with this," Larry said. "We'd have to go through case files to determine if we stepped on toes we shouldn't have, and we don't have access to those anymore. But, just so you know, regular cops don't go to the White House."

"You resisted the desire to break in and plant bugs to track the President? I'm impressed. You just limited yourselves to Embassy Row, so you violated the rights of, what, ten or twenty countries?" The words left my mouth, and Jeff and Chuckie both stared at me. I stared back. "Oh. *Snap.*"

"What?" Ishmael asked.

"You put surveillance into every Embassy around ours, right?"

He sighed. "Yes. We wanted to know what you were up to."

"You mean you wanted to know if Mister Joel Oliver was under our protection or in our custody."

"Yeah, that was part of it."

"He'll be gratified to discover that he has a fan club. And then you picked up that we had information on a notorious assassin, and what better way to prove your squad's worth than to bring down the Dingo, right?"

He grimaced. "Right. You'd have done the same in my place."

"Possibly. We can debate that at another time. But let me ask the big question. Did you happen to put illegal surveillance into the Paraguayan Embassy?"

"It's not illegal—" Ishmael started.

"Can it," Kevin snapped. "I could arrest you on a laundry list of violations, every one of which would hold up in a court of law. You've kidnapped an ambassador. The only reason we don't have all of you in handcuffs is because you did help save said ambassador's life. Keep on playing coy, and we'll show you how we do things at the P.T.C.U. Trust me when I say you don't want to know."

"Fine," Ishmael said. "Yes, we went there. We hit every Embassy within a mile radius of yours."

"And I'll wager you've also been investigating Titan Security, especially their head man, Antony Marling, right?"

Ishmael grimaced. "Yes. There's not too much to find. Titan's really good about hiding histories on anyone who matters in the company, Marling especially."

"Were you working on that before you were cut?" Chuckie asked.

Ishmael sighed. "Not officially."

"But you were unofficially, in your off hours?" I asked. They all nodded. I looked at Jeff. "We have room."

He sighed. "I'm getting officially tired of adopting strays."

"What are you talking about?" Larry asked indignantly. "Our dogs belong to us. Each one's registered and probably has a blood-line better than any of yours."

"I'd take that bet, especially in regard to my husband, but I'm in a charitable mood, so I'll just explain things clearly for all of you. We're tabling determining why your squad got the ax, for now."

"Why?" Ishmael asked, eyes narrowed.

"Because you've landed yourselves into one of the bigger conspiracies going, and you're all targets for assassination. Your missing and presumed very dead teammates are proof of that. How the rest of you are still alive is beyond me, but unless you go into some form of protective custody, you're not going to be alive much longer."

No one spoke for a moment, so we all heard the sound. It sounded like someone had dropped a heavy tin can. And then another. And another.

"Incoming!" Jerry shouted. "Grenades!"

CHAPTER 71

THERE WERE MANY TIMES I'd been grateful that A-Cs had hyperspeed, but none so much as this one.

"Into the limos! Shields on!" Jeff bellowed just before the first grenade went off, as he grabbed me, pulled me to him, and shielded me with his body.

It was a stun grenade, at least to judge by the fact that we all fell to the ground but weren't hit with shrapnel or even falling debris. It felt like the world was shaking, my vision was barely there, my ears were ringing, and I was disoriented. The calm part of my mind mentioned that this still wasn't as bad as any gate transfer when I was pregnant.

The dogs were all howling in pain. That the A-Cs weren't was the surprise. Or rather, that one A-C wasn't.

Jeff had been knocked down just like everyone else. But he recovered almost immediately. He leaped to his feet and picked me up off the ground, one arm around my waist. He went to the super hyperspeed, grabbed Reader, and flung the two of us inside the limo, onto White and Gower, who seemed to be recovering, though not as fast as Jeff had.

I got onto my knees on the seat as Jeff went back, flung Tim over his shoulder, grabbed Chuckie and Kevin, and tossed them all in on top of us. I just managed to avoid getting buried under the falling bodies. Jeff picked Len and Kyle up off the ground and flung them into the front seat.

He slammed the doors shut then raced over and tossed the flyboys into their limo. I could hear him, and he was shouting orders, in full-on Commander Mode, getting the other A-Cs up and moving. Each agent had a K-9 unit or two and dragged them into the nearest limos. Jeff grabbed Ishmael, who'd managed to hold on to Prince, and headed them for the nearest limo, which was the farthest from the one I was in.

I saw the laser shields go around our limo and the others, one by one, presumably indicating the human drivers were recovering, at least enough to hit the shield buttons.

Jeff was moving so fast he'd done all of this in about five seconds. A part of me marveled that I could see him at the super-duper speed. Most of me was just hoping he'd be fast enough to get inside one of the limos before the next grenade went off. Because while it was horrible, we'd heard at least three drop, and I knew only one had exploded. So far.

"Everyone able to see and hear?" Reader asked. There were fast assents. "Good. Len, you able to drive?"

"Yeah."

"Then get ready to get us out of here as soon as Jeff's in a limo. Kyle, get on the intercom and send that order to the other cars."

I thought everyone was in a limo, so in relative safety, but as Jeff tossed Ishmael into his limo, Prince yanked away and raced off. I saw where he was heading—for one of the remaining grenades. And I didn't think they were going to be as benign as the first one.

"Prince! No! Come here!" Hey, he was already my buddy. I tried to get out of the limo, but White and Gower grabbed and held onto me and I couldn't.

Jeff saw the dog and didn't hesitate. He ran and picked him up, as though Prince were a Pekinese instead of a German Shepherd. Which was great. Only they were now far from any of the limos.

I tried to see if they'd gotten away from the remaining bombs—only the world blew up around us.

CHAPTER 72

THE EXPLOSION WAS LOUD, and it shook like nothing I'd ever felt before. It was horrible, in a completely different way from the stun grenade. I could tell the remaining grenades had gone off at the same time, or close enough, but it felt like the whole world had exploded.

The noise was incredible—even louder than my screams, which were at the dog-only register. It rattled us even inside the laser shield. I almost bounced out of White and Gower's hold, but they both clamped down, and I couldn't get away to get out to Jeff.

"Let me go! Jeff's out there!"

"We can't go look for him until this stops," Gower said.

"Why not?" I was still screaming and felt no need to stop.

Chuckie got over to me, took my face in his hands, and forced me to look at him. "Calm down. Right now," he said sternly. "You can't help him if you're hysterical, and none of us can help him until it's at least somewhat safe to get out of the car."

"But—"

"Stop it! You don't panic, you don't freak out. You stay calm and in control until it's all over and everyone's safe. Then, and only then, do you get the luxury of freaking out, melting down, or losing control." He was quoting my mother. She'd taught me, him, both of us, that. Mom had been in this situation many times before. And she'd trained us to handle it when we were teenagers.

I took a deep breath. It was shaky, but I shoved the hysterics away. Because Chuckie was right—I couldn't help Jeff if I was a mess. I nodded.

Chuckie let go. "We can get out in a few seconds. Then we'll find him, get him to medical, and it'll be all right, Kitty. I promise."

As the ringing from the explosion subsided, there was another sound. It reminded me of metal creaking. Big metal creaking in the way it does when it's been stressed too much and isn't going to be holding on much longer. "I know that sound. That's a bad sound."

"Let's get Jeff and that stupid dog and get the hell out of here," Tim snarled.

My hand was heading for the door handle when it opened. Prince was flung in and on top of me, meaning White was on the bottom of our dog pile this time. The door slammed shut. "Kid, do what the Head of Airborne said, and get us the hell out of here."

Prince was lifted off me and placed rather gently on the floor. Jeff shoved everyone into seats and pulled me onto his lap. Kyle was on the intercom, passing along the "leave now" orders.

Len floored it and raced off, the other limos hightailing it out of there with us, as chunks of concrete started falling. They bounced off of the limos. The taxis weren't so lucky. I hoped Ishmael and his crew had good auto insurance.

Jeff looked fine, a little mussed up, but there was no blood I could see. I did the whole pat-down thing. Nothing seemed broken, out of place, wet, or otherwise harmed. "You're alive." I managed to say this without bursting into tears. Just barely.

He hugged me. "I'm okay, baby. And so's the dog. Who's too brave for his own good." Jeff patted Prince's head where he thought I couldn't see. "I was able to get us behind a bearing wall away from the blast. My ears are still ringing, and I'd bet his are, too, but otherwise, we're just fine."

I looked behind us. The garage was collapsing. "There were more bombs, besides the grenades they tossed in for us, weren't there?"

"Yeah, baby, there were. They rigged every floor. Triggered, as near as I could tell, by the bombs on our floor." He shook his head. "You called it right, I think. Whoever's targeting you realized the former cops were getting too close."

"I think it's because they did their thing at the Paraguayan Embassy after sniffing around Titan, but we can hash it out at home." My body started to shake, and Jeff hugged me tighter. I leaned against him, listening to the sound of his double heartbeats, and allowed myself to tremble—my heart was definitely racing more than his. After a bit, his double heartbeats soothed me as they always did and my body began to relax.

"What are we going to do with them?" Kevin asked as we barreled for home as fast as the traffic would allow us. The other limos were coming along, sticking close, not that I could blame them. Conveniently, we did have plenty of underground parking.

"They can room with their hero, Mister Joel Oliver. They can sleep in the Jolly Green Giant's underground chamber. They can be detained in Dulce, at East Base, or NASA Base. But they are not going home, because if they do, they're dead, and we all know it."

"I've run their backgrounds," Kevin said. "All of them are single, either never married, widowed, or divorced. None have a live-in girlfriend or partner, either. Have put protection onto the ex-wives, none of whom live in or around this area. None have children."

"That's a really odd statistic."

Chuckie nodded. "It is. We'll dig a little further, but if we're talking a dozen men with no wife or partner at home, that's indicative of a carefully selected team."

"I have a feeling they were doing more than standard K-9 stuff when they were on the force. Which may be both why they were cut and why their Chief let them keep their dogs."

"Not that they're overly impressive," Tim muttered.

"Not by comparison to what we're used to, I'll give you that. But for guys who seem to have limited resources, they did okay." I was shaken up, but not stupid. Ishmael's guys had fooled us all, more than once so far, and we weren't the only ones. "Chuckie, how many Embassies do you think actually fell for their gas leak routine?"

"From what my teams told me, all of them other than Romania and, clearly, Paraguay. Our team was not allowed into the Paraguayan Embassy. They merely handed them the surveillance equipment and slammed the door shut."

"Nice."

"Yeah." Chuckie looked at Jeff. "By the way Martini, thanks for saving us. All of us."

"I'd say it's all in a day's work, but that's not true anymore." Jeff shot Chuckie a half-smile. "Thanks for calming my wife down."

Chuckie shook his head. "She wasn't calm and she isn't calm, and you know it. But controlled, clearheaded panic is one of her specialties."

"I'm right here, guys."

Jeff hugged me as the other men started discussing potential strategies and how, or if, they should read Ishmael's team into the highly classified data that was our daily lives. "Yes, you are," he whispered in my ear. "Right where you belong. With me, in my arms."

He'd just been manly and protective and all around amazing in the extreme, and I'd thought he was hurt or maimed or worse. And somehow, he was here, safe and sound, not only acting like it was no big deal but also managing to be incredibly romantic.

I didn't care that we were in a car stuffed with other people and one big dog. I flung my arms around his neck and kissed him. And I kept on kissing him until we parked and everyone else got out of the car.

After all, what was the point of surviving death if we didn't at least get to make out heavily?

CHAPTER 73

WE MIGHT HAVE GONE FOR IT in the back of the limo, tons of people around or no, but someone rapped on the window, then opened the door.

"Girlfriend, we have a timeline."

Jeff ended our kiss slowly. "I demand diplomatic immunity."

Reader snorted. "Right. Tear each other's clothes off later. Like after we've saved whoever the hell the assassination target is tonight."

"Sometimes I really hate you, James."

"Yeah? Well, I could spend the time making out with Paul. Believe me, I'd prefer it. But, somehow, duty calls. As does your dress fitting."

Well, that damped the mood. "Fine. Do I have time to check on Jamie first?" I looked down. "And feed her?"

"Yes," Reader said with a long-suffering sigh. "Just hurry it up. We'll be taking everyone to the infirmary to get checked out." He eyed Jeff. "You should probably go into isolation."

Jeff shrugged. "I feel fine. The pain in my ears is gone."

"Right." Reader shook his head. "We need you at your best tonight, Jeff. And, I'm going to pull rank on this, too. You can help Kitty feed the baby, and then you're in isolation until it's time to get dressed."

Jeff looked like he was going to argue, but as much as I hated to admit it, I knew Reader was right. "He's the Head of the Field," I said quietly. "And I really don't want to harpoon you at the President's Ball if we can avoid it." When Jeff overstrained himself, which he'd done regularly when we worked as Commanders, his empathic blocks would break down. Soon after, if he didn't get isolation, he'd need adrenaline shot directly into his hearts. Or he'd die. One of the few things I'd enjoyed about our Diplomatic Mission was that I hadn't had to stab him with the huge needle for the past three months.

Jeff shot me a betrayed look, but he also nodded. "Fine. As you say. I'm going to use the isolation chamber in our apartment, though."

"Fine, just make sure it's clean," Reader said, and I noted he had a much more in-charge voice going. "We've had strangers in here too often in the past few days."

"Yes, sir, Commander," Jeff said, with only a little resentment and longing in his tone.

We got out of the car in time to observe the last part of the Man and Dog Reunion Ishmael and Prince were having. Clearly, the K-9 cops loved their dogs, because Ishmael was on his knees, arms around his dog, with tears running down his face, which Prince was licking off.

He saw Jeff, got up, and came over to us. "Thank you. I can't believe you did that, that you risked your life to save his. And I can't tell you what that means to me."

"You're welcome." Jeff grinned, at Prince if I was any judge. "I'm used to running after certain brave protectors who've bitten off a little more than they can chew."

"I think I should resent that remark."

Jeff put his arm around my shoulders and hugged me to him. "True enough, baby . . . but you can't deny it, either."

We zipped upstairs to the area on the fourth floor Pierre and Denise had designated school and day care center. Jeff wasn't zipping at anything close to full speed, and I realized Reader was right—he needed isolation. I chose not to mention it, as long as Jeff actually did as he'd been told, which I counted as nice personal growth for myself.

"Wow," I said as we entered and looked around. "They did this fast."

Jeff coughed. "Hyperspeed. You've heard of it. Try to keep up."

"Humph." It was easy to spot Jamie; she was sitting between Raymond and Rachel, who were in front of Denise, who appeared to be reading a story. All of them were surrounded by Poofs. I checked my purse. "Why are all the Poofs here?"

"Because I told them to protect Jamie and everyone else at the Embassy while we went after you."

Jamie made the Mommy AND Daddy Are Here! squeal. I cuddled her while Denise showed us around. "There's even a nursing area," she said, leading us to it. "Pierre thought of everything."

We discussed Pierre's amazing awesomeness as I got ready to feed Jamie. Denise left us alone while we took care of business. I could tell Jeff didn't want it to end. "James is right, you need isolation."

"I don't want to leave you alone. God alone knows what you'll get into."

"I'm going to be getting into my dress for tonight. Trust me, I know how Pierre rolls, and he's going to have us primping and prepping for, potentially, the entire time you're isolated. Go in for a few hours so you don't have to be in for days."

He sighed. "Hate it when you're logical and there's no flaw in your argument."

"Wow, you must hate it all the time."

He laughed, and we spent the rest of the time just being a normal little family. Jamie was done eating far too soon. We handed her back to Denise, then called Tito. He met us up in the isolation chamber attached to our bedroom, tested all the fluids and such, and declared them all free of Surcenthumain and other toxins.

The standard isolation chambers were always the creepiest place in any A-C facility. Dulce had a whole huge section devoted to them; when I was there, it always felt like being in the biggest haunted mad scientist lab and ancient tomb combo you could imagine.

The chamber attached to our rooms was a lot better, being more like a very solidly insulated bedroom, just one with beds that had a lot of needles and tubes attached to them. It was better by far than the ones I was used to seeing Jeff go into, but it was still a room with tons of needles and weird tubes in it. I wanted out before I even got in.

I kissed Jeff good-bye. "Be good, baby," he said. "I can't feel you in here, so I can't come to pull you out of the Potomac or toss you into a safe place."

"I'll be getting a dress adjusted, Jeff. How much trouble can I get into doing that?"

"It's you. I'd list all the potential ways, but Tito's looking impatient."

"Hilarious." I gave him one last, long kiss, then I was ordered out of the room by Tito, since my stress levels were already going off the charts.

I left the isolation room, closed the door behind me, then decided to do the other ball attendees a favor and took a fast shower. Once clean, dry, and dressed, I checked to make sure the lights on the panel outside the isolation room were the right colors. Having so ascertained, I then hit the intercom button in our room. "Walter, where is Pierre doing the dress fittings?"

"The small salon on the second floor, Chief."

I dutifully headed downstairs, but I called Reader on the way. "What's up now, girlfriend? And what took you so long to check in?"

"Jeff's in isolation, Tito said everything was fine, I took a shower, forgive me for wanting to ensure I didn't stink, and I'm heading to my dress fitting. I was wondering what you guys decided in terms of Ishmael and his crew."

"We brought over medical personnel from Dulce, and Tito has Nurse Carter helping out, too. They're checking everyone over now. So far, Reynolds, Tim, Kevin, and I have been given clean bills of health. We're also rounding up a veterinarian, at your father's suggestion."

"Considering, we probably need to get a vet on staff."

"Let's table that until, you know, after we see if we all survive tonight."

"Any progress on our assassination target?"

"You mean besides all of us? After this afternoon, I think I speak for everyone when I say we have no guesses. At all."

"I'll ponder while I'm doing the fashionista thing with Pierre."

"Do. Because time's nearly up, and we're possibly in a worse position than when we started."

"Will do, Voice of Doom. Find out if Vance told my mom anything. He claimed to know who the target was."

"Yes, ma'am."

"And let me know what he said whenever you find out."

"Oh, absolutely."

"Thanks ever, Mister Pissy."

"Sorry, just in a bad mood."

"I noticed. Why so? I mean more than the obvious reasons."

"All the stuff the K-9 unit stole from us was in their taxis. You know, the ones that are buried under rubble now."

"Crap. Have you sent agents out to check on the scene?"

"Gosh, thank God you're here, what would I do without you?"

"I'm close to getting offended."

"Don't be. Yes, we sent them. Everything was burned. We have nothing left."

"Did Ishmael and his crew look at any of it?"

"Why no, of course not. Because they were too busy playing Catch the Cat."

"I think I'm going to be offended by that remark."

"Does this mean that, should I turn straight, you're not going to run off with me?"

"No, don't worry, I'm still holding onto the dream."

"Thanks, babe, I feel better."

"But do you feel straight?"

"Doing a sound check. Nope, still gay."

"You're a tease, James, you know that, right?"

"And you're still my girl, you know that too, right?"

"I do indeed."

"Good. Then everything's still right with the world."

CHAPTER 74

WE HUNG UP, AND I JOINED PIERRE'S CATWALK. At least, that's what it felt like.

The salon was already tastefully done up in an Early American Expensive motif, presumably to fool whoever was in it into thinking American Centaurion had been around during Colonial times. Well, they had been. They just hadn't been on Earth.

It was also reminiscent of what Reader had done for my wedding, only with more black. Because, despite my hopes to the contrary, everything was in a black, white, or black and white pattern.

"Pierre, they've indoctrinated you into Armani's Black and White Army already? You've been here less than three full days."

"Oh, no, darling. But for the President's Ball everyone's supposed to show their country's colors."

Well, black and white were certainly the A-C's colors of choice. Clearly, even at the biggest shindig we'd been invited to so far, we were going in the formal version of the Armani Fatigues. I refrained from asking what our flag looked like—so far, I'd never seen one flying anywhere. Considering the A-C's color preferences, maybe it was because we flew the Jolly Roger.

I heaved a sigh. "Well, black hides stains."

As I was hustled behind the tasteful Oriental screen Pierre had clearly had brought in which was serving as the changing area, I looked at what the other gals were going to be wearing. I had to admit they looked good.

Amy, our rather willowy redhead, was in a one-shouldered white charmeuse sheath dress that managed to make her look as if she were stepping out on the red carpet, with a long, silky black wrap. Caroline was in a form-fitting confection of organza, satin, and white lace sprinkled with glittery black beads I prayed weren't actually black diamonds. Her wrap was a bolero jacket in a reversed pattern of the dress, black lace and organza sprinkled with white please-God-not-real-diamonds. Doreen was draped in what I could only think of as a black Grecian Pregnancy Toga I was fairly sure was made out of raw silk. But she was a Dazzler so, even as extremely preggers as she was, she looked gorgeous.

All the dresses were long, which made sense for the event, just not if we had to run for our lives, which I expected.

My dress options were handed back to me. I had one white, one black, and one two-toned option. "Can I just say no to the all-white one right now?"

"No, darling. Let's at least have a look."

"Pierre, white and I don't mix well."

"You look lovely in white."

"No argument. However, I will stain it in under an hour. An hour might be a generous estimate."

"She's not making that up," Caroline said.

"I'd give it about thirty minutes," Amy added.

"Less if there's a punch bowl nearby," Doreen shared.

My friends, there for me when I needed them. However, they did shove Pierre and the designer who'd apparently won the exciting contract to dress me over to the side of no all-white or mostly white ensembles.

This meant I ended up in a silk cut-velvet number that was fitted to midthigh and then hung loose. Low-cut back, rather modest yet complimentary bodice, sleeveless, but, thankfully, not strapless. The dress glittered in the light, not that I could tell how it was managing it. It reminded me somewhat of the dress I'd worn to my high school reunion, only it was more stately. Of course, I'd been chased through the desert by a psychopathic politician at my high school reunion. This boded.

Sadly, this also looked great on me. The wrap, which was along the really large and wide scarf variety, was made of the same fabric only in white, but had delicate fringe at each end. It set off the dress beautifully. I wondered if I could just carry jeans and a T-shirt with me, so I could change out of this beautiful outfit when things went all sideways. But there were never convenient changing rooms when I needed them, and even Superman couldn't find an actual phone booth these days, so I shoved that little hope aside.

"I need to see if I can run in this."

Pierre and the designer exchanged a knowing look. The designer, who was a pretty, petite Japanese girl younger than me, smiled. "The skirt's seam is actually a series of small snaps." She showed me where to pull to open the seam easily. You literally couldn't tell it was there, but I undid a couple of the snaps, and sure enough, it worked.

I stared at her. "*You* are a genius."

She laughed. "All part of the service we provide at Akiko Designs."

"Works for me. I apologize right now for how this dress is likely to end up looking when this event is over."

She shrugged. "You've paid for it. What you do to the clothes is your business. I already took pictures at my workshop." She handed me a rather large clutch that was clearly intended to accessorize this outfit. It was a black and white tiger-striped number that should have looked tacky but instead looked daring, trendy, and chic. It was also large enough to hold a Glock, Jeff's adrenaline harpoon, hairspray, and my iPod.

My shoes were simple black pumps dusted with whatever my dress had that made it glitter without my being able to tell how it was glittering. Basically, as long as there was light around, I was going to sparkle. I hoped this wouldn't make me an easier target.

It turned out Akiko had done all the dresses we were wearing tonight and had also coordinated the shoes and accessories. Pierre, being displeased with the other designers' offerings, had dismissed them to the sad ranks of not meeting his standards prior to my arrival.

I was stunned that anyone could have pulled off four different dresses, for four different body types, in such a short time, successfully. That the other designers hadn't wasn't really saying they sucked, but that Akiko had said volumes about her talent, skills, and slave-driving abilities. I looked at her closely. She was very pretty but probably not a Dazzler. I did wonder if she'd gotten some A-Cs to help her, but I decided to ask that question of Pierre when we were alone.

Our designer left with the rejects, though Pierre hung onto several of the pieces "for other occasions." As expected, he then turned us to the tasks of primping. The less said about it, the better, but it did give me a chance to ask Pierre what hairspray he favored. I'd been wanting to know since my wedding.

He winked conspiratorially. "Promise not to tell?"

"I guess not. Why? Is it so expensive Jeff'll have a heart attack if I buy a bottle?"

Pierre laughed. "Just the opposite, darling. It's very affordable."

I looked at the bottles. "They don't look affordable. In fact, they look like the most expensive hair care products on the market."

He nodded sagely. "We have heard, perhaps, of the age-old trick of pouring lesser-quality wines into higher-quality bottles?"

"Get out! So, what's the wonder spray in reality?"

Pierre shrugged. "Dove Extra Hold."

I let that sink in for a long moment. "Wow. I learn something new every day. This is, so far, the only new knowledge from the past two years that hasn't been icky, exposing decades-old secrets and lies, completely alien in nature, or terrifying."

"I live to serve, darling. I do live to serve."

CHAPTER 75

PREPPING AND PRIMPING WAS finished with enough time for us to convene with the rest of the gang in the War Room, as I currently thought of the ballroom. It was really the Doom and Gloom Room, however, since we were still exactly nowhere.

Strangely enough, I was no longer worried about it. We had the head's up that something was going down, we were all at our highest DEFCON Oh My God status readiness, and clearly the clues weren't helping us anyway. Maybe they'd all gel before everyone died. It wasn't a great plan, but it was all we had going for us.

I did have a question, though. "Mom, what did Vance tell you?"

"Absolutely nothing, kitten. He spent most of his time crying hysterically."

"Where is he now?" Maybe I could get something out of him.

"We let him go home. Politically expedient. He was escorted home. No issues."

So much for that idea. "He told me he knew who the target was. He also said he felt he was the next target, after Jack Ryan, because he had said knowledge."

"If that was true, kitten, he certainly didn't want to share it with me."

"You did the whole interrogation thing? I mean, really pumped him?"

Mom gave me a long-suffering look. "No. Because he wasn't under any kind of suspicion of dangerous activity. He was being shot at, just as you were. Meaning that I'd have hell to pay to explain why I'd been hard on him without any cause."

"I suppose." I wondered if Vance could really lie to my mother.

She was hard to fool, and she wasn't trusting. Jeff had said he'd read Vance's emotions, but he'd been fooled before—he'd had no idea any of the human drivers he'd assigned to me were traitors. So, if the lie is good enough and the liar even better, it was doable. Mom had never, ever fallen for any whopper I tried to pass, but then again, Vance wasn't her child, thank God. But that did mean she could miss things, especially since Mom hadn't been able to do the real interrogation stuff.

I decided I needed to find and question Vance myself. Should he actually still be alive and at the Ball. Then Mom dropped the bombshell.

"No one who isn't listed as an operative can wear or carry firearms. In particular, no one who's a part of the American Centaurion Diplomatic Mission can be carrying weapons of any kind."

"Well, that blows."

Mom gave me the hairy eyeball for that one. "Kevin and I are only carrying with Presidential dispensation."

"The President is okay with none of us being armed to protect him and God alone knows who else?"

Mom heaved a sigh. "He knows we have a threat, but this is standard procedure. The Secret Service will be on site, in droves. And—let me stress this—*none* of you are listed as legal law enforcement officers, meaning your carrying guns or other weapons in would identify all of *you* as the assassins. Hopefully the screening will identify whoever the actual assassins might be, not that it ever does. Now, I want all the weapons removed, and I want to see them on the table."

With much grumbling everyone dumped their weapons and, in the case of the men, shoulder holsters. To my dismay, Chuckie was among those dumping. "Why aren't you carrying?"

"Because as far as most of the attendees are concerned, I'm an international playboy, remember? My cover can't be blown for this event."

"I'm under the impression the entire population of D.C., if not the world, knows who we all are and what we do. I sometimes feel like the only people we're fooling are ourselves."

Chuckie shook his head. "I told you before, you're used to seeing the more, ah, active side of things, and that meant you were running into people who know what's going on because they're cleared for it. Some of the people that will be at the ball are cleared. Most aren't. So we have to ensure our covers don't slip."

"And you're saying they don't tell their cronies the truth?"

"Not as often as you'd think," Mom said. "Because if they're found out, they lose a lot more than their security clearances. Internal Affairs exists in each agency, and their entire jobs are to find and stop leaks, corruption, and illegal activities within their bureaus. That extends to the politicians in the know as well."

"Okay, if you say so. But can't James and Tim take in weapons?"

Reader shook his head. "Girlfriend, as far as the rest of the attendees are concerned, at this event, I'm Paul's husband. Only."

"And you need to be sure you don't tell them who we really are," Tim added, as he dropped his guns on the table. "Now drop your Glock, Kitty."

I sighed and did as requested. I had both my purse and my stylin' clutch with me. In addition to dumping my gun and extra clips, I transferred what I could from purse to clutch. I had the adrenaline harpoon in its case, my iPod, my wallet, my phone, brush, mirror, and a travel bottle of the Dove nonaerosol hairspray courtesy of Pierre. There was still room in the clutch, so I tossed in some other random things that might possibly work as weapons if push came to the likely shove.

I stared at the newspaper I'd taken from Olga's then shoved it into the clutch—since I didn't get to take my Glock there was room, and this way, if I got really bored, I'd have reading matter. In doing so, I discovered the clutch had a long strap to convert it to a shoulder bag. I decided I loved Akiko and her design skills.

Jeff arrived during the weapons dump. He looked much better than he had going in to isolation, but that could have been because of the tux he was wearing. It looked great on him, and, as always, he looked totally hot. I managed not to drool on the nice designer dress.

He and Christopher, who was also dressed for fashion success, were both looking a little smug because neither one of them regularly carried a weapon.

"No problem, baby," Jeff said after giving me a quick kiss. "I've never had an issue protecting you without firearms."

"We'll be fine," Christopher agreed.

"Yeah? Just how do you think we'll keep from blowing our covers if either one of you goes to hyperspeed?"

They looked only slightly less smug. "We'll handle it, baby."

A throat cleared and we all turned to the doorway. Ishmael was there. "What can we do to help?"

"I thought you were sending them to—" I stopped myself, just in case. "Elsewhere."

Ishmael grinned. "No human being could have done what your husband did." He shrugged. "We thought Oliver did the fluff pieces so he could do the real investigative stories, too. Turns out, every story that man prints is true."

"Sadly, not quite all—Elvis has truly left our building," Oliver said, joining us. In black tie. The suit looked good on him, though I still couldn't tell if he was muscular or pudgy underneath. "Oh, and Officer Melville, it's *Mister Joel* Oliver, please."

"You're joining us, MJO?"

"I am indeed. I was granted an invitation via your lovely mother."

"Mom, are you crazy? He's a target."

Mom shook her head. "No, I don't think so."

Chuckie nodded. "The buzz isn't saying that all the assassination attempts failed, so they're going to take out the target at the President's Ball. The operation is and has always been set for the ball."

"Okay, fine, so why have Mister Joel Oliver in danger again?"

Oliver shrugged. "I'm bait, Missus Martini. Just like you."

The logic behind this didn't have to be explained. People had been trying to kill the lot of us for days now, Oliver and me in particular. "Great, so we can draw the early bullets. Can't wait."

Jeff didn't look happy. "That isn't the entire plan you all came up with, is it?" he growled. "Using my wife as bait?"

Everyone looked uncomfortable. Jeff looked ready to go on a protective rampage. I coughed delicately. "Um, Jeff? We did this exact same thing during Operation Fugly. You were the one who suggested it."

"That was then. That was different."

"Yeah, we had about as much chance of success then as we do now. Otherwise, it was pretty much just like now, only we have a lot more innocent people to protect."

"We want to help," Ishmael said.

Reader shook his head. "Whoever's behind at least some of this knows you. If you show up, it'll give away that you're alive, which could cause the planned attempt to be aborted. We can't afford to let that happen."

"So what do we do then? Sit here?"

"Yeah." I went over to him. "You stay here and you stay safe, and you keep everyone else in this Embassy safe and you be on call, ready for action if we need you. I know your dogs could do that . . . but can all of you?"

He tried staring me down. I managed not to snort. There were exactly two people who I couldn't beat in a stare down, and he wasn't Mom or Chuckie.

Ishmael looked away. "Fine."

Amy cleared her throat. "Not to sound unsupportive of our law enforcement officers, but how do we know we can trust them?"

"Gladys will be on site," Mom replied. "Along with a number of agent teams."

"Works for me. So, who's driving us over there? I ask because we've been infiltrated and no one seems to be concerned about it."

Jerry, Walker, and Hughes came in, wearing their Navy Whites. They looked awesome. "We are," Jerry said. "We figure we can take everyone in four limos."

"There are three of you."

Len and Kyle walked in, both dressed in tuxedos—Armani, of course. Pierre had been keeping the Elves busy.

Jerry grinned. "Your boys'll drive you, Jeff, Paul, and James. We'll take everyone else."

"We get to carry," Walker added.

"How so?"

Hughes shrugged. "We're military."

Mom nodded. "They're still considered part of the U.S. Navy even though they report directly to Centaurion Division. So I was able to have an exception made."

Irving and Tito came in, sporting the team Sharply Dressed Man look. Irving was also sporting the Worried and Nervous look. "Are you sure Doreen and I should go?"

"We're going," Doreen said firmly. "I'm the only one of us who has any continuity with the former Diplomatic Corps. I realize we're all worried about saving people, but I'm also worried about our actual reason for being here. We haven't really done well diplomatically these past few months. This is an important event, and we have to show and show well."

"But no pressure!" I said cheerfully. I got a lot of dirty looks.

Tito just laughed. "I'll be there. And I promise to stay right with Doreen," he added to Irving, as he raised the medical bag he was carrying.

Michael, Naomi, and Abigail Gower arrived, all looking breathtakingly beautiful. I examined the girls' dresses. I was fairly sure Pierre had arranged their gowns, too. Michael zipped right over to Caroline, his "you so hot babe" smile already turned up to eleven.

Abigail joined Tim. She grinned at me. "Alicia's wisely sitting this one out. So I'm Tim's 'date.' "

"He's actually yours," Naomi corrected as she joined Chuckie. "Our friend the international playboy got us invited, remember?"

White, Kevin, and Dad joined us as the com activated. "Chief of Security is on premises and with the children. Commander Dyer is at Main Imageering at East Base. All other personnel are being directed to the fourth floor, per your request, Missus Katt."

"Thank you, Walter," Mom said. She looked at Ishmael. "I want you and your people, and pets, there as well." I opened my mouth, but Mom beat me to it. "Yes, Kitty, our cats and dogs are there, too. As are the Poofs, which all need to stay put."

I checked again. I had no Poofs in my purse. But Poofikins and Harlie were in my clutch. "Right, Mom, I'll deal with not having them along," I said as I quickly closed the clutch and tucked it under my arm.

Mom gave me a long look. I knew contriving to look innocent would let Mom know I was up to something, so I went for looking sulky. It seemed to work. She nodded slowly. "Good. Now, let's get going. I want us in place early, so we have a chance of stopping this operation before it starts."

While who was riding in what car was being discussed, Chuckie pulled me and Jeff aside. "I didn't want to say anything earlier, but I think we've found the point of infiltration at Centaurion Division."

"Good," Jeff said. "What are the details?"

"On the plus side, it looks as though it was only a handful of human operatives. Two were the drivers from the other day, who are still at large. The others were rounded up this morning. They were all bribed."

"How is that possible? We pay really, really well, and everyone goes through a screening process like the one you put Pierre through."

"There are more kinds of payment than money." Chuckie shook his head. "They joined because they wanted to kill superbeings. The superbeing problem is close to completely gone, and instead of getting to do something they considered exciting, they were put on straight driver duty."

"So, they got offered, what? The excitement of being traitors?"

Chuckie shook his head. "I'm still getting the intel, but it sounds like they'd been turned well before they were relegated to the motor pool."

"They'd all driven for the former Diplomatic Corps," Jeff said, sounding annoyed. He jerked. "Oh. That's who turned them you mean, right, Reynolds?"

"Right. So they were being loyal to their former bosses. They were trying to find them, it looks like, when they were approached by an outside group to work against the current regime at Centaurion Division."

"How did you get all this so fast?"

Chuckie shot me a rather disparaging look. "I didn't start searching for infiltration this week, Kitty. What happened the other day just gave us some new avenues to check."

The light dawned. "Oh. *That's* what you have Camilla working on."

"I can neither confirm nor deny."

"Good job, Secret Agent Man. Ready to go pretend to be normal for the all of five minutes before all hell breaks loose?"

Chuckie laughed. "Absolutely."

CHAPTER 76

WE LOADED UP THE LIMOS. Mom and Kevin were in their government issued big, black Escalade, Kevin at the wheel. Dad, however, was riding in one of the limos. I figured Mom wanted him with laser shield capability.

Our limo was in the lead as Len drove us out of the underground garage. "We're going to be at a hotel, aren't we?" I asked more to have something to say than anything else.

"Yes," Reader confirmed. "Same place they hold the Correspondents' Dinner."

"So they should be used to security measures, right?"

Jeff shook his head. "Maybe. But hotels have a lot of access points. They're vulnerable and hard to really lock down."

"Thanks, we needed that." I sighed. "Paul, what's the ACE situation?"

Gower looked uncomfortable and a little confused. "ACE seems calm, but he's very focused on . . . something."

"Can you share the something?"

"No, not really. I can't handle having access to all ACE does; it would blow my mind, literally. So he locks me out of almost everything, including whatever it is he's paying attention to."

Reader looked thoughtful. "So you and Kitty aren't actually in any danger. At least, not right now."

Gower shrugged. "I suppose not."

"That sort of confirms Paul and I aren't the assassination targets, doesn't it? Because otherwise, you're thinking that ACE would be stressing, right, James?"

"Yeah."

Jeff sighed. "But we already knew this. Actions over the last few days to the contrary."

"You know, if it's the usual, all the weird goings on will be related, at least somewhat. And I think we have all the clues. But none of them make sense."

"I think we've got nothing," Jeff said flatly. "All Olga did was confirm our information, let us know she knows exactly who and what we are, and get you to realize the taxi drivers were actually former cops."

"That was a help."

"Only because Richard was willing to get both of you into the taxi so you weren't shot on the street. Otherwise, they stole, then lost, the only proof we had."

"Well, we have other clues and confirmations."

"No," Jeff said patiently. "We don't. Everyone in the know is getting their information from the same source—your new buddy the tabloid reporter."

"There's more than what we got from Mister Joel Oliver, and you know it."

"Yeah, but I think it's worthless. You're placing too much faith on the so-called intelligence the Dingo passed to you."

We lived close to where the ball was taking place, so our conversation stopped as we got into the limo line. "We'll be dropping you, parking, then will call for Centaurion Division agents to guard the cars," Kyle shared.

Reader nodded. "Good. Tim and I already vetted those teams, so we should be secure, at least in terms of the vehicles."

"Too bad we can't drive them into the ballroom and just shove everyone in."

"No more chatter," Jeff said. "We're going to be live and scrutinized shortly."

We pulled up; Len stayed at the wheel, Kyle got out and opened the curbside door. There were flashbulbs going off. I tried not to cringe. Jeff got out first, then helped me, with Reader and Gower following us.

There was a paparazzi line. I wondered how his peers were going to react when they saw Oliver coming in with us, but I was too busy trying not to trip. There was nothing wrong with my shoes, but I was nervous about falling flat on my face anyway.

A long line of dignitaries flowed into the hotel. I spotted a lot of native-dress costumes, which jibed with what Pierre had said. We passed minor chitchat with those around us. I didn't see Mom or

Kevin anywhere, but I figured they were using the Covert Ops entrance.

I looked around as we inched along. It was a lovely hotel with, as Jeff had said, a million places to hide if you were an evil bad guy waiting to off someone.

There were a lot of big men in dark suits with the plastic earbuds in their ears. There had been a ton of them outside, and there were even more inside, literally acting as human guide rails. They weren't wearing sunglasses, but I got the impression they'd been told to take them off as opposed to having removed them willingly.

The rest of our group was around us now, so the four of us were in the middle, meaning I could safely ask a question. "What's with the extras from the Matrix look? There's a lot of that in this town. And I didn't know we had this many Secret Service in existence."

"These aren't Secret Service," Reader said. "I checked. Titan is providing the majority of the security personnel for this event."

"Well, that makes sense then. So, the various Goon Squads at the airport and chasing me and Richard the other evening were on Titan's payroll."

"Probably," Jeff said. "Now, can we stop the chatter? Just smile and wave."

We smiled and waved as appropriate as we edged inside. There were a lot of people, and it took a good long while to get to the main security checkpoint.

There was a bank of metal detectors. The flyboys flashed their military Get Out Of Jail Free cards and were allowed to carry in their firearms. Sadly, this meant one gun each, with no extra clips.

The rest of us sailed through without issue. It was so much nicer than one of our gates I actually enjoyed the experience. Then it was back in line, standing between two rows of yet more Titan Goons, to filter into the main room.

It seemed to take forever, but we were finally in the ballroom. Mom might have wanted us all in early, and maybe she and Kevin had managed it, but there were tons of people in the room before us. It wasn't packed yet, but based on the line that had been behind us, it would be soon.

The room was a huge oval, with a number of support columns sprinkled around, making a slightly smaller oval. The stage, which was backed by the promenade area, sat at the middle of the fat part of the oval on the far side from where we'd come in. There were extravagant buffet stations set up between the columns, with portable bars interspersed between them. Waiters cruised among the guests with trays of hors d'oeuvres and champagne.

"Swanky. Figure the bad guys are disguised as wait staff," I said quietly to Jeff.

"Why would that be?" he asked as he scanned the room.

"We seriously have to watch some TV that's not like forty years old. Because it's the easiest way to get access. And there are what looks like hundreds of staff in here." And the Dingo and his ilk had no problem killing some innocent busboy and taking his place. Plus, since Titan was doing the security, that meant they'd likely let the Dingo through. I shared this thought with Jeff, who merely grunted. I got the impression he was having some empathic challenges with this particular crowd.

This was truly a ball, so there was a large dance floor in the center of the room. Small tables clustered between it and the food and drink stations.

I was fairly sure the President and First Lady were at the far end from us. This was based solely on the fact that I could spot the Secret Service agents. They looked different from the Titan guys—more normal and less goonish for a start. There were also a lot fewer of them, which, like so many other things, boded.

There was also music playing. I was shocked and pleased that it was actually something that you'd hear on the radio—Bon Jovi's "Who Says You Can't Go Home."

Our entire contingent finally got inside. We clustered together near a table in the middle of the room. I noted that every other group seemed to be doing the same. This would have been okay if we weren't trying to foil a bad-guy scheme, but since we were, it wasn't our wisest plan.

"We need to split up and start covering the room."

"I see Senator McMillan," Caroline told me.

"You and Michael head over to him, then." She nodded and they wandered off. "Think the food or drink could be off?"

Chuckie shook his head. "No, it's tested before it comes out. All drinks are in bottles or cans before they're put into the bars."

"But that just means that a waiter or bartender could slip something in after everyone thinks the food is safe."

"Good point." Chuckie nodded to me, then he and Naomi wandered away from our group, Abigail and Tim following them. They headed to the nearest bar, and I saw the girls both cock their heads while Chuckie ordered drinks.

"The girls are reading the staff," Jeff said quietly.

"Good. Should only take them until, what, next Christmas to finish?"

The music changed, and now the Black Eyed Peas were suggesting it was time to hip as well as hop. "Let's Get it Started" blared out.

"Glad you like the music," Jeff said. "But try to focus."

"What do you mean?"

"You're rocking out."

"I'm *so* sorry. The song has a great beat."

"Dance," Reader said. "It'll help you keep an eye on the people on the dance floor."

"And the bait should be out in the open, right?"

"Right." Reader grinned at Jeff's expression. "Go dance and have fun before things go haywire. You're here to be seen, the rest of us are here to save the day."

"Yes, sir," Jeff said. We dutifully went to the dance floor and started dancing. Reader was right—because of the kind of song it was, we were doing what I considered regular club dance moves, and that gave us the opportunity to turn around a lot.

The song had definitely worked its magic—we weren't the only ones on the dance floor. We danced for several songs; whoever was acting as DJ had great musical taste, at least in my opinion. Getting to dance was great, but since having no rhythm wasn't a crime, there was no one acting wrong on the dance floor. So, dancing wasn't finding the bad guys or helping us do the diplomatic thing. I spotted Doreen working her way through the crowd, meeting and greeting and generally representing American Centaurion with a big smile, and I pointed her out to Jeff.

He sighed. "I was actually looking forward to this event a week ago. But, yes, let's go be impressively diplomatic. Maybe we'll stumble onto whatever's going on that way."

We left the dance floor and started saying hi and shaking paws. I lost track of who was who within moments. Jeff, however, was amazingly good at this. He had his charming smile, the one normally reserved for my parents, plastered onto his face, and he was making small talk as if he had been born to it. Maybe he was. Perhaps the royal genetics carried with them the ability to schmooze without missing a beat.

I didn't have those genetics, however, so when a couple of women sort of shoved me aside so they could get closer to my husband, I had two choices. My first one—shoving them hard the other way—wasn't destined to do anything but start a brawl. So my second choice had to do. I wandered off to find someone else from our group.

Sadly, I found Bryce Taylor and Langston Whitmore instead.

CHAPTER 77

BRYCE SPOTTED ME BEFORE I could move on. "Ambassador!" He reached out and grabbed me, pulling me near to him and Whitmore. "Great to see you. Lovely dress." He examined it critically. "I haven't seen one like that before," he admitted.

"Thank you. I'm wearing a private design."

Bryce and Whitmore both looked impressed. "*Très belle, mademoiselle*," Bryce said with a wink.

I decided to let his little French flirty phrase go unnoticed, especially since I hadn't been a mademoiselle for a year now, and he knew it.

"Lovely choice," Whitmore said. "Now, I know the others would like a chance to chat with you."

"Others?" Whitmore and Bryce each took an arm and led me off to a clutch of other people. Sure enough, it was the majority of my pals from the Washington Wife class and their mates. And I was alone, with no buffer.

Marion Villanova and Guy Gadoire, along with Leslie and Vance, were nowhere to be seen. Madeline Cartwright was also missing. I wondered if this was too "wild" a party for her, but I figured she was just around somewhere that I hadn't seen.

Everyone else who'd dropped by to bother us yesterday was in attendance, including Lillian "Joker Jaws" Culver. She was in a bright red dress, wearing bright red lipstick, both of which made her skin look extremely pale. Her hair was pulled back into a chignon that should have looked chic, only it and the dress were both emphasizing how bony and angular she was. She gave me a beaming smile, and I had to stop myself from jumping back to avoid the

Joker's Acid Boutonnière or whatever other tricks she had about her person.

Esteban Cantu gave me a charming, oily smile. Either his date was elsewhere or he'd come to the event stag. "Ambassador Martini, lovely to see you."

The rest of the Cabal of Evil shared their joy at my presence, other than Nathalie Gagnon-Brewer, who, formal affair or not, apparently couldn't stop going for the high score on Angry Birds.

Lydia Montgomery was here, looking both excited and a little intimidated—like the new kid at school who'd expected to be relegated to the ranks of the Losers but was, instead, being welcomed into the Cool Kids Club and wasn't sure if it would last or end up as the cruelest of jokes. Eugene was nowhere to be seen. I wondered if he was in the bathroom, puking his guts out, and envied him if he was.

"Hi. Great to see you all, but I need to find my husband." I hoped Superman, Batman, or the Flash would show up soon. I needed some support from the rest of the Justice League or the X-Men. Even Wolverine would've been overwhelmed by this mob.

"Oh, but we want a chance to get to know you," Brewer said. "We have so much we can offer American Centaurion." He nudged Nathalie, almost imperceptibly, and she nodded, still engrossed with her cell phone.

"And there's so much you can offer in return," Kramer added. Marcia was hanging on his arm and nodded enthusiastically, no nudging necessary.

"You've always struck me as much more . . . reasonable than your husband," Armstrong added. I noted that Armstrong's wife, which I knew he had, was nowhere around. So either she was with Cantu's date, or she was home.

Lydia nodded loyally. "Eugene says you're the real brains behind the American Centaurion mission."

I realized that I had three senators and a representative, let alone several other political movers and shakers, who were all under the impression that I was the weak link for American Centaurion and susceptible to their flattery and bribes. The idea was somewhat hilarious, but also insulting, and it made me mad. Good. Mad was a lot better for me than intimidated.

"We do our best to be as reasonable as possible," I said, while contemplating my escape route. "However, we don't find that same mindset often reciprocated."

Amazing. I wanted to tell them to go to hell, but instead, I was being all polite and deflecting like a pro. No one in the Washington Wife class, Mrs. Darcy Lockwood or myself in particular, would have ever believed I'd heard a word. But make me mad and put me into this situation, and here it was, flowing out as if I'd actually studied for this final exam.

The others nodded, frowny faces of support and concern plastered on. On Joker Jaws, in particular, this was not a good look. "We want to *help* you," she said, oozing sincerity like no truly sincere person ever does. "We can all remember how *hard* it can be here, when you're first starting out."

"It's so difficult to know who your friends are or aren't," Cantu added. "There are so many times you think someone you've known for years is on your side, only to find out they aren't." Wow, he was going for the Wedge of Separation between me and Chuckie awfully fast. This seemed especially odd since I was pretty sure he was at least involved with, if not in charge of, Operation Assassination.

"Oh, we do understand that allegiances can shift," I allowed. "However, we're very careful to not make quick decisions on matters of policy."

"You're such a progressive country," Lydia added earnestly. "Your religious leader, for example." The others nodded.

"Yes?" I was going to make them come out and say it. Why not? I still had no clear, gracious way to escape.

"Very progressive," Whitmore said. "More progressive than many feel comfortable with, of course."

"Really? How so?" I channeled Serene and ensured I looked and sounded as innocent and naïve as possible.

They all stared at me. "Um, ah, your country's stance on many . . . social issues," Brewer said. "Very . . . liberal."

"Oh?"

"And yet," Armstrong said smoothly, "your country seems quite . . . conservative on defense issues."

"Do we?"

The group staring continued. My Washington Wife classmates, in particular, seemed shocked. Clearly, my answers weren't what they'd been expecting. Good.

Bryce tried the flattery approach again. "You look beautiful."

"You're too kind. What's Leslie wearing?" It was a cheap shot, I had to admit, but I enjoyed it.

Bryce looked shocked and a little panicked, but he scrambled well. "Something that looks great on her." I managed not to smirk. I figured the last time he'd seen Leslie was when they'd walked through the door, and I doubted that he'd paid any attention to her clothing choices.

"Bryce is right," Marcia said quickly. "You're in a great dress." She sounded somewhat envious.

I wasn't sure if she was faking it or not, but something in her tone caused Nathalie to look up. She looked me up and down. "Your dress is beautiful, and it fits you perfectly, both in tailoring and style. If I may ask, who did the design?"

She was a former fashion model, so it didn't surprise me that she wanted to know. "Akiko Designs. She's an up-and-comer."

Nathalie's eyes widened. "You took quite a chance."

"Did I?" I laughed. "Didn't seem like it. She's extremely talented. I'm sure she's going to be big."

Nathalie smiled. "Ah, very wise. Claim her as yours now, before someone else can snap her up." She nodded as though we were fashion insiders, then went back to Angry Birds before I could share that I hadn't snapped anyone up, and the designer was free to have as many clients as she wanted.

Abner took a shot at getting the conversation back onto the track the rest of them wanted. "You know, Kitty, everyone here can help you navigate through the intricacies of D.C. life. After all, as Missus Lockwood says, we're all in this together."

"Are we?"

Joker Jaws gave her husband a sharp look. "Absolutely," she said.

"Great. Then maybe you can tell me something I'm curious about." They all nodded eagerly. I made sure I was able to see all their expressions. "I'm wondering if Titan Security is one of your clients."

Cantu and Armstrong both twitched, just a little. Bryce and Whitmore's smiles froze. Culver paused just a little too long before she put her Joker smile back on. "How do you mean?" she asked.

"They're here in full force, aren't they? I think it's pretty impressive, and I'm wondering if you helped them get the contract."

"Oh, thank you." She preened and I congratulated myself. "Yes, they're one of the many fine companies I represent. Just as I'd like to represent American Centaurion."

Really? She wanted to land us as a client? Maybe. After all, whoever controlled the A-Cs had a better shot at turning us into the War Division. However, while my suspicions about Cantu and company were confirmed, it wasn't the proof Mom or Chuckie were going to need. It was also a safe bet that none of these people would be pulling whatever triggers—the kill order had already gone out, at least so far as we knew.

"What an interesting idea. I'll discuss it with my husband."

"*Do*," Culver said. "I'll be in touch with you when?"

"Oh, don't call us, we'll call you. I'm sure we have your cards from the other day." I didn't believe they'd left any, but it was as good a line as any other.

Cantu waved at someone. "What great timing," he said, as another man joined us. "Antony, Ambassador Martini was just complimenting Titan's protective services. Ambassador Martini, please allow me to introduce you to Mister Antony Marling, the head of Titan Security."

Sure enough, the Head Dude of Evil had joined our group. Joker Jaws' smile went to Destroying All of Gotham City proportions. Everyone else seemed thrilled Marling had joined us. Other than Bryce, who looked sullen as he busied himself with the examination of his fingernails.

Marling smiled and offered his hand. "Wonderful to finally meet you. Haven't had the pleasure of meeting your husband yet, but I'm looking forward to it."

I forced myself to give him my hand. I also forced myself not to ask him why, if he was so keen to meet us, he'd spent the last few days having people try to kill me. "Pleasure."

Marling looked me up and down. "What a vision you are. *Très belle, mademoiselle*," he said with a wink.

It was fab to discover that the Cabal of Evil had their own little flirty catchphrase, but it really made me want to gag. I wondered if he'd stolen the phrase from Bryce, if Bryce had stolen it from him, or if it was just a group thing. Then I decided not to care.

"How sweet. *Merci, monsieur*." Everyone, from Marling to Bryce, looked shocked that I could toss out this simple phrase in French. I knew I had to get away from these people before I stopped channeling the Washington Wife class and went back to good old me. "Now, if you'll excuse me, it's been lovely chatting with you, but I need to powder my nose." Per Lockwood, this one still worked as the universal signal for "I gotta pee."

Lockwood appeared to be right, since the others had disappointed looks on their faces, but no one tried too hard to keep me around. Nathalie looked up from her phone again, though. "Oh, I do, too. I'll go with you." She linked her arm through mine before I could say anything, and we sailed off.

"It was very kind of you to share the name of your designer," she said as we wended our way through the crowd in search of a bathroom.

"Was it?"

She laughed. "Oh, yes. You've nothing to fear from me, I'm still dressed by Dior."

"That's nice. You look great," I added. I hadn't really paid attention, but she did look good.

"Thank you. You must be very confident, not that I can blame you. I heard there was a huge scramble from the design community to be the ones to get the chance to dress the American Centaurion Embassy."

I was lost, and this didn't seem assassination related. "I'm sorry, but what am I supposed to be confident about?"

"Why, that your designer won't move to Marcia the moment the ball is over. Because, believe me, that's going to be Marcia's first call tomorrow." Considering what I knew was coming, I doubted that, but now wasn't the time to express those sentiments.

"Excuse me?"

"Not that I believe you have any worries. Your Embassy has many women in it, meaning your designer has more opportunities to show off her skills. If she moved to Marcia, she'd only have the one client of note, and, between you and me, Marcia doesn't have the same prestige that designing for an entire Embassy does."

"You're serious?"

"Oh, yes." We found the bathroom, which was quite crowded. "I believe there's another nearby. Do you want to try that one?"

I actually wanted to ditch Nathalie. "No, I'll wait. The way my luck goes, if I leave the line, the next bathroom's line will be longer."

She smiled. "My luck doesn't run like that. I'm going to give it a try. See you back inside." Nathalie left the bathroom. As she did, I realized we'd just had the longest and most pleasant conversation of our entire relationship.

I didn't want to raise suspicions or try to leave only to have Nathalie return because the other line really was longer, so I waited. The line was indeed long, and I didn't feel like chatting because I didn't want to waste whatever little diplomatic chitchat I had left on ladies waiting to relieve themselves. But I was prepared. I pulled out the paper and read the article on Titan and Marling in full.

It might have been in the business section, but it was really a human interest piece. In addition to the personal info about how he lost his wife and children—"tragic accident" was the sum total of the description—it was revealed that he loved world travel, was fluent in several languages, loved word puzzles and anagrams and considered himself a Scrabble pro, was a huge supporter of gay rights and gay marriage, provided funding to an extraordinary number of orphanages in countries devastated by wars, was an animal activist, and had an African Gray Parrot he adored named, of all things, Rybelleclies. Apparently, the name was an anagram of his wife's name, but to me, that was taking quirkiness to a new level. A second picture showed him kissing the bird on its beak. Clearly, he was the Bird Man of D.C.

It was weird to read this article and see the good the man had done in some significant areas that mattered to me, while also knowing he'd hired a very professional assassin to kill me and was also involved in a plot to kill who knew who else here tonight. I realized if I'd read the article and met Marling before any of this had started going down, I'd probably have liked him and considered his flirty French line to be fun and flattering. Especially if I hadn't heard it from Bryce first.

Bathroom visit finally done, I folded up the newspaper and put it back into my clutch. I pulled out the strap while I was at it, and petted Harlie and Poofikins, who were both snoozing. The clutch looked just as good as a shoulder bag. I trotted out of the bathroom, feeling ready to figure out what the hell was going on again.

Sadly, I hadn't paid much attention to where we'd gone, and while there were a ton of people milling around, they weren't all heading in one direction anymore. It occurred to me that I actually had a good chance to examine the spaces outside of the ballroom with a legitimate excuse of being sort of lost if someone stopped me.

I rounded a corner close by the bathroom and heard some weird sounds. No time like the present to investigate. I walked over slowly, so my heels wouldn't make noise. There was a curtain blocking something, and the noises were coming from behind it.

I slipped behind the curtain. It was fairly dark, but not so dark that I needed to use my phone as a flashlight—more murky than anything. There were a lot of boxes piled up. They seemed innocuous. I worked my way through them, toward the sounds.

I rounded a corner and stopped dead. What I was seeing I definitely hadn't been prepared for.

CHAPTER 78

A MAN AND A WOMAN WERE in the middle of going for it in a very real and very animalistic way.

I tried to back out and knocked into a set of boxes. While they fell, the couple separated and stared at me. It was murky, but not that murky. I pulled out my phone and turned it on them, just to be sure. "Nathalie?"

She gulped. "Kitty. Ah . . ."

I looked at the man. "*Eugene*?"

He looked only slightly embarrassed but a lot worried. "Kitty, I can explain."

"Um, I'm clear on what you two are doing. It's called having an affair. I just . . . wow, let me just say that I honestly would never have guessed." In a million years.

Nathalie shrugged. "Edmund used to have time for me. You'd think running a thriving winery and being married to an international fashion model would have been enough for him. But no. And now that he's here, he spends all his time with those people and almost none with me. I have needs he's no longer meeting."

"And Eugene is?"

She ruffled Eugene's hair. "Yes. He's more man than Edmund in so many ways."

My jaw was hanging open. I expected this when it came to the Dazzlers and their whole brains over looks mindset. I was shocked to see it playing out with humans, though. "Um, what about Lydia?"

Eugene looked defiant. "What Nathalie said, in spades. I'm tired of feeling like an embarrassment."

"But you cut him dead every week!"

Nathalie nodded. "No one knows, not even Marcia. She knows I'm having an affair, but not with whom. She helps me cover, though. I'm only in the class to get to see Eugene."

"We meet up after class, each week," Eugene admitted.

"How and where?"

"Wherever we can. Lydia thinks I spend time with you at the Embassy after classes."

"So I'm your cover?" I didn't know whether to be enraged or impressed with his ingenuity. I settled for a little of both.

"Yes. Kitty, I'm so sorry," Eugene said desperately. "I wanted to tell you, but I didn't think you'd understand. Or approve."

As Caroline had said only the other day, having aliens on Earth wasn't even close to the oddest thing going on in D.C. And people having affairs was as old as recorded history, if not older. Admittedly, this wasn't a pairing I'd have ever guessed at. A question nudged. "Is that why you're always on your phone?"

Nathalie nodded. "We text all the time. I don't want Eugene to think I agree with what the others say or do. But . . ." she shrugged. "A cover's a cover, *n'est pas*?"

"True enough." I contemplated my options. "Why were you and Marcia on Embassy Row the other day?"

They both looked embarrassed. "I hadn't gotten to see her because we were delayed the other day," Eugene said. "So we'd planned to meet up . . ."

"And a friend of Marcia's lives in one of the houses between Embassies near you," Nathalie concluded. "We saw you, and I realized Eugene couldn't risk coming, because you might spot him and ask why he was in the area but not visiting you. Marcia knew your young men had spotted us, so she went for a frontal assault, so to speak, so we could get out of there without raising suspicions."

Didn't work, but then, the suspicions raised hadn't been about adultery. Well, one weird event was explained. "Any thoughts about Jack Ryan's death?"

Nathalie nodded. "I think he was murdered."

"He's dead?" Eugene asked, sounding shocked and horrified. "When did this happen?"

"This morning. No one told you?"

He shook his head and gave Nathalie a betrayed look. "Why didn't you tell me?"

"Because I didn't want you to say something incriminating in front of anyone," she replied calmly.

"Eugene killed Jack?"

Eugene looked like his world had just devolved into a nightmare of Danteesque proportions. "What the hell? I haven't killed anybody! Ever!"

"Oh, no," Nathalie said soothingly. "I didn't mean to accuse you, even inadvertently. But I'm sure Jack was killed by someone he knows, and since we've used his place more than once, I didn't want you to give the police any reason to be suspicious."

"Wait, Jack Ryan knew you two were doing the deed? And he helped you?"

Nathalie nodded. "He . . . enjoyed the whole idea of helping with subterfuge."

"He knew you were sleeping with Eugene?"

"No. Like Marcia, he knew I was having an affair he was helping me to hide, that's all."

"Who do you think killed him?"

"Whoever told him about the assassination attempt at the President's Ball." She said it so calmly, I half expected them both to pull out guns and shoot me.

"That's real?" Eugene asked instead, sounding ready to head home and hide under the bed.

"Oh, I doubt it," Nathalie said dismissively. "But someone was always dropping little hints like that to Jack, one of the group. He loved it, but he would always 'protect his source.' "

"Jack told me he'd found the info by searching through his wife's stuff."

Nathalie snorted. It was definitely on the Lockwood Ladylike Snort Scale. "Please. Pia is far too smart for that. I'm sure she was upset with Jack for panicking everyone, though."

I thought about this while Eugene and Nathalie got their clothes back in order. Pia might have been upset that Ryan had leaked real information. And maybe that's why he was killed—because not only had his information been real, but the fact that he'd leaked it had gotten back to the C.I.A.

"Shall we go back in?" Nathalie asked once they were fully dressed and Eugene's hair was brushed.

I pondered the options. It seemed unlikely they were actually involved in the big deal. But I did have a couple of other questions. "Did your husband ask you to plant a surveillance bug on me?"

She shrugged. "No. That was Jack's idea."

"What for?"

"He said they were fakes but that it would be fun to do."

"So the others, they planted on me, too?"

She nodded. "That's why Abner called you over." Her eyes narrowed. "They were fakes, weren't they?"

"No, they were real. Where did Jack get them from?"

"He said his 'source' had asked for his assistance." Her brow furrowed. "I can't believe that Jack actually gave us real bugs to plant on you."

"He did. But clearly he was being manipulated. And you think his 'source' is someone else from class?"

"I do, but I could be wrong." Nathalie looked uncertain for a moment. "If the bugs were real . . . is what Jack told us real, too?"

I had no idea what to say, so I went for the nonanswer. "What do you think?"

They exchanged a glance. "Seems possible," Eugene allowed. She nodded. "So, does that mean we're all in danger?" He sounded ready to bolt.

Nathalie looked back at me. "How did you know the bugs were real?"

I wasn't sure how to answer this. I was having a moral quandary, several of them, actually. I was saved by my phone ringing. "Hello?"

"Where are you?" Jeff asked.

"You wouldn't believe me if I told you."

"Uh-huh. You need me to find you?"

"Not sure." Eugene and Nathalie were having a quiet conversation. The gist seemed to be that, if the threat was real, they wanted to get their respective spouses and get out of here. While it was both interesting and a relief that they apparently didn't want to dump their spouses and hope the bad guys solved a problem for them, I didn't know what to do. I also had no idea how to explain to Jeff what was going on.

"Can you talk?"

"Not really."

"Okay, baby. Relax, and concentrate on what's going on." I did. "Oh. Interesting. And yeah, so you don't have to ask, I read your mind. We don't want them coming in and disrupting the ball. And you don't feel right lying to them. I can see where you are. Interesting choice. Stay put, don't tell them anything, and I'll have this handled."

"Gotcha." We hung up. Eugene and Nathalie looked at me. I smiled brightly.

"Well?" Eugene asked. "Do you think we're actually in danger?"

I took a deep breath. "I think—"

But I didn't have to share any thoughts. Five A-Cs arrived out of nowhere, looking extremely official. "Please come with us," one said, taking my arm. The others flanked Eugene and Nathalie.

"Where are we going?" Eugene asked.

"My husband is a member of the House of Representatives," Nathalie added.

"I'm lost," I tossed out, in part to not give away that these were my guys and in part because it was true.

The agents led those two off rapidly. Not at hyperspeed, but still, fast enough. The agent with me waited until they were out of sight, then walked me to a set of doors that clearly led into the ballroom. "Ambassador Martini would like you to rejoin him, ma'am."

"Will do, and thanks for the assist."

The agent smiled, nodded, and walked off. I heaved a sigh of relief and looked around. No one I knew was nearby, including Jeff. Oh, well.

I walked into the room. I was a few feet from the dance floor when someone's arm went around my waist. I looked up, expecting to see Jeff, Reader, White, or someone else from our group. But it wasn't them. I was in the embrace of Guy Gadoire.

"Ah, Madame Ambassador, how wonderful you look tonight," he said grandly, Pepé Le Pew voice on full. He twirled me around and put us onto the dance floor. Train's "If It's Love" was playing. Gadoire smiled widely. "Could it be love, Madame? I was so taken with you when we first met. Can I hope you might have felt a few flutters when meeting me?"

"Excuse me?" I managed not to gape, but it took effort. I'd felt flutters, all right. Flutters of nausea. They were threatening to come back at any moment.

"Vance has told me how feisty you are. A true original."

"Thanks, I think. Um, where *is* Vance?"

Gadoire winked at me. "Oh, waiting hopefully."

"Hopefully for what?" I had a weird feeling about this. "Um, maybe I'm getting your signals wrong, but aren't you and Vance, ah, married?"

"Oh, we are, we are. And very much in love." He winked again. "Love you might share in, yes?"

"*Excuse* me?" I wanted to ask him if he'd actually looked at my husband when he'd come by our Embassy, and if he had, how he thought he had a shot of measuring up. Then again, Nathalie was doing the deed with Eugene, so maybe bizarre pairings were the in thing in D.C.

"Vance heard through the grapevine that you take the French view of experimentation outside of the marital vows." Apparently Marcia and Nathalie had shared their theory about me and White. Lucky me.

Apparently they hadn't shared that White was, like every other A-C, amazingly hot to look at. Then again, perhaps Gadoire was going for the whole "try something you've never had" idea and was hoping I hadn't ever done dog meat. Which I hadn't, and I wanted to keep that record intact.

"Um . . ."

"And, since your little country's views are so lenient . . ." His voice trailed off leadingly.

"Um . . ."

"We were hoping you would join us."

"Us? You mean you and Vance?" He nodded encouragingly. I stared at him. "You're suggesting a threesome, the two of you and me?"

"We'd prefer it, yes. If Madame is shy, however, we would be happy to take it slowly, have you just with each of us alone, until such time as you felt comfortable to join us fully on our bed of love."

Caroline was right. Being married to an alien was totally normal compared to the people I was meeting in this town. Admittedly, if Reader and Gower had made this suggestion, Jeff would have real cause to be worried. But Vance and Gadoire were about as far away from Reader and Gower as a girl could get.

"Have I scandalized you?" Gadoire asked, sounding a little concerned and a whole lot like he thought he was earning the Casanova for the New Millennium title. I managed to shake my head. I didn't trust myself to speak.

"Ah, then, let us retire and speak with Vance." He led me off the dance floor, keeping his arm firmly around my waist. I considered bolting, but I was still too shocked to go for it. Besides, maybe this was some sort of bizarre ruse to get me to let my guard down or something.

But no. There was Vance, lounging against one of the pillars, looking expectant. He grinned at me. "So glad you're going to join us."

I tried to channel anyone I could think of—Serene, Lockwood, Pierre, Wolverine. Sadly, nothing had really prepared me for this. Neither Aunt Emily nor the Washington Wife class had covered what to do when a gay couple you suspect of some form of treason and/or dirty dealings whisks you away and, instead of trying to bribe or kill you, asks you to join them in their "bed of love." I was certain, however, that hysterical laughter probably wasn't on the list of approved reactions. Unfortunately, it was looking like all I had.

They both looked at me expectantly. I had nothing to add to this conversation, so I went for the only thing I could think of. "Why did you tell me you thought Jack was murdered?"

Vance stared at me. Gadoire's arm tightened around me. "What did you do?" Gadoire asked him. "I told you not to talk about that."

CHAPTER 79

VANCE GRIMACED. **"I KNOW YOU THINK** I'm crazy, Guy. But I know Jack wouldn't have killed himself."

"So, what, you called the ambassador and shared your wild theory?" Gadoire snapped, with an impressive glare. Not up to Christopher's standards, but then, none were.

"No." Vance shifted uncomfortably then looked down. "I knew you were interested in her. So I wanted to warn her to keep her safe."

"Wait, you came to my Embassy, acted like a complete jerk, insinuated you needed my non-Washington-insider help, and ran off the moment bullets started flying, in order to *protect* me?"

"You went to their Embassy?" Gadoire sounded furious. "We never discussed that. Wait." He looked at me. "You were *shot* at?"

"Yes, outside the Embassy. It sort of made Vance's theory seem legitimate."

"My dove, we will protect you," Gadoire said, suddenly all Mr. Pepé Le Macho Man.

It was taking all my self-control, but I was managing not to give away what I did or didn't know. I was also just managing to keep the hysterical laughter at bay, but I didn't know how much longer that was going to last.

"Protect me from the things you just told Vance you didn't believe?" I looked at Vance. "You told me you knew who the target was. You told me you were the next in line to be killed because you possessed such knowledge!"

"Vance," Gadoire said, sounding like the Stern Headmaster at Acme Academy, "what's the meaning of this? The truth, Vance. Not some wild story meant to impress the pretty girl."

Vance looked up sullenly. "Fine. I really don't think Jack killed himself. Which means that he was murdered, and the only reason I can get for why is that he warned us all that someone was going to be assassinated at this event." Vance making this leap in logic actually impressed me. I'd had no idea he could think.

"And?" Gadoire asked, Headmaster voice on full.

Vance heaved a sigh. "And, yes, I made the rest of it up. I thought she'd go for it and come with me for protection, so I could bring her home and surprise you."

"So, you really have no idea if there's an actual assassination attempt going down?"

"No," Vance said sullenly. "I also really don't know why anyone was shooting at us." He glared at Gadoire. "But it proves my theory."

Gadoire rolled his eyes. "We're in a city with half the police force it used to have. All it proves is that some lunatic was shooting off a gun in broad daylight, and those fools running Titan have no concept of how to properly protect any municipality, that idiot Marling in particular." He cleared his throat. "However, that's neither here nor there. My dear, let me apologize. I hope Vance's little fantasy hasn't spoiled your appetite for us."

"Before I respond, let me just get a couple things straight." They both nodded. "First off, am I right in thinking you're both bi?"

"Well, duh," Vance said. "Why else would we be asking you to have a threesome with us?"

"Wow, that leads me right to my next question. Why me? I mean, seriously, Vance, I've never thought you considered me worthy to empty your spittoon, let alone that you were contemplating intimacy as an option."

He shrugged. "You're Guy's type. I make concessions."

I was Pepé Le Pew's type? How had this happened? Why had this happened? Who in the Greater Cosmos had I pissed off? I knew exactly how Penny the Cat felt—repulsed and horrified with a big helping of "run away, run away!" Of course, given the choice between Guy and the real Pepé, I was voting skunk, all the way.

"So flattering. You're quite the Smooth Operator, aren't you? So, you truly have no idea who was shooting at us earlier today?"

He sighed again. "None. Your mother asked me, over and over again. But I have no idea." He grimaced. "I would have liked to have had an answer, especially after she harangued me for an hour."

"Poor baby. Maybe you shouldn't have told lies."

"Was it a lie? Someone was shooting at us."

I pondered this. "Did you tell anyone else that you either thought Jack was murdered or that you were planning to use the clever ploy of telling me you knew the assassination target and were next on the hit list?"

"No." Vance said this with a very straight, serious face. I didn't buy it.

Gadoire made the exasperation sound. "Vance, I can always, *always*, tell when you're lying. Who else did you share these wild theories with?"

He looked down. "Just the rest of the guys."

"The guys? You mean Abner and Bryce?"

"Yeah. And Leslie," he added with a grin. "She's one of the guys, too, you know."

I refrained from comment. "And you told them you were trying to get me into a threesome with you and Guy and that you were going to use Jack's murder or suicide as a ploy?" On the same day the man had died. A man who was supposedly Vance's friend. These people were really the exact opposite of "salt of the Earth."

Vance nodded. "None of them thought I was right about Jack, and not one of them believes there's going to be any trouble tonight, either. So no harm done there," he added to Gadoire. "Your relationships with their sig-o's won't be affected."

I managed not to say that, clearly, at least one of them had indeed believed Vance's theory, in which case, Gadoire's relationship with that significant other could indeed be affected. "So, seriously, neither one of you thinks we're in actual danger, despite the fact that Jack died after he called and warned all of us?"

Vance shrugged. "Abner said it wasn't possible. There's too much security here for anyone to be able to get away with anything."

Gadoire seemed to consider the possibility as real for the first time. He looked around. "I'm sure it's a ridiculous fancy, but . . ." He gave me what I was sure he felt was a seductive smile. "Why don't we all take a room here, just to be safe?"

"So, you're suggesting I take off with you two, in the middle of the President's Ball, to have a wild fling, while my husband and everyone else from our Diplomatic Mission happens to be here?"

"Yes. It will add to the excitement."

"Because a threesome with two guys I barely know wouldn't be exciting enough, true. And somehow, you don't think anyone will, say, notice I'm gone?"

"It's packed," Vance said. "If we time it right, we can be back before the President gives his speech. No one clears out until that's over because it's considered bad form and career death."

"Yeah, everyone says quicker is better." I hadn't meant to say that aloud. Oh, well. Neither one of them seemed to pick up the sarcasm, so I barreled on. "But you think it's okay for the three of us to leave and commit said career death?"

Gadoire nodded. "As long as we're back in the room when the speech is over, no one is ever the wiser." He chuckled. "After all, you've been with us quite a while, and no one has noticed."

"Oh," a voice said behind us. "I've noticed."

CHAPTER 80

"**KATHY, DEAR, WHAT ARE YOU DOING** with these gentle-men?" White asked, as he stepped around, removed Gadoire's arm from about my person, and replaced it with his own.

"Discussing an interesting proposition, Rick, honey." I wondered where Jeff was but was actually glad he wasn't the one who'd found me. I wasn't sure that his reaction wouldn't have been to pound both Vance and Gadoire into the ground. Not that this seemed like a bad plan to me, but we really didn't have the time to stop and have fun when we were trying to save everyone.

White smiled politely. "Gentlemen, allow me to clear up some points of confusion for you. If the ambassador here is having an affair, it's with me."

"Or me," another voice said from behind. Chuckie sauntered to my other side and took my free hand. "We've been having an affair a lot longer. Years, really."

"Us too," Reader said, as he and Gower joined the impromptu party. "And if anyone's taking our girl for a threesome, it's us."

Gower nodded. "It's actually written into our religious laws."

"As you noted earlier, Guy, our laws are very liberal," I added, while I wavered between relief and an even more intense desire to laugh my head off.

"But," Reader said airily, "we can't blame you boys for trying."

"We can, however suggest that you not try again," Chuckie said. "With any of the American Centaurion women. Or men. Or ani-mals."

"In case you're into them, too," I added, to make sure they were clear. I wasn't putting anything past Vance and Gadoire.

"That's also written into our religious laws," Gower said.

"Now," White said pleasantly. "Be good little boys and run along. Oh, and when you next try to visit our Embassy, please make sure you wear protective gear. The ambassador tends to be jealous."

"He's not jealous about all of you?" Vance gasped out.

"Nah," Jeff said, as he came up behind them and took both of them by the tops of their shoulders. "They're all family, or close enough. You're not." With that, he propelled them away from us and into the arms of the same A-Cs who'd taken Eugene and Nathalie away. White and Chuckie let go of me.

Jeff turned around and shook his head. "I leave you alone for five minutes . . ."

"This *wasn't* my fault!"

He grinned. "I know."

"You're not mad?"

They all laughed. "Jeff was reading you the entire time," Reader said. "He could barely tell us what was happening he was laughing so hard."

"You sure you're handling the stress well, my dove?" Gower asked.

"Do the accent," Chuckie said. "I think that was my favorite part, my leetle flow-aire."

"Dudes, he was so totally doing Pepé Le Pew! It was all I could do to contain the Inner Hyena."

"We know," Reader said. "Jeff'd be like, 'and now he's acting all protective in that ridiculous fake accent, and I can *feel* her desperately trying not to laugh.'"

"Though I'm happy the two of you aren't bi," Jeff said to Reader and Gower. "Because, believe me, the people getting the positive comparisons were you two."

"Oh, you compared favorably, too, you know."

Jeff grinned again. "Yeah." He pulled me over to him and hugged me. "You handled that amazingly well, baby."

I hugged him back. "Thanks. And I'm all impressed with the personal growth."

He chuckled as he let me out of his embrace. "Don't expect it to happen every time."

"Trust me, I won't." I sighed. "I hate to bring us back down to reality, but based on what I've gotten so far, someone in my Washington Wife class is or knows the assassination target."

"It's still not enough," Chuckie said. "Pepé and Smooth Operator only confirmed what we've already suspected. They didn't narrow the field down enough."

"Vance said he'd told the other guys—Abner, Bryce, and Leslie, even though she's a girl."

Reader shook his head. "Still at square one, girlfriend."

"So, no signs of death or destruction?"

"No," Chuckie said. "Just the usual crap that goes on at these things. You know, like what you've just gone through. Otherwise, it's been utterly devoid of dangerous activity. I don't know whether to be relieved or preparing my letter of resignation."

I looked around. "Boy, Vance was right, no one's leaving until after the President talks." I jerked. "That's it. Whoever's going down, our assassins are waiting for when everyone's paying attention to the President."

Gower nodded. "Makes a bigger impression. The music will be off, everyone will be facing the stage."

"Normally, those areas are cleared by Secret Service before things start," Chuckie said.

"Great. But Titan's running the security, so even if the Secret Service thinks it's all clear, it doesn't mean it actually *is*."

"On it," Reader said, as he pulled out his phone. "We'll check the areas that would have a clear shot of the stage." Chuckie was making calls, too.

"We need to get to my mom and make sure she has the President stall going on stage."

"Won't he need an excuse?" White asked. "These affairs are normally well orchestrated and timed out down to the minute."

"Don't care. If anyone can make the Pres stall, it's Mom."

Chuckie hung up. "I have people going with yours," he said to Reader. "But I couldn't reach your mother," he shared with me.

"Anyone see her anywhere?"

We all looked. "Nope," Jeff said finally. He sighed. "I know, I know. You want us to split up."

"I do."

The others scattered. Jeff shook his head. "You sure you don't want me with you, baby?"

"Well, I do, especially since the weird has been turned up to eleven for this entire shindig. But we'll find Mom faster if we're not together. Besides, I know you can find me."

He grinned as he gave me a kiss. "Yep. I'll just follow the shocked, horrified, and amused trail you'll leave."

"Ha ha, very funny."

We split up. It was incredibly crowded, and I was having no luck finding Mom or anyone else I knew. I spotted and avoided the Cabal of Evil, which zoomed me onto another path. I checked my phone—had a text from Reader saying Mom was advised and the Pres was stalled, so I was to go back to scouting and being baitlike. Which was nice, because I finally found someone I wanted to spend time with.

Caroline and Michael were by a support column near the stage. Because the stage was raised and there were no food or beverage stations nearby, the space they were in was like a little alcove.

"Kit-Kat!" Caroline grabbed me. "Where've you been?"

"Tell you later. But believe me when I say I'm glad to see you."

She laughed as she pulled me somewhat behind the column. "Time to meet my boss."

"Sure." I put out the paw. "Very nice to meet you, Senator Mc-Millan."

He was a little older than my parents, but unlike most of the politicians I'd met, he didn't have the "look." He reminded me a lot more of my Uncle Mort, the high-ranking career Marine, than anything else. Of course, he'd been a Marine, too, so that might have been why.

He shook my hand. "My Caroline's told me great things about you, Ambassador. And I understand you're 'related' to my wife, as well. Kelly," he called to the woman standing a few paces away, talking to another small group, "come and meet your sister."

She extracted herself and joined us. We did the intros, then she, Caroline, and I did the whole not-so-secret sorority handshake, pledge, and all the rest of the hoopla we did any time we met a sister for the first time.

Kelly McMillan was perfectly put together, blonde hair pulled back into a flattering bun, but she smiled with genuine warmth. She'd graduated from college well before we were born, but the sorority bond went past just your years in school.

Somehow through all the chitchatting we got shoved a little farther back into this alcove. The music changed again, this time a song people could actually waltz to, Rod Stewart's "Downtown Train," and Michael asked Caroline to dance. It meant someone from our group was on the dance floor, so I wasn't against it.

I thought McMillan was going to ask his wife to dance, so got ready to move on, but someone else asked her. I was fairly sure it was the Secretary of State, also known as Villanova's boss. McMillan seemed to have no issues with someone else asking his wife to dance, and they sailed off. Anyone else nearby joined them, and shortly we were the only ones in this area.

"How are you enjoying your new position?" he asked me when we were alone.

"It's . . . fine."

"How are you finding D.C.?"

"Oh, great town. So wonderful to have all four seasons. And all that."

He chuckled. "I hate it here, personally."

"Dude, really, you too? I loathe this place." I realized what I'd said and winced. Chalk one up in the Darcy Lockwood Failure Column. I had no idea why it had slipped out, other than that I liked him already and didn't feel that I was next to someone I couldn't or shouldn't trust.

McMillan laughed. "Nice to see you've relaxed around me. It's a harsh change from our beautiful home state."

"No one else seems to think the desert's pretty. But I miss it like I can't even describe."

"It's a different climate, topography, and mindset back home. You've only been here three months. Wait until you've been here longer."

"I'll like it then?" I asked hopefully.

"No. But you'll really treasure the few times you'll be able to take a vacation and go home."

CHAPTER 81

WE BOTH HAD A GOOD LAUGH, but I did have a question. "Is it that obvious that I hate it here?"

"Only because I expected and was looking for it. Transitions are always difficult. Especially if you're . . . used to being in a more . . . active role."

Chuckie and Mom had said he knew about Centaurion Division, meaning he probably knew who I was, outside of my relationship to Caroline. Still, I was supposed to be keeping the profile low.

"Yeah. How did you handle it? I mean, you're a war hero. Can't imagine a more drastic change than moving from that to what you do now."

"Oh, yes, it's very different." He sighed. "Let's stop pretending, just for a moment. When you're used to being actively involved in things, especially things like protecting innocent people from very real and very threatening dangers, focusing on compromise and diplomacy can be a rocky road to travel on. How are you really doing?"

"I suck at it. Big time. Why don't you? Is it just that you've been doing it longer?"

"No. There are times, many times, when I feel just as you do. Like I'm a failure."

"Why do you keep on? You've been a senator for a long time now. I mean, I know you have a big ranch back home. Why don't you retire and just have fun for a while?"

McMillan was quiet for a few long moments. U2 shared that "Sometimes You Can't Make It On Your Own." I agreed with their sentiments. "I think about it, periodically. Certainly when it's time to campaign for reelection."

"So what makes you go for it?"

He gave me a small smile. "Long ago, I was complaining to Kelly about some county ordinance. She got fed up and told me if I really wanted to fix things, then I needed to get involved. So I did. One thing led to another, and suddenly, there I was, on Capitol Hill, representing my entire state."

"Was it cool?"

"It was hell. War is worse, but it's also more straightforward. The other side wants to win as much as your side, and that means lots of killing, on both sides. And within that, there's strategy, maneuvering, and more. But the overall goals are simple—especially if you're fighting in the trenches. The business of politics is all compromise. You break a promise over here so you can get a more important agreement over there. It's hard not to go to bed feeling dirty."

"So, again, why do it? Why keep on?"

"Kelly asks me that, every election year. But she also asks me this—do I know the hearts and minds of my opponents?"

"Why does that matter?"

"I know my own mind, my own heart. I know that what I'm doing, I'm doing for the right reasons, to protect and serve my constituents, this country, the world at large. But I don't know and can't know my opponents' hearts and minds. Or at least, so far, I haven't believed any of them are more committed than I am, more willing to make the hard choices, more able and willing to call foul when it needs to be called. And until that time . . ." He shrugged. "I don't do this so much because I want to, but because I haven't yet found someone I trust with the job more than I trust myself. And I know I'm not the only one in government who feels like that. There are more of us than I believe most people think. It only takes a few high-profile bad apples to ruin the entire barrel."

I looked around the ballroom while I digested this. The former Diplomatic Corps had screwed their own people, as hard and as viciously as they could, for what had turned out to be decades. They hadn't been willing to step down, ever. White, however, had been a great leader, for a long time. And he stepped aside when he didn't feel he could lead the hearts and minds of his people as well as Gower could. But he didn't step down until he knew Gower was ready.

Jeff and Christopher had done the same thing, left jobs they'd loved and worked hard to get, because there were others they could trust with those jobs—and they were needed elsewhere. Because

White had felt there was no one else we could trust to take over the Diplomatic Corps and do the job that needed to be done.

"So," I said slowly, "you're saying that sometimes you need to do the job you hate, that you don't think you're good at, because there's no one better available, and at least you know that you'll do the best you can."

"Yes. I'm saying that unless or until you can trust someone else, you have an obligation to do the job, and do it well, to the utmost of your ability. At least, if you're a leader," he added. "Though I think it applies to everyone."

"Even if you think you're better at doing the real protection stuff?"

"Even then. And, who knows? You might surprise yourself, if you give it a chance. Understanding people's motivations is a huge part of this job, and from what I gather, you're quite good at that."

"I suppose." I wasn't doing so well with motivations right now; none of us were. I looked at McMillan. "Can I ask a hypothetical question?"

"Certainly."

"Why do you assassinate someone?"

This earned me a long look. "I don't, but I understand your question. There are a few reasons, all of them political. To remove someone from office, to make a statement against what your target stands for, or to remove someone standing in the way of what you want."

"That last one, why do you feel it's a political reason?"

He shrugged. "Most human motivations can be boiled down to very simplistic emotions or desires. Love, revenge, money, power. There are others, of course, but you can probably boil them all down to those few." He chuckled. "Money can boil down to power and revenge can boil down to any of the others. So, I guess that leaves us power and love."

My mental wheels were finally turning. But the answer was still out of reach. "Okay, that all makes sense. So, why assassinate someone, as opposed to merely killing them?"

"You mean, why was JFK shot publicly?"

"Yes."

"To make that statement. And access, of course. Most people of high political importance have a great deal of security around them at all times. Usually it's only at big events where there are so many people that an assassin can take their shot."

"You mean an amateur assassin, right?"

"Right."

Almost there. "So, what if you didn't want to make a statement? What if you didn't want anyone to know?"

"It's difficult to kill someone and not have the police take an interest. While there are sadly many unsolved murders, the police do their best to solve every case they can. Especially high-profile ones. Killers tend to get caught."

"Amateurs, yes. But not the professional ones." I could feel it, the answer to the question of what was really going on, but my mind couldn't quite wrap around it. I scanned the crowd.

"Ah, then we're talking straightforward murder for hire. That's a different thing. Your professional assassin doesn't want to get caught, of course, or make a statement—if a statement's being made, the assassin isn't the one really making it. He or she is merely doing a job."

"The person paying them doesn't want to be found out, either. That's part of why they hire a professional."

The room was packed, but I finally spotted Leslie dancing with Bryce. They looked extremely comfortable with each other, both laughing and smiling. They smiled a lot alike. I wondered if Leslie still wanted to talk to me or if that had all been some sort of weird thing going on around Ryan's death.

"Exactly."

"So, it's safe to assume that some suicides are actually murders done so well that the police are fooled?"

"Yes, I'd have to say that's a likely assumption."

"So, what do you think about the current police situation in the city?"

"I think it stinks. I'm not a fan of Titan Security. For a variety of reasons."

I looked at his expression. Everyone I knew seemed to trust him. And I knew something he didn't, which I was fairly sure no one, including Caroline, had briefed him on. "Titan hired people to . . . watch you while you're in Paraguay."

"Oh, I know. Can't stand them. I do not approve of turning the protection of city, state, or country over to private enterprise. Possibly because I'm an old soldier, so to speak, but more because I think it's incredibly dangerous to our liberty, as well as providing no protection for those who're likely to need it most. Antony Marling and I agree on some things, but not this one."

"I'm with you on that sentiment. But there's more than that. The Titan guards with you in South America . . . they're not . . . what you think they are. And definitely not who you think they are. If you see them in the room, avoid them, and let me know."

I got a shot of the McMillan Gaze, which was reputed to be something prisoners, soldiers, and the faint of heart cracked under back in his war days. It reminded me a lot of my mother when she was seriously pissed. Ergo, it didn't affect me all that much. I'd grown up with this look, usually when I came home late from a date.

"Just what are you trying to share, young lady?" Young lady, not Ambassador. Yeah, he was trying the Parental Gambit.

I could play the game, but time was short, we were on the same side, and I still didn't know what was going on. "Peter and Victor are actually some of those professional assassins we were just talking about."

His eyes narrowed. "You have proof?"

"Right now, only my word. The real evidence was destroyed earlier today." And, I realized, that was exactly why the garage had been blown up. If the bombs and resulting building collapse killed all of us at the same time, it merely meant it was doing double duty. I had a feeling the Dingo was still alive and that he was here, right now.

I ran his clue over in my mind. Despite all evidence to the contrary, I knew he'd been telling me what I wanted to know. But the quick brown fox jumps over the lazy dog still made no sense in terms of anything going on, unless Prince was the target, which seemed more than farfetched.

McMillan shook his head. "You can't afford to get into a pissing match with Titan. And by you, I mean American Centaurion. The big security companies are your enemies in more ways than one."

"Yeah, I know what you're trying to find down in the Chaco. We want to stop that program, too."

He looked grim. "My entire congressional team wants the project found and stopped. We're so close, but every time, we're just a little too late. And now I know why."

"What do you know about Marling? I mean that the papers don't print."

McMillan shook his head. "Before this conversation, I'd have said we both agreed on the philosophy of increasing help to local, state, and national protection agencies and differed on the paths to take. Now? If your intelligence is correct, it shades everything I know. But why would anyone hire assassins to be a part of the protection team? Doing that kind of clandestine work seems more suited to spooks than to killers."

"Aren't plenty of spooks killers, too?"

"Yes, but not normally as a professional choice. You have to make hard decisions when you're in the thick of things, but that doesn't mean you murder for a living. I know you know that. Because I know you had the misfortune to meet Leventhal Reid before he . . . died."

I looked him right in the eye. "The story is that he was after a group of college coeds while he was high on meth and was subdued by county sheriffs. Unfortunately, to save the girls, the sheriffs had to kill him."

"It's a good story, and you tell it very well." He leaned closer and dropped his voice. "I'm close friends with your uncle; we served together for a time. Who do you think he turns to when he needs political approval to pull a particularly brave young lady's fat out of the fire?"

"I can guess."

"Reid was the worst kind of politician, and man, there is. You did the world a favor. But you didn't do it because you were paid to, did you?"

"No." And actually, Jeff had killed him. To save me. But that distinction wasn't important right now.

Some people passed by and waved at McMillan in that way you do when you know you have to be polite but you really don't want to stop to chat, let alone hang, with the wavee. He gave them a curt nod in return, and we went back to looking like party guests.

"Who was that?" I asked as much out of interest as to sort of change the subject.

"The head of the ATF. We're not on good terms right now. Of course, I don't get along all that well with most of the Alphabet Agencies, at least, not with the people in charge of them, your mother excluded. All of whom are in the room with us now. Should be a fun party."

And there it was. Total clarity.

CHAPTER 82

BUT I HAD TO BE SURE BEFORE I leaped into action. "Senator, a related hypothetical. What if you wanted to kill some specific people, but you absolutely didn't want anyone to know that they were the ones you wanted killed?"

"A diversionary killing, you mean?"

"Maybe. More that you don't want the cops able to determine who the real intended targets were, so that the cops don't figure out that you gave the order to terminate." The few cops left, that is, who would be so overworked they'd take the first easy answer they could find, because doing otherwise would mean they, like the K-9 team, would be cut.

"Terrorist attack is your best option," he replied without missing a beat. "It focuses everyone on the larger threat to national security, while leaving you free to kill off anyone you don't like. Of course, you'll kill many other innocent people along the way, but that's essentially the point."

"Yes, it is. And they'll get at least a double out of it, too."

"I beg your pardon?"

I looked around again and spotted Doreen and Irving just coming off the dance floor. I waved them over and did the fast introductions. "I need you two to stay with the senator and pay attention. Sir, you need to look for anyone on your congressional teams, the one going down to South America for sure, but possibly others. Any of them who are in agreement with you on the private security issues and their related projects. Anyone who the two Titan employees you know would also know by sight."

I got one more long look, then he nodded. "Should I get Kelly out of here?"

"I'd love to get everyone out of here. I'm just betting we won't be able to." I was sure I was giving off stress vibes. I wanted to really focus, in case Jeff was involved in a particularly deep and interesting conversation, but before I could, the music went to something really dull and undanceable, and the dance floor cleared. Caroline, Michael, and Kelly rejoined us, Amy, Christopher, and Tito in tow, which was great. But Leslie Manning followed them, which wasn't.

"Kitty, there you are."

"Hey, Leslie." I did the required introductions.

"Where's your husband?" she asked when I was done.

"Around. Somewhere. I'm sure."

"Well, then, can I steal you away for a minute so we can talk?"

It was say yes or tell her she'd won the Worst Timing in the World Award. I voted for the former. "Sure. Where's Bryce?"

"Around." Leslie looked worried. "I need to talk to you now, while he's busy."

I needed to get the rest of the team focused on what I'd figured out, and I needed to do it without Leslie catching on. She might have information about what was going on, or this might be her way of suggesting I share the bed of love with her and Villanova.

"Sure. Oh, Ames, your earring's sort of screwed up. Let me fix it." I got up close to her. "The quick brown fox jumps over the lazy dog equals the Alphabet Agencies."

"Huh?" Amy said, as I fiddled with her earring then moved away. "Uh, thanks, Kitty." She put her hand to her ear, a confused look on her face. Oh, well, I'd tried. Hopefully Leslie's weirdness would be brief and I could get back and get everyone moving on getting the obvious targets protected.

Leslie was watching me; I couldn't pass any other information without her seeing it. "Be right back. I promise."

We walked off. "Thanks, Kitty," Leslie said. "I appreciate you being willing to help me."

"I have no idea what you need help with, and I didn't exactly promise to help. I said I'd talk to you at the ball. So talk, what's going on?"

We passed Bryce who was talking to Marling. They were behind a column and seemed to be arguing, albeit quietly. I turned and headed us closer to them. Leslie noted where I was looking. "You know about Jack?"

"There's a lot about Jack going around right now. Which 'about' are you referring to?" We were close to Marling and Bryce. Marling looked annoyed.

". . . don't want to keep on doing this," Bryce hissed. "We're tired of pretending."

Marling saw us, and his expression shifted to pleasant. "Ah, how nice to see you ladies."

Bryce spun around, eyes narrowed. But he smiled when he saw us. "Hey."

"Hi," Leslie said. She seemed uncomfortable. "We were just going to powder our noses."

Bryce smirked. "The ambassador does that a lot." He shot Leslie a look I could only think of as annoyed. I was fairly sure he hadn't wanted this conversation interrupted.

I shrugged. "It happens."

"We were discussing animal rescue," Marling said. "I believe that's something you have an interest in?"

I didn't know what they'd been talking about before we joined them, but for sure, animal rescue wasn't it. I wondered if Marling was making a veiled reference to the K-9 dogs. But I decided not to press the issue, since I still had no idea what Leslie wanted. "I'm all for saving helpless animals. I understand you're a bird man."

Marling beamed. "Yes, my Bellie." It was interesting—when he smiled like this, his eyes, which were gray, had an almost pearly sheen to them. I wondered if he'd chosen his parrot in part because it was gray in color, too. The look was very pretty, though I couldn't tell how it happened. Maybe the light hit his eyes differently when he was really smiling honestly. I wondered if other people's eyes did that. If they did, I hadn't noticed, but then that didn't necessarily mean anything.

"I thought her name was, um, longer." There was no way I was going to get Rybelleclies out with proper pronunciation.

He laughed. "It is, but I use her nickname more. You like birds?"

I didn't all that much, but I wasn't going to tell him that. "Birds are fine. I'm more of a cats, dogs, and horses girl."

"Ah, well, with your name, at least the first is understandable."

"Yes." I tried for something else innocuous to say, since "hey, are you the one planning to kill everyone" and "what's the status on the supersoldier projects you're managing" didn't seem like a wise gambit. "Interesting, what you can come up with when you're making an anagram, isn't it?"

Marling nodded, the pearly sheen leaving his eyes as they went back to their regular gray. "True enough. Keeps my late wife near me."

"Sorry, didn't mean to bring up sad memories."

He shook his head. "Not your fault; you haven't had to go through losing your husband yet."

This was getting uncomfortable, so I was relieved when Leslie took my arm. "The powder room calls. We'll catch you when we get back in," she said as she dragged me off. "No need to have to hear him wax rhapsodic about that stupid bird."

"I suppose. It's an interesting name."

"It's stupid," she snapped. "I think it shows a lack of creativity, if all you can come up with is an anagram of your name when you're trying to be clever."

I contemplated this as we moved through the throngs of people. It was kind of clever, really, though I had to figure there would be a more normal name someone could make out of Cybele Siler. It was a weird name, just as weird, really, as what Marling had named his bird.

"What's going on with you and Bryce?" I asked while I played around with the letters in my mind.

"Oh, the usual," she said. We left the ballroom. I was still turned around, but I was pretty sure this wasn't the way Nathalie and I had gone.

"What's the usual?" I braced myself for her to suggest that I sleep with her, Bryce, Whitmore, and Villanova on their extra large bed of love.

"Oh, he's always complaining about something," she said as she looked around. I got the impression she hadn't censored that remark. Sure enough she turned back to me and smiled. "You know how it is."

"I guess. Um, you know I know about you and Marion and him and Langston, right?"

She shrugged. "It's complicated." Like the anagrams. I visualized the letters as if sitting on a blackboard, waiting to be used. What else could you do with them?

"I'll bet. Look, are we actually heading for the bathroom?"

"No, I just wanted to get away from them so I could talk to you."

"So talk. Really, I don't know why you're coming to me with a problem or whatever it is, instead of your friends. Are you and Bryce having a spat or something?" As I said his name I realized I could spell it out with the letters in Marling's wife's name.

I thought about it. Could Bryce be Marling's son? They didn't look that much alike, but they didn't look that different, either. Without a picture of his mother to compare him to, it was hard to say.

Leslie nodded. "You're the one who can help me. They can't. Great dress, by the way."

"Thanks." I jerked. The flirty compliment. It wasn't usual at all. Maybe Bryce wasn't imitating the head man at Titan to suck up but because he'd heard the head man at Titan toss that bon mot off regularly as he was growing up.

If Leslie noticed that I'd stiffened, she didn't let on. "So, have you heard about Jack?"

"That he supposedly killed himself, yes." I looked at the remaining letters in my mind. They didn't spell Taylor, because there was no 't.' "Leslie, are you in trouble?" I had a feeling she was, because I had a feeling she was pretend dating Marling's supposedly dead son. But I wasn't sure. I had to figure out what the other letters spelled.

"Possibly. Do you believe Jack was a suicide?" Her voice sounded tense.

I figured this was a test before she told me whatever the heck it was she'd been wanting to, which was hopefully a full indictment of Marling and Bryce. But as my father had always taught me and Darcy Lockwood had reinforced, when asked a question you don't want to answer, shoot a question back as your reply. Plus I was distracted with doing anagrams in my mind. "What do you think?"

She looked around and moved me farther away from where people were. We were by the stairs that led to the parking garage and something that called itself a disposal shaft, which I assumed meant it was the garbage chute. She stepped closer to me. "Jack Ryan didn't kill himself, he was murdered."

Time was undoubtedly running out, so I just went for it. "Right, because he'd discovered there was going to be an assassination attempt at this event." S-L-I-L-E-E were the letters left. Slyly? Yeah, but it was spelled wrong and made no sense. I flipped them around. L-E-E-S-L-I. That sounded kind of normal, but not quite.

"No. Because he warned the wrong people to stay away."

"Okay, I'll bite. Who shouldn't he have warned? Bryce?"

Leslie stepped closer. I noticed she had gray eyes. "Well, yeah, that was a mistake. But he made a bigger one."

"Oh? What?" As I asked this, my mind flung the remaining letters from Cybele Siler into a coherent word—they spelled Leslie. My mind was whirring, and it tossed the letters for Antony Marling up onto my mental blackboard. "Who else did Jack talk to that he shouldn't have?"

She smiled, and the light near us gave her eyes a pearly sheen. "You." She grabbed the handle nearest us and yanked it up as she shoved me, hard. The doors slammed open, and I fell backward, down the garbage chute.

CHAPTER 83

AS I FELL TIME SLOWED WAY DOWN. My mind shared that Antony Marling could be arranged into Taylor Manning as I saw Leslie slam the chute doors back down.

I'd have marveled at Marling's ability to hide his children in plain sight, but I was too busy trying to come up with a plan for how to not crack my head open or break every bone in my body as I fell.

I was actually grateful she'd picked the garbage chute—I'd already have smashed into something hard and unforgiving if she'd chosen the stairs. She'd hit awfully hard, though. I was used to A-Cs hitting with that amount of strength, but not humans.

For whatever reason, I clutched at my purse, a little too tightly, and heard a disgruntled sound. Right, I had Poofs with me. Time to see what they could do with this situation. "Harlie, Poofikins, Kitty needs help!"

There was a blur and a feeling of really fast movement, and then I landed. Onto a big ball of fur. I rolled off and hugged the two Poofs who'd gone Jeff-sized. "Good Poofies!"

They purred. It was very loud when they were this size, but I didn't care. It also sort of echoed up the garbage chute, but again I didn't care. It was a much better sound than listening to all my bones break. "Wow, Poofies, what a wonderful smell we've discovered."

Poofikins picked me up gently in its jaws, and then we all jumped down off of the big garbage can piled high with food, wrappers, and other things I didn't want to contemplate. Harlie had my once lovely wrap in its jaws and dropped it on the ground. It was gross, but I shook it off and put it on. Who knew? I might need it. I hooked the clutch's strap over my neck. It might not be my regular purse, but why mess with tradition?

Once I was on my feet, the Poofs went back to small and disappeared. I checked my clutch. They were in it, grooming each other. I couldn't blame them.

Checked my phone—no bars. Not a surprise, since I was sure I was at least a couple of floors underground, and there was a lot of exposed metal down here. I felt reasonably steady and checked my dress. Black really did hide stains. Headed off to find an elevator or stairway so I could get back to everyone else.

I was lost in moments, but I forged on, naturally ending up at a dead end. I heard a heavy step behind me and turned around slowly. I was expecting to see a human, Peter the Dingo Dog, Surly Vic, another person holding a gun. But it wasn't a person standing there. It was a ten-foot-tall creature, encased in metal.

It was sort of humanoid, in that it was standing on what I was fairly sure were legs and had what appeared to be arms. Or armlike things. It had five of them, so it was hard to be confident, but I went with arms because it had some really horrible-looking pincers, nails, and other weapons of mass destruction at the ends, sort of forming fingers, but only if Edward Scissorhands had done the rough draft.

I could tell it had started life as a parasitic superbeing, though, because of the formation of its so-called head. It wasn't a head so much as a roundish thing with spikes sticking out of it. No human could make this up—even in his wildest nightmares, Michael Bay wouldn't make a Transformer that looked like this. Though I'd have given a lot to see Optimus Prime, or even Bumblebee, right about now.

The metal did look very flexible, which boded but not well. I contemplated if I had a chance of running, but the question of "where to" loomed.

"Say hello to the next generation of soldier," a familiar voice said from behind the supersoldier. Even with all that had gone on, whose voice it was came as a surprise. This event was really testing my ability to roll with the shocking revelations.

"Madeline Cartwright, interesting to find you here."

"Is it?" She gave me a disapproving look as she stepped around the so-far still monster. She had both a gun and a remote control. It didn't take rocket science to guess what the remote controlled.

"Yeah, it is. Sorry to disappoint."

She looked me up and down. "I knew you'd survive something that would and should kill a normal person. Nice dress, though."

"I'm lucky that way." I wondered if she knew I wasn't a normal person anymore and really prayed she didn't. "And thanks, it's a designer original."

"If you were going to live out the night, I'd tell you to ensure that you kept the designer on retainer."

"Good to know. So, you and Marling are working together? Or is it just a family affair with him, Bryce, and Leslie, and you're crashing that party?"

She rolled her eyes. "Please. Antony thinks he's so clever, hiding his children within the political hoi polloi. Anyone with the slightest brainpower can fiddle around with their names to come up with who his offspring are. I mean, you figured it out, right?"

"Yeah." At the last minute, but I wasn't going to share that with Cartwright. I wondered if Olga knew and then realized that of course she did. She'd given me the paper that held all the pertinent clues. No chance of seeing Olga here, though. She was wisely sitting this one out. "They must resemble their mother."

"Yes, for the most part." She smiled. "My sister was brilliant."

"Your sister? How has that secret been kept from the Pentagon?" Or Mom, Chuckie, or anyone else?

She chuckled. "Unlike my bother-in-law, I changed my name to something completely different, no anagrams."

"Wise."

"Then I married a nice man who worked for a nice general. It was fairly easy after that. Besides, decades ago, no one was using computers to track. And I've been a model employee."

"True enough. I have to be honest, out of everyone I've dealt with, you didn't hit my radar as being the Dominatrix of Doom. Um, good job. I guess."

She smiled. "Thank you. Love the title. I may use it, with your permission. In private, of course."

"Go for it. So, before you kill me or whatever, would you mind clearing up a couple of things?"

She checked her watch. "Yes. We have time."

"We do?"

"Yes. You're dying on stage, so to speak. It will be quite dramatic. I believe experiencing your death in this way should short your husband out, empathically and possibly mentally, too. He'll either be useless or so out of control that he'll end up dead, one way or another."

"Nice." I decided not to ask what she thought everyone else with us would be doing. If I didn't focus her on them, then maybe they'd have a shot. "So, why were assassins hired to kill me?"

Cartwright snorted. It fell much more on my side of the snort house. Pity. I tended to prefer those who snorted like I did. "You were identified two years ago as a problem. You've been nothing but a thorn in our sides. And everyone who's gone up against you has died or been imprisoned. Or run off."

"Yeah. You still in touch with good ol' Rue and Ronaldo Al Dejahl?"

"No. But I'm sure they'll be back."

"Me too. Bummer though that idea is. So, back to the assassins. It seems like overkill, so to speak, especially since it alerted us that something was going on."

"So what? You were supposed to be alerted."

"Really? Hadn't seen that one coming," I admitted.

She nodded. "We let just enough leak so that the reporter would scramble to warn the world. Unsurprisingly, he went to Reynolds." The way she said Chuckie's name, I knew she'd absolutely planned some horrible way for him to die.

"Why leak that? We're actually prepared."

Cartwright laughed. "There is no way you're prepared for this. Either our enemies will all die, shortly, or they'll fail to save all those people and lose their jobs. I personally can't wait for your mother to get offloaded."

"Stay away from my mother."

"Or you'll what? Kill me? I have the gun and the remote control."

I needed more information, so I let her have that one. "True enough. So, who all is in on this with you? I mean, clearly you're in it with Marling and the kids. Who, as I think of it, are pretending to have a relationship with their sibling." I was too wired to gag, so I saved that reaction for later, taking the optimistic view that I'd have a later.

"Why not? They're pretending to have relationships with Marion and Langston."

"Get out! So, they aren't gay, either one of them?"

"No. They're very adaptable. Marion and Langston were both vulnerable and in useful positions."

"Wow. Are they, um, you know . . . actually a . . . um, real couple?"

"Who can tell? Antony's machinations have certainly affected their psyches. Among other things." She sighed. "I'd be upset, but they've been too useful."

We were, I realized, gossiping, and she seemed to be enjoying it. It dawned on me that she probably didn't have a lot of friends, if any, she was surrounded by people she was faking out, everyone liked to let their hair down every now and again, and every super-genius liked to have *someone* to impress, especially if they'd been doing most of their genius stuff in the shadows for a very long time.

"Amazing. Do they know you're their aunt?"

"No. Their mother died when they were young. It was better that we broke emotional contact."

"How'd she die?"

Cartwright looked sad for a moment. "Early experiments with the supersoldier program. It was very unstable when we first started."

"Bummer. Why hide the kids, though?"

"Antony was concerned that they'd be used against him. So he hid them to be safe."

"Interesting the way things change. So, was Ronald Yates involved? At the beginning, I mean."

"Oh, yes. He's the one who approached us first." She smiled fondly and even looked a little misty. "He was a great man." Uh-oh. I knew what was coming. Decades ago Cartwright would have been young—hard to believe, but reality said it was so—and that meant she'd have been Yates Bait. And I'd killed him.

Sure enough, she looked at me, and her eyes narrowed. "And you killed him." Right on cue.

"He was dying anyway. Mephistopheles was all that kept Yates going."

She gave me a long look, then nodded slowly. "True enough."

I was shocked to my core, but I chose to not show it. "So, Cantu, Armstrong, Kramer, all the rest of the Cabal of Evil, how much do they know?"

She laughed again. "I do love your names for things. Everyone else says you use the names to belittle or because you're not bright enough to remember the real names, but I think you do it because you have an interesting worldview."

"Thanks, I think you're the only one who feels that way." It was the weirdest thing, in an entire day of ultra weirdness, but I was sorry she was evil. I was actually enjoying the conversation. "The names just sort of come to me, it's not like I even try. But everyone else seems to find my names for things wince-worthy at best."

"Not everyone appreciates those of us who can think outside of the box."

"True enough. So, the others, are they patsies, informed helpers, or what? And, seriously, what is Lillian Culver's damage? You want a supersoldier? Just clone and enlarge her, and the world will run screaming in terror."

Cartwright gave a belly laugh. "I know! She's horrible. And clueless, for the most part. She, like the others, is aware of the supersoldier projects, as you call them. But they're not aware of what powers the soldiers possess." She patted the beast next to her. "They're truly amazing."

"I can believe that," I said quickly. "But seriously, Cantu and Armstrong aren't in on this? I really thought they'd been helping Cooper a few months ago."

"Yes, and you see how well *that* turned out."

I laughed. "Yeah, good point."

Cartwright nodded. "They underestimated you, completely. I warned them that they were, but, you know, you're a woman, and a young one, so how could you possibly outthink brilliant men such as they?" Her sarcasm knob was definitely turned to eleven.

"You've had to put up with that kind of crap thinking for a long time, haven't you?"

"Yes. I'd tell you that you get used to it, but I frankly see no reason to lie to you at this point. It never stops. Your mother deals with it, too."

"Yeah. I suppose. Mom seems to ignore the barriers like they're not really there."

"Just as you and I do. We all play the game. All smart, capable women learn how, sooner or later."

"True enough. So, Paraguay and France, supersoldier headquarters?"

"In a way."

She didn't seem to want to elaborate, and I wanted to keep her talking. "I'm curious. How are you going to ensure all the people on the congressional fact-finding teams who are close to exposing this project are silenced?"

"What's your guess?" Cartwright sounded genuinely interested.

"You have the Dingo and his partner, possibly more assassins, upstairs, waiting for the right cue. Probably when the President takes the stage. They'll shoot not only Senator McMillan and his congressional team, but also the heads of the Alphabet Agencies. It's blamed as a terrorist attack—you'll probably lay it on the Al

Dejahl terrorist group since they're supposed to be wiped out and you have that connection with Yates."

She nodded. "Go on."

"Then, in the midst of the chaos, Spiky here and its buddies will show up, to save the day. They may accidentally step on a couple of folks the snipers missed, but the people who are most likely to point that out will be dead. Titan shows that it's better than the police, who, if they manage to arrive, will be killed or useless, and Titan takes over all police duties here . . . and then expands to cover the rest of the U.S, and then the world."

"Well done."

"Question, though. How will you explain all the Titan goons who basically did nothing?"

She shrugged. "They'll take their share of damage. They need to be better than the police, but still, not better than these." She patted the supersoldier again.

What was it with the evil geniuses and killing their own guys? Goons clearly needed a union or something. I decided not to ask about this, though. "I think the plan to get rid of all the heads of the various agencies is kind of genius. It'll definitely throw everyone off the real scent. Your plan?"

This earned me a rather fond smile. "Yes, it is."

"How many assassins do you have? I mean, I realize the Dingo's good, but that good?"

"You need far fewer snipers in this situation than you'd think. Three or four is more than enough."

"Who are the third and fourth?"

"People much more reliable than the idiots I have to work with on a regular basis." She checked her watch and shook her head. "Time's up. We need to get into position so things go according to schedule."

"One last question? Please?" Keep 'em monologing, stay alive, that was my Motto of Mottos.

She sighed. "Fine. One."

"Why are you doing this, all of this? What's in it for you? Money? Power? Or something else?"

"That was more than one question."

I managed a smile. "Sorry. But they're all related to the main question. Why are you, you specifically, doing this?"

Cartwright stared at me for a few moments. "Why do you do all that you do?"

"Protecting people seems like the right thing to do."

"Really? The people who lie, cheat, steal, do worse? You like protecting them?"

"I guess I don't think about it, when I do it. I'm usually protecting people I care about."

"Really? Who at this gala event, aside from your friends and family who accompanied you here, do you actually care about?"

"The President."

"Why?"

"Um, because he's the President, and he's a good man."

"Really? You know him personally?"

"No. My mom does. She likes him."

"He's her boss. Of course she'll say she likes him. It's politically stupid to say you don't like the man you're hired to protect. Who else?"

I thought about it. "Senator McMillan and his wife. I care about them."

"Why so? Because you've grown up with him as senator? What does that mean, in reality?"

"No. I like him because he's decent. He's a real person, still the man he was, despite being here for so long. I admire that. And, like you, he seems to actually, I don't know, get me. No one else in this town has, just him and you." I now had the cherry and whipped cream for the top of my weirdness sundae.

"So, if I told you that I wouldn't kill him or his wife, would let all your family and friends leave in safety, would you still try to stop me?"

"Yes."

"Why?"

"Because what you're doing is wrong and will harm more people than just the ones I know and care about."

Cartwright nodded. "I believe it's good to know where you stand before you die."

"Where do you stand?"

She shrugged. "I want respect. I'm the brains behind Titan Security, despite what my brother-in-law would tell you. I'm the one who comes up with the ideas and then sees how to make them a reality. But someone else always gets the credit. I'm tired of that, tired of catering to men who haven't got the brains to advance their careers without my help, tired of listening to them take credit for my work over and over again. The only thing that gets you respect in this town is money or power, preferably both together."

"If you turned the others in, you'd be lauded as a hero."

"No, they'd turn state's evidence and we'd all go down." Cartwright shook her head. "No, unfortunately, this is the only way. I am sorry, though."

"About what?"

"It's going to be horribly painful for you. It has to be, in order to ensure your husband is destroyed. I imagine it will destroy your child, too. Which is a pity, but sacrifices must be made."

"Just like your brother-in-law sacrificed his children?"

"Yes, in that sense. Well, I've honestly enjoyed talking to you."

"Odd as it sounds, me too." I readied myself and focused on the inner me. If I was ever going to need hyperspeed, now was the time.

"No more lives left for Kitty Katt," Cartwright said as she aimed the gun at my gut. "See you in Hell, Missus Martini."

It turned out that the shot rang out before I could run.

CHAPTER 84

CARTWRIGHT FELL FORWARD. The back of her head had a big hole in it. I looked behind where she'd been standing. "I think," Adriana said, as she lowered her smoking gun, "that Grandmother would not like her new friend to be dead."

"Olga is your grandmother?"

"Yes."

My mind was working at high speed for a variety of reasons, adrenaline high being the biggest. "She's trained you in the old KGB ways, hasn't she?"

"Of course. It's a dangerous world, and Grandmother won't be in it with me forever. She wants to ensure I'm protected."

"No argument from me. How did you know where I was?"

She shrugged. "I followed you." She smiled. "Grandmother agreed it would be nice for me to get to enjoy the party."

"Thank you for the save."

"You're welcome." She picked up the remote. "It's not on a kill switch, thankfully." She handed it to me.

I looked up at the monster. "It's conscious, isn't it?"

"We feel sure that it is, yes. In its own way."

"Any guess for how to destroy it?"

"I think the better question would be, is this the only one here?"

I thought about it. "Of course it's not. Think they're all down here?"

"I don't know. I followed you down the garbage shaft."

"Seriously?" She didn't look even slightly mussed. I was wearing the latest in garbage encrusted wraps, I didn't have to look in a mirror to know that my hair was most likely a disaster, and, upon a quick scan, my skirt was already torn.

"Yes." She indicated the large, but fancy, black bag she had slung over her shoulder. "I carried what we thought I might need with me."

"Should I even ask how you got all that through security?"

"Probably not at this precise time. I think we should save everyone else now."

"Amen to that." I took Cartwright's gun. "Oh, how nice. It's a Glock. Full clip, too. Handy." I stepped around the body and felt something follow me. I looked over my shoulder. The supersoldier was right behind me, like the ickiest, scariest dog in the world. "I guess it's, um, attached to the remote."

"At least we'll know where it is."

"Good point."

We took a look around. The hotel was huge, and we weren't in the parking garage, we were in a basement of some kind. While it was actually quite spacious from a height perspective—the supersoldier didn't have to bend over, and there was at least two feet of clearance between its head and the ceiling—it was, naturally, one of those rat maze basements, because my luck wouldn't allow me to fall into a wide-open room with exits clearly marked unless there was a nuclear bomb set to go off in less than a second.

"We should hear something, wouldn't you think?" I asked as we crept along, the supersoldier making far less noise than I'd have expected. I checked its feet. "Wow, rubberized soles. It's nice to see today's evil geniuses going Old School and really adding on those extra touches that mean so much. Craftsmanship and attention to detail are always appreciated."

"If they're stationary, we won't hear anything," Adriana said.

No sooner were the words out of her mouth than I spotted light reflecting off of something very shiny. We both flattened against the nearest wall. The supersoldier did the same, although, with all its arms, prongs, blades, and such, "flattened" was more of an attempt than a success.

We were near a hallway. I listened but didn't hear anything, so I risked a look around the corner. I was rewarded with a great view of a platoon of supersoldiers. I counted eleven, meaning my personal robotic pal made the even dozen. These people were really into the number twelve for some reason. I was sure it would end up having some weird, evil bad-guy significance in numerology or something; it sounded like the way they rolled.

The supersoldiers resembled each other, though a quick count showed that some had different numbers of appendages. I gave up counting the different extras on each one. Bottom line was they were all ten feet tall, encased in what I knew even without asking was a special kind of hard-to-destroy metal, each with a parasitic superbeing inside.

What I didn't see was anyone in charge of them.

But before I ran out and got shot by someone I merely hadn't seen, I examined the remote. There were a lot of buttons on it. None of them were marked. Naturally. I considered hitting some at random but decided I was thrilled to still be alive and unscathed.

This left us with a couple of guns as our entire assault force. I didn't feel like channeling General Custer.

Nothing for it. I did the silent motions to tell Adriana to stay put and stepped out. Sadly, Spiky wasn't clued in to hand signals and stepped right out with me. I froze, waiting for someone to speak or shoot. Nothing.

Adriana joined me. "I think we're alone here."

"Huh. Cartwright was pretty confident she was going to kill me." I considered this. "And she'd have been right if not for your grandmother."

We stepped closer to the other supersoldiers, and as we did, Spiky took its place with its brethren. They were three abreast in four lines.

As we walked around the platoon, I heard a bonging sound. It sounded far away. "What's that?"

Adriana cocked her head. "I believe that's a fire alarm."

"Huh. You think that was the signal for them to attack?"

"I doubt it. Fire alarms tend to make people run out of the building."

The light dawned. "Amy figured out my clue!" As I said this, I heard the sound of voices in the distance. Adriana and I looked at each other and moved so that the platoon hid us. I took my shoes off; she did the same. I considered and ripped the bottom of my dress off, though I held onto the skirt, just in case.

I heard a scream. It sounded like a scream of rage more than grief. "They've found Cartwright's body," I whispered.

She nodded. "They'll come looking for us, then."

I studied the remote. "God, I wish Chuckie was down here with us. He'd probably have a decent guess for how this works."

"It has to be simple enough for the average person to use."

"Does it? These are the prototypes." I looked back at the remote. There were twelve buttons on the top, arranged three across in four columns. There were also buttons on the sides, three of them, where it would be easy for someone to use their thumb to activate. No time like the present to find out. I hit the button I thought corresponded with Spiky.

Of course, I had no idea which way was up for the remote. I found out, though. Because I'd actually activated a soldier at the back, not the front. It stepped around and stood right next to me and Adriana.

The voices were coming closer. I hit the button for the supersoldier that had moved. It didn't make it go to the off position, as I'd hoped it would. Instead it activated in a way we hadn't seen yet—it was much more "awake" than Spiky had been. Not good.

"What the hell?" It was Leslie, and she sounded pissed. Adriana and I dodged behind nearby supersoldiers. The activated one just stood there.

"Here, Kitty, Kitty," Bryce called. Hilarious.

I couldn't see them, ergo I wasn't in a position to shoot, so I hit the button for the activated supersoldier again. It moved from where it had been and headed toward where the voices had come from. It stopped walking. But I hadn't pushed anything.

"Stop playing around," Marling said. "We know you're here. I have no idea how you were able to get the drop on Madeline, but I have the master remote."

Well, that was bad news. I could see Adriana. She shook her head, vehemently. I took this to mean she didn't believe Marling. I considered. Cartwright hadn't seemed the type to allow someone else to have the master anything. So either Marling was lying, or he and I both had masters.

I heard footsteps, and Adriana disappeared from my view. I took this as a hint to keep moving. The supersoldiers were wide as well as tall, so they did provide good hiding, but there were three people looking for two of us.

"Found the bad Kitty," Bryce called out. He was really enjoying the cat jokes a little too much. He also had a gun trained on me. I wasn't going to be able to shoot before he could.

But I could press buttons without him noticing. So I pushed the three on the side.

CHAPTER 85

THE SUPERSOLDIERS CAME TO LIFE. This was good in that Bryce was too busy to shoot at me. Of course, he was too busy screaming and running, because whatever I'd hit had said "KILL" to these things.

They were flailing and stomping around. No projectiles going yet, but getting trampled was just as crappy a way to die as getting shot.

Adriana leaped out of the way of a couple of metal feet, which meant she was exposed. I ran and grabbed her. We both hit the ground as bullets flew around where she'd been. I'd used hyperspeed without thinking about it. I hoped that was a good thing.

But since the hyperjuice was flowing, might as well continue to use it. I ran toward Marling. Of course, I overshot. Oh, I hit him. We just kept going until we did my standard hyperspeed move and slammed into a wall.

On the plus side, this knocked him out. I grabbed his remote and ran back. Overshot. Ended up in front of the stairwell just as the door opened to reveal Amy and Caroline.

"What are you two doing here?"

"Following that bitch Leslie Manning," Amy said.

"To back you up," Caroline added.

"Caro and I saw her come back in the ballroom without you, and we knew she must have done something to you."

"Ames and I figured we'd be more useful here. The others are handling the evacuation. Chuck and some of the others are after the people who started shooting after the fire alarms went off."

"Was anyone hurt?"

"Nope. Senator McMillan took over, and everyone listened to him," Amy said proudly.

"Yeah. He and Ames figured out your clue, and we got rolling," Caroline added. "Nice to know all your friends from high school are as smart as you and Chuck, Kit-Kat."

Amy beamed. Well, one good thing had come out of this—Amy and Caroline had clearly bonded. Amy's expression went back to pissed off. "We'll have to congratulate each other later, Caro. Where's Leslie?"

Crap. "Um, follow me. Or the sound of screaming." I turned around and ran off.

This time I slammed into a supersoldier. Well, it was sort of what I'd been aiming for. It grabbed at me, but its hand, or handlike thing froze when it got near me. I had no idea why.

There were walls down in this part of the rat maze already. I hoped we weren't going to destroy any bearing walls and then figured, if this fight continued for too long, of course we would. But maybe I could get things under control before that happened.

Bryce and Leslie were shooting at the supersoldiers near them. I had no idea why. The bullets were ricocheting everywhere. "Stop shooting, you morons! You of all people should know bullets won't work!" They ignored me, but they ran out of ammo fast and went back to running and screaming.

The metal monsters were well programmed. They had the three humans surrounded, and they blocked every exit. I'd only gotten in and out because of the hyperspeed. Which I hoped meant they weren't programmed for it.

I jumped away from the supersoldier I'd run into. It turned away from me and went after Adriana. "The remotes!" Adriana yelled as she rolled and dodged. "They control them! Do something!" I hit some more buttons.

Not a good choice. Whatever I'd done flipped the "Fire Now" switch. I ran and grabbed Adriana and managed to turn us so that instead of running into a wall, we zoomed around and ran into Amy and Caroline. We all went down in a pile, and the remotes flew out of my hands. I realized I'd dropped Cartwright's Glock where I'd left Marling. I had no idea where my skirt was. I wasn't exactly batting a thousand, though my wrap and fancy handbag were somehow still with me.

"There's one coming after us!" Caroline shouted.

There was, and it had everything aimed at us. It fired—and the projectiles slammed into a shield.

I looked up to see Naomi and Abigail, holding hands and clearly concentrating. Adriana and I scrambled to our feet, I grabbed Amy, she grabbed Caroline, and we trotted to the Gower girls. You only had to teach me three or four times—I didn't want to knock the Gowers over.

"Can you stop them?" Adriana asked.

"No, I lost the remotes."

"That means you're not safe anymore. They seem programmed to not harm the one holding the remote control."

"We have limited range," Naomi said, sounding like talking was taking a lot out of her. Not a good sign.

"Okay, let me out or whatever. I'll be back."

Abigail nodded. "Hurry."

I breached the shield and ran for where the remotes had gone. Sadly, Bryce was diving for the one nearest to me. No problem. I slammed into him and didn't worry about hitting a wall. Once we stopped I hit him in the face, just for fun. It hurt. And he didn't go down, though he seemed a little dazed.

I pulled the wrap off, wrapped it around his neck, and tied it around an exposed piece of pipe. Then I kicked his chin, which sent his head back into the wall. He sagged, and I took off.

Unfortunately, Marling wasn't where I'd left him, nor was Cartwright's Glock, and neither Bryce nor I had grabbed the remote. I sighed and trotted back at human regular speeds.

Marling had one remote and Leslie had the other. Not good. They had all the supersoldiers firing on the girls. There was no way the Gowers were going to be able to hold a shield against this onslaught for long.

I went for the weaker link and tackled Leslie from behind. Happily, she lost her grip on her remote, and it skittered across the floor. Unhappily, a supersoldier I was fairly sure was Spiky stepped on it.

This caused the supersoldiers some issues, which Marling had to handle. I couldn't really give this any attention, though, since I was busy discovering that Leslie was actually not weak in any way.

I wasn't sure if she'd ingested a Surcenthumain cocktail, but I should have been able to beat the crap out of her, and it wasn't happening. "Did you do something special to yourself, Leslie?"

She smiled—a weird smile. "No. *I* didn't do a thing."

She hit me in the gut, and I went flying. I landed on the skirt part of my dress that I didn't even remember dropping. I grabbed it and scrambled to my feet. Leslie faced me and seemed to ready herself.

She cracked her neck, and it didn't look or sound like a human neck cracking.

"You're not really Leslie, are you? I mean, not in what I'd call the human sense."

She ran at me as fast as any A-C. But I didn't think that's what she was. Titan had made some real leaps in technology with the supersoldiers. Who was to say that they hadn't also been working on androids? Amy's dad had been trying to create a zombie army that looked like every guy I knew, after all.

As she headed toward me, I used my skirt like a bullfighter. It worked. She missed me. "OLE!"

She skidded to a stop, spun, and went for me again. I used the skirt, but she was smarter than the average bull, because she hit it. I wrapped it around her head, twisted, did a spin, and let go.

She and my skirt went flying. She slammed into a supersoldier, which grabbed her and flung her back. Right at me.

As Leslie slammed into me and as we hit a wall, I noted that my skirt had hooked onto the supersoldier, making it look as if it were waving a fancy silk flag whenever it moved. I had no time to appreciate the humor, though.

Leslie really didn't seem any the worse for wear, so I stopped fighting the way I'd been trained to and started to fight like a girl. I clawed at her face and pulled her hair, only I did it with A-C level strength. Sure enough, skin and hair came off. To reveal bone laced with circuitry. "Ick!"

It didn't stop her. She grabbed my throat, lifted me off my feet, and started to squeeze. "My father's a genius, haven't you heard?"

Bryce joined us. He looked no worse for wear either. He smiled at me. "Father does excellent work, doesn't he?"

"He does," I managed to choke out. "But why?"

Marling heard my question. "My children died, just like the reports all say. But I had some of their DNA. I was able to replicate them. Not all the models worked well. But once Gaultier made his advances . . ."

"Ewww." The only reason I didn't gag was that Leslie seemed to have cut that function off along with most of my air. I gasped as my lungs made it clear they were close to exploding.

Marling noticed. "Let her breathe."

Leslie grimaced, which was freaky looking now that her skin was off, but she loosened her grip on my windpipe considerably. I was still up in the air and it wasn't comfortable, but air was coming in and going out, and that was good enough for the moment.

I took a deep breath, then figured it was time to go back to getting the bad guy to monologue for a while. "You mean they're made from like real people bodies?"

"In a sense. I grew new children from their cells."

"Clones? Or rather, clones put over an android, or vice versa?"

"For the nonscientifically inclined, yes. As they aged, I made . . . adjustments. You may have interrupted Gaultier's plans, but you've hardly stopped us."

"You know *Aliens 4* sucked, right?"

"Only because the filmmakers insisted on having the plucky humans win. You know it won't work like that. Even though you've gotten lucky in the past."

"So, you and Gaultier, best buds for life or bitter rivals?"

"Oh, we were good friends. I quite enjoyed Ronald Yates, too."

"Nice to know you were all members in good standing of the Club of Evil Geniuses."

He chuckled. "Well, it's worth it to share data with some people."

"Did Madeline know about your offspring?"

"Of course. She and Ronald Yates suggested we try replicating them in the first place. And Gaultier knew—he and I shared information rather freely, since we weren't in competing businesses. No one else alive knows, however. Well, all of you know now, I suppose. But you'll be dead soon."

Marling had the supersoldiers back under control. I could see the Gowers' shield start to flicker. We were about to run out of time.

"How can you do something like this?" Amy asked. Good, she was embracing our team's reliance on keeping the bad guys monologing. Leslie still had me up in the air but, thankfully, still wasn't squeezing hard. Either she didn't want to go against her father's wishes, or she wanted me to see my friends die before she killed me, or both. I bet on both.

Marling nodded to Amy. "I respected your father. It's too bad you were always a disappointment to him."

"You and my father are both disappointments to humanity. I'm flattered to be someone neither one of you respects. I don't understand why you made androids of your children, though."

"Because I love them," Marling said simply.

"Then why didn't you make an android of your wife?" I asked.

He turned to me, eyes flashing. "How dare you?"

"Blah, blah, blah. You didn't love your kids, not like you loved your wife. If you had, you wouldn't have made these monstrosities to stand in for them."

"We're perfect," Leslie said.

"Well, you were," Bryce snickered. "Now? I think you need to go in for an upgrade. Make her prettier, would you?" he asked Marling.

"Bryce really is an amazing creation. No one would believe an android could be such a total tool."

My girls all laughed at this. Bryce flushed. Yeah, Marling did really great work. What a waste.

Leslie's eyes narrowed, but she was glaring at Bryce. They were looking at each other, not me. I probably wasn't going to get a better chance. I'd pay the price later, but right now called for pulling out all the stops. I focused and forced myself to rev up to what I'd been at when things were going sideways during Operation Confusion.

Cartwright had shared how this group planned to destroy my husband and likely my child too. They wanted to destroy all of my friends and family, everyone I cared about. And they wanted to hurt Jeff and Jamie in ways that would ensure they died in agony, ripped apart by their own powers, because they loved me.

It took no time for me to focus on the one thing I knew would bring the adrenal rush faster than anything else: rage. I saw red and knew it was time to channel Wolverine's patented Berserker Rage.

I grabbed Leslie's wrist and focused all my strength as I bent and twisted. I pulled my neck free as her wrist snapped. It broke off in my hands.

She screamed while I landed on the floor. I threw the hand at her and ran. Bryce just missed me. I was at the speed I'd been when I'd been kicking butt and having the Poofs eating bad guys underground in Paris. Maybe I just did my best work under the earth and pissed off beyond belief.

Naomi and Abigail grabbed the others, and I grabbed them as their shield flickered out. I dragged them behind me as I slammed through walls, pulling them with me. I risked a look behind. The girls seemed attached and okay. But the supersoldiers were following us, weird weapons blazing, slashing, or whatever some of them actually did.

It was interesting. I had complete control when I was revved up to this level. The fire alarms were still blaring, and that meant no elevators would be working, or if they were, they were ferrying passengers from the higher floors. The garbage chute might work, but it was iffy. That left the stairs. I had to figure the Gower girls had used up all their reserves, meaning they'd all be moving at human speeds, but my job was to stall so they'd have time to get away.

I dumped them in front of the stairwell door. "Get out of here and get some help! That's an order."

With that I turned around and launched myself at the supersoldiers heading for my friends.

CHAPTER 86

I HIT THE FIRST ONE, grabbed an extremity of some kind, and used the momentum to swing myself onto the next in line. Did this a couple of times and ended up on the sorta-shoulders of one of them.

I grabbed its head portion and twisted. It was hard; I really had to put my back into it. But I felt it start to give.

"Don't let it out!" Marling shouted. "They're only controllable while they're in the suits!"

Oh, really? Interesting. I didn't stop pulling and twisting, however. It felt the way I imagined riding the mechanical bull would, only a lot more stressful, and with no drunks cheering me on.

"Stop!" Bryce screamed. "They'll kill us if they're out."

"You and Leslie aren't really alive," I shared while I ducked low to avoid a shot from one of the other supersoldiers.

"They're as alive as you are," Marling said as I finally got the lid off one really hard-to-open can. Naturally the smell was horrendous. I didn't stop to sniff the roses, therefore.

Instead I threw the helmet portion at Marling and hit him, knocking him to the ground, I assumed because I was working faster and throwing more strongly than he'd been prepared for.

The superbeing inside the metal shell was trying to get out. I didn't have a lot of time and fewer options. But from what our latest set of genius loons had said, these things likely had Mephistopheles' DNA in them. I opened the clutch and grabbed the hairspray. I didn't bother with spraying, just ripped off the top and dumped the whole bottle in.

I jumped off as the thing started screaming in a way that was so far from human I could barely recognize it as real. But real it was.

It flailed around, slamming into two others. It was still able to use its weapons, and it did, against its brethren. They, in turn, fought back. I couldn't tell if Marling was controlling them or not, then saw that I'd hit him in the head with the helmet, and he was knocked out. Nice to know he was still human, to use the term loosely.

I ran and grabbed the remote before Bryce or Leslie could reach it. It was like they were moving in slow motion, which meant I was revved to my highest level. I had the remote, which was great. But I still had no idea how to work it.

Considering how the supersoldiers had reacted when the other remote had been destroyed, I knew it had to be protected. Plus, it was the only thing that would control them. I didn't want to lose it again, either. I considered my options and dropped it into my clutch, where I probably should have put it in the first place.

The Poofs weren't in there anymore. I had no idea where they'd gone, but clearly handling metallic superbeings was beyond them, and they'd wisely headed for the hills or the nearest Poof Condos.

Standing still had given Bryce and Leslie time to reach me. They both slammed into me and tackled me to the ground. They reared back, presumably to start the android version of ground and pound, but they were ripped off of me before any punches landed.

Jeff was roaring, already at "lion takes over the veldt," but I hadn't heard him because the supersoldier fight was making so much noise I couldn't hear anything else. I knew he was roaring, however, because of his expression, which was seriously pissed.

He had each of them by their necks and slammed their heads together repeatedly until I saw them both essentially short out. He was moving so fast he was blurry, meaning he was functioning at his super-duper level. His jacket was off and his shirt was open. I didn't have time to try to figure out why or enjoy the sight of his awesome pecs and abs. Fugly fighting was so rarely fair.

I could tell that someone else was in here, beyond Marling, who was still out, and the supersoldiers, which were still blasting and slamming into each other. He was moving fast, faster than Jeff, but I could just tell it was Christopher.

Well, Superman and the Flash were here, and just in time. I looked around for Batman. Sure enough, I spotted Chuckie, coming in with the rest of the humans. I got up, ran to him, and shoved the remote into his hand. "It controls them. I have no idea how. They won't hurt you if you're holding it." Then I ran back to Jeff.

I arrived in time to see metal pipe wrapping around three of the supersoldiers as if it were a really fast snake. The one whose head I'd ripped off was down, twitching. The two it had been fighting were down as well, but they weren't out.

Jeff and I went to these and started ripping parts off. "How do we get rid of these things?" Jeff asked.

"I poured hairspray into the Headless Horse Thing. Which I think killed it. It at least hated it a lot. But Marling said they're uncontrollable out of the suits, so I don't know that we want to pull any other helmets off unless we have some of those snazzy self-contained nukes loaded with alcohol handy."

"Coming right up," Tim shouted from behind us.

Christopher joined us. "No more pipe," he said. "But I have party favors." He had two of the nukes.

"We just carry these things around all the time?"

"No," Christopher snapped, Glare # 5 in place. "Doreen insisted we needed to call for some."

I took them while he and Jeff ripped heads off. Helmet off, nukes in, helmets slammed back down. Then the three of us dashed off and stood in front of the others.

The explosions were interesting in that the metal didn't dissolve or anything. But it was clear from the weird movements of the metal that whatever was inside had been blown to smithereens. Icky crud exiting through the cracks the supersoldiers had made in each other's armor was also a clue.

"Creepy." The remaining supersoldiers turned on us as the three Christopher had tied up broke free. We all ducked as pipe shrapnel flew all over. "Oh, good." The supersoldiers went into formation and started for us.

"Dammit, that's wrong," Chuckie snarled under his breath as he ran in front of us. The supersoldiers stopped. They seemed confused. Chuckie fiddled with the remote, and all of a sudden they looked the way they had when Adriana and I had first found them: turned off. We all breathed a sigh of relief.

"Is there a way to stop these things other than that remote or us shoving self-contained nukes down their necks?" Jeff asked.

"No clue," Chuckie said. "I'd assume their creator knows, though."

I looked down. There was water on the floor. "The supersoldiers have rubberized soles. We can't electrocute them."

"But we can *be* electrocuted," Jeff mentioned.

As he said this, I saw Marling stagger to his feet and grab some

wires the fighting had exposed. He was about to yank when shots
rang out. The bullets knocked his hand away from the wires.
"Freeze," Reader said. "I didn't shoot you dead for a reason. But
that doesn't mean I can't or won't."

Marling looked down at the very crumpled remains of Bryce
and Leslie. "You killed my children." The water wasn't to them yet,
but if they were still able to function, Marling was the most amazing scientific genius in the history of the world. Jeff had literally
smashed their heads flat.

"No. You killed them, and your wife, a long time ago, because
you were doing the whole tampering with things man is not wont
to and all that jazz. These aren't really your children and never
were. You wouldn't have done all the things you did with them, to
them, made them do what you have, if you believed they were human."

"How can you say that?" he asked me. "I care for them. They're
mine."

"Yeah? Why didn't you clone your wife, then?"

"She . . . her . . . Madeline forbade it."

"Right, the same Madeline who, along with Yates, suggested
cloning the kiddies didn't somehow also suggest cloning her brilliant sister? Pull the other one."

"We didn't have the right DNA for Cybele."

"I'll bet. So, using whatever excuses passed muster, you didn't
clone your wife, who I definitely believe you loved very much.
Speaking of those you love very much, where's your parrot, Bellie?
The one you named after your wife?"

Marling stared at me. "Safe at home in her cage."

"Exactly. She's a living thing you love. So you have her safely
out of it. You haven't made a clone of the bird."

"Water's rising and spreading," Jeff murmured. "And he feels
like he's just come out of the Washington Wife class."

I knew what that meant. "How do we destroy these supersoldiers?"

Marling laughed, and it was the laugh of a crazy man with nothing left to lose. "You don't." He looked right at me. "Trust me.
Compared to what else is out there, these are your friends." Then
he yanked on the wires as the water reached his feet.

CHAPTER 87

I GRABBED CHUCKIE AND BOLTED, Jeff and Christopher right there along with me. They grabbed Reader and Tim as we ran by them. The A-Cs down here had already grabbed whatever stray human was near them and headed for the stairs.

The lights went out, which wasn't too surprising. "I dropped the remote," Chuckie shouted as we got into the stairwell, right before he started gagging.

"We need that!"

No sooner were the words out of my mouth than I felt something move past us. It felt fluffy. It *was* Fluffy, back in a flash on Chuckie's shoulder with the remote in its mouth.

"Good Poof!"

Fluffy purred at me, then went into Chuckie's pocket, remote still in its mouth.

The ground was shaking. I looked behind us. Sure enough, the supersoldiers were marching after us. "Um, Fluffy must have activated something." They stepped right on the remains of Bryce and Leslie, smashing the rest of them as flat as their heads. I was too revved up to have this affect my stomach, but I had a feeling I'd be having vomit-inducing nightmares soon enough.

The supersoldiers caught up to us and stopped walking. "Great," Jeff said. "What the hell are we going to do with them?"

"They seem benign unless activated," Chuckie said.

"Not if we crack their crispy shells and let the chewy goodness inside out."

"We can't leave them here," Christopher pointed out.

"Not a problem," Tim said. He was speaking softly to someone. I looked. He was talking to Harlie and Poofikins.

"There you two are!" They purred at me, then disappeared. "What's going on?"

"Once you disappeared after giving Amy the big hint about what was going on, we all regrouped," Reader answered. "Senator Mc-Millan had us start evacuation procedures. Doreen was communing with someone."

"Someone?"

"Not ACE, per Paul. But whoever the hell she was talking to told us to get the nukes, she was directing the Poofs including telling them to help the rest of us, and so on." He shook his head. "She's almost as bossy as you are, girlfriend."

"Hilarious. So, Tim, what's coming?"

"We're going to airlift these things out of here."

"How? We're underground."

"Why don't you let Alpha and Airborne handle this?" Reader asked pointedly.

"Because none of you are fast enough to escape the electrified water."

A whole lot of A-Cs arrived, carrying equipment. "Ambassadors," Chuckie said carefully, "I believe it would be best if you rejoined the other guests."

"Et tu, Brute?"

He grinned. "Seriously. Get out of here."

"You're not coming?" Jeff asked.

Chuckie patted his pocket. "I'm the only one who knows how to work the remote. Besides, the international playboy running away when things are bad isn't going to surprise anyone who notices."

"Yeah, Bruce Wayne always uses that excuse, too."

Reader kissed my cheek. "Get upstairs. We'll handle this. Carefully."

"You'll find Madeline Cartwright's remains somewhere around here. She was the one in charge."

"Not Marling?" Tim asked.

"No, not from what I learned." Not from what I'd seen, either.

"Okay, we'll get her, too." Reader turned away from us and looked at the wreckage. "Can we get some lights?" Lights came on. "Great. Okay, Reynolds, let's see if you can make these things help with cleanup."

Jeff took my hand, and he, Christopher, and I headed upstairs, at human normal. I assumed the guys had burned out their hyperjuice.

I'd certainly burned out mine. I could feel the exhaustion trying to shove in. "This feels weird."

"Walking upstairs like humans, being really tired, or us leaving the rest of the work to James and Tim?" Jeff asked.

"All of the above."

"Yeah," Christopher said. "But . . . it was interesting."

"What was?"

"Watching how Senator McMillan got things under control."

"He was a war hero, so it's not like he's not used to giving orders."

"Yeah. And he sits on Capitol Hill now."

"He said it was because he didn't know for sure that someone else would do a better job. That sometimes you have to do the job you don't want to, because you're the only one who can, or the only one you can trust to do it right, to the best of your ability."

"We'd never have been able to stop this if we weren't actually invited to the event," Jeff said. "We had access only because we're diplomats."

"True enough. The former Diplomatic Corps was helping not only the Cabal of Evil but the League of Really Whacked Out Evil Super-Geniuses, too." I filled them in on what I'd gotten from Cartwright and Marling. "So, the only reason we could stop this is because we're doing their jobs now."

Jeff put his arm around my shoulders. "Yeah, baby. And we probably wouldn't have been able to save the day if you weren't taking the Washington Wife class, either."

"I suppose not."

"Why were the androids even *in* that class?" Christopher asked.

"I'm not sure. I think in part to spy on the spouses of those in the Cabal of Evil, in case they learned too much. Some to keep an eye on what we were up to. Some, I'd guess, so they could be more human."

"Didn't work," Christopher said.

"No, it did. Marling may be winning the award for World's Most Maddest of Scientists, but he did really good work. It took fighting with them for me to realize they weren't fully human." Which begged its own set of creepy questions.

"How many others like them are out there?" Jeff asked, voicing Creepy Question Numero Uno, as we finally reached the level the ball had been on.

I stepped forward and grabbed the door handle. "No idea. It's a problem for another day. At least I hope," I said as I opened the door. To find myself face-to-face with Peter the Dingo Dog and his happy cousin, Surly Vic.

Shocking no one, they had guns out and trained on us. Time to see if Chuckie was right and I actually had profiling skills. "Your employers are dead."

Peter shrugged. "We were paid to do a job. Turn around and go back downstairs."

"No."

He stared at me. "Then we'll shoot you here."

"Yeah? There are a ton of people on site paying attention. Everyone's jumpy. Gunshots will absolutely demand attention, and you don't have silencers on those guns, probably because you were originally supposed to create a 'terrorist attack,' and that's better if it's really noisy. So, I know why you want us to go downstairs. Not gonna happen. What's going to happen is you're going to put your guns away and leave."

"Why would we do that?" Surly Vic asked.

"Because you two owe us, and it's a blood debt."

"I repaid that," Peter said.

I snorted. "No, you didn't. Passing me the clue was great, but that's not repayment for my husband saving your life and the life of your cousin there."

"You told him to."

"Yes, but he did it. He didn't have to. Any more than you have to actually kill us. This operation is in shambles, none of which is your fault. You're the best there is. No one who matters will care that you didn't complete your assignment after the people who'd paid you were dead. You'll still have more work than you can probably handle."

"There is such a thing as honor."

"Yeah, there is. And if you kill us, any of us, then you've lost your honor. We saved your lives after you'd tried to kill us multiple times. If that doesn't say 'you owe us,' then let me mention that us letting you go is more than fair."

"We're letting them go?" Christopher asked, sounding as shocked as the assassins in front of me looked.

"Yes. Because we have honor, too. They were doing a job. It's not a job I approve of, but compared to everything else that's going on, at least the goals are clean and clear. They're paid to kill someone; they kill them, no freaky androids or supermonsters hiding in their closets. So," I said to Peter, "you let us live and go away, and we don't tell the authorities that we've seen you or that we've let you go." Because I knew without asking that the authorities, who were Mom and Chuckie, would not be happy with this compromise.

"We could kill you and complete our work, and no one else would know," Surly Vic said.

"You'd know. You'd owe a blood debt to us for the rest of your lives. And while you might take the three of us out, there are a lot more of us than there are of you. You'll owe all of American Centaurion, and the ones left behind will find a way to make you pay, in blood, for the rest of your lives."

Peter's eyes narrowed. "How do we know you won't attack us the moment we put our guns away?"

I looked right into his eyes. "Because I just gave you my word. You leave, you don't kill anyone here, you don't come back hunting us down, you get the hell out of Washington, and you leave Titan's employment, and we let you go and tell no one that we've seen you or that you've made this bargain with us."

He said something to Surly Vic in their native tongue. Surly Vic replied in kind. It was clear they were arguing. I cleared my throat, and they both looked at me, midargument. "Antony Marling and Madeline Cartwright are dead. Titan's about to be taken down by the federal government. Think of me as your friend when I say this: You need to put distance between yourself and that company right now."

Peter looked at me for a few seconds. Then he holstered his gun and barked something at Surly Vic, who holstered his as well. "As you say," Peter said slowly. "This evens our debts. You have given me important information just as I gave you, and you have saved us and we have spared you." His eyes flicked to Christopher.

"He's my husband's cousin. They feel the same way about each other as you and Vic do. And you tried to kill my baby and my friends."

"Ah." Peter nodded. "Then we will call it even in all ways." He gave us a fleeting smile. "Until we have the misfortune to meet again, may you have pleasant days." They spun on their heels, and took off at a trot I was fairly sure they could keep up for days.

"You know Jeff and I could have killed them before they could pull their triggers," Christopher mentioned.

"Yeah, I figured you could."

"So, why let them go?" Jeff asked.

I looked up at him. "Because, sometimes, it's better to make a political compromise that leaves both sides feeling like they won."

Jeff bent down and kissed me. "Spoken like a true diplomat."

CHAPTER 88

WE MADE OUR WAY TO THE BALLROOM. Everyone was milling around and being ushered back inside by a lot of A-Cs. The Titan goons were nowhere to be seen.

"What happened to the Titan Force of Doom?" I spotted Doreen, Irving, and Tito and headed to them.

"Jeff, Paul, my dad, and I cleared them out," Christopher said. "They were getting in the way of us actually being able to protect people and evacuate."

"How about the Cabal of Evil?"

"No reason to hold them," Jeff said. "But I'm sure Reynolds and your mother will find some incriminating evidence once they go through Titan's files."

Amy spotted us and ran over, Caroline, Adriana, Naomi, and Abigail with her. She hugged Christopher tightly, then looked at me. "Are you sure I'm human?"

"Yes," Christopher and I said in unison.

She shook her head. "How would we know? I mean, my father was apparently best buds with that raging nutcase. What if . . . what if I'm not really me?"

I figured if that were the case Chuckie would have known, but maybe not. "You have emotions."

"So did they," Jeff said quietly. "That's why I killed them. Not because they were androids, but because I could feel that they wanted to kill you."

"Great," Amy said with a sigh. "I'm not going to sleep well."

Doreen took her hand and smiled. "You're human. Trust me." White, Gower, Michael, and most of the rest of our males filtered in and joined us, Len and Kyle among them. Adriana's eyes lit up as the boys arrived.

I examined Doreen closely. "You're communing with ACE, aren't you?" She shook her head, a little smile on her face. I thought about it. "Oh. What's your baby's name?" Sure, the baby wasn't born yet, but that hadn't stopped any of the others from wanting their identities established before birth.

"Ezra Ira, after Irving's grandfathers." Doreen grinned. "I think we'll be changing our religious views about knowing the sex of our babies."

"Probably wise," Gower said. "Richard, would you help me draft that?"

"Oh, you'll be fine without my help, Paul," White said as he gave me, Jeff, and Christopher hugs.

"We need to get home. Soon," Doreen said meaningfully.

Tito put his hand on her stomach. "Yep." He shook his head. "I'm not sure I approve, by the way. Not that I was consulted."

"Approve?" Jeff asked.

"Consulted about what?" Christopher asked.

I thought about it. "ACE kept Ezra inside Doreen—so Ezra would be able to communicate with Jamie and Serene and his mother—didn't he?"

"Something like that," Doreen said. "I didn't realize until things started to go down, of course."

"Yeah, ACE works in all those mysterious ways. So, Ames, stop worrying." Amy still didn't look convinced. A thought occurred. "Where's Mister Joel Oliver?"

"Right here," he said, coming up. "Just finished getting all my shots. Great stuff."

"Can you please take a picture of Amy here?"

"Certainly. Why?"

"Humor me. Doesn't have to be great. Use a digital camera if you have one here."

"Of course I do. Several. And film cameras, too, of course."

"Good to know you're ever the artist."

Christopher laughed as Oliver took some snaps of all of us. He put out his hand and took the camera as soon as Oliver was done. He grinned. "Everyone's exactly who and what we think they are. So, now you have proof from more than one source, so stop stressing." He gave Oliver back his camera and pulled Amy back into his arms.

She sighed with relief, then looked around again. "Does something like this happen every time you guys go to a formal event?"

"You've seen my wedding video. Yeah, pretty much."

Doreen and Naomi nodded emphatically. "We're going to keep that designer in business," Abigail said with a laugh.

"That settles it," Amy said firmly. "Justice of the Peace."

"Huh?" Christopher said.

"Screw the big wedding. My parents are gone, thank God in the case of my father, and I spent all night with people pretty much acting all scandalized because we're living together and not married, like it's nineteen-fifty or something. Let's just do whatever your version of going to a judge and saying 'I do' is."

Gower and White exchanged a very meaningful glance. "You're sure?" White asked.

"Totally sure," Amy said.

Christopher shrugged. "It's up to her. I don't care as long as it abides with our religion."

"Conveniently," White said, "we even have our favorite photographer present. Mister Joel Oliver, if you would?"

"What, now?" Christopher's expression was priceless. Oliver clearly thought so, too, since he took a few quick snapshots.

"Yes," White said, with a totally straight face. "Why wait any longer?"

Amy looked at Christopher's face and laughed. "Let's do it back at the Embassy. I think all of us could use a shower before the not-so-big event."

"I'm all for a shower!"

Jeff laughed and hugged me. "Only my girl." He nuzzled my ear. "Love your focus on the priorities."

"No shower any time soon for Jeff," Tito said, Doctor From Hell voice going.

"Why not?" I looked at Jeff's chest. I could see a bruise over his hearts. "When did you get shot with adrenaline?"

"Right before we went downstairs to save you," Christopher answered. "Jeff really overdid it. As usual."

"So did you," Tito said calmly. "I didn't give you adrenaline. This time. But you're headed for isolation, too, Christopher. So, let's get back home."

"Can't yet," Caroline said, interrupting Christopher's protests that he was fine. "The President's taking the stage."

"Can Doreen wait?"

Doreen nodded. "Yes. I want to hear what he says."

My father joined us. Kevin and Mom were near the President. The President started speaking, reassuring everyone that the fire, which had broken out in the basement and had consumed much of the lower levels, had been contained. It was the usual "let's all calm down, the danger's past" speech. Chuckie, Reader, and Tim joined us while the President was talking. We got the "it's all good" sign from them and the "yes, I still have the remote" sign from Chuckie. Good. I looked back at the stage.

"And, I would be remiss if I didn't thank our good friends from American Centaurion," the President said, smiling in our direction. "Their fast actions ensured that we all were able to evacuate safely, and their Embassy staff were instrumental in helping contain the fire before it could spread throughout the hotel."

True enough in its way. We got some applause. "In particular," the President went on, "I'd like to thank both Chief Ambassadors, Jeffrey and Katherine Martini, for once again proving that when America needs a friend, American Centaurion is always there."

"Like a good neighbor," Gower whispered to me. I cracked up as we got a spotlight. We all looked awful—our clothes were disasters, and everyone's hair looked worse. But I didn't care. Because I knew our hearts and minds, and we belonged here. Besides, clearly, this town needed us.

The President then went on to thank the brave police force and firefighters who'd come to the call, and he announced that, in light of many things, he was requesting the police force be reinstated to full power, with additional slots being created. This got a lot of applause in the room.

"Oooh!" Doreen grabbed Irving's arm. "I think it's time. Like now."

"We'll get the limos," Len said. "Can we give you a ride home?" he asked Adriana.

"Absolutely." She smiled at me. "Grandmother expects me to be late."

"Len, Kyle, take Adriana out for some ice cream or something."

"Us too?" Michael asked, arm around Caroline.

"Sure."

"Great, as long as Amy's not getting married tonight," Caroline said.

"No," Amy said with a laugh. "We'll wait until everyone's home."

"What about everyone else?" Abigail asked meaningfully.

"I've called for a floater gate," Reader said quietly. "We just need to get Doreen down to one of the limos."

"Works for me. Jeff and I will stall people here. You all get going."

"You want me, Matt, or Chip to wait for you?" Jerry asked.

"Nah," Jeff said. "We'll manage. If you want, once Doreen's safely home, go out, too. Might as well end the night on a high note."

"Yeah. We can always call a taxi."

This earned some chuckles, and our group wandered off, determining who was going home and who was going out. My dad gave me a kiss. "Tell your mother I'm going to go back with Doreen. Irving's asked me to provide some Jewish support."

I kissed him back. "Will do, Dad. Dad?"

"Yes, kitten?"

"Thanks for loving me just the way I am."

He smiled. "As far as your mother and I are concerned, kitten, no one could make you more perfect than you are." Dad trotted off and caught up with Reader and Gower.

Oliver was still standing there. "MJO, what's your plan?"

He smiled. "I'd like to stick with you, Ambassador. You're good for my career."

Jeff sighed as he buttoned up his shirt and tucked it back in. "Let's go find your mother, baby. Yes, yes," he said to Oliver, "tag along. But take an unauthorized picture of any of the kids or, worse, print one, and I'll kill you."

"I understand, Ambassador," Oliver said with a twinkle. "We'll discuss authorized pictures another time."

We headed off toward where we'd last seen Mom, Oliver trailing us. We got stopped by a lot of people who seemed to feel the President's speech had been a none-too-subtle hint for them to say thank you to us. We shook a lot of paws and said a lot of "our pleasures." Oliver took a lot of pictures. Some people actually had us pose with them. None of them knew what we'd actually done, but it didn't matter. We'd clearly gotten the Presidential Seal of Approval stamped on us.

Right as we reached Mom and Kevin, who were with the President and First Lady as well as a tonnage of other people, Missus Darcy Lockwood rushed up to us. "Oh, Missus Martini, it's such a thrill to see you here. You're, as you know, my favorite student of all those in my Washington Wife class."

I looked right at her and smiled sweetly. "I'm sorry. I don't believe we've ever met." Then I turned my back to her and went and hugged my mother.

Best. Party. Ever.

CHAPTER 89

WE GOT HOME LATE, took care of Jamie, looked in on Doreen, Irving, and Ezra, who'd arrived with absolutely no complications whatsoever, then headed to bed.

Well, I headed to bed. Jeff headed to isolation. Christopher was already there. It was weird having both of them sleeping in the room attached to the nursery, but it was that or send them both to Dulce, and I just couldn't do it.

I slept like a log, and Jamie didn't wake me up in the night. I decided not to worry about it. It was a little harder doing all her routine without Jeff's help, but it wasn't impossible. I was still tired and fuzzy from the energy expenditure the night before, so I was moving more slowly than normal, but we had nothing to be on time for, so it didn't matter.

Jamie and I had slept in late, so late that I discovered Amy and Caroline had gone shopping with Pierre. I was glad they'd bonded. I really was. But I felt really alone. The Embassy was essentially deserted—everyone was over at Home Base, briefing Senator McMillan on all we'd learned. Why I hadn't been invited was probably due to my sleeping like the dead, but it still rankled.

After wandering the Embassy like a pathetic, lonely ghost, I went back up to my apartment. Jeff and Christopher had a couple of hours before they were going to be out. I heaved a sigh as my phone rang.

I grabbed it. "Hello?"

"Kitty? It's Bernie."

"Hey! I'm so glad you called!"

"Wow, talk about a wild party last night, huh?"

"You and Raul made the President's Ball after all?"

"We sure did! I even saw the President congratulate you and your husband. Boy, he's sure a hunk and a half."

"Thanks. Why didn't you come see me? I didn't spot you once last night." Not that I'd actually been looking.

"Oh, I didn't see you, either, until the President pointed you out, and I didn't want to come up and have you maybe think I was only saying hi because you're kind of a celeb right now."

I snorted. "It wouldn't have bothered me."

"Great. Well, I was wondering, you up for a play date today?"

"When?"

"How about right now?"

"Now works. Just need to get our stuff together."

"Um . . ."

"Um?"

Bernie sounded embarrassed. "I get why you have bodyguards and all that. But I was hoping to meet up at a park that has a lot of moms and nannies and kids. I just . . . your dudes kind of stand out. I think they'll freak the other parents out."

The boys had had, like the rest of us, a long night. And I was perfectly capable of going to a play date by myself. Besides, Chuckie, like everyone else, wasn't here to tell me no or to take the boys. "Sure thing. Name the place, and Jamie and I will be there!"

"Wicked!" She gave me the name of the park, then, when I shared I had no idea where it was, laughed and gave me the directions to get there, and we hung up. It was fairly close, actually within walking distance if I was willing to hike it. Which, after the prior few days, I wasn't. But I decided to go for it anyway.

I hurried us into our coats, grabbed the diaper bag and my purse. I contemplated putting my Glock into it, but if it fell out or Bernie saw it, that was worse than having the boys along. I had the same thoughts about the stroller. It would make some things easier, but it was heavy as hell, and I couldn't really manage it on steps without help, especially now when I felt totally drained and exceptionally human. Besides, the guys who'd been trying to kill me were undoubtedly long gone.

"Poofies have to stay here," I said. A lot of disappointed mewling hit my ears. "No, I mean it. Guard Jeff and Christopher." An animal I couldn't explain would probably also freak Bernie out. And I really wanted her to continue to think I was a normal gal like her, at least for a little while longer.

I felt like I was sneaking out of my own home, but it wasn't as though there was anyone to tell where I was headed. Well, Walter. But he probably needed the rest.

I got us outside without slamming the door. Sure the Embassy had great soundproofing, but I didn't want a slamming door to upset the new parents.

We reached the sidewalk, and I headed off. I looked up at the Romanian Embassy. I was fairly sure Olga was sitting by the window. I waved to her and had Jamie wave, too. We walked on.

After a couple of blocks, not having the stroller along was shown to be a really stupid plan. Enhanced or not, my purse, the diaper bag, and Jamie all felt really heavy after I'd hiked with them for a couple of minutes. The exhaustion let me know I was really not up to sprinting at human, let alone enhanced, levels, and walking was a poor idea, too. But that's what taxis, real ones, were for. I gave up and looked for an available one.

A couple went by with fares, but I lucked out on the third one. It pulled over and we got in. "Mitchell Park, please."

The driver grunted and took off. It didn't take very long; Bernie had been right, it was close. "Thanks," I handed the driver a $10. "Keep the change."

Jamie and I got out and looked around. It was a nice park, lots of foliage, lots of trees. I didn't see a lot of families around, but maybe they didn't do Sundays in the park around here too much.

We followed the sidewalk in. Soon I spotted the landmarks Bernie had given me to find her, and we went onto the grass. Now I was glad I didn't have the stroller—there was no way I'd have managed it on the wet and bumpy ground.

"Kitty!" I turned to see Bernie stepping out from the bushes.

"What were you doing in there?"

She laughed. "Jordan lost a toy." She tickled Jamie's tummy. "There's the precious girl."

I looked around. "Where is Jordan?"

"Raul wanted to meet you, so the baby's with him." Bernie clapped her hands twice in front of Jamie. "Can you come to Bernie?" she asked with a big smile.

Jamie grabbed hold of my jacket and made fussy baby sounds. "Oh, come on, Jamie-Kat. You remember Bernie. She was in Mommy and Me with us." I tried to hand her to Bernie, but Jamie held on and screamed.

I cuddled her. "We were gone for a long time last night. I think she just wants Mommy time."

Bernie looked disappointed. I looked around again. "Where the heck are Jordan and Raul?" I didn't see anyone.

"Over here." Bernie headed off around the bushes she'd emerged from. I followed her. She went between a couple of big trees, and I lost sight of her. There were a lot of big trees here as well as really tall bushes, so it was shaded. In the summertime it would have been nice. Right now, it was cool enough that it made me shiver.

I went where Bernie had to see her standing there. There was no sign of Jordan or a man who might be Raul. There was, however, a gun. In Bernie's hand. A gun with a very professional looking silencer on it. Pointing at me and Jamie. We were standing very close to Bernie, and I couldn't be sure she wouldn't shoot Jamie if I tried to run.

"What the hell?"

"I'd like the baby now," Bernie said calmly. "You can hand her to me and then I can kill you where she doesn't see it, or I can kill you in front of her and then take her. Your choice."

Something Cartwright had said the night before clicked. She'd indicated there were at least three assassins, maybe four. Peter the Dingo Dog and Surly Vic were only two, and they were clearly a team. They hadn't had someone else tagging along last night.

"Is there really a Raul?" I tried to rev up, to get enraged, so I could do something. But I was still drained from all the energy expended the night before. Tito hadn't put me into isolation because I'd hidden how tired I was from him. That now seemed like a really bad life choice. I didn't have enough adrenaline to trot, let alone sprint.

"Yes. Unfortunately, he was detained by the police last night. Someone with sharp eyes pointed him out. One of your bodyguards, as a matter of fact."

"But they didn't recognize you?"

"I did a fast fade."

"Ah. Is Jordan really your son?"

"No. It's amazing how easy it is to borrow a kid from day care, if you fake the right paperwork. His parents have no idea he's gone to Mommy and Me with me. And by the time they figure it out, you'll be long dead and I'll be long gone."

"The people who hired you are dead."

She shrugged. "Some of them, yeah. The ones who want your little girl there? They're very much alive."

I thought about things. "You were the one who planted the eighth bug on me, weren't you?"

"Eighth bug? Didn't realize you were that popular, but yeah. It was simple to do, too. You're far too trusting. But then, you were easy to read. Lonely, feeling out of sync with everyone around you. I only had to get a little bit of information on you to see how easy it would be to earn your trust. Dress like you, talk like you, act like you, presto, you're desperate to have me as your friend."

She was right on the money. My people-reading meter had been off a lot recently. Probably because I'd been focused on what I didn't like about being here as opposed to what I did.

"You aren't the one who rigged my limo, are you?"

"Nope."

"But you're the one who shot at me when I was out around Sheridan Circle the other day."

"Nope. That was Raul. That cab showed up at a very inconvenient time." Pity the K-9 squad's cabs had been destroyed. No save was coming in that form.

"So, who's paying you?" Whoever it was had certainly gotten their money's worth. No one knew where I was, and Bernie had done such a good job with me that I'd left every single form of protection at home. And Jeff was in isolation, so unable to pick up how very, very frightened I was. I'd been an idiot, and my baby girl was going to pay the price for my stupidity.

Bernie shook her head. "Assassins code—we don't kill and tell. Now give me the baby so she doesn't have to see you die." She pointed the gun right at the center of my chest. She was so close she couldn't miss, but just far enough away that I wouldn't have a prayer of knocking the gun out of her hand.

I heard the "thwap thwap" sound a gun with a really good silencer makes. Bernie stared at me as I swung my purse at her gun and knocked it away. She had two holes in her head, but I didn't want to chance that she'd involuntarily pull the trigger.

A man ran up, holding a gun with a silencer on it. I realized it was my taxi driver. "Guess it's a good thing I tip well."

He kicked the gun away from Bernie's hand, squatted down, and checked her pulse. "Dead. Good." He stood up and took my arm. "Let's get out of here."

"We're leaving the gun?"

"Yes. Let the police find it. We'll give them an anonymous tip in a few minutes."

I looked up at him. He wasn't wearing a disguise but I realized I hadn't recognized him before. "Malcolm Buchanan? What are you doing here? Aside from saving my life, I mean."

"My job." He took the diaper bag, put his arm around me the way Jeff did, and hustled us to the cab.

"What took you so long? To kill her, I mean."

"I waited to see if you could get the information on who her client was out of her."

"Ah. Um, what's going on? Who the heck do you work for?"

"Someone who knows you really well." He tucked me and Jamie into the back, then got in and drove off.

He didn't take us directly back to the Embassy. I considered everything as we drove around. "Why did I notice you the other days? But not today when you picked me up?"

"I wasn't hiding from you the other days. I didn't want you to notice me today, so you didn't."

"Huh. I'd say that sounds conceited, but clearly, you're good at what you do." We went to a shopping center miles away from Embassy Row. "So you were following Bernie? When I saw you outside Mommy and Me?"

"In a sense. I've had you under surveillance. So when I spotted people who were following you, it became my job to find out who and what they were." He pulled up near a pay phone. "Stay in the cab. That's an order."

"Calling in the tip to the police?"

"Yes." He made the call; it was brief. Then we headed off again.

"You broke cover when Raul or whoever he really is was shooting at me."

"My job is to keep you alive. In case you weren't sure." Buchanan had a sarcasm knob, too. Nice to know.

"So, you aren't a cop. And you're not from American Centaurion."

"Correct."

I pondered. Chuckie hadn't seemed to know him, but Buchanan had said he was hired by someone who knew me well. Very well, since I was alive only because he'd been around. "Can I see your badge?"

"No. You don't need to."

"Right. Because I'll bet I know what it looks like." I dug my phone out and dialed. "Mom?"

"Yes, kitten? I'm in the middle of a high-profile meeting."

"I just wanted to say thank you."

"For what?"

"For Malcolm Buchanan."

Mom was quiet for a few moments. "Are you and Jamie okay?"

"Only because you know me really, really well."

"I *am* your mother."

"Thank God."

Mom laughed. "I love you, kitten. And from now on, do what Jeff, James, and Charles tell you to, okay?"

"Love you, too, and I will do. Um, what happens to Malcolm now?"

Mom barked a laugh. "Get used to your shadow. Just never rely on it."

"Gotcha. Thanks Mom. You're the best." We hung up. "So, do you hate the Washington Wife class as much as I do?"

"More. I'm not married." We were at a stoplight. He looked back at me and winked. "Tell your husband to stay on his toes."

I felt my cheeks get hot. Great. Buchanan chuckled the rest of the way back to the Embassy.

CHAPTER 90

BUCHANAN DROPPED US AT the Embassy door. "See you around," he said. "Oh, and remember that no one's who they seem in this town. Stick with the people who like you for who you really are and you'll be all right."

"Thanks." He waited until I got the Embassy door opened and I waved good-bye before he drove off.

"Kit-Kat!" Caroline called as I walked in. "Where the heck have you been?" She and Amy were both wearing shirts that said "D.C. Babe" on them.

Amy waved clothing at me. "We have one for you and one for Jamie, too!"

"We got them for the other girls, too," Caroline said. "You think it'll be okay if we give one to Adriana?"

"Yeah, as long as you have one for her grandmother, too. Who we should really visit at least once a week."

"Already on the schedule, darling," Pierre said as he joined us, D.C. Babe shirt on.

"I see you're part of the gang."

He grinned. "The requirements were charm and hotness. Our lovelies insisted I fit the requirements."

I laughed. "Perfectly."

Pierre clapped his hands twice in front of Jamie. "Is our precious ready to come to her Uncle Pierre for a while?"

Jamie squealed. With joy. I handed her to Pierre, who started dancing with her. The girls were chattering about where they'd gone and how I had to go there with them next time.

Tito joined us. "Christopher's already out of isolation. He's over at Dulce, giving his intel. Jeff's due out in a couple of minutes, and they want the two of you over there once he feels up to it. James said that you two shouldn't have sex first."

I laughed and headed upstairs, the sound of my friends' laughter echoing behind me. I ran into Nurse Carter coming out of our rooms. "Hey, I didn't know you were still here."

She looked a little embarrassed. "I think I'm staying. Staff nurse. Doctor Hernandez needs the help, and I have nothing to go back to Paraguay for. Your friend, the one who doesn't trust anybody, said to tell you he's cleared me."

"Works for me, and I'm glad you're staying. Go downstairs and demand your D.C. Babe T-shirt. It's a new Embassy dress code requirement."

She laughed and headed off. I went in to find Jeff waiting for me. He had his pants on, but happily, not his shirt. The sounds of "I Just Can't Get Enough" by the Black Eyed Peas was playing in the background.

I chuckled and dumped my purse on the floor. "You changed the playlist."

"Yeah. I like your 'My Husband's A Hottie' playlist more for some reason."

Katy Perry's "E.T." came on and I laughed. Then I heaved a huge sigh and let all the negative crap I'd been carrying for the last three months float away on the air. "It's really good to be home."

Jeff cocked his head. "Want to tell me about it?"

I wrapped my arms around him and snuggled my face between his pecs, enjoying the feeling of his hair, skin, heartbeats, as well as his arms around me, while he kissed the top of my head and Katy sang about how great it was to be in love with an alien. I wondered how she knew. "Not right now. Now's just for being together."

Washington, it really isn't like any other town out there. But then, we're not like any other people out there, either. And I wouldn't have it any other way.

Coming in December 2012:
the sixth novel in the *Alien* series
from Gini Koch

ALIEN VS. ALIEN

Read on for a sneak preview

THE MARTINI COMPLEX WAS HUGE. It contained both the ginormous house Alfred and Lucinda lived in, an almost-as-big guesthouse, and a servants' quarters that would make most millionaires drool with envy. It also took a good five minutes to drive from the entry gate to the main house. Under these circumstances, that wasn't a lot of time to prepare for unwanted visitors.

"We really need to get anything remotely incriminating or telling hidden and out of the way."

Amy shot me a look that plainly said she thought I was crazy. I got that look a lot, from just about anybody and everybody these days. "Kitty, you're acting like we're running a meth lab or something. This senator knows about . . . everyone, right?"

"Right." He did. Armstrong was one of the people who had a very high security clearance, which included getting to know about the Alpha Centaurions who lived on Earth. But he wasn't our friend in any way, shape, or form, and I didn't want him finding some hidden weakness. "But still . . ."

My phone chose this moment to ring. I checked. Not the senator, but, indeed another number I'd become familiar with. "Hi, Malcolm, what's up?"

Thankfully, Malcolm Buchanan had been assigned by my mother to be my permanent watchdog. He'd saved my and Jamie's lives at the end of Operation Assassination. And now, wither I went, so Buchanan went, too. In the case of this situation, he was housing in the servants' quarters.

"You have company coming."

"Yes, we know. Not thrilled about Senator Armstrong's arrival, but there's nothing I can do about it."

"Well, get ready," Buchanan said. "Because there's a lot more than one person in the limo that's just pulling up at your front door."

"We have more than one coming in," I shared as I slammed my phone closed. "How are we going to handle this?"

"I'm getting the door," Kyle said. He nodded to Len. "You're backing me?"

"Of course."

Len and Kyle had been on the USC football team when we'd met in Vegas right before my wedding. Len had been the quarterback and Kyle had been on the line. They'd both given up promising pro careers to work with the C.I.A.'s ET division. Therefore, in addition to being big, athletic guys, they both packed heat. Ostensibly Len was my driver and Kyle was my bodyguard, but both boys weren't fans of anyone who tried to kill me, in part because those people also tried to kill the boys at the same time.

I contemplated allowing them to open the door with an impressive show of force. Unfortunately, I had a pretty good idea that such a cheerful greeting wouldn't be likely to be included in the Diplomat's Handbook.

Jamie gurgled. She hadn't seemed like she was in pain for the past couple of days, so, hopefully, she was fully recovered from cutting all of her baby teeth at the same time. I felt outnumbered and unprepared, and I missed my husband more than I would have thought possible. I opened my phone again and dialed.

"Hey, baby, I was just thinking about you. How're my girls doing?" Jeff had to ask because he had had to have such strong blocks up in his mind to protect him from our emotions while Jamie was in pain. I really hoped it was time to take those blocks down.

"I think Jamie's fine. I'm stressed out of my mind. Jeff, are you in the middle of anything you can't get away from?"

"We're just doing some paperwork with Reynolds."

"Great. Can you all get down here, right away? We're about to have an impromptu visit from Senator Armstrong and I don't trust his motives at all."

"Neither do I. We'll be there right away. You want Reynolds along?"

"Please. I have no idea who else is coming, but Malcolm said he saw more than one person when he called to warn me."

Jeff grunted. "He's not in the house, is he?"

"Spend needless jealousy on Malcolm when you're here, okay?" I lowered my voice. "I miss you. Use the fast hyperspeed."

"Love you, baby. Be right there."

We hung up. I kissed Jamie's head and handed her to Amy, then headed after the boys. Martini Manor was so huge it was easy to catch up to them before they reached the main entryway. And just in time—I got to them as the front doorbell rang.

"Boys, let's remember that while we don't like the senator, we aren't allowed to act like we're Al Pacino in *Scarface*."

Both boys shot me betrayed looks. Their expressions shared that, yet again, this kind of "fun" was not something they thought they'd signed up for when joining the exciting ranks of C.I.A. operatives.

But they soldiered on. Kyle got the door, Len flanking him, just in case Armstrong actually had a carload of mercenaries along for the ride. Of course, I wouldn't have put it past him, or any of the rest of the Cabal of Evil.

Amazingly enough, Armstrong was in the doorway, no gun or grenade in sight. He was carrying an expensive-looking attaché case and, as always, had the Senior Senator from Wherever look going strong. Even though we were now in the Diplomatic Corps, I still didn't pay a lot of attention to politics, but the thought occurred that Armstrong probably had his eye on the White House.

This unsettling notion got pushed aside as Armstrong strode in. Armstrong wasn't the issue—his companions were.

Guy Gadoire followed Armstrong across the threshold, beaming. My mouth fell open. "My darling Missus Martini. You look radiant as always." He raced over to me as I slammed my jaw shut.

Gadoire was a lobbyist for the tobacco industry. He spoke in a fake French accent that made him sound like a less appealing Pepé Le Pew. He was also bisexual and had, along with his partner, Vance Beaumont, suggested I share a "bed of love" with them only a few weeks prior. Despite all this, somehow, he was not on my list of Potential Adultery Options.

"Guy, what are you doing here?"

"You are surprised to see me, my dove?" He grabbed the hand I hadn't offered and kissed it. Based on his hand kissing alone, I never wanted this man's lips near mine. Gadoire was the only man I'd ever met who could make kissing your hand seem completely charmless and unappealing.

The boys stared at him. They'd heard about him, of course, but this was their first real introduction to Monsieur Love, as I called him in private.

"Ahhh . . ." Gadoire tended to make me speechless, though not for the reasons he assumed.

I heard footsteps behind me and Gadoire's eyes lit up. I looked over my shoulder to see Amy arriving. She didn't have Jamie with her. I counted that in the win column.

Gadoire let go of me and turned the "charm" on Amy. "And who is this lovely vision with you?"

"I'm Amy Gaultier. Ah, White. Amy Gaultier-White." Amy and Christopher had gotten married right before Jamie's teeth arrived and she still wasn't used to being married, partially because she'd spent more time away from her husband than with him. But, as she said, that's what you did when your best friends needed you.

Amy made the mistake of offering her hand. Gadoire snatched it to his lips like he had to kiss hands or die.

She gave me the "oh, my God this is gross" look, but smiled sweetly at him when he straightened up. "Monsieur Gadoire, I've heard so much about you from Kitty."

Gadoire winked at me. "I'm sure you have."

I managed not to gag. "How's Vance?" I hadn't missed anyone from my Washington Wife class while in exile in Florida, but it was polite to ask about someone else's spouse.

"He's well. Looking forward to seeing you again."

"Excuse me?"

No sooner were those words out of my mouth than Vance Beaumont sauntered in. Vance was one of those perfectly put together people the rest of us privately hated. I wasn't so private in my hatred, but that didn't stop Vance from grabbing me and giving me a big hug.

I managed not to go rigid or shove him away, but this wasn't a typical greeting for the two of us. "Hi, Vance."

"Kitty . . . if there's anything I can do, I just want you to know I'm here for you."

"Huh?"

Vance put the Frowny Face of Concern on. I didn't buy it for a New York minute. "We'll talk about it later."

"Talk about what?"

Armstrong cleared his throat. "Guy and Vance are aware of the . . . situation I need to discuss with you, Ambassador." He looked around. "Is there somewhere private we can go to talk?" He pointedly looked at Amy and the boys, and it was clear he didn't want them along for whatever chat he had planned.

"Whatever we need to talk about can be discussed with Amy, Len, and Kyle. They're all part of our diplomatic mission."

Armstrong shook his head. "I believe you'd prefer to have this conversation in private, Ambassador. Very sure."

Something about his tone and expression made me want to pull my Glock. However, my purse was in the room Amy and I were sharing, and besides, if I didn't want the boys to use extreme force, it was worse if I did.

What I really wanted was backup. I'd called for it. So why wasn't it here already? Surely they'd had enough time to get to a gate and over here by now.

The gates were alien technology that resembled airport security terminals more than anything else. They allowed you to travel pretty much anywhere in moments. The main gate hub was in the Dome, out in New Mexico, but there were gates all over. The majority of gates were in restroom stalls of every airport in the world, even the tiny ones. For homes, however, if the bathroom wasn't used, the basements were.

So, Jeff and whoever else he was bringing along should have zipped down to the Embassy's basement, calibrated, stepped through that gate and out the gate in the basement of Martini Manor. By my count, they should have been here by the time Armstrong got through the door.

But no, I was still backup-less. There was also no way I was having a three on one meeting with this portion of the Cabal of Evil. "I like to live on the edge, Senator. Why don't you share your news?"

Amy cleared her throat. "Why don't we get out of the hallway?"

I really wanted to get Armstrong's info and get him back out the door, but I had to admit I wasn't being gracious or diplomatic. "Good point, Ames."

Amy led us to a nearby study. This was Martini Manor—there was a nearby anything depending on your definition of "nearby." In this case, it was only halfway down the hall.

As with every other room in the house, the study was done in what I called Early American Expensive. The older generation of A-Cs were traditionalists to their cores, and they'd happily adopted Earth traditions the moment they arrived.

It was also decorated in Modern Hunk, since Jeff, Christopher, and Chuckie were all sitting in the lovely club chairs this room contained, looking for all the world like they'd been here for hours.

I would have leaped on Jeff, but I caught Chuckie's eye and he gave me a look I was familiar with—the "play it cool" look. Know a guy more than half of your life, you know when he wants you to act nonchalant.

Amy was clearly in on the news, because she didn't look at all surprised. Armstrong, Gadoire, and Vance, however, clearly hadn't been expecting this kind of company.

Armstrong, unsurprisingly, rallied the quickest. "Ambassador Martini, how good to see you."

"Senator," Jeff said with a nod. "I didn't realize you were bringing along additional visitors."

Armstrong managed a weak Campaign Smile. "Well, you've got additional people too. Nice to see you, Mister White, Mister Reynolds."

Christopher gave Armstrong a cold nod. Chuckie smiled without any warmth. "I'm sure you weren't expecting us, Senator. But it's more social this way, isn't it?"

Armstrong shook his head. "I'm not here on a social call, in that sense. Ambassador," he said to Jeff, "what I have to discuss affects you and Missus Martini. Are you sure you don't want to ask your associates to wait outside? I have to stress that it's a very private issue I need to discuss with you."

I always turned right back into Missus Martini any time Jeff was around. Supposedly I was the co-Head Diplomat, but no one seemed to buy that story, other than Jeff, who steadfastly insisted I was his equal.

"If it's so private I have to ask why Guy and Vance are here," I said, before Jeff could respond.

"We're here to help," Gadoire said. Vance nodded. They looked serious and concerned, and a part of me wasn't so sure it was an act.

Amy and I looked at each other. "Help with what?" she asked.

"Again, it's a private matter for the ambassadors," Armstrong said. He gave Chuckie a long look. "Though Mister Reynolds might want to remain, as well."

"All of us," Jeff said. "There's no one here we need to hide anything from."

Armstrong sighed. "When you change your mind, I want you to remember that I requested privacy." He put the attaché case on a nearby table, opened it, and pulled out a large manila envelope. The rest of us crowded around the table. Jeff was behind me and he took and squeezed my hand.

Armstrong pulled some pictures out of the envelope and spread them out on the table.

We all stared.

"Whoa," Kyle said finally.

"Wow," was Len's contribution.

Jeff, Chuckie, and Christopher didn't make a sound. Neither did I. I was still trying to process what I was seeing.

"Kitty," Amy whispered, "what did you do?"

Gini Koch lives in Hell's Orientation Area (aka Phoenix, Arizona), works her butt off (sadly, not literally) by day, and writes by night with the rest of the beautiful people. She lives with her awesome husband, three dogs (aka The Canine Death Squad), and three cats (aka The Killer Kitties). She has one very wonderful and spoiled daughter, who will still tell you she's not as spoiled as the pets (and she'd be right).

When she's not writing, Gini spends her time going to rock concerts with her daughter, teaching her pets to "bring it," and driving her husband insane asking, "Have I told you about this story idea yet?" She listens to rock music 24/7 and is a proud comics geek-girl willing to discuss at any time why Wolverine is the best superhero ever (even if Deadpool does get all the best lines). You can reach her via her website (www.ginikoch.com), email (gini@ginikoch.com), Twitter (@GiniKoch), FaceBook (facebook.com/Gini.Koch), or Facebook Fan Page (Hairspray and Rock 'n' Roll).

Gini Koch
The Alien *Novels*

"This delightful romp has many interesting twists and
turns as it glances at racism, politics, and religion en route.
Darned amusing." —*Booklist* (starred review)

"Amusing and interesting...a hilarious romp in the vein of
'Men in Black' or 'Ghostbusters'."—*Voya*

TOUCHED BY AN ALIEN
978-0-7564-0600-4

ALIEN TANGO
978-0-7564-0632-5

ALIEN IN THE FAMILY
978-0-7564-0668-4

ALIEN PROLIFERATION
978-0-7564-0697-4

ALIEN DIPLOMACY
978-0-7564-0716-2

ALIEN vs. ALIEN
978-0-7564-0770-4
(Available December 2012)

To Order Call: 1-800-788-6262
www.dawbooks.com

DAW 160

Diana Rowland

My Life as a White Trash Zombie
978-0-7564-0675-2

"Rowland's delightful novel jumps genre lines with a little something for everyone—mystery, horror, humor, and even a smattering of romance. Not to be missed—all that's required is a high tolerance for gray matter. For true zombiephiles, of course, that's a no brainer."

—Library Journal

"An intriguing mystery and a hilarious mix of the horrific and mundane aspects of zombie life open a promising new series...Humor and gore are balanced by surprisingly touching moments as Angel tries to turn her (un)life around."

—Publishers Weekly

And don't miss:
Even White Trash Zombies Get the Blues
(July 2012)   978-0-7564-0750-6

To Order Call: 1-800-788-6262
www.dawbooks.com

Tanya Huff

"The Gales are an amazing family, the aunts will strike fear into your heart, and the characters Allie meets are both charming and terrifying."
—#1 *New York Times* bestselling author
Charlaine Harris

The Enchantment Emporium

Alysha Gale is a member of a family capable of changing the world with the charms they cast. She is happy to escape to Calgary when when she inherits her grandmother's junk shop, but when Alysha learns just how much trouble is brewing, even calling in the family to help may not be enough to save the day.

978-0-7564-0605-9

The Wild Ways

Charlotte Gale is a Wild Power who allies herself with a family of Selkies in a fight against offshore oil drilling. The oil company has hired another of the Gale family's Wild Powers, the fearsome Auntie Catherine, to steal the Selkies' sealskins. To defeat her, Charlotte will have to learn what born to be Wild really means in the Gale family...

978-0-7564-0686-8

To Order Call: 1-800-788-6262
www.dawbooks.com

DAW 200

Tanya Huff

The *Confederation* Novels

"As a heroine, Kerr shines. She is cut from the same mold
as Ellen Ripley of the Aliens films. Like her heroine,
Huff delivers the goods." —*SF Weekly*

A CONFEDERATION OF VALOR
Omnibus Edition
(*Valor's Choice, The Better Part of Valor*)
978-0-7564-0399-7

THE HEART OF VALOR
978-0-7564-0481-9

VALOR'S TRIAL
978-0-7564-0557-1

THE TRUTH OF VALOR
978-0-7564-0684-4

To Order Call: 1-800-788-6262
www.dawbooks.com